BEFORE I
WAKE

BEFORE I
WAKE

Eric Bowman

G. P. Putnam's Sons / New York

G. P. Putnam's Sons
Publishers Since 1838
200 Madison Avenue
New York, NY 10016

Library of Congress Cataloging-in-Publication Data

Bowman, Eric.
Before I wake / Eric Bowman.
p. cm.
ISBN 0-399-14263-0
I. Title.
PS3552.0875714B4   1997   96-35481 CIP
813'.54—dc20

Printed in the United States of America

1 2 3 4 5 6 7 8 9 10

This book is printed on acid-free paper. ∞

Book design by Gretchen Achilles

BEFORE I
WAKE

1

Can you keep a secret?

The reason I ask: Trust is a primal issue for me. The psychologists call it a "lingering dysfunction" of my "difficult formative years." Right-o. And since we're all encouraged these days to take responsibility for ourselves and all our actions, I am more than willing to accept their diagnosis.

Yes, I tell them, I admit it freely: I trust no one. Most of all *doctors*.

So, as you can imagine, who *you* might be and why I should trust your ability to keep a confidence are matters of legitimate concern.

One last question before we proceed: If I share my secret, will you hear me out or turn and walk away? My worry is simple, if not obvious: the possibility of your disapproval when all one hopes for is empathy or understanding. And in this harsh, uncaring world why should any man stick his neck out if he thinks it might result in a sudden loss of contact with his head?

Perhaps I'm too quick to anticipate your response. Judge not lest ye yourself, etc., etc. After all, your capacity for fun may well exceed my meager expectations.

And so, just this once, I *will* take the doctors' advice and speak directly from the heart:

Take it from me: Murder is everything it's cracked up to be.

: opening of an untitled manuscript by Terence Peregrine Keyes

The anchorman hit the pavement at a speed later estimated by inept use of a mathematical formula—the press being more intrigued by the *idea* of a rate of descent than its accuracy—to be one hundred and seventy-nine miles an hour.

He would have dropped considerably faster if his body hadn't glanced off the canary-yellow awning over the Sixty-ninth Street service entrance of the four-star restaurant next door. The canopy's steel alloy frame partially deflected the hurtling body and saved the life of a Puerto Rican busboy who had just stepped outside to sneak a smoke. Hearing the fabric rip overhead, Julio Torres froze like a cat and so became the only eyewitness to the meteoric punctuation mark that ended Mackenzie Dennis's stellar career.

Naked, cruelly disfigured by the impact, Dennis was not immediately identified. After landing headfirst, the man who had for the last five years been one of the most instantly recognizable faces on American television achieved instant anonymity.

As it happened, ten yards away, in that ground-floor bistro sat a stunningly well preserved socialite, who three years before had repeatedly—and, truth be told, with more enthusiasm than skill—banged Mackenzie Dennis over the course of one turbulent summer. The woman could easily have identified the body had the maitre d' not discreetly closed the eatery's blinds and instructed his busboys to cover the mangled corpse with one of their trademark mauve tablecloths.

Not until the first patrol car arrived did the building's doorman realize that the shattered window thirty-five floors above belonged to the newscaster. One officer immediately called for backup and planted himself next to the jumper. The doorman led his partner through the co-op's Venetian marble lobby, up the gilded elevator to the penthouse, and used his passkey to enter Mr. Dennis's apartment when he responded to neither the doorbell nor the house phone.

Patrolman Dwight Dodds quickly determined that no one remained in the apartment, and that the involvement of a celebrity warranted the swift attention of superior brass, so he stepped back into the hall and used the house phone to notify the 19th Precinct, Upper East Side, Manhattan.

The dispatcher routed Dodds to robbery-homicide, who bounced him to the squad's commanding officer, Lieutenant Lloyd Coxen, just returning to his Brooklyn duplex from dinner with his in-laws. Coxen subsequently placed an urgent series of calls up the chain of command: to his captain, the investigative coordinator for Manhattan North Detective Operations; the Deputy Inspector, senior officer for all of MNDO; their division captain, the Detective Borough Commander for Manhattan; and finally the Chief of Detectives for NYPD at One Police Plaza.

By the time he phoned back the sergeant on the desk at 19th homicide, Coxen had already decided to bypass the next detective in his rotation and assign the jumper to Jimmy Montone. Although currently off-duty and working days, Montone was hands down the best man in all of Manhattan North to handle a high-profile situation. Coxen ordered him paged and summoned to the scene post-fucking-haste.

The lieutenant ordered his squad to keep Dennis's name off all department communication frequencies, which were constantly monitored by the city's news-gathering organizations.

"We are not having a circus here," said Coxen, "until we know the fucking elephants are in the goddamn tent."

And that was how Detective First Grade James Montone—the department's fair-haired boy since his celebrated arrest of serial killer Wendell "the Slug" Sligo—first came to be involved in the case that would leave his arrest of the Slug, or any other potential obituary epithet, in the dust.

As Montone popped a handful of Tic-Tacs, the cabbie, a dreadlocked Caribbean, took the curve on Park around Grand Central like he was driving an Indy car. Montone slid across the seat and slammed against the side door and the Tic-Tacs went flying.

"For Christ's sake!"

"You said hurry, mon."

"Fast is good. Alive's better. "

They hit the straightaway on Park. Montone leaned back and rubbed his forehead, trying to gear himself up. Lieutenant Coxen's page drove a stake through the heart of his night off, the beeper pulling him right out of the middle of a revival of Orson Welles's *Touch of Evil* at the Angelika Film Center. Now there was no telling when he'd get to bed.

He had been planning a quiet dinner, take in an early show, maybe a round of golf in the morning, until Carla in Public Relations leaned on him to meet with this British writer. Montone had never heard of Terry Keyes before, but Carla said he'd written a couple of bestsellers and the PR Office, ever mindful of the department's positive new image, wanted to offer full cooperation.

"He's working on a book about homicide," Carla told him. "He asked to meet you *specifically.*"

So Montone reluctantly gave up the first half of his evening and cabbed down to the Time Cafe on Lafayette, fully expecting to regret his decision, but Terry Keyes turned out to be a stand-up guy with a refreshing grasp of police work. His questions were insightful, pragmatic and unsentimental, a far cry from the swarm of magazine hacks the Information Office used to sic on him after his arrest of the Slug: humorless dweebs with their microcassette recorders and college psychology courses who'd seen too many cop shows.

"To be honest, I don't know how you do it, Jimmy," said Keyes. "Day in, day out, you're face-to-face with aspects of human nature that would give people nightmares the rest of their lives. Hell of a way to make a living."

"If it was easy anybody could do it."

"Is it ever a distraction or get in your way?"

"What's that?"

"Recognition from the big cases you've worked on?"

"I don't think about it much."

"Does it ever work to your advantage?"

"Occasionally. Somebody's seen you on TV, they might confide something."

"So fame does give you an edge."

"You use whatever you got. Job's tough enough."

As they talked he'd been trying to think of which movie star Terry Keyes reminded him of: sturdy, medium height, sharp-looking but down-to-earth, a working-class guy. He drank black coffee, not *caffè latte,* and dressed like a human being, not one of these downtown night crawlers. Creased khakis, T-shirt, warm-up jacket, baseball cap. Working-class English accent, dark blue eyes—Mel Gibson, that was it.

Keyes studied him for a moment, then smiled sincerely. "I know you've had a lot written about you in the past, but if we're going to do this together I don't want any 'all in the line of duty' bullshit. That's public relations. I hope you're not offended by that."

"Not at all."

"This book's about hard procedure; some poor son of a bitch gets himself killed, you step into the middle of this bloody wreckage, which no average citizen in their right mind even wants to know about."

"Not on their best day."

"You turn what you see into information and move it around until the pieces make a picture of a killer."

"If we catch a break," said Montone.

"Chance favors the prepared mind."

"Sometimes you make your own luck."

"And exactly how you go about doing that is what I want to learn from you."

"Sounds reasonable."

"If it's agreeable to you, Jimmy, I'd like to watch you work one case from start to finish. Every last detail. Truth is in the accumulation of details. How does that sound?"

Take him along on some calls, walk him through a few case files; why not, Montone decided. Murders were way down in the district, it wasn't like he didn't have the time. If access was what the department wanted to give Terry Keyes, he could accommodate them.

"Sure, why not?"

They shook hands on the deal. Keyes picked up the tab and they walked outside together. Keyes waved down a cab.

"You married, Jimmy?"

"Never been."

"Like the ladies, do you?"

Montone shrugged, noncommital.

"Well, I've got a girl waiting for me uptown even as we speak. She's one of these marathon partygoers. Taking me to another one tonight. Ever had a girl like that?"

"Not for long."

Keyes laughed. As he got into the cab Montone gave him a business card with his home number, asked him to call tomorrow and they'd arrange a time to begin their collaboration.

Montone walked over to the Angelika to catch the nine o'clock show of *Touch of Evil*. He'd been spending his nights off alone at the movies for longer than he cared to remember, a habit no one knew about. His life had turned inward and solitary over the last few years, a process he observed with clarity, understood without confusion and yet seemed powerless to affect. He'd seen it in other officers, a brooding that crept in like middle age, memory laden with too many snapshots of the worst that humans could do to each other.

Terry Keyes got that on the money: nobody in their right mind would want this job.

In the middle of the scene where Charlton Heston rescues Janet Leigh from the motorcycle gang, his beeper started buzzing. Who else but Orson Welles would have cast Charlton Heston as a Mexican cop? Who else but Lieutenant Coxen would ruin the rest of his night off with such perfect timing?

The cab slammed up to the curb at Sixty-ninth Street. Two patrol units blocked the corner, top lights running. He saw a crowd gathered outside a restaurant where'd he'd once taken a date he was trying too hard to impress. Montone hung his shield around his neck, walked past the uniforms at the corner and found the first patrolmen on the scene standing beside a pink tablecloth. The jumper's feet stuck out the back; Caucasian male, adult. A puddle of blood dripped down into the gutter.

"Call came in, ten forty-six," Patrolman Dwight Dodds told him, reading off his notes. "Busboy's coming out the door here, almost takes it on the head. We roll up at ten fifty-one. There's glass all over the sidewalk. Doorman spotted a window out, thirty-fifth floor."

Montone crouched down beside the jumper and lifted a corner of the tablecloth, stains still spreading. Checked the back of the hands and forearms; no cuts. He pulled the cloth back further and took a good look at the guy. Noticed the tiny glass fragments embedded in the forehead. Study enough faces hit by subway trains, point-blank bullets, poor bastards hanging by their belts in a welfare flop, and you learned to see past the trauma for the face that used to live there.

"Shit. You know who this is?"

The two patrolmen glanced at each other.

"We got a pretty good idea, Jimmy," said Dodds.

"Doorman says he had no guests. Everybody who signed the lobby register after seven is accounted for. Thick walls in this building. Neighbors heard nothing," Montone told Lieutenant Coxen, as they rode the elevator to the penthouse.

"What do we got inside the apartment?" asked Coxen.

"I was waiting for you."

Montone smiled his boyish smile and popped a couple of Tic-Tacs.

"What is that, cinnamon?"

Coxen held out his hand; Montone shook out a couple more.

"I bagged the hands and feet," said Montone. "Wanted to load the body in the wagon before any press got here."

"We get our pictures first?"

"We got our shots. Donatello from the squad showed right after me; had his camera in the car. I didn't want to wait for CSU."

"Long as we're covered," said Coxen, waving it off.

"Called in ten units backup, all the entrances are secured. Tried to keep the vic's name off the scanners, fat chance. We'll need big-time crowd control once the TV trucks show."

Coxen silently approved. The business of violent death on the Upper East Side of Manhattan—Fifty-ninth to Ninety-sixth between Central Park and the East River; arguably the greatest concentration of private wealth in any police jurisdiction in the world—generated more sustained local scrutiny than presidential politics. Montone had been down this road before; that's why he was Coxen's first and only choice for the job.

"I knew Dennis a little," said Montone. "He did a story on me a couple years ago. One of those network magazine shows."

"After the Sligo business?"

Montone nodded. Coxen had transferred into the squad after the Slug was already in Attica.

"So he's the one who made you a household name, huh?"

Montone shrugged.

"Good guy?" asked Coxen.

"Hard to read. Like he was on camera all the time. Followed me around for a couple of shifts, his trench coat seemed more real than he did."

"Think we can keep this zipped up, Jimmy?

"Sure. And I hear Madonna's gonna get her virginity back."

The doors opened and they exited the elevator. Coxen spoke to the two uniforms standing in the marble foyer; one of them, a veteran sergeant holding the logbook, signed them into the scene.

"Nobody else goes inside but CSU. Let me know the minute Captain Jakes gets here."

Coxen turned back to Montone.

"Let's make it fast, Jimmy; I got a shitload of calls to make," he said wearily, running down the list in his head; network presidents, ex-wives, the mayor.

Montone walked in ahead, signaled Coxen to wait in the entry hall that fed into a sunken living room, thirty by twenty. City sounds drifted in through the smashed window straight ahead.

Plush white carpet. Black leather sofas, matching recliner. A shelving unit with three Emmys and a handful of other awards Montone didn't recognize. A sixty-inch rear-projection TV dominated the center of the room; home theater deluxe; two VCRs, Dolby stereo amplifier, CD and videodisc player. Three speakers hung on the wall above the set. Two large modern abstract canvases, soft slashes of grays and black, bracketed the opposite wall.

Montone pulled on rubber gloves as he stepped forward cautiously, looking for footprints in the rug.

"Here," he said, pointing.

Montone followed the tracks to a door which he nudged open. Master bedroom, lights still on. Sleek black furniture on a hardwood floor; Japanese style. Bed made, undisturbed; paisley silk bathrobe laid across it, belt unknotted. No clothes on the chair. Closet doors closed. Montone crossed to an adjoining room.

Black tile, spacious; a big-ticket bathroom. Recessed lights. Double sinks; gold fixtures. Cedar sauna, big enough for two. Whirlpool bath. Multihead shower stall. Water beaded on the glass door, the shower floor.

Montone opened a black wicker hamper in the corner; two days' laundry inside. Socks, underwear, shirts. Workout gear, still moist.

He walked back through the bedroom , took a left down the hall to the next door. A gym; one mirrored wall behind a rack of free weights. Black industrial carpet. A treadmill, three Nautilus stations, high-end equipment. Something caught the light on a stool near the mirror.

A small black-framed mirror. Razor blade beside a loose pile of white powder. A short steel straw. Traces of two lines on the glass.

The last door down the hall led to an office, paneled in black walnut. Bird's-eye maple desk, an IBM PC, and beside it another extension of the three-line phone system he'd seen in the other rooms. An encyclopedia open on the desk. Oxblood chaise in a reading nook between inset bookshelves; biography of Robert Louis Stevenson on the side table. Tasseled bookmark—a White House souvenir—wedged in at page 75.

Photos of Mackenzie Dennis with a roster of who's who notables covered one wall; politicians, newsmakers, movie stars. Lower down were shots of Dennis in extreme sporting events; white-water rafting, vertical rock climbs, off-road races. More photographs of Dennis against war-torn backdrops; life before the anchor desk.

He retraced his steps to the living room and around the edge of the carpet to the other side of the apartment.

"The Chief wants an opinion; if it's a homicide, he's coming down," said Coxen, dialing his cell phone again in the entryway.

Montone held up a finger: another minute.

He walked through an archway into a rectangular dining room. Keys on a heavy silver ring bearing the insignia of Dennis's network lay on the bare table. A weathered leather saddlebag hung on the arm of a chair, one of those cowboy briefcases. Jimmy threw back the flap, found a wallet with Dennis's picture ID, a laptop computer, some loose correspondence and a shuttle ticket for tomorrow morning to Washington DC. No phone or address book, no appointment calendar; Montone guessed that Dennis kept electronic versions on the laptop.

Swinging doors led to a large kitchen; spotless cooking island in the middle, copper pots suspended above a restaurant-quality range. A knife, fork and salad plate bearing the remains of a meal lay in the sink. On the counter an empty bottle of Sam Adams Pale Ale rested beside a set of Henckels carving knives in a butcher block. Inside the fridge he found four cardboard Zabar's take-out containers.

Through a second door he entered a maintenance hall with a garbage chute, broom closet and laundry room leading to the service entrance. Dead-bolted. Montone unlocked it and turned the knob. The door opened onto a landing, stairs leading down and up one more flight. He examined the side of the door; tacky to the touch around the bolt. He took the stairs up; another door opened to the roof, unlocked.

A garden covered most of the roof, potted trees, loose gravel and redwood decking, cushioned chairs and lounges. Montone walked the perimeter. The adjacent building to the south ended three stories below. A fire escape ran down its outside wall to an alley below. Except for the difference in height, the narrow gap between the buildings looked accessible. Montone trained his pin spot flashlight on the gravel where the ladder met the roof; scuffed in a few places, tar exposed. Looking closer, he spotted two irregular scratches on the inside of an eighteen-inch red brick lip that circled the roof's border.

Montone went back inside and stood in the living room, sifting through the pieces he'd found, starting to get a feel. Coxen, just finishing another call, gave him an impatient look.

"Captain Jakes is downstairs; we've got news trucks pulling up outside."

"Here's one possibility. Guy comes home from work, throws his keys and satchel on the table." Montone pointed to each room as he ran it down. "He goes into the bedroom, changes clothes. Works out in his gym down the hall. Toots a few lines of blow—"

"Shit."

"Let me finish. Goes back to the bedroom, lays a robe on the bed, takes a shower. He's planning a quiet night, some takeout, maybe watch a ball game. Instead, for no particular reason, he walks out of the shower buck naked and tosses himself out a thirty-fifth-floor window."

"In deep despair over what exactly?"

"Or," said Montone, holding up a finger again. "He comes home, works out, has a sandwich and a beer. Then while he's in the shower somebody who climbed up on the roof and at some previous time gained access long enough to lay some duct tape across the dead bolt on the service door, enters his apartment. He takes out a guy, six one, one eighty, who was fit enough for vertical rock climbs and competitive ten Ks, without any sign of a struggle. Drags him into the living room, unconscious or already dead, and throws him hard enough to bust through a sheet of tempered glass."

"Already dead?"

Montone held up his hands. "You're gonna kill yourself by taking a run at a window, I don't care how intent you are on dying, instinctively you're gonna shield your face." He crossed his arms in front of his head to demonstrate.

"So?"

"Body had glass splinters in the forehead. Nothing in the hands or arms. His head hit the window first. I think he was already out."

Coxen chewed it over. "You left out the blow. Maybe the guy's flying. Thinks he's Superman."

"You ever watch this guy on TV, Lou?"

"Sure. Hundred times."

"He thought he was Superman without the blow. Had an ego makes Steinbrenner look like a squeegee guy trying to clean your windshield."

"Maybe he keeps it for guests."

"Or maybe it's planted by the perp who gives him the heave-ho. Detail like that gets in the tabloids, people think it's an explanation. Like no wonder he jumped."

"If it's there it shows up in the blood panel."

"All I'm saying is, whether he's using or not, word gets out it's here and the damage is done."

The elevator door in the vestibule opened. Two teams of detectives from the Crime Scene Unit at the 23rd Precinct stepped out, kit bags in hand, already wearing gloves. The sergeant had them sign the logbook and waved them through, but Montone signaled them to hold up outside. A strange look on his face.

"What?" asked Coxen.

Montone heard a low steady hum cut through the street noise. He stepped toward the TV, scrutinized the monitor. A thin crack of static rippled across its big screen. A tiny green LED light glowed at the bottom of the frame. He checked the components of the system and spotted more green lights bouncing across a signal indicator on the VCR.

Montone leaned down, studied its control panel. Reached in with a pencil and pressed a corner of one button.

A whir of internal machinery ejected a videotape from the player. He lifted it out; no identifying marks on either side. A quarter of the tape had distributed to the other spindle.

"Was he taping something?" asked Coxen.

Montone checked the channel indicator. Set to 3. Glanced behind the VCR and found a three-pronged cable running out the back; yellow, white and red mini-plugs in the VIDEO IN ports.

"Not off the tube he wasn't," said Montone.

He pushed the tape back into the VCR and hit rewind. The four CSU guys were edging up to the door, trying hard not to look interested. Montone nodded toward Coxen.

"Excuse us for one second, fellas," said Coxen, closing the door in their faces.

Coxen joined Montone a few feet in front of the big screen. They waited. The tape finished rewinding. Montone used the tip of his pencil to touch play. Tape roll on the screen appeared, then black; then an image popped into view.

Mackenzie Dennis faced out from the monitor; the shot cropped him across his bare chest, just below the shoulders. He was in this same room, a corner of one of the abstract canvases visible behind him. His eyes steady, focused on the camera lens. Hair wet, slicked back. No visible emotion on his long, pale, familiar face; not the confident, seen-it-all anchorman mask, but a blankness, remarkable for how much seemed absent.

"I am guilty . . ." began Mackenzie Dennis. Tension in the voice, pitched higher than what they were used to. ". . . of so many things. But principally, crimes against the truth."

Montone watched his eyes closely; they never wavered from the lens.

"I have abused the trust you placed in me. I have done this by routinely promoting a false vision of the world with no correspondence to reality. I have willingly participated in a conspiracy against the truth. I have committed these acts of deception of my own free will, in exchange for wealth and cultural power. What is worse, I committed these crimes—to you, my viewers—in the guise of a trusted confidant whom you invited into your homes."

"What the fuck . . ." whispered Coxen.

"The stories I have told you were half-truths or outright lies. Instead of facts I gave you fallacies. In place of genuine emotion I gave you false sentimentality, all calculated to blind you to the truth.

"My intention wasn't to inform but to distract you with worry about issues that have no real impact on your lives, to feed you misinformation that serves the interests of the wealthy and powerful in our society. I have let myself be used by forces that only want to control your thoughts, take your money and subjugate you to their will. Be warned; we are not sages or soothsayers; we are fearmongers."

Dennis's eyes looked heavy now, mesmerized. As he paused Montone leaned forward, straining to hear what else the microphone picked up.

"I willingly bartered my soul to these enemies of the common good. I sold you out. I beg your forgiveness for my crimes. This punishment is just."

They heard a break in his voice on the last line, emotion surfacing. Then silence. Montone kept watching his eyes.

Mackenzie Dennis rose unsteadily to his feet. His genitals flashed briefly into view. He staggered slightly and then disappeared from view. The tape continued to run.

Coxen glanced over at Montone as he moved closer to the speakers, holding up a hand for silence, trying to listen.

Moments later, so shockingly loud it drove them back a step, they heard the crash of the window breaking. No voice, no scream. Then the wind and the indifferent sounds of the city filtered through the broken glass.

The tape continued to run—a corner of chair, a slice of painting; no other sound or movement—for two and a half minutes, before it cut to black.

The hat wasn't right, its decorative spray of roses wobbled around whenever she turned her head. Wide-brimmed floral hats were one of the "signatures of the summer season"—she'd been so quoted in *WWD* herself—but tonight Tyler Angstrom felt less like "a leading arbiter of style" and more like a hostage to the whims of female-averse designers.

Tyler snatched a flute of champagne off a passing tray and grabbed a miniaturized quiche. Since they refused to serve any *real* food, she needed something to fuel her relentless nervous system. Clothes draped on her in a way that made strong women weep, but alone in front of the mirror Tyler knew her figure owed more to the dispensary of prescription drugs in her medicine cabinet than it did to genetics.

Her five-year run as a high-end fashion model had done little to generate feminine confidence; quite the contrary, by the end she felt as androgynous as a Martian. Her ears stuck out like Dumbo's and her features, fine-boned and striking, would have been described on anyone less than her five foot nine as "elfin." Tyler's modeling assignments had invariably taken her to second-rank outposts in the fashion empire; Germany, Palm Springs, Miami before Miami was Miami. Paris and Milan remained rumors. And no matter where she went, people in the business treated her like chattel. It sucked. She hated it. She quit.

A blast of disco music drew her back to the mob scene in the Grand Ballroom below. Whenever this top fashion rag wanted to celebrate a meaningless achievement—this was some sort of trivial anniversary—it established new standards for wretched excess. Balloons and confetti swirled in the air. With explosions of light, a gauntlet of paparazzi greeted the arrival of each new industry aristocrat. Giant blowups of past covers from the magazine loomed above the throng.

Tyler leaned over the mezzanine rail and scanned the crowd, searching in vain for her date. After she had introduced him to everyone in sight when they first arrived, Terry had disappeared off her radar screen for nearly two hours. Easy enough to lose someone in this crowd, but his absence plunged her into deep anxiety; she now calculated the chance of a romance developing between them at less than zero.

A best-selling British author with smashing good looks and the one elusive virtue guaranteed to bring Manhattan to its knees: originality. Why in the world would Terry make a play for her when he had the whole field to choose from?

"We have to stop meeting like this."

She turned. Terry Keyes stood directly behind her, smiling slyly. Black linen double-breasted suit, ebony walking stick, and the confidence to carry it off.

"I was beginning to think you'd ditched me," she said, opting for honesty, a risk that on occasion paid big dividends.

"My dear, I haven't been able to take my eyes off you," he said, doing a Cary Grant impression as he took her hand and joined her at the balcony.

"And would you like some cheese with that bologna sandwich, sir?"

He laughed. Good.

"It's true, Tyler," he said, gazing at her with open amusement. "And I've been absolutely amazed. You must know every single person in this room."

She looked down at the party. The thought depressed more than pleased her. "I better know them. I put the damn guest list together."

Excitement rippled through the crowd near the red-carpeted entry; some movie star husband-and-wife team were ascending the stairs. Strobe flashes sent high shadows flying up the walls.

He leaned over and put his elbows on the rail beside her. "They put on a bloody brilliant show, don't they? If a bomb went off in this room America could lose her entire ruling class. And you're not even supposed to have one."

"Don't tell anybody."

"All the fortunes they've built. All the secrets they're carrying around. By God, Tyler, you must be one of the few people here who know what most of them are."

"That's what they pay publicists for, Terry. To keep them."

He leveled her with an intimate, knowing look. "Do you kiss and tell?"

Tyler looked away as she felt color rise in her face like a rush of blood pressure.

"How about kiss, then tell?" He laughed; she thought it sounded both charming and cruel. "I don't know if you're ready for me."

"You probably didn't get to date much in prison," she said, flustered.

"No, dear. You spend most of your time inside trying to avoid dating." He slid a hand smoothly around the silk wrap on her hip. "But come to think of it, I would like to, Tyler. Very much indeed."

"What?"

"Date you."

He ran his hand over the curve of her waist as he brazenly looked her up and down. Surrender must have registered on her face, because he produced a Plaza Hotel room key from his pocket.

"I've got champagne chilling in the room. If you think you've fulfilled your professional obligations."

He dropped one of his hard hands across her thigh while the other pressed against the small of her back, creating an exquisite angle of pressure. Her knees started to buckle. He gripped her firmly around the waist and started for the elevator, keeping the urgency simmering. People seemed to be noticing them but she no longer cared.

As the elevator doors closed a commotion rippled through the crowd below—a shout, an anguished "NO!" and other exclamations of alarm as small groups bolted for the Oak Bar, a television set, confirmation.

CNN already had a live feed from the scene outside the restaurant on Sixty-ninth Street.

2

THE FIRST NATURAL LAW:

Because the condition of man is a condition of war of everyone against everyone, every man has a right to everything, even to another's body . . .

To this war of every man against every man, this also is consequent: no action can be unjust. The notions of right and wrong, justice and injustice, have there no place. Force and fraud are the two cardinal virtues . . .

In revenge, men must not look at the greatness of evil past but at the greatness of the good to follow. The bonds of words are too weak to bridle men's ambitions, avarice and other passions, without the fear of some coercive power . . .

In such condition of war there is no place for industry, no account of time, no arts, no letters, no society, and which is worst of all, continual fear and danger of violent death, and the life of man solitary, poor, nasty, brutish and short . . .

THOMAS HOBBES, *Leviathan* (1651)

When men quit the state of nature and entered into society, they agreed that *all but one of them* should be under the restraint of laws, and that he should still retain all the liberty of this state of nature, increased with power, and made licentious by impunity. This serves to demonstrate that men are so foolish that they take care to avoid what mischiefs may be done them by polecats or foxes, but are content, nay, think it safety, to be devoured by lions.

JOHN LOCKE, *Two Treatises of Government* (1690)

: excerpts in a notebook found among the possessions of Terry Keyes

By half past midnight they also knew the following: The one distinct footprint Montone found imprinted in the living room carpet matched a pair of shoes in Dennis's closet, there were no incoming unscreened messages on his answering machine and the redial button on his phone connected them to a young woman named Louisa Fernandez, who had for the last five months been working as the anchorman's personal assistant.

Miss Fernandez made it to the apartment shortly after one o'clock that night. She was a spectacular-looking twenty-six-year-old native of Miami, with a butternut tan and the kind of lustrous cascade of thick brown hair you see in shampoo commercials. Her parents were Cuban-born but Louisa spoke unaccented English and presented a perfect example of the pulled-together, ambitious career girl that New York still hauled in by the thousands. Louisa did not strike Montone as characteristically hysterical, but she cried long and hard when he broke the news about her boss.

They spoke in the foyer outside the apartment, Montone taking notes, handing her a fresh supply of Kleenex, glancing occasionally at the hem of her pleated navy skirt, which had been riding steadily north on her bare brown legs ever since they sat down. He recognized and dismissed his attraction to her as an instinctual response to grief in someone so young and beautiful.

"I never knew anybody that died before," Louisa said.

Louisa described a job that sounded like a 1950s housewife, without any of the long-term benefits or job security. The network paid her a rookie patrolman's salary to run the guy's errands, take in dry cleaning, buy his Christmas presents and just maybe, on occasion, Montone speculated, perform the most traditional matrimonial service.

Louisa told him she had purchased the take-out food Montone found in the refrigerator and brought it over at approximately six-thirty. She used her own key to get in and saw no one in the apartment. Then she'd gone out to dinner with some friends and returned home at eleven-thirty to find a message from Dennis on her machine—logged in at 7:35 p.m.—asking her to pick up weekend tickets for a

Broadway musical. Nothing to suggest he was planning a dive out the window.

"When did you see him last, Louisa?" asked Jimmy.

"I spoke to him last at the studio at about five, before the broadcast. That was our routine, check in at the end of the day. He asked me to pick up the stuff from Zabar's."

"Anything unusual about the order?"

"No; usual stuff."

"Did he mention any plans he had for the evening?"

She shook her head. "He said he was tired. He had to do the show from Washington tomorrow—I guess it's today now, isn't it?—and he wanted to get some rest." She squeezed out another tear.

"You notice anything unusual at work yesterday?"

She thought for a moment. "No."

"He speak to or mention anybody you didn't know?"

"I was running around most of the day—that's not what you asked. No, nobody that stands out."

"See anybody hanging around the apartment? Stairwells? Elevators?"

"No."

"He get any crank calls? Crazy letters from fans? Anybody fixated on him that way?"

"No. I mean, maybe he did. Not that I knew about."

"Did he own a video camera that you were aware of?"

That threw a jolt into her. She turned two shades paler under the tan. Pain spread across her face; she put a hand to her forehead. "Shit."

Montone waited. A fat tear splashed onto her knee.

"My mother is gonna kill me. She's gonna kill me and then she's gonna die of a heart attack."

Montone kept quiet. One of the guys from the squad, Mike Murphy, chose that moment to step out of the elevator. He was about to say something when Montone waved him into the apartment. Montone handed Louisa another Kleenex.

"You found the videotape, didn't you?" she said, eyes red.

Montone nodded, but aside from that he barely breathed, realizing he was about to hear either the easiest confession he'd ever solicited or maybe something even more interesting.

Louisa dropped her voice about an octave, leaning forward,

looking up at Montone from under her hair. "They warned me about him when I interviewed for the job, okay?"

"Who did, dear?"

"Some girls at the office. I was working as a temp and one day I'm in my cubicle, typing, and he comes to talk to me, out of the blue."

"Mr. Dennis did."

"Mack. Everybody called him Mack. Do you have any cigarettes?"

Montone had one out for her and lit in about two seconds; although he no longer smoked he always carried a pack for perps, informers, witnesses. Louisa took a deep drag and leaned forward over her crossed legs. The flat she was wearing lolled off her top foot, flapping back and forth in a lazy rhythm, highlighting the tendons in her instep. The starch had gone out of her, taking with it enough of the refinement she'd been putting on for the real girl to come through; a sly earthiness that made her sexual relationship with Dennis more explicable.

Montone's first operating principle: Wait long enough and keep your mouth shut and people will reveal themselves to you.

"So he says to me his assistant just quit on him, he's looking for a replacement. Describes what I'd be doing. I'm biting my lip to keep from saying yes too fast."

"And some of the girls warned you, what, that . . . there might be more to the job than what he'd told you about."

She nodded, glad that he was helping, without sounding like what she'd done was wrong or even that surprising.

"So about a month goes by and we, you know, one night we became intimate. He initiated it and I . . . I know it's like a completely bad idea so I'm trying not to make anything more of it than what it was . . . but I guess I went along with it, didn't I?"

"Which was what?"

"About once a week. On a slow night when he wasn't wearing out one of his tuxedos. He'd call. I'd come over."

"Did you ever go out together?"

She blew smoke, angling her head like that was a funny question. "He was my boss."

"Ever spend the night?"

"No. I had to get up early and go to work in the morning."

"How'd you feel about him?"

She looked as if she didn't understand the question.

"Did you like him?"

"Oh. No, not much. He lived in his own world, you know? Center of the known universe. I walked in on him doing weight lifter poses in front of the mirror in his gym one day? He didn't even seem embarrassed, stays right in the pose and says, 'Not bad for forty-eight, huh?' " She rolled her eyes.

"Ever see him do any drugs?"

"I never even saw him have a second beer."

"Now what about this videotape?"

"Okay. This one time about two months ago Mack brings out this video camera, sets it up on a tripod near the bed and, you know . . ." She looked at the floor, turning a shade red, and flicked at the cigarette even though the ash was down to the nub.

"He taped the two of you making love."

"Yeah. And then he wanted to watch afterwards. He got off on it but it gave me the creeps. I guess he was more used to seeing himself on TV than I was."

Nice; a little irony. "It made you uncomfortable."

"I went to Catholic school, okay? I asked him to erase it, he promised he would and says besides, he'd never show it to anybody. Now it'll probably end up on *Hard Copy*. I figure I'm already going to hell for this anyway. I mean, I'm in trouble, right?"

"You have a boyfriend, Louisa? Dating anybody right now?"

"No."

"Any exes hanging around, holding a torch for you?"

"No." She sounded annoyed by the suggestion.

"Where were you at about ten forty-five?"

"Still at the restaurant."

"With five of your friends, right?"

"Right."

"So it's pretty likely you didn't push your boss out that window."

Her eyes widened. "Somebody pushed him?"

"Did I say that? No, I said *you* didn't."

"Oh. No. God. Course I didn't."

"So what's there for you to be in trouble about?"

She appeared to relax, looking around for a place to put out the cigarette. Montone looked too, saw nothing in the piss-elegant entryway, so he took the butt from her, smiled politely and walked it into the apartment.

The two CSU teams, wearing gloves and cotton booties, were crawling over the living room, now crisscrossed with long plastic runners, vacuuming for fibers, dusting the home theater components for prints. One of them had Dennis's computer open on the dining room table; Montone made a mental note to catalog its contents.

Murphy was standing in the kitchen with Hank Lopez, one of the night shift guys who'd come in, maybe the laziest detective in the squad. Lopez was giving him the evil eye; he must've been next on the chart and Coxen passed him over, Montone realized. No wonder. Lopez nursed a grudge if you borrowed a pencil.

Murphy, fat, easygoing Murph, had a smirk on his big florid mug as Montone carried the cigarette to the sink and doused it with water.

"So he was boinking her, right?" said Murphy.

"Get your mind out of the gutter, Murph." Montone dropped the butt in the trash. "No more than once a week, tops."

Murphy laughed that wheezy smokaholic laugh of his and held out his hand; Lopez handed him a five.

"You want to believe the best about somebody and look where it gets you," muttered Lopez.

"Yeah," said Murphy, pocketing the bill with his plump, clever hands. "He was one of my role models, too, Hank. That guy could fucking *read.*"

"I wasn't talking about him," said Lopez, with a nice view of Louisa's crossed legs.

"She says he owned a video camera," said Montone, then lowered his voice. "And unless he recorded over it, there's another video in here I want to see worse than *Batman.*"

"The two a them?" asked Murphy alertly. "Need some help, Jimmy?"

Montone found a cabinet full of tapes in Dennis's office, labeled in ways that indicated they featured Mackenzie Dennis broadcast highlights. Montone had a patrolman box and tag them so he could take them home and make sure there weren't any other surprises.

In the desk's bottom drawer, resting neatly on some files, Montone found a Hi-8 Panasonic camera. The tripod he located in a closet behind the desk. He called in the crime unit to dust the camera, desk and tripod, feeling fairly certain they'd come up dry.

Montone walked out to Louisa again. One of the CSU boys had just finished fingerprinting her. She looked up at Montone, worried, as if mug shots and a lineup were next. Montone explained it was a standard procedure so they could eliminate her prints from any they found in the apartment.

He asked for her key to Dennis's apartment, told her anything of a personal nature she'd left inside would be available to her as soon as they'd finished their investigation. She pulled the key off a University of Miami key chain. Montone pocketed the key and gave her his business card, with the voice mail number circled, in case she remembered anything, saying he'd probably need to speak to her again.

Louisa wiped the stubborn ink off her fingers with another Kleenex, took his card and studied it, as if trying to memorize the numbers. Montone recognized that she was reluctant to leave, go home to an empty apartment and lie there awake thinking about this man she'd slept with hitting the sidewalk. He gently cupped a hand on Louisa's elbow, guiding her into the elevator.

"Jesus. It didn't even occur to me," she said, halfway down, staring at the floor.

"What's that?"

"I'm out of a job."

Montone waited a beat. "Not that it's any of my business, but can I give you a piece of advice, Louisa?"

She looked at him, nodded, slightly slack-jawed.

"Anybody from the media tries to buy your story, and they will, tell 'em to take a hike. They're gonna come at you now twelve ways from Sunday; people you never heard of, trying to be your new best friend. Just know you don't have to answer any questions, not even if I'm asking them, not if they make you uneasy. If they do, you hire a lawyer, he'll answer 'em for you; that's what's they get paid for, to take the heat.

"This guy, you picked up his shirts for him, you bought some cold cuts; now he's dead and you move on with your life. You seem like a nice girl. Nobody ever has to know about you and him, or anything about any videotape, because they won't from me."

She picked at a loose thread on her sleeve, glanced up at him, her face knotted, trying not to cry.

"Thanks" was all she could manage.

"You remember that."

The doors opened. The crowd outside had grown to over two hundred people; a line of uniforms held back a pack of media pressing at the front entrance. The sight confirmed Louisa's worst fears. She started to crumble.

Montone told Louisa to stay put, walked to a patrolman he knew, and then he waved the building's stout little doorman over. He laid a trusting hand on the doorman's shoulder, lowered his voice, read his name tag.

"Artie, I'd appreciate it if you could escort the young lady out of the building without any hassles from our friends outside."

"Basement; not a problem," the doorman said, hyperefficiently. "Service entrance feeds into the alley on Sixty-eighth. Not even staked out yet."

Montone turned to the uniform: "You put her in your unit, drive her home, see her up to her apartment. Check out the closets, look under the bed, make her feel safe before you leave. I want a car outside her building the rest of the night and drive-bys all day tomorrow."

Montone led them back to where Louisa was waiting, explained the plan, took her ink-smudged hand in both of his and offered his sympathies, privately hoping that the person who had pushed Mackenzie Dennis didn't decide, by whatever twisted reasoning, that her number was up next. The doorman and the uniform walked Louisa down the stairs.

Top brass filled the far end of the lobby; Captain (Dapper) Dan Jakes, wearing one of his fifteen-hundred dollar suits, flashing 18-karat cuff links, was calming down Flannigan, the Borough Commander, and Bill Foley, the Chief of Detectives, who had just rolled in from downtown. Coxen hung back behind the group, glancing over at Montone, waiting for the egos to sort out who was going to handle the press conference. Dapper Dan saw Montone near the elevator and waved him over.

Eric Bowman

"The network's already flying flags at half-mast, for Christ's sake," the Chief said. "They pulled the president out of some awards dinner in Beverly Hills; he's catching the red-eye. This guy is a personal friend of mine."

"We're getting behind the curve here," said Foley, glancing nervously out at the crowd.

"Anything from the girl, Jimmy?" asked Dan Jakes.

Montone shook hands all around. No introductions; they all knew him and liked seeing him there. Since they were all more politician than cop now, it reassured them to know one of the department's shining lights was on the job.

"Found a video camera. Apparently he got a charge out of watching himself mambo.

"We got a case here," Montone went on, running down the pertinent details for them. "We don't have any witnesses or suspects, but we got a case. Murder one."

Silence dropped like a rock, everyone waiting for the Chief to react. He studied a well-manicured hand.

"Gotta give 'em a statement or they'll hang around all night," the Chief said, with a nod back at the press outside.

"Run it down, Jimmy?" asked Dan Jakes.

"Somebody moved the camera and tripod after Dennis went out the window. Nobody saw glass come down before the body, so he didn't break it first himself, with a chair say, then put the camera gear away, then jump. We won't know if it's the same camera I found till we check the tape, but I'm guessing it is. Somebody put it back in the desk. And they smoothed out the carpet, too; no indents from the tripod."

"Why the fuck would somebody do all that?" asked Coxen, irritably. His stomach grumbled; he winced, perpetually halfway to an ulcer.

"Gimme a break, Lou, it's only been two hours." Montone looked to the senior guys for a little relief; the Chief stayed stone-faced.

"What about this taped confession?" he asked. Jakes and Flannigan had already been upstairs to see the tape; the Chief hadn't.

"This guy made one hell of a living making it look like he wasn't reading when he was reading."

"Reading what, in this instance?"

"Cue cards maybe. Behind the camera. This 'confession' sounded like it was scripted to me."

"So you're saying it's no suicide. Definitive."

"Two things: Jumpers go feet first and they almost never go butt naked. This guy took a header, plus, from what I know of him, he's got way too much self-esteem."

The Chief looked out at the news crews again on the far side of the lobby's glass wall. Hot spots of wandering light caught reporters jostling for a good frame, getting ready for their close-ups.

Dapper Dan gestured to Montone: Thanks, Jimmy. Give us a minute.

Montone walked back across the lobby, wishing he still smoked, and watched them confer like a crew of umpires trying to make a tough call in the deciding game of the World Series. The Chief did most of the talking, a lot of it with his hands. Finally, something decided, Dapper Dan and Coxen walked to Montone, while the big boys went outside to face the cameras.

"We want you out front on this, Jimmy," said Dan.

"Open checkbook?" asked Montone, with a pointed glance at Coxen.

"Open checkbook. Task force. We want exceptional clearance. Send a message we're on top of it."

"I wouldn't say homicide to anybody tonight, Cap. They get the facts, that's it. And I wouldn't say word one about that tape. Zip it, lock it and send it to the Cave."

"Good call," said Dan, flashing his cuffs. "It's your case, Jimmy. We'll need a statement from you for the news. You know the drill."

"Let me know who you want on the team," said Coxen.

Montone nodded gravely, shook both their hands before he followed the chiefs outside.

A tall silver-haired old man stood across the street, half a block down from the crowd. He looked like a respectable Upper East Sider on his way home, but closer scrutiny would have revealed frays at the seams of his clean Burberry raincoat and rounded heels on his sturdy brogans.

When he'd heard about the anchorman's death on the radio in his hotel room, the old man had quickly riffled through his notebook of clipped newspaper stories.

There it was, a party photograph on a three-week-old society page; Terry Keyes standing just over the dead newscaster's shoulder.

The old man had immediately walked north along Fifth Avenue, driven by an instinct that what he'd been waiting for had begun. Television trucks congested the streets around the site. The crowd expanded steadily.

"They saying he jumped," a Hispanic man explained to a blank-faced girl. "That's where he landed, right there. I seen them cleaning up the blood."

"He was pushed," said the old man to himself, in a flat British Midlands accent.

"On the radio they was saying it's suicide," said the girl.

"Pushed," said the Englishman, staring up at the broken window. He carried an unsettling presence, a shroud of stillness, in-penetrable. The young couple glanced at each other warily and moved on.

The Englishman stayed for an hour behind the barricades, watching everything.

"At approximately ten forty-five this evening, Mr. Mackenzie Dennis fell from his thirty-fifth-floor apartment window," said Montone. "Officers from the Nineteenth Precinct responded within minutes. Mr. Dennis was pronounced dead at the scene; his body was taken to the medical examiner's office, where an autopsy will be performed tomorrow."

The reporters jamming microphones in his face shouted a solid wall of questions about the possibility of foul play. Montone waved them off, regretfully indicating he wanted to be more help but his hands were tied: they knew how it was.

"Sorry, folks, that's all we've got."

Uniforms closed the gap as Montone slipped back inside the building.

"Were you surprised to get this case, Jimmy?" called out a reporter.

Montone looked back over his shoulder, smiled confidently. No surprise there.

"Of course you drew the case, Jimmy," whispered Terry Keyes.

Ninety-nine percent probability.

"Well begun is half done."

Sitting on a chair one foot in front of the set in his Plaza suite, Keyes hit the mute button on the remote as CNN cut to its reporter on the scene. Keyes looked at the luminous hands of his Rolex. Two-fifteen.

He glanced back at the girl in the bed; snoring lightly. She'd reliably passed out only minutes after Keyes dissolved a two-milligram dose of Rohypnol in her third glass of champagne.

Keyes silently rose and entered the walk-in closet. He removed from the dresser a small black satchel—heavy with the clothes and hardware he had used earlier—and folded it inside the garment bag he'd made a point of hanging in plain view on the hook of the open closet door. He knew the garment bag had caused the girl no undue concern, part of the romantic surprise he'd created for her.

If she'd seen what was in the satchel her evening would have ended far less happily.

He stepped back into the bedroom, opened the girl's large beaded handbag and took out her Filofax. Glancing at her driver's license, he noticed, without surprise, that she had lied about her age. After making sure the phone numbers and addresses he wanted were inside, he slipped the notebook into his suitcase.

He propped the note he'd written along with a single red rose on the pillow beside her, hung the tab with a breakfast order on the outside knob, shouldered his bag and padded silently down the back stairs to the Fifty-eighth Street exit. No one saw him go.

After walking twenty blocks to the south and west, he dropped the black satchel into a Dumpster parked at a construction site. As he moved out of sight, a garbage truck turned the corner for collection, right on time.

Tyler woke at seven when a waiter knocked on the door. Vision blurred, head throbbing, she hadn't the slightest idea where she was.

Her eyes picked up the rose on the pillow, then tried to focus on the note:

6:00 am
My Darling Tyler,
    What a fabulous night! Sorry I had to leave but I'm off to work; the habits of a disciplined life die hard and you looked so beautiful and peaceful that I hadn't the heart to wake you.
    You mentioned another party tonight. Yes. Tremendous. May I bring along a new friend? He's a bachelor; maybe we can fix him up with that model friend of yours you were telling me about. What was her name? The one with the dreadful harassment problem? Holly, wasn't it?
    I think she might like this friend of mine. He's a famous police detective.
    Talk later.

    Yours, Terry

She finished the note, pulled on a robe, told the waiter where to set down the tray, stumbled into the bathroom and threw up prolifically.

Slumped on the cold tile floor, drenched in sweat, Tyler realized she still clutched the note in her hand. She smoothed out the wrinkles, and after reading it a second time, she retrieved a vague physical recollection of being thoroughly and repeatedly ravaged. The memory clouded but the note sounded cheerful, as if *he* thought they'd had a pretty good time. He called her "darling" and said she looked beautiful. Not altogether bad news. Even more encouraging was the mention of getting together tonight.

Tyler glanced over and saw herself in the floor-length mirror.

Livid bruises marred her wrists and upper arms. Turning, she realized the oval splotches on the inside of her thigh were finger imprints. A sinking sensation ran down into her belly as she experienced an involuntary flash of memory; the two of them, entwined, how strong he was, bending her down and over—

"Oh God."

She felt sick again, shivers racked her body. Tyler looked up and saw dark water beading in a discolored patch near the corner of the ceiling where a fragment of paper had curled away from the wall.

You bruise easily, she reminded herself. Don't make more of this than you need to, because the good news is you may have a boyfriend.

Montone had the first key in the door when he heard the phone ring inside. He opened all three locks, rushed into his living room, set down the box carrying Dennis's computer and tape collection and caught the call just before the machine picked up.

"Montone."

"Jimmy; Terry Keyes."

"Hey, how you doing?"

"I'm not calling too early, am I?"

"No, not at all." Jimmy glanced at his watch: five minutes after eight.

"Good, good. Jesus, Jimmy, I just saw you on the news."

"Yeah? How'd I look?"

"What can I say? You're the real deal. I mean, this is amazing. We were at this big party last night when the news about Dennis came in and it was like a bomb went off."

"People see somebody on TV a lot, they feel like they know him," said Montone.

"But I did know him. I met him about three weeks ago. We talked on somebody's dock for, I don't know, must have been half an hour."

"Where was this?"

"Some party in the Hamptons. One of these society ordeals my editor's always dragging me off to."

Montone sat down. "What was he like?"

A thoughtful pause. "Carried himself well. Bit of a pontificator, aware of his own importance. Polite, but guarded. He wanted to make sure who he was with before he revealed himself."

"Any drugs at that party?"

"Good Lord, do people still do drugs?"

"You'd be surprised."

"I think he was drinking white wine. Didn't strike me as an addictive type; too vain for self-abuse. And a major pussy hound."

"No kidding."

"He must have hit on everything under forty with a pulse and a handbag."

"He there by himself?"

"That was my impression—I'm sorry, Jimmy, you must have a million things on your mind. I just wanted to thank you again for your offer to help. I thought I'd get the machine."

"Offer's still good. You want to come and hang with us on this one today, it could be exactly what you're looking for."

Keyes paused; cautious, respectful. "Are you saying what I think you're saying?"

"Don't quote me yet."

"Foul play."

"It's a possibility. You wanted to follow a case from start to finish."

"Only if you're sure I won't be in your way."

"Like you said, you knew the guy. Maybe you'll shake something loose that helps us out."

And you knew him too, didn't you, Jimmy?

"I'm happy to help in any way I can."

Montone gave him the address of the medical examiner's office, where the autopsy was scheduled for eleven.

He'd have to run the idea by Murphy and the rest of his team, but if there was going to be a book on this case, unlike the half-dozen cheapies that flooded the market after he brought down the Slug, Montone was all for letting an author in on the ground floor. Better to control the flow of information than have the guy running around loose on his own. The brass didn't even have to know about it. After spending a few years in this city's public eye, Montone had learned a trick or two about controlling the spin.

Montone switched off his phone and headed for his bedroom. Completing their initial canvas and closing down the scene had taken all night. A two-hour nap and he'd be good to go.

Terry Keyes set down the cellular phone on the ledge of the roof but kept his binoculars trained on Montone until he walked into his bedroom and closed the blinds. The one-bedroom apartment was on the sixth floor of a building on Thirty-seventh between Eighth and Ninth.

After becoming aware of James Montone during the last year of his incarceration, Keyes had read every word ever written about the detective. Most of the books about the Sligo case were shallow, unreadable attempts to cash in on the immediate sensation of the case, but his study only began there. Montone fit the profile he was looking for perfectly. No psychoanalyst ever brought more scrutiny to bear on a subject.

Wendell Sligo himself had proved to be an invaluable source of information.

With his computer, Keyes had hacked into Montone's bank records, credit reports, pension information. Montone had been born and raised in Queens, but he paid twenty-three hundred a month for the privilege of sleeping in Manhattan, while most of his colleagues made the daily commute from suburbs in Queens, Rockland County, Staten Island. Keyes knew Montone wouldn't take that ride back across the Triborough Bridge; he'd tried too hard to build a life on the fashionable side of the river.

Working-class background. The golden boy who caught all the breaks and closed the big cases.

The hero who brought the Slug to justice.

That cocky, confident smile on TV.

But I know the price you've paid for your fame, Jimmy. I know about those visits to the department psychologist.

The night sweats. The waking visions of that girl in the van.

When we're through with the dance you'll look back on those days like a favorite summer.

Keyes stood on the roof of the building on Thirty-ninth in which he had rented a top-floor office. The name in the lobby directory read "Howard Kurtzman, Capital Investments." Kurtzman's home address was an apartment on Flatbush Avenue, a safe house Keyes had set up during his last visit to the States.

Mr. Kurtzman, as the building's manager would have described him, was a short, pudgy middle-aged man with a prominent graying mustache. He wore a hearing aid and glasses with thick black frames that magnified his bright green eyes, walked with a slight limp and spoke with a pronounced Brooklyn accent. Since taking the office last fall, Mr. Kurtzman had never lodged a complaint, seldom came into the office and always minded his own business, which was why neither the manager nor anyone else in the building ever gave him a second thought.

Keyes capped the binoculars and walked downstairs. Making sure the corridor was empty, he entered Mr. Kurtzman's office and locked the door. He set the thick black glasses down on the desk and removed the tinted seagreen contact lenses. He applied spirit gum remover to the edge of the mustache, then retrieved a lukewarm raspberry Snapple from his bag, which he drank through a straw.

He ordered flowers for delivery to Tyler Angstrom at her office. As he ate a bag of ripe cherries and piled the pits in an ashtray, he modemed his laptop computer to an on-line stockbroker service, surveyed the day's market trends and made three prudent plays.

During his American book tour the previous fall Keyes had opened brokerage accounts in three different cities. In the intervening months he aggressively worked his stocks and commodities from London, averaging ten thousand dollars' income a week, rolling profits back into the accounts.

At the same time, Keyes had quietly shifted his prior holdings to the States. With the advance from his new book in hand, he had a quarter of a million dollars in a number of cash and investment accounts established under a variety of names. Over twenty-five credit cards issued in those names had been waiting for him in rented post office boxes when he arrived back in New York.

To begin work on his magnum opus. The definitive statement about murder in America.

Keyes set Tyler Angstrom's Filofax down on the desk and paged through it; names, home addresses, answering services, private phone lines, faxes, computer on-line access codes, all written in her schoolgirl-neat hand. In another section she had broken down the list into sociological categories, an index for the purpose of organizing party invitations: Film, Fashion, Society, Publishing, Fortune 500, Media.

He had singled Tyler out after reading about this list in a magazine profile of her. His subsequent research had been exhaustive. He knew her habits. He knew her patterns. He knew her weaknesses.

The woman's aggravating compulsiveness had proved to be exactly as useful as he had estimated: Keyes had in his hands a compendium of the city's elite. Switching on his office Xerox, he photocopied every page, arranged the duplicates in a three-ring binder, carefully replaced the originals and dropped Tyler's Filofax into a large plain envelope.

Keyes plugged his phone into a black box in the top drawer of the desk. He hit play on a handheld microcassette recorder and set it beside the mouthpiece: New York street sounds issued from the tape. While the black box routed the call through one of fifty pay phone numbers he had randomly collected from around the city, Keyes dialed the new home number of Holly Mews.

The poor girl had changed it recently after receiving a series of disturbing phone calls.

He heard her voice on the answering machine: cheeky, teasing, unduly confident.

"This is Holly. You know what to do and when to do it."

He held the tape recorder to the phone and left thirty seconds of street noise, then added some deep breathing before hanging up.

Slipping on a pair of surgical gloves, Keyes lifted two newspapers from his briefcase. With a pair of scissors he cut out an assortment of individual letters from their Mackenzie Dennis stories. He arranged them on a sheet of common copier paper, waited for the glue to set, then folded the note into a dime-store envelope and affixed a stamp.

Using bold block letters, he addressed the letter to "Ms. Holly Mews."

He unlocked a cabinet door and checked a stack of two VCRs inside; the tape he was copying had finished. He removed the duplicate Hi-8 videotape from the lower deck. The tape went into a bubble-pack envelope, already stamped and addressed.

Keyes removed the mustache, Mr. Kurtzman's clothes and the padding from his waist. He locked the glasses, gloves, contact lenses and electronic gear in the bottom drawer of the filing cabinet and changed back to Terry Keyes; black jeans, black Nike Air high-tops, a white Gap T-shirt, tan linen jacket. He put on a NY Yankees baseball cap and a pair of Ray Ban Wayfarers.

Exiting the office, he took the back stairs down to the street and walked east on Thirty-ninth. Just for fun he placed another call to Holly Mews's answering machine from a pay phone in front of his building.

As he continued along his way he dropped the letter to the girl, holding it by the edges, into a mailbox. When he reached the crowded post office on Third he entered and dropped the bubble-pack envelope in a local mail slot.

3

Dear Mr. Sligo,

I am organizing a visit to your part of the world in order to conduct some research on the book I am writing. Any volume that aspires to present a survey on the phenomenon of murder in the United States, as this one does, would fall woefully short of its stated mission if it failed to include an extensive profile of yourself.

Fully aware that you have offered cooperation to a number of writers and journalists in the past, I am equally certain of your disappointment in the lack of insight or compassion shown to you in their resulting work. In order to set to rest in advance whatever reservations you may feel in response to this request, I have taken the liberty of enclosing my two previously published works, confident that you will find in them sufficient evidence of my sincerity and innate understanding of your situation.

I am particularly interested to speak with you in person, Mr. Sligo, and I will be in touch with you again shortly to see when such a time during my visit might be conveniently arranged.

Respectfully yours,

Terence Peregrine Keyes

: letter found among the personal effects of Wendell "the Slug" Sligo
at Attica State Penitentiary

Upon first viewing the body, the chief medical examiner offered Montone a characteristically dry opinion on the cause of death.

"This looks like a man who fell from a thirty-fifth-floor window," she said.

The forty-two-year-old daughter of a Chinatown merchant, Dr. Rayfen Lee carried a spotless reputation as the sharpest no-excuses pathologist on the staff.

Half an hour later she had Mackenzie Dennis zipped open from collarbone to gut. As she worked, narrating the procedure into an overhead microphone for later transcription, a wealth of detail accumulated to substantiate her first impression. Massive blunt-force trauma. Crushed foresection of the skull. Dozens of bone and glass fragments driven deeply into the brain. Multiple fractures of both shoulders, legs and arms. Pelvis pulverized; internal organs massively ruptured. Spleen nearly liquefied. The undigested contents of his stomach were consistent with the Zabar's takeout they'd found in his refrigerator.

She pointed out a pale circle of skin around the ring finger of his tanned right hand.

"He wore a ring here," said Dr. Lee. "Married?"

"Wrong hand," said Montone.

"Wrong guy," said Murphy.

Blood, bile and urine samples, extracted early that morning, were already undergoing analysis. Montone wanted the results from those tests as quickly as possible. At his urging, Chief of Detectives Foley had put in a call to the ME's office authorizing a rush. Some results would be available by the end of the day. Those that would normally take weeks should now be available in days.

With difficulty Dr. Lee had been able to dissect intact tissue sectionals from brain, liver and kidney.

"Think you should run high-pressure liquid chromatography on those," Montone suggested.

"You're looking for barbiturate?" she asked, raising a sleek eyebrow above her mask.

Montone nodded. Murphy stared at him; it was the first he'd heard of the involvement of any drug other than cocaine.

"Any particular derivative?" asked Dr. Lee.

"Amobarbital."

Dr. Lee nodded and handed the tray of glass tile specimens to her assistant. "Ultraviolet spectrophotometry. Flame ionization. High-pressure chromatography."

The assistant made some notations and carried the tray off toward the lab.

"If you're looking for long-term abuse there's no intravenous damage," said Dr. Lee.

"This would likely be a one-time thing," said Montone.

Dr. Lee leaned forward and alertly scanned the backs of Dennis's hands and arms. "Intramuscular perhaps."

She lifted and extended the victim's left arm, then pulled down a magnifying lens suspended on a retractable frame above the table and trained it on the upper tricep. With a steel pointer she drew Montone's attention to a pinprick crimson dot in the center of the muscle.

"Maybe here," she said.

"Pretty hard to self-administer in the back of your own arm, isn't it?"

"Yes. Not impossible."

Something else caught her eye; she pulled the lens down to just above the neck and studied the skin closely, then used the pointer to show Montone two slight, thin red abrasions that overlapped each other, running horizontally across the base of Dennis's throat. She tracked the lines around to the back of his neck, where they were only faintly visible, concealed by massive trauma from the fall.

"These are consistent with ligature striations," she said.

"Jesus. He was strangled?" asked Murphy, leaning in behind them.

"Twice," said Montone.

Terry Keyes sat waiting for them on a bench in the corridor outside. He had politely refused Montone's offer to visit the morgue during any part of the autopsy. Exposure to that sort of anatomical detail would only fuel his already too vivid imagination, Keyes told them sheepishly.

The three men went for coffee at a diner down the street from the morgue. Keyes presented Montone with a hardcover edition of his most recent book, *Flatlander,* by Peregrine Keyes. He inscribed it as they sat in the booth:

To Jimmy, May you always get your man. Best wishes, Terry.

Murphy turned the book around in his hands as if it were a slightly dangerous object. "What is this, like a novel?"

"Very much so. In fact, it *is* one."

"No kidding. How'd it do?"

"Five weeks on the *New York Times* bestsellers list," said Keyes, matter-of-factly.

"Good for you," said Murphy. "They gonna make a movie?"

"A studio bought the rights."

"Yeah? Who's gonna be in it?"

Montone cringed slightly: Murphy was a lot of things, but suave wasn't one of them.

"They haven't gotten around to that yet," said Keyes, friendly. "I've been advised not to hold my breath."

Murphy balanced the book on his palm, as if trying to weigh its value by the ounce. "Where do you get your ideas?"

"Oh, you know. Here and there."

"Peregrine, that's an unusual name. What kind of name is that?"

"It's my middle name, actually. Publishers seem to prefer it, that's why it's on the book. Certainly wouldn't be my choice. My real name's Terence. Terry."

"So which is it, Terry or Perry?"

"Either one," said Keyes, with an agreeable smile. "Or both."

"Terry-Perry?"

"A peregrine's a bird, isn't it?" said Montone.

"Yes. A breed of falcon."

"The kind they hunt with. I read something about this."

"So what's this supposed to be, a castle?" asked Murphy, pointing to the illustration on the book's jacket; a Gothic stone structure framed against a bleak sunset horizon.

"It's a prison."

"No shit. Hope it's not autobiographical," said Murphy, laughing and wheezing a little.

"It is, actually," said Keyes calmly.

Murphy quieted instantly, then set the book down.

"I got the impression you weren't aware of my background, which frankly surprised me," said Keyes, looking directly at Montone. "It's all these magazines ever seem to write about. If your Information Office didn't tell you I thought you ought to know."

"You did time," said Montone evenly.

"Twelve years. In that one there," said Keyes, pointing to the book jacket.

"No shit," said Murphy.

Montone wanted to ask what he went away for, but waited. Better to hear him tell it.

"I had a troubled childhood, not that that's any excuse. The usual delinquent indiscretions, petty theft, vandalism. But I pulled it together in school. With the attentions of an interested teacher I tested high enough to attract a scholarship to university."

Murphy uneasily shifted his weight in the booth; Montone felt like the seat panel might pop him into the air like a teeter-totter. Ever since Murphy stopped drinking and started eating, he'd been spreading out faster than Orson Welles.

"The night before I'm to leave for Cambridge this old friend of mine, without telling me, sets me up with a prostitute. We go out, he gets me pissed to the gills and then takes me to meet this girl he knows under a pier at the beach; the most beautiful he's ever seen, straight off a centerfold. This was his idea of a joke, to give you some idea of the company I was keeping. Captain of the bloody soccer team. What he'd actually done was dig up a streetwalker from Blackpool. What you might charitably call a 'skank.' "

"Plenty of those around," said Murphy, regretting he'd opened the whole thing up to begin with.

"I'm alone, waiting under the pier when this woman steps out of the dark. And she's like Medusa; foul-mouthed, strung out, vicious. She grabs me and starts demanding I give her the money she's owed. I didn't know anything about their arrangement but I hear my mate up on the pier, laughing himself sick. Only I'm so snozzled I can't stay on my feet, let alone convince her I've been had.

"The woman slugs me, knocks me right to the ground, then sits on my chest. Spewing venom right in my face. I'm pleading with her to get off me, I can't breathe, I think I'm dying. She sticks a hand down my pants and starts fondling me and when I don't respond—how could I, under the circumstances—"

Terry's hand shook slightly as he stirred his coffee. Looking down into the cup, face flushed, disturbed by the memory.

"—she goes berserk, slapping me, swinging her handbag, and I haul off and catch her flush in the jaw. A solid punch. I meant to hit her with all I had, no question about that. She falls backward and hits her head against a rock in the seawall. I was out of my mind with anger. I stumbled over on top of her and hit her again. Then once more. I hit her those three times."

He stopped stirring the coffee, holding the spoon frozen above the cup.

"She died instantly when her head hit that rock. I had no idea. I crawled down to the water, violently ill. Apparently I was screaming. A policeman found me a few minutes later, lying near her body, so drunk I could barely speak. My friend, the only witness who might have supported this version of events, ran off before anyone saw him.

"It was those last two punches. That's what they built their case on. I hit her after she was dead. Didn't know that at the time, obviously, but there it was."

"You go to trial?" asked Montone.

"Court-appointed lawyer talked me into pleading guilty without one. Case drew a lot of attention when a London newscaster did a series of television reports: the lower-class lad who'd been given every chance to succeed and still managed to fuck up his life.

"After that the university dropped me cold. My friend the soccer player refused to testify on my behalf; claimed he hadn't even been there. He had his own scholarship to worry about. He went on to quite a career; used to watch his games on TV while I was inside. After running me through some tests, this expert psychologist decided that I had known exactly what I was doing at the time of the crime. With all that weighing on him the judge decided he should make an example of me and handed down the maximum sentence. Fifteen years. I didn't even appeal. I felt so low I thought I deserved whatever they did to me."

Keyes looked at them both with naked honesty. "They'd probably all look at me today and tell you prison was the best thing that ever happened to me. If I hadn't gone inside I never would've straightened myself out. Started writing on the prison newspaper. Gave me a second chance at life, let me find a meaningful career, whereas if I'd stayed out in the world I would've self-destructed eventually. Maybe even done more damage, to myself or someone else.

"I'm not bitter, but I'm not so convinced. Even if it was the best thing, what does it matter? It came at the cost of that woman's life. Black and white. A day doesn't go by I don't see her face. Miserable as she was when our paths crossed, she must have had her own hopes and dreams. In time maybe she would have turned herself around. Who knows?"

No one spoke.

"These things happen," said Murphy, the philosopher, with a dismissive wave of a hand.

"You had to kill a man in the line of duty once, didn't I read that somewhere, Jimmy?"

Montone nodded.

"How'd you take it?"

"Bothered me at the time. Not anymore."

"See, this isn't the same. It doesn't fade. That's why I couldn't look at that body on the table today. Why I write the things I write about. It's your job to stop people from killing each other, or when they do, to make them pay for it. As I see it, my job's trying to understand why it happens in the first place."

Keyes went quiet. A waitress refilled their cups as they sat in silence. Murphy glanced at Montone, trying to get a read on his reaction so they could be in sync. Montone still looked neutral.

"That's this con's story," said Keyes, matter-of-factly. "My side, anyway. I would have told you straightaway if I'd known. Most people I meet know about it already, so I seldom bring it up. Thought you ought to hear it from me. And if you feel any differently about working with me I completely understand."

Montone waited another beat. "You're sorry for what you did."

"I hope that's apparent."

"You paid your debt."

"That's what they tell me."

"We were all young and stupid once, weren't we, Murph?"

"Now we're old and stupid."

"So you squared your account. I got no problem with that."

Keyes looked at them, grateful, not groveling, glad they weren't finding him wrong but not like he needed their approval.

"Thanks for the book," said Montone, taking it from Murphy.

"My pleasure."

Nobody said anything for a moment but there was shared relief they'd whistled past an unpleasant possibility. Murphy's response, habitual; he reached for a menu.

"You wanna eat something?" he asked.

"When a high-profile crime like this breaks, the department puts a team on it. Six detectives, full-time, but the whole squad'll put in time as-needed."

They were in Murphy's unit, driving up Park Avenue South, heading for Broadway in the Fifties. Murphy at the wheel, Montone, riding shotgun, turned to face Keyes in the back, who held an open notebook in his hands.

"How many detectives in the squad?"

"Thirty. Three sergeants, one lieutenant; he's squad commander."

"But you're in charge of this investigation."

"That's right."

"See, Jimmy's the closest thing we got in the detective division to a rock star," said Murphy, one hand holding a cigarette out the open window, steering with two fingers.

"Fuck you very much, Murph."

"My pleasure."

"Seems to me your reputation's well deserved, Jimmy," said Keyes. "More closed cases, more arrests, high conviction rate."

"I can't take all the credit," said Montone. "Lot of people involved. Murph here deserves at least one or two percent himself."

"At least."

"So—I don't mean to overstep my privilege here—are you treating the Dennis case like a homicide?" asked Keyes.

Murphy looked at Montone for a cue on how to react.

"We can't make that call yet but visibility is so high everybody from the Chief to the mayor wants what we call 'exceptional clearance.' That means we have an open checkbook; unlimited overtime, lab work, phone dumps from the Bureau."

"Phone dumps?"

"If we want to run records in and out on a particular number on a particular day—"

"His home, his office, his girlfriend," said Murphy.

"FBI does the legwork, on contract. Costs five hundred bucks a pop, but under these circumstances we don't even have to ask the lieutenant. Department calls this kind of operation a task force; a dedicated detail working this one case."

"And the scene itself, the apartment, what's your procedure there?" asked Keyes, scribbling on his pad to keep up.

"First we collect physical evidence; hair and fibers, fingerprints, and try to keep the brass from stepping all over our work. Department doesn't use civilians like those numb nuts in LA who fucked up the O.J. deal. We've got trained detectives from CSU, Crime Scene Unit. They post a run number for the investigation and shoot down from the Twenty-third. What they come up with is sent to our own lab at SRD, that's Scientific Research Division, for analysis. Everything's in-house.

"The same time, we canvas the building, neighbors, employees, anybody who might have seen or heard anything. We're sending teams back today for a recanvas, people who might have been out when we came through last night. Or sometimes a detail breaks loose when they've had time to think about it. First forty-eight hours are crucial; after that, memories start getting funky."

"Do you check around the neighborhood, other buildings?"

"We're checking out the building next door, since so far there's no way anybody gets to that penthouse using the lobby or stairs; it's a secure building, lots of VIPs. If, and understand I'm not saying anyone did, if somebody did get to him there's a chance they came onto the roof from the building next door."

"You really consider every possibility, don't you?'"

"Every death, even if it looks like suicide, you look at it for homicide. These are the questions you ask. Did he jump? Did somebody give him a nudge? Fact of life up here; you get high-rises you're gonna get jumpers."

"Tell him about the guy last year," said Murphy, already laughing. "Mr. Touchdown."

"Mr. Touchdown?"

"Wealthy businessman. Big sports nuts. Personal friend of Joe

Namath. His business goes in the toilet, the wife leaves him, his girl-friend leaves him. Then his dog leaves him. He straps on a Jets helmet and takes a dive from the nineteenth floor."

"He's at the fifteen, the ten, he's at the five—touchdown!" said Murphy, exploding into a coughing fit.

"Twenty-nine years he never missed a game," said Montone. "You never know."

When they stopped laughing, Keyes asked: "But so anyway, you think there is the possibility Dennis didn't jump."

"I'll tell you something else; people don't usually commit suicide when they're naked."

"Why?"

"Hard to say. They aren't talking," said Murphy.

"Maybe they don't want to embarrass whoever might find them."

"That's considerate, isn't it?" said Murphy. "Splash your brains all over the wallpaper but don't let 'em find you with your dick hanging out."

"Lot of guys, they came to our squad from Harlem, South Bronx, they've been up to their elbows in junkies, hookers, career criminals," said Montone. "Now suddenly they're dealing with millionaires, tax-payers. You can't treat these people the same way, but some guys can't make that adjustment and, let me tell you, the days of beating some perp with a rubber hose are long gone. You have to kill 'em with kindness."

"It's good to help people," said Murphy.

They were in an elevator; the emblem of the network Mackenzie Dennis used to work for adorned its buttons as well as the blue blazer of the young female page escorting them. Murphy fiddled with his tie, trying to make a good impression. Keyes continued to take notes.

"So one of the first places we go is the victim's place of business," said Montone. "Get a feel for what was going on in that part of his life."

The door opened, depositing them on the top executive floor. Floor-to-ceiling windows offered spectacular panoramas of the city. The page led them to a settlement of secretaries. Montone produced his business card for the receptionist. She pointed them to a brace of leather couches and picked up the phone. Moments later a pair of massive doors swung open and a man inside caught a glimpse of them in the waiting area.

"Good God, is that Terry Keyes?"

The network president—youthful if not young, short, impossibly tan for April—breezed past his secretary to where Terry was sitting, shook his hand vigorously and slapped him on the shoulder. They appeared to be fast friends. Keyes was quick to introduce the detectives and explain why he was there.

"So this bum's with you, is he?" the president said, a little too loud. "Come on in, guys. Grab a chair. Terry, it's a damn shame Tina's not here; I know she'd love to see you."

Keyes followed the president—a man named Ted—back into his office; Montone and Murphy trailed. Without being asked, Ted explained how he and Terry knew each other: One of his network's primetime magazine shows had produced a story on Keyes when he was promoting his book. Ted took an interest and invited Terry out for a weekend in the Hamptons.

Ted hit a button on his desk, releasing a magnetic catch. The gigantic doors swung silently closed. Ted perched on the edge of his desk and energetically fed himself jelly beans from a cut crystal Baccarat jar. Montone noted a gold wedding band on his finger.

Right beside the jelly beans, turned out so visitors couldn't miss it, stood a gold-framed glossy photograph of a sapphire-eyed, honey-haired blonde. Montone recognized the woman; an actress who'd starred in a TV series a few seasons back. One of those shows where everybody managed to get into bathing suits at least once an episode.

"So I'm on a dais at the Beverly Wilshire last night, waiting to give my speech for a charity Tina and I have supported for years, when I get the call about Mack. Naturally I headed straight to the airport. Sit, sit, please," he said, waving his arm at the Mies van der Rohe sofa and chairs.

Murphy and Keyes sat down. Montone remained standing at Ted's eye level, and let him keep talking. Tina was the blonde in the photograph; he already had that figured and hadn't even asked the guy anything yet.

"We're all deeply, deeply shocked by this. Mack was a dear friend, a great talent. Tina and I considered him part of our family. He'll be terribly, terribly missed." Which was more or less the same quote Ted had given in that morning's press release.

Ted waited a decent interval, thoughtfully examining and then eating another jelly bean. Montone noticed there were only red and black ones in the jar, tastefully complimenting the room's decor.

"Was his job secure?" asked Montone.

"I'm not sure I understand the question," said Ted, slightly offended, as if Montone had spoken ill of the dead.

"Was there anything about his job situation that might have contributed to a sense of uncertainty or despair about his future?" His tone stayed neutral, unpatronizing.

"Let me be very candid. Can I tell you there hasn't been recent concern about the numbers on our evening newscast with Mack? No. This is a business. We have stockholders to answer to. Enough to warrant a change of the kind you're suggesting? The answer would be: Not yet."

Montone digested that doubletalk as he jotted something in his notepad. "Would you say he had many friends here?"

"Mack was an extremely popular figure. Real team player."

"Any enemies you're aware of?"

Ted stopped him in his tracks again. "Are you suggesting there might be more to this than suicide?"

"No, sir. I'm asking you if he had any enemies."

Ted took a moment to consider. "Mack was an ambitious man in a highly, highly competitive arena. He worked his way up to that anchor desk in a comparatively short period of time. I can't sit here and tell you he didn't bruise a few egos along the way."

"Any names you can think of?"

"None that come immediately to mind. Everybody takes a few hits from time to time. We don't play touch football in this business."

"No personal grudges? No disgruntled husbands?"

Ted's tan turned a shade darker and he stopped eating jelly beans. "May we speak frankly? We're all grown-ups here, aren't we, guys? There were rumors of indiscretions. Mack was an extremely, extremely attractive man. Unmarried, as you undoubtedly know. Beyond that, I couldn't begin to give you any specifics. People don't tend to confide in me about these things at the water cooler."

"That's very helpful, sir. Thank you."

"You should know I've given instructions to my staff and everyone in the division that they are to cooperate with you one hundred percent," said Ted, coming off the desk, sounding slightly relieved, ready for them to go.

When they were back in the elevator, Montone said: "Didn't tell me you knew the guy."

"Didn't know that's who we were going to see," said Keyes.

"So you been out to Ted's house on the Island, Terry," said Murphy.

"Couple of months ago. East Hampton, I think."

"Nice layout, I bet."

"Yeah. I think Mackenzie Dennis fucked his wife," said Keyes.

"I think so, too," said Montone, matching deadpans.

"The one in the picture?" asked Murphy. "Healthy."

"Very, very."

"Mack was a real team player," said Murphy.

"Seems like Ted's got his hands full," said Montone.

"Not that, over the course of the weekend," said Keyes, "the same thought didn't occur to me."

Montone smiled, shoved a stick of gum in his mouth, looking at the floor numbers click down.

"Great minds think alike," he said.

Keyes smiled back, as if they were both members of the same secret order.

An hour of inquiries with studio personnel gave them nothing aside from educated guesses that Mackenzie Dennis had slept with two other women who worked in the office. As they were leaving the building, while Murphy stopped to pick up a soda and a couple of candy bars at the lobby newsstand, Montone made a call on his cellular to the precinct. Keyes used a pay phone to call Tyler Angstrom.

"Oh Terry, I'm so glad you called, God, thank you so much for last night, I had such a fabulous time and your note was so sweet—"

"You're very welcome."

"Everything was perfect, perfect, perfect. And the flowers, Terry, they're here on my desk, they are exquisite."

"I'm so glad you like them."

"What a wonderful surprise; the day has been a complete disaster because after I got to the office this morning I realized I'd lost my Filofax—"

"Your what?"

"Address book, phone book, client list, my *everything*, my *life* is in that book, I'm paralyzed without it and even though I keep a spare copy at home it hasn't been updated in *ages* and I didn't have time to go home anyway so I was literally paralyzed—"

"How dreadful for you," he said, holding the phone away from his ear; her voice could pierce Kevlar.

"Total despair all morning, except for your gorgeous flowers— and last night, which was so *marvelous*—but thank God there's a happy ending because a cabdriver dropped it off an hour ago: I must've left it in a taxi, can you believe it? Who says this city doesn't have a heartbeat?"

Christ, she's easier to take unconscious.

"Listen, Tyler, I'm afraid I've got to run, but are we still on for tonight?"

"Absolutely, darling."

"I've spoken to that friend of mine I mentioned in my note, the police officer? As it turns out, he is a huge fan of Holly's and he would love to meet her—have you had a chance to speak to her?"

"I just did, after I got my book. She changed her number the other day, those crank calls she'd been getting, I think I told you—"

"Yes; terrible."

"Well the bad news is she got *another* one this morning, at the *new* number—"

"How awful."

"—which is supposed to be unlisted so I think she's spooked about even going out in public, but the good news is when I told her your friend was a detective Holly said she'd really like to talk to him about this."

"He'd be more than happy to help; shall we say eight-thirty then?"

Keyes glanced across the lobby to see that Montone was finishing his call, and quickly hung up before the woman started gushing again. He crossed to Montone while he was near the newsstand.

"Jimmy, I just talked to my girlfriend Tyler, she's a publicist, I went to that party with her last night?"

"Yeah."

"She says there's another big bash tonight, an opening of a restaurant owned by these supermodels, and she's got this girlfriend who's a top model herself, Holly something or other."

"Yeah?"

"Anyway, I had mentioned to Tyler I might be working with you and somehow when they were talking your name came up—look, here's her picture."

Keyes lifted a copy of a fashion magazine from the newsstand rack. On the cover a sultry brunette—a face Montone recognized instantly from billboards and ads—was giving her best come-hither, in a strapless white leather number that appeared to have been applied by a spatula.

"This is the friend?"

"Holly Mews, that's it," said Keyes, looking up her name in the table of contents. He let Montone take the magazine. "So to make a long story short, apparently Holly knew who you were and she tells my girlfriend that she really wants to meet you."

Montone stared at the photograph. "This girl is single?"

"That's the rumor. Which only goes to prove one of Terry Keyes's Natural Laws of the Universe."

"What's that?"

"No matter how good-looking a woman is," said Keyes, lowering his voice, "somebody somewhere is tired of fucking her."

Keyes left them outside and walked off to another appointment. Montone drove east, taking the Fifty-ninth Street Bridge, as Murphy talked him through the dailies' coverage of the Dennis case. Even the *Times* put his obituary on the front page. The *Daily News* ran a recent photo of Dennis out on the town with a spectacular-looking woman on his arm, fishing for an obscure but lurid innuendo with the headline: "DEATH IN THE FAST LANE." Inside, the *Post* used Dennis's jump to tentpole one of its apocalyptic editorials: If a man like *this,* one of the *media elite* who has achieved *everything,* decides to take his own *life,* what does *that* say about our *decadent liberal culture?*

Every story gave great signifigance to Montone being in charge of the investigation, citing his involvement as a strong indicator of foul play. The *Times* included the notorious file photo of a wounded Montone bringing the Slug into custody.

By the time Murphy had finished checking out the sports sections, they were heading north on the Clearview Expressway. He picked up and studied Terry Keyes's signed book again.

"Seems all right, this guy," said Murphy, looking at his photograph on the jacket.

"Seems that way."

"Wouldn't have figured him for a perp."

"Me neither."

"But hey . . .

"You never know," said Montone.

Murphy was quiet for a while. "Think I'll run a BCI on him. Check with Interpol overseas. Make sure he's clean."

"Couldn't hurt."

"He'll never hear about it, will he?"

"Not unless you tell him."

Murphy paged through the book. "Maybe I'll read this when you're done with it."

"Sure, Murph. And let me know if you're not going to be using your ballet tickets this season."

"Something comes up I can't make it, you're my first call."

"What a pal."

"Fuck you, too. So happens I went to the ballet once. The wife drags me. Lincoln Center. These great seats. Chicks with legs up to here; I'm thinking, this ain't so bad. And what I couldn't get past? You hear their feet clumping all over the place. Every time they make a rush across the floor it's like a herd of buffalo."

A ramshackle building inside Fort Totten, an underutilized US Army base east of the Throgs Neck Bridge, contained an NYPD facility known informally as the Cave. Home to the two sergeants and twenty detectives of TARU—Technical Assistance Response Unit—who specialized in high-tech electronics and analysis. TARU officers conducted surveillance operations, planted bugs, wired informants or cops for undercover work and were generally considered to have the tightest lips in the department—a large part of how the Cave got its nickame.

Normally Montone would have taken any videotape from an investigation to the newsroom at Fox 5. He had contacts there, both on and off the air, who were always ready to help if they could get a jump on a story for their trouble. But Montone had convinced downtown that Dennis's "confession" should be held back; only the killer, if there was one, would know about it. The tape had been sent by secure courier last night straight to the Cave.

Montone and Murphy sat with Detective Tammy DePietro in a cramped, darkened cubicle before a wall of video equipment. An image of Mackenzie Dennis from the suicide video—embedded with a boxed display of digital time code in the lower left-hand corner—filled a monitor at eye level. Detective Third Grade DePietro, Montone's favorite officer in the unit, a short, peppery girl from his old neighborhood, took them through the tape at superslow motion, one frame at a time.

"There it is again," she said, freezing the image, pointing to the time code, which read 00:01:35.26. "That's definite eye flicker."

"Rock it back," said Montone.

Using the control knob, she rolled the picture back and forth; at this speed, when viewed repeatedly, a small but distinct left-to-right movement of Dennis's eyes became apparent.

"So he's reading," said Montone.

"I compared it to some tape we pulled of his broadcasts where he's working off a TelePrompTer. Identical motion. And there's six other eye movements like this on this tape. One time, here, let me find it . . ." She punched in a time code on the keyboard; the picture zoomed ahead, then stopped precisely at that number. "Right here. Watch his eyes."

She eased the image slowly forward again. Dennis's eyes trailed momentarily down and to camera left, then back up toward the camera, slightly to the right.

"There's a pause in what he's saying here, too," she said.

"Run it again; sound off, regular speed," said Montone.

As Dennis moved his lips, Montone picked up two yellow legal pads and re-created the motions of a person holding cue cards, talking it through. "First card goes down and to the left. He stops to watch the card go down, then his eyes come back up to catch the next one."

"Exactly," said DePietro, stopping the tape. "Whoever's in the room with him is changing the cards."

"Perp's right-handed," said Montone to Murphy.

"I think maybe he was trying to let whoever was going to see this know what was happening."

They watched the end of the tape in silence, as Dennis disappeared. She stopped it before the window broke.

"That's great work, Tammy, we owe you one."

"How 'bout it, babe?" asked Murphy. "Mets-Dodgers? First-base dugout?"

"I'm over baseball," she said. "US Open. Agassi. Center court."

Murphy and Montone looked at each other, deadpan.

"What do you think, Murph? Little steep?"

"We'll have to consult our ticket broker."

"One last thing I want to show you," said DePietro.

She punched in another number and ran the tape back to the moment where Dennis stood, in slow motion again.

"You're not talking about his johnson, are you, Tammy?" said Murphy.

"I've seen better," she said, cop-tough. They laughed.

Dennis slowly rose again from the chair and moved off camera.

"Coming up," she said, dead serious, leaning closer to the screen. "The wall, here, in the corner."

She slowed the tape down to single-frame advances. Finger poised. Montone moved closer to the monitor.

"There." She froze the picture and pointed.

A shadow flicked across the back wall between the paintings, caught in a wafer-thin fraction of time. A long, straight line, attached to a loop.

The shadow of a noose.

Keyes exited the the Number 6 Green Line at Twenty-third, walked up to street level and headed west on the north side of the street. Checked his watch: 4:20. On schedule. He kept a room at the Chelsea Hotel, under his own name, and among other things he needed a change of clothes. He crossed Seventh Avenue but before he crossed south on Twenty-third, something caught his eye and stopped him in his tracks.

The man sat behind the window of a coffee shop directly across the street, cradling a cup in his hands, staring at the hotel's entrance. Keyes moved closer until he could confirm the familiar craggy profile under the cowlicked white hair.

The old bastard had followed him to New York.

Keyes moved out of the line of sight as questions crowded him: How long has he been here? What does he know? Why would he show up now, outside my hotel, on this day?

He stepped back to a newsstand and paged through a newspaper as he ran a regimented check on his emotions, reining them in with brutal efficiency.

Think it through: What harm can the man do to me in this country when he couldn't touch me at home? He carries no authority here, without resources or meaningful contacts. How can he be more than a minor inconvenience? Keyes swiftly saw a way to turn the situation to his advantage.

Glad you could make it, old boy. Our score needs settling anyway. And as long as I'm about my business here, this time I'll finish the job.

He could abandon the Chelsea without any hardship. That's why he'd gone to the trouble of developing contingencies. The meddlesome bastard would never get near him again.

Keyes crossed back around to Seventh, circled blocks out of his way and entered the rear of the hotel.

When he looked down from the window of his room, the old man was gone.

4

HOST: They must have absolutely loved you over there.

KEYES: The bloody wonderful thing about Americans is that the more you rip into them the more they love you, as long as you sound like an upper-class twit.

(Audience laughter)

No, it's absolutely true. Some dim glandular memory of their colonial past surfacing; they think it's the voice of authority speaking.

(With upper-class-twit accent) It's not so much the callow depravity and violence of your culture that so greatly disturbs us, per se, but that you go about it with such utter disregard for manners.

(Laughter)

It's true!

HOST: You told them that, did you?

KEYES: And a whole lot more. I'm telling you, Barry, if you go on TV over there and you sound even remotely like Alistair Cooke they think you're the voice of God. Can you imagine what God *would* say, if he had the chance?

(Upper-class accent again) Now let's see: America, yes. You've corrupted the Third World by exporting your naked materialism, degraded the experience of human tragedy into raw spectacle for your nightly newscasts, perverted the worldwide standards of female beauty into an endorsement for anorexia, spawned a generation of boorish millionaire athletes who've made a mockery of the very concept of good sportsmanship and taught the rest of the world that every problem can be solved at the point of a gun.

Hmm. Not bad for two hundred years' work.

(Laughter)

And don't even get me started on their lawyers!

HOST: (Laughing) You said all that to them?

KEYES: Good God, man, someone's got to try and stop them.

HOST: So they're having you back again soon, are they?
KEYES: Next week. I can't wait.
(Laughter)

: transcript of an appearance by Terry Keyes on a British television program,
The Late Show, *prior to his second trip to America*

The crowd outside the restaurant snaked along Fifty-seventh and around the corner inside a line of velvet rope. Bouncers had staked out a narrow path to the street so celebrities could walk the gauntlet from their limos to the entrance. On the wall above the marquee, idealized bas-relief profiles of the restaurant's four supermodel owners gazed up into the New York night; Mount Rushmore with lip gloss. Below them, in syncopated lights, the name of the place flashed cheerfully: THE FACE.

Montone flashed his badge and squeezed through the mob to the front doors. He spotted Terry Keyes waiting inside, wearing a black double-breasted suit, next to a pretty, anorexic blonde who stood half a head taller. Terry saw him approach, spoke to the bouncer at the door, and the man waved Montone into the foyer. They shouted introductions over pounding dance music from the interior; Montone could feel its hollow thump skip through his ribs.

The blonde's name was Tyler and she wasn't as young as she appeared from a distance. Netted black lace clung to her arms and legs and she wobbled on high heels, smiling nervously, holding on to Terry's arm. She seemed sexy enough in a malnourished sort of way, but Montone thought her outfit looked dumb and he wondered why Keyes was with her.

"I think Holly's inside," she shouted next to his ear.

All Montone could see ahead was a dark mass of swaying bodies, arms waving on a dance floor. Terry put a hand on his shoulder and leaned in.

"Bloody awful!"

Montone smiled in agreement. They pushed inside. The music took on more character here, a repetitive hook floating over the insistent throbbing percussion. Swirling lights cut through the dark, punctuated by strobes that lit up angular slices of dancers.

Half the crowd's still outside and they're over code limits already, guessed Montone. And the fire inspector's probably at the bar having drinks on the house.

Beyond the dance floor the space opened into a cavernous dining room, its moody lighting curdled with smoke, furtive groups bunched around tables. Tyler led them in that direction. Skirting the dance floor, they put the pummeling speakers behind them and conversation became possible again. As their eyes adjusted, more details of the partygoers clarified; most of them were young or, like Tyler, desperately trying to appear so, and wearing casual black. Montone shouldered their drink orders to the bar while Tyler and Terry secured a table.

When he returned a woman was bending over between their chairs, her back to him; tight black jeans, thick auburn hair spilling over a black silk muscle T-shirt. He set the drinks down and she turned to face him, Tyler saying something that he missed, gesturing in his direction.

"Hi," she said.

Montone wouldn't have recognized her from the magazine cover. She was wearing no makeup, only a light sheen of lip gloss; her hair was tousled, casual, not teased into an artificial mane. The smile seemed genuine and warm. Her blue eyes didn't hold the defiant sexual charge of the model's pose. They looked lively and playful, suggesting humor, even mischief. She's younger than she looks, he thought, shaking her hand. A dry, cool touch, long fingers, nails sensibly short. No rings.

"Can I get you something to drink?" he asked.

Holly casually waved the bottle of beer she was holding—No thanks—then leaned in, touched his arm and spoke close to his ear. "I have an uncle who's a policeman."

He leaned toward her and she tilted her head, offering a perfect ear.

"I have an uncle who's a model," he said.

She looked at him skeptically, reserving the possibility he was teasing.

"True story. Ed Sancola. He owns a Big and Tall shop in Rochester. They call him Big Ed. Older guy, keeps fit. Likes to model suits for the ads he takes in the local paper. People come in, they recognize him. He says, 'I'm my own best customer.' That's the line he uses in all his ads. Even does his own TV spots for cable. In Rochester Uncle Ed's what you might call an extremely minor celebrity."

She laughed freely, liking his story, then leaned in to his ear, lightly brushing against his shoulder, taking her turn. He caught a scent; fresh soap, a light floral perfume.

"My uncle, he's my mother's sister's husband."

"You're kidding me."

"No, I mean I'm not related to him by blood," she said, giving him a little shove.

"Thank God for that."

"He's a, what do you call it, a desk sergeant?"

"You could call it that. Where's this?"

"In Providence." She brushed a fugitive strand of hair away from her face.

"Rhode Island? Is that where you're from?"

"Born there. We moved to Florida when I was in high school."

"I've never been to Rhode Island. It as small as they say it is?"

"Like you wouldn't believe."

"Always surprises me to see it on a map. I'm thinking, why go to all the trouble?"

"No room for Big and Tall shops in Rhode Island," she said. "Big Ed would be out of his element."

"He could always open a Small and Short shop."

She gave him a sly look and took a pull off her beer. Montone glanced down at the table. The blonde—what's her name, Tyler—had turned in her chair, chatting animatedly with a short black woman Montone recognized from television. He didn't see Terry.

Montone was blinded by a flash of light as a photographer took a picture. From behind Keyes clapped an arm around Montone's shoulder as another shot was taken.

"More privacy back there," said Keyes quietly, subtly tilting his head back and to the left.

Montone looked in that direction and saw an open rear door leading to a courtyard.

"Do you smoke?" Montone asked Holly, leaning in again.

"Used to."

"You want to get some fresh air?"

She looked toward the rear door. Hesitated.

"You wanted to talk to me about something, Holly?" he asked, more directly.

A darker set of thoughts clouded her features. She nodded and started toward the door ahead of him. Keyes shot Montone a thumbs-up as he followed her outside.

The courtyard was almost empty, a few small groups clustered under oversized beige umbrellas, but they were effectively alone and the faint pulse of the music barely reached them here. Holly stopped alongside a fence near the back, hooked the heel of one cowboy boot on a lower rail and finished her beer, looking solemn and inward. Montone stood across from her and waited for her to speak.

"I remember when you caught that crazy guy. The Slug, wasn't that what they called him?"

"Wendell Sligo."

She nodded seriously. "I saw you on the news a lot. I must have read everything they ever wrote about the case in the papers and magazines. I don't know why but I couldn't get it out of my mind. Is that too weird?"

"Lot of people felt that way."

"I felt kind of odd about it but my sister said it's just normal human curiosity. She even wrote about the case in one of her books. She's a psychologist; the one with the big brain in the family."

"Which one are you?"

"I was the tall, goofy-looking one."

Not anymore, thought Montone.

"I'd just moved to the city. Living by myself for the first time. I guess I was scared, too."

"He's a scary guy."

"He killed how many people?"

"Fifteen."

"Jesus. You knew one of them, didn't you?"

"Police officer," he said. "She was working undercover."

Sheila hadn't entered his mind for months. The pain must have shown on his face.

"That must have been awful for you. I'm sorry."

Her sympathy felt genuine. Montone nodded. She looked away. Biting her lip. Tense.

"So what's going on, Holly?"

"I feel kind of foolish talking about it. Compared to all that, it seems sort of ridiculous."

"What?"

"I guess it's part of my job. A lot of the girls in this business attract people who fixate on them. Obsessive types."

"Nutcases."

"They write to you, send flowers. In their minds they build up a whole relationship with you."

"They see your picture, this image of you, they confuse it with the person."

"Right. They don't understand that it's like acting. We're playing a part, but for some people it just pushes the wrong buttons."

"City's full of creeps who need their bolts tightened."

"Usually they're harmless."

"So what makes this one different?"

"A few weeks ago I started getting these phone calls. I usually screen when I'm home but I'd hear them come in on the machine. No voice, whoever it is never leaves a message, but there's more to it than just a hangup. They'd last for a while, over a minute. Just somebody there. This . . . presence."

"How often?"

"At least once a day. I didn't even notice at first, I'd fast-forward past it when I didn't hear anything. After about a week I realized what was going on when whoever it is started calling a few times every day."

"Number's unlisted?"

"Yes."

"Could you hear anything in the background?"

She thought for a moment. "Sometimes street sounds. Sometimes . . . nothing."

"Any breathing?"

"Usually toward the end. Not heavy, just . . ." She demonstrated; slow, focused breaths.

"Man or a woman?"

"I assume a man."

"Do you have a feeling one way or the other?"

"Look, I don't want you to think I'm naive. This has happened a couple times before, you change your number, it's no big deal."

"Okay. So what makes this different?"

She hesitated again. "I guess I'm concerned about this getting out. Maybe what this person is after is publicity. My sister said that's something to be careful about."

"And if you took this to the station, filed an official complaint, there might be some chance of that, is that your concern?"

She nodded reluctantly, mindful she might be offending him.

"We're talking here as friends, you're asking my opinion," he said. "Nothing you say goes beyond that confidence unless you want it to. Fair enough?"

"I feel like I can trust you."

"Good."

Satisfied, she reached into the back pocket of her jeans and took out a square white envelope, greeting card size, and handed it to him without a word. Montone opened it carefully, tugging out the card inside by its edges.

Letters from newsprint had been cut from a newspaper and neatly arranged in a row. Upper and lower case mixed without any discernible pattern.

beauty is betrayal

He turned it over; blank on the back.

"When did you get this?"

"Last Friday," she said.

"Where did you find it?"

"In my mailbox."

The postmark showed cancellation had taken place the day before delivery; the zip code indicated processing occurred at the FDR post office on Third between Fifty-fourth and Fifty-fifth, a branch that Montone knew handled more daily volume than any other in the country.

"This where you live?"

She nodded. "Downtown. Tribeca."

"Alone?"

"Yes."

"Does anyone else have access to the mailbox?"

"I have the only key."

"Ever given it to anybody to pick up your mail?"

"No."

"Have you ever received anything like this at home before?"

"No."

"There anybody out there you have any reason to suspect? Somebody from work? Maybe an old boyfriend?"

"Not that I can think of."

"Maybe somebody you rejected. Think about it a second. You may not even have been aware you were doing it; the person could have built this whole fantasy in their head. Anybody come to mind?"

She thought for a moment. "Not really. People have this preconception about models, that we're all out partying at the hot clubs every night or sleeping with rock stars. A few of them are, I guess—you can't help what people think, but with the kind of hours I work? I'm usually up at five in the morning, freezing my tail off at some crummy location."

Montone smiled.

"I'm not asking for sympathy, but my social life for the last year you could print on a matchbook."

"How long have you lived at this address?"

"About eight months."

"You give out your address to a lot of people?"

"Only friends or family. I don't get a lot of mail at home. I use a post office box for business."

"That's smart."

She shrugged; a New York gesture.

"Have you shown this to anyone else?"

"No."

"Your friend Tyler?"

"She's not my friend; she's my publicist."

"Can I keep this?"

"Of course." She watched him slide the card back into the envelope and pocket it. "So do you think there's a connection? Between the card and the calls?"

"Something like this, I don't like to encourage any speculation until I have all the facts in front of me. I take it you reported these harassment calls to the phone company?"

"Sure. Like they're going to do anything."

"They're supposed to report it to the police; it's a state and federal offense."

"The problem is, whoever it is never says a word."

"That doesn't matter; if they're bothering you it's still harassment. And what NYNEX can do is set up a trace line," he said, taking out his pen and notepad. "You get one of these calls, you hang up and hit five-seven, that activates the trace."

"Really?"

"I can set that up for you. What's your number?"

She gave it to him.

"The thing is I just changed it again three days ago. After the card showed up? Totally unlisted and I already got another call this morning. On the machine."

"Same deal?"

"Yeah."

"What time?"

"About eight. I was out at a shoot; I heard it when I got home."

"Did you erase the message?"

"No." Her eyes brightened with excitement. "Hey, you want me to play it for you?"

"You mean now?"

"Why not? Unless hanging around with the terminally hip is your idea of a good time."

"I could skip that."

"Escaping from a party is always more fun than the party. Anyway, meeting you is coolest thing that was going to happen to me tonight."

"You want to say goodbye to your friend?" he asked.

"I told you, she's not my friend. What about *your* friend?"

"I barely know the guy."

"Then let's blow this pop stand and grab a cab."

"I've got a car."

"A *police* car? I always wanted a ride in one."

"Detectives' unit. Not a blue-and-white."

"Under cover; even better."

She took his arm and led him briskly through an ivy-covered rear gate leading to a long narrow path that flanked the restaurant and took them down an alley to the street.

"Didn't that uncle ever take you around up in Rhode Island?"

"No, I *told* you," she said, mock-exasperated. "He was a *desk* sergeant."

"Doesn't mean he didn't know how to drive."

At his seat near a window inside the restaurant, from where he had watched their entire conversation, Terry Keyes waited until Montone and the girl had cleared the gate. He backtracked to find Tyler in a conversational knot near the dance floor, took her aside to say he felt a migraine coming on—not to worry; he had medicine at home, but he had to take it quickly—with regrets, quickly excused himself and left the party before she could summon a response.

"What's this for?" she asked, pointing to a brightly lit box attached to the dash.

"Siren box."

"Can we turn it on?"

"No."

"Against regulations?"

"Something like that."

"Do not use to impress girls," she said, in mock officialese.

"Somebody must have showed you the manual."

"Are you on duty right now?"

Holly curled up on the passenger seat, facing him, ignoring her seat belt, as they drifted into traffic heading south on Seventh Avenue.

"I'm on call."

"What does that mean?"

"If they need me they call. Here." He pointed to the radio. "Here." He showed her his pager. "Or here." He lifted his cell phone from the inside pocket of his jacket.

"Reach out and touch someone. What kind of pistol is that?" The jacket had shifted, revealing his shoulder holster.

"Sig-Sauer."

"Nine-millimeter?"

"Yeah."

"Automatic?"

He gave her a look. "Yeah."

"What's the magazine capacity?"

"Fifteen."

"I thought they only carried nine rounds."

"That's the two twenty. This is the two twenty-six."

"Aren't you guys supposed to use thirty-eights?"

"Used to be standard issue. Until they decided us 'guys' were walking around with less firepower than the average teenager. What, you go to college on some kind of weapons scholarship?"

"My dad used to hunt a lot. I always thought guns were kind of cool. I know that's not very PC."

"What's your father do?"

"Owned a carpet store. Retired now. And I didn't go to college. Like I said, my sister has enough brains for both of us."

"You know how to shoot?"

"Sure. He used to take me to the range when I was kid."

"You're still a kid."

"I'm twenty-four, Mr. Old Guy."

"You look nineteen."

"Thank you."

"I'm thirty-four, for the record."

"Old Guy." She leaned back and grinned confidently at him.

"Are you familiar with the phrase 'Youth is wasted on the young'?"

"I'm way too young to grasp that concept, Officer."

"I rest my case."

They rode in a full silence, creeping through the snarl of Times Square. Montone stole a glance and watched the field of lights play off her features as she looked out at the undulating waves of nightlife on the street. Floating on some private feeling, an enigmatic smile on her lips, she looked like she held a powerful secret. Remote as she seemed at that moment, Montone felt a barrier inside himself give way and for the first time the possibility of her fell within his reach.

Two taxis just ahead of them braked sharply, narrowly avoiding a collision. The drivers, one Asian, the other West African, rolled down their windows and began screaming at each other in their separate languages. When traffic stalled behind them, Montone popped the siren; the drivers looked up, startled, like shoplifters caught with the goods. They dove back into the shells of their cabs and scuttled off, the other vehicles in their way parted and, as the light turned green, they sailed away from the pack down Broadway. Montone didn't turn off the siren for another six blocks.

Holly's loft, the southwest corner of the fifth floor, offered views of the Hudson to the west, and south toward the Battery. Tall, valanced windows lined both walls. Montone asked her to keep the lights off and looked out in each direction, trying to determine who might have a view looking in.

"You might want to consider buying some shades for these," he said.

"What I wouldn't give for one free day to shop," she said, returning from her open-plan kitchen with two glasses of a California chardonnay.

"When that day comes, maybe you can pick up some furniture while you're at it."

"You don't like the minimalist look?"

"I like a place to sit down."

"I'm never here. I have a bed." She shrugged, as if the fact that the rest of her needs were therefore satisfied would be self-evident.

Weight-bearing Ionic columns marched the length of the L-shaped space. They leaned against opposite columns and sipped their wine. She stared remotely at the floor. The reason they were there seemed for the moment forgotten and the silence grew uncomfortable.

"Want me to guess what's in your refrigerator?" he asked.

She looked at him quizzically, brought back by the novelty of the idea. "Okay."

"Bottled water. White wine. Cranberry juice. Frozen yogurt. Vitamins. Maybe some take-out containers from the local Chinese. A brand-name vodka, in the freezer, probably Stoly Crystal. A bag of store-bought ice. One of those facial ice-pack things. And some film."

"You peeked."

Montone protested his innocence. "Swear to God."

She led him back to the kitchen, footsteps echoing on the bleached hardwood, and opened the refrigerator.

"I threw out the Chinese yesterday," she said, showing him that everything he'd named, along with a few other items, was inside. "How did you do that?"

"The wine's obvious," he said, waving his glass. "Everybody in New York has bottled water. Every girl I've ever met keeps cranberry juice for some reason. You're so skinny I figured you had to treat yourself to some kind of indulgence—I went with frozen yogurt."

"Nonfat."

"The vodka's a no-brainer. The film, that's because of the camera bag hanging on the door over there. The ice is left over from the last time you had people over for drinks, which was probably last night judging from the unwashed glasses in your sink. The ice pack was a guess, based on your profession. How much time you spend putting makeup on and taking it off and so forth and the early hours you mentioned."

She opened the freezer section and pointed.

"Aha! You missed the frozen chicken," she said, picking it up and looking at the label. "And apparently so did I, since it's been in here for about three months."

"I would've bet you were vegetarian."

"Nope. Confirmed meat eater."

She tossed the chicken back inside and closed the refrigerator door.

"Your mind work like that all the time?" she asked, mock-wary.

"It better."

She frowned slightly, chewed on her lower lip again, then led him across the length of the loft to the partitioned bedroom at the far end of the layout.

The bed, lush with cream-colored linens and quilted down throws, looked slept in. Clothes littered the floor. A single Stickley chair sat before a vintage Mission vanity with inset mirror. An empty black Tumi rolling carry-on stood at the entrance to a walk-in closet, poised between arrival and departure.

Holly sat on the edge of the bed and picked up a sleek black answering machine, message light blinking.

"Two of those calls came in this morning," said Holly. "This is the one I saved."

She hit play and they waited, silently, Montone standing away from the bed, as the tape respooled. When it racked to play, Holly turned up the volume and held up a finger for attention.

Street sounds; traffic, horns, a blast of bus exhaust. Footsteps, pedestrian chatter. A loud two-beat, rhythmic squeak, repeated four times. A distant whistle. A man's ragged voice, singing, also distant, strangely distorted. Then the slow, insistent breathing Holly had described, cutting through the generalized din. Followed by a slow hang-up.

"Let me hear it again," said Montone.

She reset the message and held the machine up toward him as he moved closer and listened a second time.

"Pay phone. Manhattan, definitely," he said. "Street level, on a corner; you can hear the traffic patterns changing with the streetlight. Someplace busy enough so there's a cop with a whistle nearby. No construction going on."

"Sure it's Manhattan?"

"Near a bus stop, probably one of the avenues; the bus went straight by without slowing, no turn."

"Which narrows it down to, what, only about a thousand phones?"

He closed his eyes and replayed the possibilities. "Recognize anything about that singing?"

She shook her head. "Sounded like a street person."

"I'd like to keep that tape."

"Sure." She popped it out and handed it to him. "I've got another one here somewhere."

As she rummaged through a shoe box beside her bed, the phone rang; she stopped, looked at the machine, realizing there was no way to screen the call without a tape. Montone took a step backward toward the door, an offer of privacy. She waved a casual okay, slid her hair to one side with an elegant crane of her neck and answered the phone.

"Hello? . . ." She looked up at Montone. "Hello? . . ." Eyes widening, she nodded and pointed at the receiver.

Montone put a finger to his lips, stepped silently over, took the phone from her and held it to his ear. He heard no traffic at the other end of the line, only a leaden silence along with, as she had described, the sensation of a physical presence. Then slow, deliberate breathing.

Montone pressed the flash button. "This is the police operator. Ma'am, is this the caller that's been harassing you?"

He held the phone out to her and nodded his head vigorously.

"Yes," she said, into the mouthpiece.

Eric Bowman

"We have activated a trace. Any further unauthorized calls to this number will result in arrest and prosecution. Please hang up now, Ma'am, and we will stay on the line to complete the trace."

Montone hit the flash button again and listened. He still heard faint street noise but the breathing had stopped.

"What happened?" she asked, breathless.

Montone covered the mouthpiece. "I think he dropped the phone and ran. Didn't even hang up."

"Really?"

"I think we scared the shit out of him."

Holly put a hand to her face to suppress a nervous laugh, something prankish and collusional connecting them now. The throaty honk of a tug on the river drifted through the open bedroom window. When the horn sounded a second time, Montone heard it over the phone line. He moved quickly to the window and looked out.

"What is it?" she asked.

Montone laid the phone down with the receiver still off the hook and started for the door. "Stay on the phone. Lock the door after me."

Montone ignored the slow-moving elevator and sprinted down the stairs, two leaps per flight. He exited the side of the co-op into an east-west alley and circled back around to the corner, unsnapping the catch on his holster. He slowed his step and strolled casually across the street, toward the pay phone that he'd spotted from the window, isolated in a greasy pool of streetlight.

The receiver had been carefully laid down, not dropped, on the steel shelf below the phone. Using a handkerchief, he picked up the handset and looked up and across the street at the brightly lit windows of the loft.

"It's me, Holly, are you there?"

"Yeah?"

"I'm coming right back. Buzz me in."

A slight, confused pause. "I already did."

Montone looked down and saw the front door of her building just swinging shut. He dropped the phone and ran, drawing the nine-millimeter with his right hand. The door handle wouldn't yield. He scanned the intercom box, did not see Holly's name listed and jammed the heel of his palm against the entire row of buttons. A scratchy male voice responded, then the buzz of the lock release. He threw the door open and barreled into the narrow foyer, gun arm extended, pointed to the floor.

With his back to the wall he inched ahead, stifled his breathing and listened; a door opened a floor or two above, scuffling footsteps in the hall. Eyes searching. No one on the stairs.

Straight ahead, the moon-faced porthole window of the elevator stared blankly at him. Motor grinding; the elevator was on the move, going up, trailing cables. He sprinted up the stairs, winding around the elevator column. On the third floor he saw pale orange light sluicing out of an open doorway; an owlish middle-aged man peered at him, halfway across the threshold, in T-shirt and house slippers; the scuffling he'd heard. Montone showed his badge, waved the gun, the man slid back inside and silently shut the door.

Montone ran up the last two flights, passed the straining elevator and stationed himself in a shadowy corner outside Holly's door. The elevator ground to a stop and went silent. The doors opened, affording Montone only a cross-section view, a narrow angle of inside wall. He heard clicking, something shifting its weight in the car. He raised his piece and edged forward, the interior coming into sight.

A gray rat stumbled over the edge of the doors, corpulent body wobbling over its feet, hideous denuded tail snaking behind. A large feral cat pounced after it and swatted it against the wall. The rat lay still, bleeding from a number of wounds, paralyzed with terror. Reacting suddenly, the cat turned and stared at Montone, cold eyes alert and fearless. As the elevator doors slid closed behind it, the rat, claws clacking, turned frantically and scrabbled away, racing for darkness. The cat leaped after it, disappearing down the stairs.

Somewhere far below Montone heard a door slam, but he decided not to go after it. He holstered his piece, knocked on Holly's door, identified himself, and she let him back inside.

From the roof of the building across the street, through binoculars, Terry Keyes watched Montone reenter the loft. They touched this time, his hand on her shoulder, solicitous; hers on his arm, taking his hand, anxious for reassurance.

Splendid how they're getting along. Practically made for each other.

He watched as they talked it through, Montone walking her to the window and pointing down at the phone, then toward the front door, retracing his steps.

Keyes had to lower the glasses and lie still for a moment when Montone looked out the window toward him. Keyes counted a full minute before edging up over the lip of the roof again.

Montone was questioning her, the girl shaking her head, gesturing at the intercom box on the wall beside the door, demonstrating for him how she had admitted whoever had been downstairs into the building. Keyes wondered, but couldn't tell, if he told her about the rat.

Fifteen minutes passed as they drank another glass of wine to come down off the adrenaline. Keyes didn't need to hear them to follow the conversation; his strategies for safety, her confident assertions of self-reliance, showing him the triple locks, the state of the art anti-intruder bar on the door.

Then Montone gave her his card, wrote his home number on the back. Her hand found his again at the door as he left, awkward, as she planted a grateful kiss on his cheek.

When she locked the door after him, Keyes put down the glasses and rolled onto his back, laughing so hard his chest convulsed, tears came to his eyes and he had to cover his mouth.

5

Leviathan by Thomas Hobbes
The Culture of Narcissism by Christopher Lasch
Model: The Ugly Business of Beautiful Women by Michael Gross
Fodor's Guide to Miami
My House: Life in the NFL Combat Zone by Cody Lawson
Awaken the Giant Within by Anthony Robbins
The Anarchist Cookbook
How to Find Anybody Anywhere
Handbook of Hypnosis for Professionals by Roy Udolf
Criminal Intent by Erin Kelly
Black Heart: The Capture of Wendell Sligo by David Fellows

*: inventory of books found in the New York City office rented by Terry Keyes
under the name Howard Kurtzman*

"Doorman in the next building says he let in a cable TV installer around two-thirty on the afternoon Dennis takes a header," said Murphy, displaying a DD5 interview form he'd pulled from the stack on his desk.

The task force—five detectives and a handful of uniforms—centered around Montone's desk in the detective squad room, all shuffling through their notes for the morning briefing.

Terry Keyes observed the entire meeting, jotting down notes while he sat unobtrusively near the door. When Montone had discussed with the rest of the squad having Keyes watch them work no one raised any objections.

"Description?" asked Montone.

"White male. Hard hat, carrying a toolbox. They've had a lot of problems in the building, rats chewing the cable, there's been a parade of repair guys in and out."

"So, generic repairman? That's it?"

"Nobody else eyeballed him inside. The doorman saw him leave about quarter after three. Pat's checking to see if the company had a scheduled service."

Pat Feany was the first man Montone had requested for the team. In addition to being a first-rate detective, he had a famously bad marriage which made him willing to work ungodly hours. He hung up a phone at his desk behind Murphy in the bullpen.

"Cable company had no service calls on that block of Sixty-ninth on the day," said Feany in his whiskey baritone.

"That's it?"

"Canvas was a dry hump, Jimmy."

"Anybody see a truck or cable company van parked outside?" The crew checked their interview sheets; nobody had an answer. "Come on, Murph."

"I'll check the stacks again," said Murphy, paging through the DD5s.

Pat Feany stood up and paced, straightening his natty tie, sharp black eyes darting around.

"If somebody does him, how's he get out of the building?" asked Feany. "He's got three or four minutes, tops, after Dennis goes out the window before the shitstorm reaches the apartment. You're saying he hides this video camera, puts the chair back, smooths out the carpet."

"Maybe."

"Maybe he goes in the kitchen and makes himself a root beer float," said Murphy.

"One calm, collected motherfucker," said Feany, lighting a smoke.

Montone pointed to the sketch of the building on the blackboard near his desk. "That still leaves him time to go up on the roof, climb down to the fire escape next door, take the stairs to the street and get out before the first patrol's even on the scene."

"How's he climb down to the other building?"

Montone pulled a photo out of the crime scene file and held it up. "This is the brick border around the edge of the roof. See these scratches? They're fresh. Maybe he's got some kind of hook, attached to a rope. That gets him down within reach of the fire escape."

"What is he, a fucking ninja?"

"You take some uniforms, Pat, send somebody down that wall on a block and tackle and check it out. Go over the roof next door, dust the fire escape, send some guys through the alley to see if he dropped anything. What else have we got?"

As a political consideration, Montone had requested Hank Lopez be put on the detail, to square the lieutenant passing him over on the original assignment. Because Lopez didn't know his butt from a gopher hole, Montone had paired him with Detective Frank Fonseca, the squad's rising star. A fresh-faced, earnest, hardworking rookie who'd recently transferred in from narcotics, Frankie had a gift for cultivating sources and a dogged dedication to details that reminded Montone of his younger self. With his wide-ranging circle of informants, both confidential and civilian, Frankie had already earned the nickname "the king of contracts."

Lopez and Fonseca ran down their background check on Mackenzie Dennis: no recent threats, no prior violent incidents, no previously noted security concerns, no unusual insurance polices, no hidden financial difficulties, no network rivals with murderous intent.

Dennis's parents, retirees living in South Carolina, had been notified and were flying up to claim the body for burial. Dennis also owned a second home out on Long Island. Montone told them to contact Suffolk County Sheriff Department, have them seal the house and arrange access; he planned to drive out and inspect it himself.

Fonseca brought up two small details from forensics: A small pebble found near the apartment's service entrance was a match to the loose gravel scattered on the roof. The only fingerprints they lifted in the kitchen, on doors and windows or on the VCR belonged to Dennis and his assistant, Louisa Fernandez. Hair and fibers had also come up with matches to both of them—one from the girl in bed—and no one else.

During their report a patrolman walked a large paper sack into the room and handed it to Montone. When Fonseca was finished, Montone lifted a stick out of the sack and held it up for the squad to see: three feet long, thick as a broom handle, a wire loop attached to the end. A line ran from the loop down the handle, controlling the tension of the wire.

"Dog pound sent this over," said Montone. "Called a noose. They control strays or dangerous animals with it. The perp used one of these, or something like it, on Dennis."

Montone demonstrated on Murphy, as they had previously discussed, slipping the noose around his neck and drawing it tight.

"Jump somebody from behind, the vic can't move, can't see who or what's back there. Tighten the wire with this hand, you'll get a blackout in twenty seconds."

He lifted the loop off of Murphy. "Say he takes Dennis down when he's coming out of the shower. Pops him with an injection; a very precise dose so he knows exactly how long he'll be out. During that interval the perp sets up the camera. When Dennis comes around, perp leads him into the living room, lays out what he wants. Our guy's groggy, freaked out, he agrees to anything he thinks is gonna keep him alive. Perp turns on the camera, holds the cue cards in one hand, probably a gun with the other to keep him talking.

"When he's done, soon as Dennis stands up, the perp slips the loop back on him; autopsy said he was choked twice. Now he's through with the guy, he shows him no mercy. Chokes him till he's out again, rushes him over and throws him through the glass."

No one responded. Keyes made a sketch of the noose on his pad.

Montone set the choker down on his desk. "Let's run pet shops, supply houses for any recent buys of these things. Maybe we get lucky. That's it."

The squad went back to work, two detectives stopping to examine the choker. Terry Keyes approached Montone as he cleaned up the files on his desk.

"I'm gonna go out for coffee, you want to come?" said Montone.

"Sure."

"How did you figure out that he'd used a noose like that?" asked Keyes, as they turned onto Lexington Avenue.

"Dennis had ligature marks on his neck but he didn't die of strangulation."

"But how could you tell he'd used precisely that sort of device?"

"The killer controlled him but kept his distance; Dennis never got close enough to fight back. He was a strong guy but there were no signs of a struggle on the hands; bruised knuckles, tissue under the nails, that sort of thing."

"Still, it's pure speculation, isn't it?"

Montone hesitated, then decided to further confide. "On the tape there was a shadow of a loop on the wall."

"Really? You saw that on the video?"

"Super slo-mo. It was there for a split second."

"I didn't realize you had those kinds of technological resources."

"We're talking about a VCR; not exactly high-tech."

"So what does that tell you? Maybe your killer works with animals."

"Maybe. The case is thin; no witnesses, not much physical evidence. Most people who kill make a lot of mistakes because they're not thinking clearly or they're just stupid. This guy's not stupid."

"What about a motive?"

"Not too concerned with that just yet. Nail somebody on physical evidence, you've got plenty of time to worry about why. And frankly, who gives a shit? You kill somebody, what difference does it make why you did it? That's the DA's job. The damage is done."

Keyes nodded but didn't respond. Montone pulled his jacket shut, suddenly in a bad mood; the weather had turned, wind up, clouds rolling in, rain on the way. As reliable as a barometer, the old wound on his lower left thigh began to throb, as if an animal were gnawing the bone.

"You have to give me your word you're not going to talk to anybody about what you hear in these briefings," said Montone, lowering his voice.

"That's what we agreed to, absolutely."

"Not your girlfriend, not anybody. This is sensitive material, the tape, this confession, we're holding that back from the public for a reason."

"You don't want anyone to know it's a murder."

"Part of the reason. We got sickos out there who'd come in and confess to the Lincoln assassination if they thought it would get them on *Live at Five*. We also try to hold back some information that only we and the person who did this know about."

"I understand. And I appreciate your confidence all the more."

"I know we had an arrangement, but we're taking a chance having you in there."

"Jimmy, I don't want to cause any problems and I'm not going to do anything to violate your trust. The second you're uncomfortable with my being around, let me know and I'm out of your way."

Montone hesitated, looking up and down the street. "As long as we're clear."

"A project like this takes a long time. I'm not going to publish one word about it until well after the case is closed. That's a promise. I'll put it in writing if you like."

Montone waved him off. They stopped in a bakery, bought coffees and Danish and kept walking. A tall, striking brunette crossed the street in front of them, bringing traffic to a halt without breaking stride or betraying any awareness of the attention she drew. The two men watched her until she disappeared into the crowd.

"There is a God," said Keyes.

They started walking again.

"How did you and Holly get along last night?"

"She's a nice girl. Nicer than I would've guessed, actually. Some of these models, you see 'em in restaurants up here all the time."

"Genetic mutations," said Keyes.

"You can hear the wind whistling in their ears."

"Did you go out with her after the party? I lost track of you there."

"We spent some time. I drove her home."

"She tell you about her situation?"

"I gave her some advice. Commonsense sort of things."

"Are you going to see her again?"

"I don't know—what is this, a dating service?"

"Stranger things have happened. I know: I've seen them."

"Between Holly and me? What are you, nuts?"

"I'm dead serious."

"She's being harassed. Probably an occupational hazard and maybe I can help her out a little, which I'm happy to do, but that doesn't mean anything's going on between us. And I don't mix business with my personal life."

"Pardon my asking, Jimmy, but do you have a personal life?"

"I've got interests."

"Seeing anyone right now?"

"Not at the moment."

"You're not going to stand there and tell me you're not attracted to her."

"I'm not dead, for Christ's sake."

"Good. Then keep an open mind."

"Come on, how in the world would a girl like that be interested in me?"

"You'd be surprised."

Montone paused. "You know something I don't know?"

"Only what she told Tyler this morning."

"Told her what?"

"That she liked you. That she's very appreciative. That she'd like to know you better."

"She said that?"

"That's what I'm trying to tell you, Jimmy; you made a very big impression."

They stopped to wait for a light. Montone glanced at a newsstand and spotted Holly's picture on another magazine cover; gorgeous, glamorous, unattainable. He felt a slight shiver of disassociation, as if he had momentarily stepped into somebody else's life.

"Oh my God," said Keyes.

Montone turned around; Keyes wasn't looking at a newsstand but at a window of the electronics store on the corner.

Mackenzie Dennis's videotaped confession was playing on every one of the television sets in the display. Jaded New Yorkers all around them on the sidewalk had stopped to watch, openmouthed, stunned by his degraded appearance.

Montone's beeper went off. He pulled out his cell phone and punched in a number.

"Shit."

The tape had arrived in the morning mail, addressed to one of the station's five o'clock anchors. Montone examined the bubble-pack envelope in the news director's office while Murphy and Feany canvased the mailroom. Sheets of rain rattled the windows as the spring storm coursed quickly over the city.

The postage had been canceled that morning at the FDR post office on Third, the largest branch in the city. Stamps, not metered; whoever sent the package dropped it one of the wall slots. The handwriting was in characterless block letters, thick black ink, probably a Sharpie. No other distinguishing marking. The envelope could have been purchased at any of a thousand stationery stores.

The news anchor, a middle-aged woman with stiff hair and a brittle smile, had met Mackenzie Dennis socially on a number of occasions but she worked for a rival network and could think of no compelling reason why he would have singled her out for delivery. As they spoke, Montone realized the anchor and her news director were still under the impression that what they'd received was a suicide message and that Dennis himself had arranged to send it to them posthumously. No one at the station had noticed the shadow of the noose.

And by now every other local station and national tabloid trash show had picked up the excerpts they had broadcast and were beaming them coast to coast. The confession of Mackenzie Dennis immediately became the epicenter of the nation's televised attention. The angle proved irresistible: Suicidal news anchor accuses media of lying to the public. The media loved exploiting nothing so much as a story about how the media exploited the news.

Dennis's story burned a white-hot hole in the news director's headline-sensitive brain (they titled it "His Final Story"), and that was why he had rushed the tape onto the air without first calling the police.

Destroying the man's reputation, emotionally devastating his survivors, not to mention materially damaging a homicide investigation; those sorts of niceties didn't apply to a story this sensational. If any human misery ended up on video these days the public's right to immediately see it superseded every other consideration. No money had changed hands, which in their minds absolutely justified releasing the video as a "responsibility to our viewers."

These people seemed prepared to be indignant that the police were even expressing an interest, but Montone hid his disgust, questioning them evenly. He could need their cooperation again. The killer might decide to send them something else.

The release of the tape told him this much: Whoever had done this crime wanted the publicity, which raised the stakes to a much more ominous level. Montone had realized this perp was smart right from the jump. Now it looked like he had a plan.

"You see the body language in there when I first went in?" Montone asked Keyes, when he walked back to where the writer was waiting in the newsroom.

"I didn't notice," said Keyes, glancing back at the glass windows of the news director's office.

"Arms folded. Shoulders up. Chins out to here."

"Well defended."

"Ready for a fight. What does that tell you?"

"They don't know what they've got. They still think he committed suicide," said Keyes quietly.

"You learn fast."

Holly Mews was waiting at the precinct's front desk when they returned. Leather jacket, black T-shirt, shades, tight jeans and cowboy boots. Four uniforms and the desk sergeant were falling all over themselves trying to fix her coffee. She looked pale and tense and carried a manila envelope under her arm. As Montone approached she walked over to him, away from the pack, eyes downcast.

"Is there someplace we can talk?" she asked quietly.

He led her upstairs and into one of the small rooms the detectives used for interrogations. Keyes followed them up, looking concerned for her, but she wanted to talk to Jimmy alone so he waited outside in the squad room. Murphy and the other detectives were more than a little interested and cornered Keyes with questions about who she was and what she wanted with Montone.

"You all right?" he asked.

"Not really," said Holly once the door was closed. "I told you I use a PO box for all my mail—only my family and a few friends know my actual address."

"Right."

"So I found this in the mailbox at my apartment this morning."

She handed him the manila envelope. Her hands were shaking. Montone held it by the edges and emptied its contents on the table.

The first thing he saw was a five-by-seven black-and-white photograph of Holly standing in her loft near a window in the kitchen area, holding a mug in her hand, staring thoughtfully at something, maybe a newspaper, spread out on a table. She wore jeans and no top, her hair wet and combed back, just washed. Early-morning light from the eastern windows flooded the room, sending crescents of shadow along her sharply muscled back to the rounded, stone-smooth curve of her breasts. Her lithe, graceful stance and clear lack of awareness that she was being photographed gave the picture a sensual sheen that Montone worked to block from his mind.

Holly herself was framed from the knees up, in sharp focus, with everything around her slightly fuzzy; the shot had been snapped with a long lens, probably from a window or the roof of the building across the street. The picture stock was glossy, a standard commercial brand, slightly curled at the edges; Montone guessed that it had been developed and printed by hand in a private darkroom.

The only other item in the envelope was one sheet of common white copier paper. In its center, as in the last note she'd recieved, a few words had been assembled out of letters cut from a newspaper.

beauty is merciless

Holly sat down and lit a cigarette.

"What the hell is that supposed to mean?" she asked, angry and frightened.

Montone didn't respond as he examined the envelope. Addressed to "Ms. Holly Mews." Blue ink. Printed letters. Stamp canceled at a midtown post office. Mailed yesterday from somewhere in the city. His mind touched momentarily on that package sent to the TV station—also mailed yesterday, from another local office twenty blocks to the south and east—but the writing and ink were distinctly different, and without more to firmly connect the two his thought did not linger.

"You think it's from that guy you saw last night? The one making the calls?" She crossed her legs, the top one swinging nervously.

"Possibly."

"You don't think it's obvious? This creep's been watching me from the roof. Following me around. Now he's taking pictures—"

"I know it seems likely—"

"Who knows how many more of these he has? He might have been up there for weeks—"

"We try not to make those kinds of assumptions until we find out everything we can."

Holly lowered her head, fighting back tears.

"I'm not going to let some freak ruin my life, I'm not, I mean, I didn't do anything. I thought about what you said and I didn't reject anybody, I don't have any crazy ex-boyfriends, I'm nice to people I work with, I have a good reputation—"

"I'm sure that's true —"

"This is just some insane wacko who picked me out of the blue."

Montone waited, then spoke gently. "You're on magazine covers. You look a certain way. Some of those pictures can be kind of provocative."

"That's just my job."

"I'm not saying there's anything wrong with it or that you're in any way responsible, but it could still set somebody off. There doesn't have to be a rational reason. And it doesn't necessarily mean that this person wants to hurt you."

He didn't tell her there were a thousand freaks in a city this size with imagined relationships to women they saw in print or on video. Vivid, meticulous interactions, more real to them than the people in their lives. These images talked to them. Inner voices told them how to respond. Every once in a while, in one of these men, the voices shouted down the sound of the world and their private hell spilled out onto the street.

"You said yourself, girls in your line of work get reactions they can't control from guys all the time. They have problems like this pretty regularly, right?"

A moment later she nodded, staring at the floor.

"What can I do?" She took off her shades and looked up at him. Her eyes were red and strained from crying.

"Can you tell what morning this might have been?" he said, looking to the photograph.

She thought for a moment. "I think I wore those jeans on Monday."

"This last Monday."

She nodded.

"I want you to think back over that day. Go through your appointment book, re-create the day in your mind. Did you meet anybody or see anybody unusual, in places or ways that stand out in your mind? Don't answer right away. Think about it for me. I want to test these for prints—I'll be right back."

He gathered up the photo and note and started for the door as she took out her appointment book.

Montone grabbed a forensics kit from supply, went into his office and checked the photo, paper and envelope for prints, then examined the first card she received, which he'd been keeping in his desk. He lifted only one partial from the photo, which he suspected belonged to Holly; he would take her prints before she left for comparison.

He stood the card and the letter side by side and studied them with a magnifying glass. The letters in each message came from different newspapers but because of similarities in spacing and layout seemed clearly the work of the same hand.

beauty is betrayal

beauty is merciless

Might be part of a quote from poetry or fiction. He put in a call to a professor of English literature contact at Columbia but got the machine and left a message. The man had been an effective witness in a homicide they closed last year; he seemed to get a thrill out of the idea of detective work, a typical reaction for people who didn't have to do it for a living.

Murphy knocked and came into the room as he was finishing, Terry Keyes close behind him. Montone casually dropped the photo, note and card in an evidence folder before they could see it, and locked it in his desk.

"What's our position on the videotape?" asked Murphy.

"Reporters downstairs?"

Murphy nodded.

"We didn't know about it," said Montone.

"You want to check with downtown about that?"

"I'll call but they'll go with it."

"Have we reached any conclusions regarding said video?"

"We're reviewing it. We'll have a statement later."

Murphy stole a glance toward interrogation. "You fighting crime in there, Jimmy?"

"Crime-related."

"Because if there's anything I can do to help—"

"Goodbye, Murph."

Murphy left the room. Montone closed the door and motioned for Keyes to sit by the desk.

"Has Holly said anything to your girlfriend I ought to know?" he asked.

"Is she in some kind of trouble?"

"Between you and me, enough to worry about."

"This is that harassment thing," said Keyes.

"I don't think she's being harassed. I think she's being stalked."

"What's happened?"

"She's gotten a couple of threatening notes in the mail and somebody's watching her from the building next door. I chased a guy away from outside her place last night."

"Jesus."

"I'd like to know if she's said anything to anybody else."

"I'll ask Tyler, I'll call her right away."

"Problem with a deal like this is the freak hasn't broken any laws and there's only so much I can do officially until that happens. Hopefully it won't come to that. Sometimes they just go away."

"This is awful. What can she do? What can we do?"

"She can hire a bodyguard. Buy a dog. Leave town for a while."

"Maybe she should date a policeman."

Montone gave him a look. "I'm trying to be professional here."

"How is that inconsistent? You obviously care about her."

"She's a nice kid. I don't want to take advantage."

"No, of course not." Keyes nodded thoughtfully. "I just had a thought; Tyler and I are going out to the Island for the weekend—maybe we should take Holly with us, get her out of here for a couple days. As you suggested."

"I'm supposed to drive to Bridgehampton in the morning. Dennis had a house out there."

"So come to dinner with us Saturday. Spend some time with her. You want her to feel safe, don't you?"

"I want her to *be* safe."

"Let me talk to her about it. Would you be comfortable with that?"

Montone hesitated. "All right."

After five minutes in the closed room with Holly, Keyes came back to Montone's office.

"What time can you leave?" he asked.

"Sorry?"

"Holly's going to drive out with Tyler this afternoon. If you can get away tonight, I thought I'd wait and drive out with you."

"This is all right with her?"

"I got the impression she'd like to spend some time with Tyler alone. Shoulder to cry on. Female bonding."

"Guess I could leave late tonight. Grab a motel out there. See the Dennis place in the morning."

"Holly says she's got the use of a friend's house. Some deep-dish fashion photographer. Anyway, the place is huge, lots of bedrooms, right on the beach, and you're invited."

"I wouldn't want to impose."

Terry sat next to him and lowered his voice. "Jimmy, can I give you a piece of advice?"

"What?"

"She likes you. She's grateful. She knows how busy you are, and yet here you are, gallantly taking the time to help her out."

"It's not such a big deal."

"She seems like a genuinely good person. Levelheaded, wants to do the right thing. Hasn't been spoiled by her success, are we in agreement here?"

"Yes."

"Not to mention she is a dreamboat goddess out of fucking Greek mythology."

"What's your point?"

"Tyler told me her last two relationships ended so badly she called in the Red Cross. Men in the same business, real swine. She's sworn off the smart set. Wants to meet someone from the 'real world.' "

"Call this the real world?" said Montone, finding the idea laughable.

"Compared to what she's used to, you're bedrock. So my advice is, I think you need to stop underestimating yourself."

Montone grinned in spite of himself and couldn't think of anything to say.

"Is this a workable plan?" asked Keyes.

"Definitely."

"What time do we leave? I'll meet you here."

"Nine o'clock."

Keyes shook his hand, gave him the high sign and left.

Montone held Holly's hand, pressing each finger into the ink, then onto the paper in turn. Her composure recovered, she regarded him with a wry half-smile as he worked that made Montone worry about what Keyes had said to her. He felt as gawky as an eighth-grader under her silent scrutiny. The frank, casual way in which she offered her hands bordered on intimacy. Montone glanced up at the one-way mirror on the wall behind her with an unreasonable rush of paranoid suspicion that the squad was camped out back there watching them.

When they were finished he handed her tissues and rubbing alcohol and she cleaned her fingers, smiling quietly. Montone sensed a shifting in the ground between them, as if she now possessed some secret knowledge of him, and he wasn't sure he liked it.

No suspects had emerged from her recollection of the last few days, and as they talked it occurred to Montone that her earlier discomfort had been displaced by the reassurances given by her attractiveness to him, a more familiar dynamic that tilted the playing field back to level ground.

This is her normal experience, he reminded himself; men continually off balance, eager to please, extending courtesies out past their usual limits. Beauty has a force like gravity and the women who possess it develop a sixth sense about its effect on the people they encounter. Montone saw no way to counter this new term of engagement. Holly remained gracious, even inviting of his attention, holding only her private center in reserve. For whatever reason, and to no ill effect, the rules of courtship now governed their every move.

He walked her down to a rear exit in order to avoid the television crews that had assembled near the front desk for reactions to the Dennis tape.

"I'm going to call downtown, make sure they put a patrol car on your street this afternoon. They can't park but they can do regular drive-bys. If you're uncomfortable about going up to the apartment alone I could have somebody meet you."

"I'll be fine, thanks."

"I don't want you to worry. Guys like this, you know, they're cowards, it doesn't necessarily mean anything."

"You don't have to reassure me, Jimmy. You've already done that." She'd never used his first name before. He could tell it was a conscious decision.

"Okay."

"I guess I'll see you tonight, then."

"Safe trip."

They shook hands. He watched her walk to the corner and waited until she hailed a cab.

Montone placed a conference call to Captain Dan Jakes and Will Flannigan, the Borough Commander. They backed his play on the Dennis video, so he went down to give a statement and answer questions in front of the station. Television reporters routinely used the precinct's imposing stone edifice to lend some weight to their stand-ups. Montone had long ago learned that what worked for them worked equally well for NYPD, so he positioned himself on the top step where they could frame him against the fortress.

He also knew how to punch up his responses into sound bites that would actually make the news. The Dennis "suicide tape" would lead most of tonight's local and even national broadcasts, providing him with a unique opportunity to talk directly to the killer. Montone knew nothing about who or where this man might be but he felt certain he would be watching.

He began by discouraging the idea that the department had any knowledge of the tape prior to its appearance on the air, assuring them that if they had known about it they certainly would have made it available to the public.

He made it clear that the department at this point considered Dennis's death an apparent suicide, an idea which the emergence of the tape, to their way of thinking, only tended to support.

He denied the existence of a special task force, saying only that due to Dennis's prominence in the community, a number of detectives had been assigned to expedite the investigation. They were pursuing a strong lead, for instance, which suggested that Mr. Dennis had made prior arrangements to mail the video to the television station after his death.

He cautioned members of the press against leaping to any reckless or premature conclusions about the unfortunate occurrence; Mr. Dennis had survivors who deserved sympathetic consideration during this difficult time. The statement made by Dennis in the tape, which had already been transcribed and widely disseminated, was obviously that of a man in the grip of serious emotional distress.

As such, Montone stated emphatically, they assigned "no special significance to the *content* of the statement itself."

Montone didn't know who he was up against but he was confident his discounting of the tape's "message" would run counter to the killer's expectations. If the man had murdered Dennis to make a statement of his own, or if the speech he'd fed to his victim *was* his statement, then Montone wanted to do everything he could to nullify its impact.

The perp had gone to painstaking lengths to make this death look almost, but not quite, like a suicide. The man had left so many subtle but unmistakable markers to the contrary—the disposition of the camera, the lines of blow, the single stone from the roof—that Montone concluded they weren't mistakes at all; they'd been deliberate and provocative. The killer was throwing down a direct challenge for anyone sharp enough to interpret his signs correctly: he *dared* them to see this as a murder, the work of a superior intelligence.

With nothing else to guide him, Montone sensed he might be able to get at this guy by ignoring the bait. Stick with the suicide theory, eliminate the idea of a murder from public perception. If he guessed right, that might diminish the killer's pride of achievement, inflame his ego, piss him off, and if this perp got angry enough he might be provoked into a more reckless attempt to assert the importance of his "contribution."

A *grinder,* that's what his high school hockey coach had called Montone. There were plenty of more talented skaters on the squad and most were more physically gifted, but none had half his determination. Aware of his limitations, Montone modeled his police work after the athletes he had always admired the most; lunch bucket guys who take their shifts, do their minutes and never for one second get out of high gear.

Keep grinding and maybe you get an edge. Grind and you wear down your opponent. Don't stop, don't talk about it, do it. Sooner or later they'll make a mistake and in that moment the game is decided.

He made a note reminding himself to tell Terry Keyes that grinding was the heart of a murder investigation.

At eight o'clock as he was heading out the door for home Montone got a call from Pat Feany asking him to come over to the building next door to Dennis's on Sixty-ninth. Murphy jumped into the car with him out front and they drove together.

"Got that BCI on your pal Terry from Interpol," said Murphy, fishing a folded telex out of his jacket.

"How's it read?"

"He did the big stretch for manslaughter. Seems like it squares with what he told us. Paroled in '92. Three years off for good behavior. Model prisoner."

"Maintained his parole okay?"

"Clean as a choirboy. Not a single beef since. Went off the books two years ago. Case officer practically wrote a poem about him."

"That's good," said Montone, realizing he had wanted the report to come back clean.

"Juvie record's not on the sheet but I could track it if you're interested," said Murphy.

Montone waved him off. "You run immigration?"

"He was in the country for eight weeks last September, October. Official reason for the visit says 'book tour.' He came back in again about a month ago through Kennedy, with a work permit this time. 'Book research.' Estimated stay, six months."

"Stands up, doesn't it?"

"Hey, he turned his life around," said Murphy, putting the telex away. "Good for him. One less fuckup in the world."

Pat Feany had the alley between the buildings roped off and work lights set up on the adjacent roof, where Montone and Murphy joined him. He first showed them the roof-access door, up a short flight of stairs from the service elevator. The super explained that the stairwell door was always kept locked and only he and bulding residents had keys. The area around the bolt was tacky to the touch, just like the door to Dennis's service entrance.

"Say he comes in as 'cable guy' on the afternoon of the day and tapes the lock," said Feany. "What's his next move?"

"He goes over to the roof of Dennis's building," said Montone, looking up the stairs. "He picks the lock to Dennis's service entrance and tapes that, too."

"Why?"

"He's scouting. Saves him having to sweat it later when he's on the clock."

Montone led them up onto the roof. The other two detectives on the team were combing over a taped-off section under the lights near the fire escape.

"How's he get across?" asked Murphy, looking at the twelve-foot gap between the buildings and the thirty-five-floor drop to the alley below.

"The 'cable guy' comes in with a toolbox, right?" said Montone, leading them over to the edge.

"That's what the witness said."

"In that box he's carrying a rope attached to some kind of hook. He tosses the hook up onto the lip of the roof next door; that's where the scratches on those bricks around the lip came from. He lowers himself onto the rope, swings across to the other fire escape and climbs up. Comes back the same way."

Feany looked skeptically down over the edge. "In broad fucking daylight. No one sees him."

"People don't look up in this city, Pat."

"Swings across like Tarzan."

"The fact that the perp's got balls does not seem to be in question here. He probably packed whatever else he needed for the job in that toolbox and stashed it somewhere inside the building. Anybody see him walk out with it?"

"We know he left. I don't know about the box," said Murphy, making a note to ask.

"So he comes back at night, swings across, whacks the guy, swings back," said Feany, still unconvinced.

"You got another scenario?"

"How's he get back in here past the doorman at night?"

"This building has a parking garage, doesn't it? Security's probably not airtight and he probably knew it. Maybe he taped another door. Check it out."

"This asshole went to a lot of fucking trouble," said Feany, lighting a smoke.

Montone knew Feany had a bad feeling. He felt it too. They were accustomed to the panic, disorder and stupidity that characterized most of the crimes they investigated. This kind of logic and cold precision broke hard against the grain, suggesting a confidence and presence of mind that left them all uneasy.

"Got something here," said Frank Fonseca.

They moved to the taped-off section of roof and Fonseca showed them what he'd found, lifting it from the ground with a long pair of forensic tweezers; a small, glittering red octagonal flake, cut from paper or a pliable synthetic.

"Maybe some kind of sequin?" offered Fonseca.

Montone examined the red chip through a magnifying card he took from his wallet, and held it up to the light.

"Think there'd be a hole in it. Something to attach it to something."

"To what? An evening dress?"

"Check with the super, see if they ever have parties up here," said Montone.

"Maybe Cher was his accomplice," said Murphy.

"I don't think it's a sequin," said Montone, turning it around. "I think it's a piece of confetti."

Montone pulled up outside the station at nine-fifteen and dropped Murphy off. Terry Keyes waited for him on the sidewalk near the precinct garage, carrying a weekender duffel. He threw the bag on the backseat, climbed in beside Montone, and they drove away. It didn't strike Montone as unusual at the time that Keyes had been standing so far from the front doors.

As Murphy entered the station, Ida, the elderly civilian receptionist at the Welcome Desk, asked him if he'd been with Detective Montone. Murphy told her he was driving out to Long Island for the night to inspect the Dennis beach house in the morning.

"Is Detective Montone planning to stop back in at the station before he leaves?" asked Ida.

"Why?"

"Gentleman here to see him," said Ida, nodding back at a tall, white-haired man seated near the door.

"He have an appointment?"

"No."

"He want to talk to another officer?"

"No."

"What's he want, Ida?"

"I'm sure I don't know," said Ida, clinging to her civil-servant ignorance like a badge of honor.

Murphy looked at the man, sitting bolt upright, staring straight ahead with an almost military bearing. He considered going over to have a word with the guy, but at the end of a double shift on a Friday night Murphy decided against it. He still had the long drive home out to Rockland County ahead of him, and the turnaround for tomorrow barely left him with enough time for a microwaved dinner, a kiss for his two adorable, chubby daughters and a six-hour flop. He told Ida to take a message and headed upstairs to the squad room.

When she told him Montone wasn't coming back, the old man scribbled something on the back of a business card, left it with Ida and politely asked her to please have the detective call him as soon as possible on "a matter of some urgency."

None of which left much of an impression on Ida's limited field of memory, although as he spoke she remembered enjoying the sound of his crisp British accent. She'd neglected to mention to Murphy that he was an Englishman.

Ida stuck the card in Montone's message slot without reading it and Deputy Inspector Peter Henshaw of Scotland Yard left the station house.

6

My only memory of Dad: lying in our one-room flat in Blackpool at the age of four, while Karen, my mother, serviced the man in the bed beside my crib. He wore a green-olive uniform and dropped his hat on the floor beside me. Candlelight sparkled off brass insignia on its brim, mesmerizing.

He was an American GI. I don't know his name and his memory is bound up with Karen's mythology about him. She claimed they'd had a romance three years before and I was the result. He came back to England to visit from time to time, this being one of those occasions, and wrote to her often, although I never saw any letters. After leaving the service she told me he intended to join the police force in some large American city and that one day we would be moving there to join him.

I was frightened by the noises they made but kept very still, for good reason, because if I made a whimper while they were fucking Karen would lock me in the crawl space inside the bedroom wall and the cycle of abuses would begin again. A teaspoon roasted on the hot plate that served as our kitchen was her favorite disciplinary tool.

When they finished Karen made a trip to the loo down the hallway. The man rolled over on the bed and stared down at me in the crib. I could smell liquor and sex on him.

He asked me my name. I asked him if he was my father. He laughed, baring long, irregular teeth.

He whispered to me that Karen had told him a secret and he wanted to share it with me, but I had to promise not to tell anyone. I agreed.

"Your daddy's the Devil," the man said.

He dropped a handful of coins in the crib and said it would be our little secret. I never saw him again.

: excerpt from Flatlander *by Peregrine Keyes*

Terry Keyes waited in the car, double-parked, while they made a quick stop at Montone's apartment so he could pack a bag. Twenty minutes later they were headed east through thinning Friday night traffic on the Long Island Expressway; windows open, radio picking up a West Coast ball game, cool night air streaming through the car.

The highway took them past Montone's old neighborhood near the Whitestone Bridge; a grim, deteriorating blue-collar eyesore. The houses, most of them cheap, postwar structures, had not aged well and few owners had the pride or the money to maintain them.

"You grew up out here, didn't you, Jimmy?"

"That's right."

"You come back much?"

"Only passing through. Not too many happy memories."

"Looks like the neighborhood I grew up in."

"Not too many get out. The ones that don't never change."

"How'd you manage?"

"Hockey scholarship. Small college upstate."

"Your family still live out here?"

"My dad's dead. My mother moved to Tampa a long time ago."

"Brothers and sisters?"

"Only child."

"Really? Me too," said Keyes. "What did your father do?"

"Industrial chemist," said Montone. "He was part of the team that invented Styrofoam."

"That must have been worth a fortune."

"Not to him. Company owned the patent. They were just contract workers."

"What did he get for his troubles?"

"Liver cancer. He died when I was four."

"That couldn't have been easy."

"It wasn't."

"I didn't know my father, either," said Keyes, sitting back, one foot on the dash, his face moving in and out of the light from oncoming cars.

"Why's that?"

"For starters my mother didn't know who he was. There were a number of candidates but she couldn't seem to make up her mind which one planted the flag. In her more lucid moments she clung to the idea that he was American."

"She still living?"

"Honestly, I don't know. I was twelve when I last laid eyes on her; a custody hearing when she signed me over to the care of the state. She was so heavily medicated she didn't even know who was kissing her goodbye."

"You went into the system."

"Foster homes. Juvenile detention. Punctuated by brief but eventful stays on the street. Pretty dreary stuff; it's all there in my book if you're interested."

"Brought it with me," said Montone, nodding back toward his bag. "Haven't had a chance to get into it yet."

"A little light reading for the beach." Keyes smiled.

"I was in a foster home for a couple years. My mother got sick. I ran kind of wild myself there for a while."

"Probably don't need to read it then," said Keyes. "I didn't realize we had so much in common."

"Sports, that's what straightened me out. Coach took an interest in me. I really caught a break."

Yes, you did. The first of far too many.

Half in shadow, Keyes watched him through unblinking eyes.

"Your mother was a hooker?" asked Montone, after another pause.

"The term suggests a degree of career direction the poor woman didn't really possess. Professionalism eluded her. 'Hooker' would have been a step up."

"I'm sorry to hear that."

"I got off on the idea of an American father. Constructed all sorts of fantasies about who he might have been. War hero. International spy. Slumming movie star; for a while I convinced myself he was Steve McQueen, making a war picture on location. So taken with Mum he wore the uniform home from the set. She worked as an extra on a film that shot in Manchester once, so it's a good bet she screwed somebody from the unit. Probably an electrician."

Montone listened carefully, surprised that he didn't sound bitter. He didn't sound amused, either.

"Movies, you know, they created our view of the world over there," said Keyes.

"Here too."

"But you already lived in the middle of these modern wonders; they only amplified what you saw every day. Our little empire had been torched to the ground. We'd run out of dreams; American movies gave us a whole new reality. That's all we saw in prison. I made a study of it."

"How so?"

"You'd be amazed. America sends a lot more out into the world than you realize. You can't see it here, Jimmy, you're insulated. Have you ever been overseas?"

"No."

"They watch *Monday Night Football* in London. There's a McDonald's around the corner from the Kremlin. MTV rules the Third World. The heart of Europe's no bigger than Texas; we're overmatched. Movies, television, fashion, music, food; everything starts here now."

"But you've got all that history, tradition."

"And American pop culture is a bloody steamroller with Mickey Mouse behind the wheel. No contest. 'History' didn't stand a chance. More people know who Michael Jackson is than the name of the president of their own country. The French are still trying to fight it, naturally, but the war's over. Euro Disney is here to stay."

They rode without speaking for a while, passing the exits for Kennedy. Keyes was a good driving companion, comfortable in silences, letting the conversation conform to the rhythm of the road.

At a quarter to midnight they reached the turnoff to the Montauk Highway. Following Holly's written directions, they headed south toward the ocean past the town of Water Mill, off the highway and down winding country roads that took them past hidden mansions, weekend estates tucked away behind security walls and lush stands of mature trees.

They found the house at the end of a twisted sandy lane, standing on a bluff directly above a broad white sand beach, a modern three-storied collision of glass and long arms of timber, encircled by landscaping that casually complemented the natural ground cover and sea grasses. Their arrival activated motion-sensor lights above the garage. One car, Tyler's late-model BMW, sat in the drive.

Tyler greeted them at the front door and led them into a soaring entry hall. Montone could smell slightly sour red wine and a hint of grass on her breath when she kissed him hello. She seemed a little unsteady on her bare feet. She was wearing a loose, loud, flowing caftan and still managed to look overdressed, reinforcing his initial impression from the other night that the woman was slightly ridiculous. Terry seemed comfortable with her, at least physically, leading Montone to conclude she was probably uninhibited enough to be memorable in bed.

As she walked them through the round sunken living room, crammed with white leather sofas and pretentious objets d'art, Tyler rambled about the "glorious house" and its "gorgeous location," and was explaining how the famous photographer and his architect had consulted an expert in some ancient mystical Chinese art called "feng shui," when Holly appeared on a balcony above them.

"He built it so he'd have somewhere to take his girlfriends when the wife was out of town," she said.

"Telling tales out of school," said Tyler.

"Were you one of them, dear?" asked Keyes, amused.

"Not in this lifetime," she said, coming down the stairs. "I think that's why he lets me use the place."

She showed Montone to a downstairs bedroom, where he dropped his bag while Tyler took Keyes upstairs. The walls were lined with large framed photographs that Montone guessed were the owner's artwork; empty forbidding black-and-white landscapes, depressing portraits of New York City street life.

"This the guy?" he asked, pointing to the pictures.

"Yeah." They looked at them for a while. "What do you think?"

"Not sleeping with him was a good call."

Montone opened a sliding door, exiting onto a deck that fed down to the beach. The air was warm and welcoming. As he stepped near the edge of the deck a row of motion-senstitive spot floods along the rear of the house winked on, illuminating a broad slice of the waterfront, setting the white foam of the breakers aglow. The muted drumming of the surf sounded as foreign to his ears as another language.

Holly stepped onto the deck after him. Her hair was down; she wore an oversized green cable sweater, black tights and a pair of fleeced moccasins. Montone guessed that she'd already gone to bed, coming back out when they arrived. There'd only been one wineglass on the living room table and Holly, he could tell, hadn't been drinking.

"You okay with this?" she asked.

"I don't know. I could've been spending the evening in a Blimpie's on Forty-fourth Street."

She smiled and moved to the opposite rail of the deck. "I know you're involved in something important right now. You really didn't need to come."

"I've got legitimate business out here tomorrow anyway. If it was a problem I would tell you."

"Once I got here the whole thing seemed so far away, I don't know, I started to feel kind of silly. I went to bed early so I wouldn't have to think about it."

"Feeling that and having it actually be that way are two different things."

"Being alone with Tyler for nine hours makes you want to sleep for about a week," she said.

"So it's not just me."

"Everybody has that reaction to her. She means well, I think she has a good heart. She's just not very . . . likable."

"I've been wondering what Terry sees in her," he said.

"She's just crazy enough to be good in bed."

"That was my guess too."

"Plus he hasn't known her that long. Poor thing; three weeks for her is a major relationship."

"I'd have to wear earplugs. Like those guys that wave the planes into the jetways." He lifted his arms, mimicking the motion.

She laughed and seemed to relax slightly, leaning over the rail.

"So peaceful out here," she said.

"You feel safe now?"

"You bring your nine-millimeter?" she asked, with a crooked smile.

He parted his jacket to show her.

"Yes. I feel safe. And not because of the gun. Thank you, Jimmy."

They heard a sharp squeal from somewhere above them in the house, what could have been a cry of pain, but then it was followed by a peal of laughter—Tyler's voice, unmistakably—and then a series of enthusiastic vocalizations, punctuated with an occasional piercing "Yes!"

"Oh my God," said Montone.

"She's a screamer."

They looked at each other and started to laugh. Realizing they were directly below the bedroom window the sounds were coming from, Holly tried to keep them both from laughing out loud, which only made it that much harder. Tyler launched into an operatic series of whoops and hollers, throwing in a few "Oh Gods" for good measure. On the deck they made the mistake of looking at each other again and now they were in serious trouble.

Montone doubled over, trying desperately not to make a sound, gasping for air. Holly abandoned any attempt to contain herself and slumped weakly against the rail, weeping with laughter. As Tyler screamed again both of them melted helplessly onto the deck.

"She's gonna set off the smoke alarms," whispered Montone.

Holly's hysteria hit a new level. She waved her hands frantically, then crawled down the stairs of the deck, trying to catch her breath, and dropped to the sand. Montone pulled his jacket off and buried his face in the material, trying to stifle himself as he stumbled down the stairs and fell to the ground beside her.

"Why doesn't he kill her and get it over with?" she gasped.

They crawled weakly away from the house toward the sea until they were far enough for the sound not to carry and the laughs finally broke from them, big and steady as the waves until they both collapsed, rolled onto their backs and waited for the condition to subside.

"That was better than sex," said Holly, drying her eyes with the sleeves of her sweater.

"Or whatever she was having."

"You think they heard us?" she asked.

"She wouldn't have noticed World War Three."

"He didn't make a peep, did he?"

"He couldn't get a word in edgewise."

They laughed one last time, then lapsed into a spent, contented silence. The row of lights along the back of the house blinked off, leaving them in a wash of pale moonlight reflecting off the bone-white beach.

Montone turned and propped himself up on one arm to look at Holly. She had stretched out in the sand, relaxed and still, arms behind her head, looking up at the sky. Neither spoke for a while.

"It's weird, isn't it?" she asked.

"What's that?"

"The way people meet. How their paths cross."

"Definitely."

"Makes you wonder if there's any purpose or pattern to things or is it all random electrons flying around, bumping into each other."

"You didn't tell me you were a philosopher."

"Aren't you, with all the things you must see? Life and death. Doesn't it make you ask those questions?"

"I think about 'em, sure."

"The Buddhists believe people's paths are already all laid out for them. You may not even know you're alive but your path keeps taking you where you're supposed to go."

"Where are you going?"

"I don't know. I feel kind of ignorant about it really. I started working when I was sixteen."

"You're not ignorant."

She turned on her side to look at him, mirroring his posture. One slender bare foot slid out of her shoe and burrowed into the sand. Her perfect face looked younger to him in that unreliable light, less guarded than before, and he sensed that another barrier between them had fallen away. They were quiet again for a while.

"Did you ever have to kill anybody?" she asked softly.

"Once."

"Can you talk about it?"

"Narcotics bust. I had the suspect on the floor, handcuffed. Thought we had the situation contained. This other guy came through a connecting door to the next apartment, guns in both hands, firing. My partner got clipped. I just reacted."

She looked at him searchingly, as if his face held more of the answer than what he'd told her.

"Did it bother you?"

"Not that much. It was him or me. He was the bad guy. Not the kind of thing I walk around regretting."

"Was it like that when you caught Wendell Sligo?"

"Different."

"How?"

Montone thought carefully before he answered. He hadn't talked about this with anyone for a long time.

"I'd been looking for the man who did those murders for a year and a half. There was a team of us, working the case. We hadn't come close to identifying him yet, but from what he did to his victims we put together a detailed profile of who he might be."

"How?"

"Once we realized we were dealing with multiple killings by the same person, the department sent me down to take a course at the FBI Academy at Quantico. There've been enough of these kinds of murders now, they've developed a system for analyzing the patterns. They teach you a certain way of looking at the victims, the way the crimes were committed. They tell you things."

"What did they tell you?"

"He was killing prostitutes, taking these girls right off the street, but the profile said he was shy and reclusive, which meant he wasn't talking them into going with him and that meant he had to overpower them quickly. So we knew he was physically strong but that his appearance wouldn't be that memorable or threatening, because no one had ever noticed him at the scenes."

"He looked like a science teacher."

"Sligo's a big, husky guy but there was something so ordinary about him you wouldn't notice him sitting next to you on a bus. After we took him down the papers started calling him the Slug 'cause he had this languid, easy rhythm about him. The name made good headlines but that was just his way of blending in. The Quantico profile told us to look for a guy with exactly that anonymous quality."

"What else did it tell you?"

"Said he was a white male in his early thirties who lived by himself and had never been married. Most likely an only child. Above-average intelligence, high school graduate from somewhere in the area, probably with a degree from a two-year technical training school in engineering or electronics. That he had a job as a tradesman or some kind of repair work and probably worked alone. That he drove a customized van that he'd remodeled himself."

"Really? It could tell you those kinds of details?"

"I can't tell you why exactly, but it works. Psychology, intuition, it all sort of comes together. We knew that as a kid he would have shown signs of trouble that nobody noticed or paid enough attention to."

"What kind of things?"

"Starting fires, torturing animals. Probably a bed wetter. When he got into his teens and hormones kicked in he'd have started taking more chances to see what he could get away with; petty theft, peeping in windows, maybe even breaking and entering. He would have had at least one prior arrest for some kind of sexual misconduct. All of that turned out to be on the money. He'd been busted for attempted rape of a prostitute at nineteen but the case was tossed on a technicality. The profile also said that subsequent to that arrest he would have been clean for at least five years before the killings started."

"Why?"

"Because he was smart. Because he'd let his impulses run away from his ability to control the behaviors and had gotten caught. So he pulled back, learned from his mistakes, sharpened up his games. Maybe even tried to go 'straight' for a while, even date somebody. Convince himself he was normal."

"So he was conflicted."

"At that point. He knew exactly what was inside him and how wrong it was. The whole time he was obsessing about killing. Visualizing. Getting his kicks. The images terrified and excited him. He fought it, but nothing could make him let go."

"And he lost the battle."

"These ideas had a grip on him that ran too deep. When they're tied into sexuality like his were, and there's no chance of dealing with it therapeutically, there's almost no way back. And once he gave in to it and committed that first murder, he found out he had a taste for it. The feelings of power and control only reinforced his fantasies. He wanted more."

"Fifteen people."

"And he never would have stopped. You talk to this guy—he's intelligent, soft-spoken, obviously well educated. But to this day he expresses not one shred of remorse about the victims."

"How is that possible?"

"Something goes wrong inside these men. It's not that they don't know the difference between right and wrong. Sligo's not crazy in that sense; he seems completely rational. But the victims they do these things to aren't real to them."

"This is the kind of thing my sister writes about."

"The shrink?"

"Psychologist, yeah. She thinks they're born that way. Usually people say it's the result of abuse when they're kids. But if that's true, why don't they all turn into criminals?"

"You were right," said Montone. "Your sister is smart."

"Still doesn't explain why, though."

"At any given time there might be fifteen or twenty of these men out there, actively killing. At some fundamental level they're no longer what you'd consider human."

"They're monsters."

"Wendell Sligo, who is in maximum isolation at Attica until the twenty-second century, gets five marriage proposals in the mail a month from women he's never even met."

"That's insane."

"And every afternoon from two to four he plays bridge with three other serial killers. All housed in the same yard to protect them from the rest of the prisoners. Between them these four killed thirty-nine people."

"How did you catch him, Jimmy?"

"An outside security camera at a bank near where the last victim was taken had his van on tape. Didn't show the driver, didn't show the girl anywhere near it, but the van was there in the parking lot for over an hour around the time she disappeared and we had the detail about the van from the profile, so I ran a check on the plates. The computer didn't show any recent record, the one assault he'd been brought up on was dismissed so it didn't come through, but his address put him in the center of an area where most of the victims had been taken. Not much to go on but I was willing to try anything.

"I drove out to his house that night. Working-class neighborhood in Yonkers. As I got there Wendell was coming out of his house, moving slow, wearing this oversized army-surplus jacket. When I saw him I had a gut feeling this was our guy, but instinct told me not to get out and talk to him. He walked back to a locked garage behind the house and came out driving the van. He didn't see me so I tailed him.

"He drove around Westchester County for a couple of hours, kind of aimlessly, until he passed through a stand of woods where one of the earliest victims had been found. A wilderness sanctuary off the Taconic Parkway, an out-of-the-way area, with no reason to go there at night.

"I was about to call in backup and pull him over, when he turned off the road. I couldn't take the same turn or he would have made me, so I drove on and stopped about a hundred yards up the road. I called the state troopers and followed the path on foot he'd driven back into the woods. The van had stopped about a quarter mile in. Quiet. Real dark in there.

"I heard him moving through the brush some distance away when I got up to the vehicle. Windows were tinted black, couldn't see anything inside. I wanted to pull back and wait for the troopers before we tried to take him but then I heard something move in the rear of the van. The back door was unlocked.

"She was one of ours. Working on our detail, on the street in East Harlem, undercover, dressed as a hooker. Somehow he'd taken her a couple hours before. No one saw him do it. I'd been on the move the whole time, didn't even know she'd been reported missing."

"Did he know she was a cop?"

"He found her badge. He had her bolted through the wrists and feet to a metal pegboard in the back of the van."

"Oh my God."

"The van was his killing ground. Place was tricked out like a surgical theater. Stainless steel. Soundproofing. Corrugated floor. Scalpels, power tools, IVs, tanks of oxygen and nitrous oxide. He could keep them alive for days that way."

Holly winced involuntarily. She looked pale and upset. Caught up in his own story, he hadn't been paying enough attention to her reactions.

"I'm sorry, I'm telling you way more than you need to know."

"She was still alive?"

"They didn't write about that afterwards."

"Oh God. And you knew her."

"Yeah. She was a friend."

Montone looked up at the sky, then closed his eyes and found himself back in the moment. He hadn't descended into that cloistered nightmare for a long time. He felt a tremor building in his hands but he needed to keep talking.

"We went out for a few months, couple years before this when we were both still on patrol. Sheila was from the neighborhood, you know? Tough, feisty. It was no great romance, we kind of both knew that, so there were no hard feelings. And we stayed friends."

"I'm so sorry."

Montone nodded, looked away.

"He had two girls that night. He was carrying the other body into the woods to his drop site. She was already dead. I heard him coming back. I closed the door and stepped away. When he reached the back of the van and opened the door I shined my flashlight on him and told him to get on the ground. He turned around slowly to look at me, ignored what I said to him. His expression never changed, as if he wasn't even interested. I was so angry I had no feelings for him at all; I didn't care if he lived or died. And that made me hesitate."

"That's how he hurt you."

"He had a derringer in a rig up his sleeve. As he brought his arm up it whipped out into his hand and he fired. Hit me right above the knee. I fired at the same time but my shot went wide and caught him here, in the shoulder, which was lucky because he was wearing body armor under his jacket. Wouldn't have hurt him at all with a center shot. He went down, dropped the gun and didn't offer any resistance. Thing was, he couldn't handle pain. He only liked giving it.

"I got him cuffed to the door handle. Sat down, set a tourniquet on my leg and waited for the troopers. Wendell started crying. This fucking beast whining about how much his shoulder hurt. I wanted to kill him. I'd let my guard down for a split second, because I hated him and what he was, and the son of a bitch almost took me out. That was the longest ten minutes of my life."

Tears formed in his eyes. He blinked, trying to see through them.

"I put a blanket over her, tried to keep her talking. You could already hear the sirens."

Montone took in a deep, shuddering breath.

"She didn't make it. I kept thinking if only I'd pulled him over earlier. The whole time she's lying in there with the life running out of her. Maybe it was too late anyway, that's what the doctors told me. Her name was Sheila. Sheila Marks. Sligo had videotapes of all his victims. He'd play them for the others while he worked on them. The tape of Sheila was running on this TV he had set up in the back."

Holly took a deep, halting breath and wiped the tears from her eyes. "Oh my God, Jimmy."

"I shouldn't have told you. I'm sorry."

"I asked. I wanted to know."

"You didn't need to hear that."

"Maybe you needed to tell it."

As Montone considered the idea he reached a hand down to rub his left leg above the knee, aching from the damp ocean air.

"Was it that leg?" she asked.

"I couldn't work afterwards. Took a disability leave. Six months. I couldn't stop seeing her lying there."

She moved over to him, cupped her hands on his face and kissed him tenderly. Her eyes looked sad and compassionate, willing enough to wrap them both in forgetting. Montone felt a stab of irrational regret, knowing they would become lovers and that the poignancy of longing for her while she remained beyond his reach would fade. He could still cite a hundred reasons to her why they should wait, move forward from this moment more slowly or not at all, but as her kisses set off the explosiveness of their chemistry all his fine reasonings were swept aside.

The warmth and taste of her breath, the smell of her hair, felt immediate and shockingly real, but her sincerity dissolved his last resistance. He wanted her more than the minor grace of maintaining his own good intentions.

"Should we go inside?" he whispered.

"No," she said, pulling off her sweater.

He unsnapped his holster and set it carefully in the sand, within reach.

Fifty yards away, from the highest window of the house, through the magnifying eyepiece of a night-vision pocket scope, Terry Keyes watched them make love on the beach.

He extended a pencil-thin, parabolic microphone another three inches outside and checked the meter on the palm-sized Nagra recorder to make sure the sounds they made were registering as clearly as had their conversation.

It occurred to him that if they were going to be a while he might still have time to plant a microphone in Montone's bedroom, where they would now surely spend most of the night.

Don't get greedy. Everything's on track. You've got more than you need already.

A stertorous snore from the next bedroom interrupted the broadcast whispers of the lovers. The idiot woman had been so loaded by the time they arrived that the pill he'd slipped into her wine had put her under within fifteen minutes. Not fast enough to spare him the indignity of servicing her first, but that served the purpose of legitimizing his interest in her. At least she had found within herself a budding appetite for pain. Still, the thought of even that much contact with her deeply disgusted him.

If only they knew how I suffer for my art. And they will.

Montone woke at the sound of voices. His arm reached for Holly; then he remembered that after the last time they'd made love she crept back at first light to her own bedroom for the sake of appearances.

"The only time," she promised, kissing him, then stopping to flash him once at the door.

Out of habit his hand next found his holster in the stand beside the bed. Seven-thirty. He climbed out of bed, tried to loosen up his damaged leg. A heavy fog obscured the beach; he could barely make out the waterline in the gray, diffused light.

After a shower he found Holly and a worried Terry Keyes in the kitchen drinking coffee. Tyler had taken ill during the night. Some kind of devastating intestinal flu, maybe an attack of diverticulitis.

Or maybe a little too much dago red and prescription medicine, thought Montone. He'd be willing to give odds she had a pill habit.

Whatever the reason, Keyes seemed concerned enough to cut their weekend short and drive her immediately back to the city. She had left some medicine she needed at her apartment, and if need be, could get in to see her doctor. When Keyes went upstairs to bring Tyler down to the car, Montone and Holly could barely look at each other. Neither wanted their elation at suddenly being left alone together to undercut an appropriate concern for Tyler's condition.

"Do they know?" he whispered.

"Not a clue," she said.

He kissed her once, a delicious, conspiratorial feeling between them.

Keyes helped Tyler slowly down the stairs. She looked drained, frail and white as cotton.

Worse than a hangover, Montone realized; she's desperately ill.

He carried their bags to the car and opened the door so Keyes could help her in. Tyler could barely mumble a goodbye and wasn't even strong enough to fasten her own seat belt.

"Terribly sorry about all this," said Keyes, as they stowed the bags in the trunk.

"Nothing to be sorry for. She's lucky she has you to take care of her."

"Burns the candle a bit at both ends, I'm afraid. Very tense girl. I'm really only just getting to know her. Must be the strain of her job, I suppose."

"Anything else we can do?"

"We'll be fine. You and Holly getting along all right?" asked Keyes.

"Yeah, good. Had a nice talk last night."

"Do you have to go back to work today, or can you spend some more time with her?"

"Hadn't thought about it yet."

"It's just I don't really like the idea of her being out here alone. That was the whole point of her getting away, wasn't it? Having people to stay with."

"If I head back in I'm sure I'll bring her with me. She needs a ride now, anyway."

"And if you do decide to stay," said Keyes, with a hand on Montone's shoulder and a sly smile, "best of luck to you, old boy."

Keyes winked, got into the car and drove off. The last thing Montone saw was Tyler's pale, ravaged face leaning against her window. He waited until they were out of sight and went back in the house.

He followed her voice upstairs to where Holly was waiting for him in bed. Although every bit as urgent and erotic as the night before, now they took their time, patiently learning each other, extending their senses, taking delight in what they discovered. Near the end they fell into each other's rhythms like athletes and climaxed together so powerfully all they could do afterward was laugh.

Montone sat at the counter and in amazement watched Holly move around the kitchen. She'd put her hair up and wore only an oversized white shirt with the sleeves rolled. They didn't say much. Watching her fix French toast and a fresh pot of coffee, he decided he'd never seen a more enchanting sight in his life. She'd glance over at him every once in a while as she worked, see the pleasure on his face and grin.

"Are you having a moment?" she asked.

"What?"

"You look like you're having a perfect moment."

"Is that what this is?"

"I think so."

"Well," he said, "one in a lifetime ain't bad."

His innate cautiousness had already led him to examine a hundred implications of their intimacy and he'd come to the startling conclusion that none of them justified the concern. If his life had been too rigid to accommodate this possibility, then his life had to change.

Ever since Sligo he'd denied himself too much, maintaining a rigid, almost ascetic discipline, as if he didn't deserve his dreams. The department shrink, a woman he visited twice a week for over a year, told him it was because he felt responsible for Sheila's death. She was right, of course, but knowing it never seemed to change anything. Now, five years later, out of nowhere his dreams had been exceeded, effortlessly, and he wasn't going to turn away from this gift he'd been given, however improbable it seemed.

Montone made certain the house's security system was working and as a precaution left his second gun, a department-issue .38, with Holly before leaving at quarter to ten for his appointment with Suffolk County Sheriff. Mackenzie Dennis's country house was about a twenty-minute drive east into the Hamptons. Not one of the opulent jewels that studded the coast but a relatively modest Cape Cod cottage tucked into the woods on the northern, less fashionable side of the highway.

Two Suffolk deputies, Phillips and Eichler, waited for him in the driveway. They'd already obtained the keys from the real estate company that managed the property, and a woman from the office waited for them at the door.

The house and grounds had been secured the morning after Dennis's death, the deputies told him. No one had been allowed inside since, although Montone suspected the deputies had helped themselves to a good look. If there was some departmental advantage to be gained by contributing to a front-page investigation, no self-respecting cop was going to pass up that opportunity.

Flush with his fat network contract, Dennis had purchased the property only a few months before. The real estate agent said he'd been working with a decorator to get it ready for the "season," the eight weeks at the end of every summer when the New York elite migrate en masse to this scattered collection of fashionable towns and villages.

Only a few pieces of furniture had been moved into the house, all of them bearing slipcovers. No mail, no newspapers. The beds were all unmade. The woman from the real estate company wasn't sure if Dennis had ever even spent a night there.

"What a tragedy," she said, at least twice.

She asked Montone if he happened to know anything about Dennis's will and the disposition of the property. He politely informed her that if she was so eager to handle the resale she ought to speak directly to Dennis's lawyer. The woman went slightly pale and left him alone for the rest of the time he was there.

He found little trace of Mackenzie Dennis in the house. No personal possessions. He hadn't even had time to plaster pictures of himself on the walls. Certainly no one had made any obvious attempt to gain entry; a high-end alarm system connected to a private security service was already in place and operable. The killer hadn't been here. Montone quickly decided the house had no bearing on the investigation, wrote a few notes for his report and told the deputies they could release custody to the care of Dennis's estate.

Nice, sleepy little district out here, Montone thought, walking back to his car, looking off into the soft woods. Not a bad beat to work for law enforcement; a few weekend drunks, crowd control at celebrity polo matches, some off-season breaking and entering, maybe an occasional domestic. The assaultive, kinetic violence of the city, so imprinted into his nervous system, felt like a distant planet.

For a moment he envied these deputies their country life and clean air, imagining his days off spent on a small boat out in the Sound, fishing in the morning, cruising up for a casual lunch at some dockside restaurant. A frosted mug of cold beer on a hot summer day. Steaming lobsters on a sunset beach campfire, watching the seasons change, settling in for a sleepy winter after the big shots took their ongoing party back to Manhattan. The reverie carried him halfway back to Water Mill.

Holly found a place in most of those imaginings without his even trying to put her there. Strange how fast he'd let her in, how hopeful she made him feel. He warned himself against buying the dream before they made it real enough to warrant the investment.

Pulling back, withholding his private nature from the people who cared about him, now there was something he knew how to do.

What are you saving yourself for? he asked himself. What are you waiting for?

By the time he parked in the drive, he couldn't wait to see her again. He could go back to worrying about covering his ass for the rest of his life if it didn't work between them. Determined that this time the thing wouldn't fail because he didn't let the woman know who he was and how he felt about her.

Life wasn't issued with a guarantee. When the main chance comes you have to take it.

He parked the car and walked in calling her name.

Straight ahead he saw her long bare legs dangling in the air, three feet off the ground.

Still, slowly twisting.

He ran into the living room and looked up to see the rope hanging from the bottom rail of the balcony banister. Clothesline. Ending in a noose.

He saw her face. Blue, features distorted. She was gone.

"No. No, no, no."

Not again.

Cop instincts kicked in—*Don't touch anything*—but he overruled them. He ran to the kitchen, grabbed a knife from a butcher block. A chair had been kicked over in the living room, near where she was hanging.

Don't do this.

He lifted and set the chair beside her, jumped up, held her around the waist, reached up and cut the line.

The loose dead weight of her sagged onto his chest and shoulders. He gently collected her, stepped down, laid her softly on the floor. She still wore the same white shirt. Her upper body was already cool, blood pooling in her legs. He pried the rope free from her neck and felt for a pulse, knowing full well he wouldn't find one. There were vivid, purple scratches along both sides of her neck.

"Oh God. Oh God."

He closed her terrible voided eyes and held her and let the grief come close to breaking him inside. He hovered on that black edge for what felt like forever, realizing that if he fell from here he might never make it back.

He wanted to follow her. He tried to.

But just before the tears came he shut them down. Steel plates crashed into the gap between him and that irrevocable pain. All knowledge of her—memories, emotions, physical sensations—he willed out of his mind. Whatever Holly had been, essence, soul, spark, didn't exist anymore and nothing he could do would bring her back.

His thoughts found a simple track to follow and clung to it ferociously.

He would find whoever did this. That was his job. He had work to do and these first moments were the most important. He looked at his watch: 11:20. She'd been dead for at least half an hour.

He laid the body back down and stood up.

Leave the chair and the knife where they are. Find a phone. Call it in.

Procedure.

Phone in the kitchen.

Don't touch anything else.

The operator quickly connected him to Suffolk County Sheriff. Detective James Montone, NYPD homicide, reported a murder. He never mentioned the word "suicide," which was duly noted by the dispatcher. Deputies were on their way. He asked them to send Phillips and Eichler, the officers he'd met at the Dennis house, the investigation already taking shape in his mind.

One more call: Murphy, in the 19th squad room. An excruciating minute of hold before he picked up.

"Mike, I'm in trouble."

"What's up?"

He ran it down. Not the whole story but enough for Murphy to read him correctly.

"Jimmy, do you want us out there?"

Montone didn't understand the question.

"Are they connected? Dennis and the girl?"

"Maybe. I don't know."

"Because I can call a chopper. We'll be there in an hour. I'll bring the team."

Montone didn't answer, stunned by Murphy's suggestion that the killings linked up; it shimmered like the silvery glimpse of a fish in a stream, yes—

"Jimmy, listen to me: If we take jurisdiction we can control the scene, do you understand what I'm saying? If you're in trouble, we can make it ours."

He turned to look at her. Something nagging at him . . .

"Jimmy?"

"Hang on a second."

He laid the phone down and walked back to the body. What was it?

Her hands cupping his face.

He spotted a ring on her right hand. Middle finger. Thick gold, a large blood-red stone, a signet ring.

She wasn't wearing a ring last night.

Montone hurried back to the phone.

"Murph, go to my desk."

He heard Murphy put the call on hold.

Dennis's hand on the autopsy table. A band of white flesh at the base of his right ring finger.

"I'm there," said Murphy, coming back on the line.

"The murder book, top drawer. There are shots of Dennis's office, the desk area."

He heard Murphy locate the file, page through to the photos.

"Okay," said Murphy.

"There's a photograph in one of them. On the wall behind the desk. Color. He's accepting some kind of award."

"Got it."

"There's a ring on his right hand. Third finger."

A pause. "I can't see it that well."

"Use a magnifier. Top right-hand drawer."

He waited.

"Looks like gold. A red stone."

Montone let out a breath. "They're linked."

"We're coming out."

"Do it. Do it."

"Jimmy, listen to me, don't touch anything. Go outside and wait for the locals—"

"Just get here."

Montone hung up the phone, started for the door, then stopped.

"No," he said quietly. "You've left something."

He walked back to the living room. Stifled an impulse to lower the shirt, which had bunched up around her waist. He looked around the living room.

Upstairs. Something on the edge of the balcony.

Sirens in the distance, approaching. Not much time.

He took the stairs.

A hand-sized microcassette recorder stood upright on the tiled floor, near where the rope was tied to the rail. The tape inside had spooled through to one side. Something recorded.

It was what he'd expected to find.

Her suicide message.

7

FORENSIC PSYCHOLOGICAL ASSESSMENT
October 14, 1980

Subject is a Caucasian male, age nineteen. Father unknown. Relationship to mother, still living, is hostile and remote. Working-class background, with extensive history of juvenile deliquency. Subject is recipient of full academic scholarship to Sidney Sussex College, Cambridge. Standard intelligence tests indicate genius-level IQ. Subject stands accused of murder in the second degree, awaiting trial.

Subject shows little or no remorse for his actions. He appears to be a hypersensitive person who is overly responsive to criticism and quick to project the blame for his troubles onto others. He demonstrates an excess of ego involvement bordering on grandiosity and general manifest hostility. MMPI Test results are strongly suggestive of a Narcissistic Personality Disorder and poor impulse control, which is consistent with a high potential for violent acting out.

Subject is fully competent to understand the charges against him and assist in his own defense. He suffers from no mental disease or defect that, in the event he is convicted, would excuse him from responsibility in committing the crime of which he is accused.

: found in a notebook owned by Inspector Peter Henshaw, Scotland Yard

The more evident truth, far less appealing to popular liberal sentiment, is that hardened criminal personalities are the end result of choices made exclusively by the self. Social and environmental conditioning are, at best, secondary factors.

Consequently, every criminal act made by such personalities should be considered volitional and willful. The individual must bear complete accountability for the consequences of their actions under the law.

We find a useful example in the case of mass murderer Wendell Sligo . . .

: underlined passage in a copy of **Criminal Intent** *by Erin Kelly, found in the office rented by Terry Keyes in the name of Howard Kurtzman*

Montone gave his statement to the first arriving officers and informed them he had strong reason to believe the crime he'd discovered was connected to the Mackenzie Dennis case. Phillips and Eichler arrived in the second car on the scene and, as he had hoped they would, boosted Montone's credibility with the first team. Reluctant to contravene his authority, the four deputies worked with him to seal off the house and set up a perimeter for the investigation.

Additional units were summoned to set up command and control on site, settling in a guest room over the garage. Although they insisted on calling in their superiors before turning over control of the scene, the deputies agreed not to go inside the house until the NYPD task force arrived and all jurisdictional issues were resolved.

Within half an hour Murphy, Pat Feany and Frank Fonseca approached by helicopter along the water. Deputies patched into their radio and talked them down to a landing on a broad section of beach west of the house. Murphy informed Montone that a second chopper with three Crime Scene Unit investigators was not far behind them.

By this time the Suffolk County higher-ups had arrived, along with Suffolk County homicide. After a tense five-minute face-to-face on the deck behind the house, the locals agreed to let NYPD take the lead. They were up to speed on the Dennis case and knew Montone by reputation; none of them were eager to be perceived as obstructing a high-profile investigation.

Montone instructed the Suffolk detectives to spread out and search the area for the approach angle the killer might have taken to the house. He led his own team inside; Feany and Fonseca covered the upstairs rooms while he worked with Murphy downstairs. They found no evidence of forced entry or any indication that the house's sophisticated security system had been compromised or bypassed.

When they were alone in his bedroom Montone closed the door and took Murphy quietly aside.

"I slept with her last night," said Montone. "In here. Again this morning, upstairs."

Murphy paused; not surprised exactly but far from happy to hear it.

"Okay."

"I was out of the house an hour and a half. My time's accounted for, deputies were with me at the Dennis house—"

"That's not going to be a problem."

"Mike, somebody's trying to set me up. This is personal."

"How?"

"They're not going to be able to fix time of death to the minute." When Murphy didn't respond: "They're going to find my semen in the body."

"Jesus, Jimmy."

"She said she was on the pill. It sounds stupid now but it didn't seem like a problem at the time . . ."

"You don't have to explain."

"Whoever did this followed her out here from the city. Probably the guy I chased away from her apartment the other night. He'd been stalking her, Mike. Making calls. He took pictures of her, sent one to her in the mail along with a couple of threatening notes."

"I wasn't aware of that," said Murphy, noncommittally.

"He followed her here, then watched and waited until we were all out of the house."

"Where's Keyes and his girlfriend?"

"She got sick during the night. They drove back to the city this morning about nine o'clock."

"We'll have to get them in for prints—"

"The point is, this is the same guy who did Dennis. He stole the ring off his finger and put it on hers. He's rubbing my face in it."

"Yeah."

"I'll tell you something else. He sent the first note to her *before* Dennis was killed. He had this all blocked out. How is he going to know I'll draw the Dennis case?"

"I'd have to think about it."

"How's he know I'm going to hook up with the girl when I hadn't even met her yet?"

"You think you're the connection?"

"You think it's a coincidence?"

"I don't know. Have to think about it."

"It's personal, Mike."

Murphy lit a cigarette and cracked open the sliding door to the deck. Suffolk deputies were fanning out to examine a section of nearby beach. Montone wondered if they'd make anything of the imprints in the sand where he and Holly had made love, or if the rising tide already washed them away.

"You got any more good news you want to tell me?" asked Murphy.

Montone remembered. "I gave her my spare piece before I left. The thirty-eight."

"She know how to use it?"

"Yes."

"You find it yet?"

"No."

Murphy stubbed out the cigarette. "What am I supposed to tell Pat and Frankie?"

"Can we keep it in-house?"

"I don't know, Jimmy."

"We can claim the body, do pathology back in the city."

"We would anyway," said Murphy, then paused and lowered his voice as he closed the sliding door. "Are we having a discussion about suppressing evidence?"

Montone thought it through, his mind wheeling like a hunted animal. "No. No."

Pat Feany called them out to the living room. He'd found the tape recorder at the top of the stairs, picked it up with a handkerchief and brought it downstairs. He set it on the living room table and pointed out an NYPD serial number stenciled on the side of the case.

"This look familiar to you?" asked Feany.

"It's mine," said Montone. "Brought it with me last night. It was in my bag, in the bedroom. I didn't take it with me this morning."

Feany and Murphy exchanged a look; Feany appeared to read a lot from him. He'd seen the girl with Montone at the station house the day before, and moved intuitively into a respectful, protective under-standing of his colleague's predicament.

"You want to listen to what's on here, Jimmy?" asked Feany.

Montone hesitated, took a pen from his pocket and pressed the rewind button.

"Was this chair like this?" asked Feany.

"No," said Montone. "It was tipped over. I stood on it to cut her down."

"Tipped over like this?" said Feany, placing the chair on the ground near the body.

"Half a foot to the right."

Feany moved the chair into position. "How's that?"

"That's good."

The tape clicked as it completed rewinding. Montone used the pen to hit play.

Tape hiss, followed by a brief silence, then muffled sobs.

Her voice.

"Beauty . . . is a lie."

She was crying openly, softly, only able to utter a few words at a time before stopping to control her emotions, her voice constricted and strained, with lengthy pauses in between each sentence.

"Instead of honoring the natural gifts I was given, I have allowed my beauty to be used . . . by an industry built on deception and the exploitation of women's emotional vulnerability. . . . I've sold my physi-cal gifts to the highest bidder . . . like a common whore."

There followed a long trailing series of quiet, fearful sobs.

None of the men in the room moved. Frank Fonseca came out of an upstairs bedroom to show them something he'd found but stopped instantly when he saw the looks on their faces. He sat down on the stairs to listen along with them.

"They have used my image to . . . create fear and insecurity . . . in other women . . . in order to profit from the sale . . . of products they don't need that are worse than useless . . . Oh God, please . . . please . . ."

She cried again, helpless with fear.

Montone slowly sank down onto the sofa and covered his face with his hands.

They heard a click as the recording stopped, then another as it started again, with her voice slightly more composed.

"I have allowed my physical body to be distorted and manipulated in an attempt to encourage men . . . to believe in fantasies and false perceptions that promote a vision of human sexuality that is degrading, deceitful and dehumanizing. I confess that by willingly taking part in this . . . conspiracy I have committed criminal acts . . . and profited in ways that I now see were corrupt and damaging to myself, to women and to society.

"I am sorry for my crimes."

On the tape a moment later they heard the chair fall to the floor and the anguishing, desperate rattle of her failing attempts to breathe.

"Turn it off," said Montone. "Turn it off."

Keyes pulled into the garage of Tyler Angstrom's building at five minutes after one o'clock in the afternoon. In accordance with his timetable, the injection he had given Tyler in the car was just beginning to wear off, and as he slipped into her parking space she returned to a groggy consciousness.

He made a point of calling the doorman down to help him escort her from the car to the elevator and up to her apartment, describing to the man in detail his concern about how ill she had seemed throughout their long drive back from the Hamptons.

After insisting that she put in a call to her doctor's service, Keyes slipped Tyler another sedative in a glass of water and tucked her into bed. He strolled into the living room, turned on the tube and sat down with a turkey sandwich and a diet soft drink to wait for the first stories about the "tragic death of a supermodel" to appear.

He wondered whether the police would call him before the story broke, then bet himself a piece of the chocolate cake in Tyler's refrigerator that, despite the emotional hardship of her death, Montone would still retain the presence of mind to follow through on what he perceived as his duty.

The call came at one-thirty from Montone himself, who told him what had happened.

"Oh my God, Jimmy. Oh my God, I can't believe it . . ."

"Did you see anyone while you were driving away? Any cars parked on the road to the house? Anyone walking?"

"Not that I can recall. Jesus Christ, she was . . ." Keyes began to cry;

so convincingly he almost believed it himself. "She was such a beautiful girl . . . I'm sorry, I'm sorry."

"It's all right."

"But I mean, how are you, are you all right?"

"No, not really."

"Jimmy, I am so sorry. Are there people with you? Someone you can talk to?"

"Yes."

"God damn it, why did we have to leave? Why? Why? It's not fair."

"It's not your fault. There was no way to know."

"No, we should never have left her alone. That was the whole point of her being there. Doctors make house calls; I should have had someone in to see Tyler. There must be one fucking doctor in the Hamptons who would have made a house call."

"You can't blame yourself," said Montone.

Keyes made an effort to contain his grief. Montone waited.

"Is there anything I can do, Jimmy? I feel so terrible. What can I do to help you?"

"We'll need to get your fingerprints, yours and Tyler's. Help us sort out whatever we find here."

"Of course."

"No hurry; sometime in the next couple of days. She still sick?"

"Dreadfully. She slept most of the ride in. Sleeping now. We have a call in to her doctor."

"When she's feeling up to it then."

"What about you, old boy? Are you coming back to town today? Do you want some company?"

"There's a lot to do out here."

"Listen, you call me anytime, day or night, if you need to talk, hang out, get drunk, whatever you want. I'm here for you."

Montone paused. Keyes thought he detected the first break in his stoic reserve, confirmed when a moment later he heard a wave of weakness alter his voice.

"I appreciate that."

Keyes ended the call, put his feet up, cracked his knuckles and took a big bite of the chocolate cake he'd set waiting by the phone, untouched until the bet was won.

"Mmm. Worth the wait."

The CSU detectives arrived in the second chopper, assumed control of the interior of the house and went to work. When they had the photographs they needed, Montone waited on the rear deck with Pat Feany while morgue attendants removed the body. Murphy had contracted with Suffolk County to transport Holly back to the city and into custody of the NYC coroner, going out of his way to commend their entire organization for their seamless cooperation. They wanted Suffolk personnel to feel appreciated so there would be no leaks coming from that direction; the first reporters had already begun to arrive, kept a half-mile away by a police checkpoint.

Montone and Feany lit cigarettes and stared out at the waves as sunlight broke through the sluggish marine layer for the first time that day.

"He put the rope on her and stood her up on the chair. Tied it off so her feet were barely touching," said Montone. "Then he put a gun to her head, maybe my gun, held out a piece of paper and made her read it. When she was finished he kicked the chair over."

"And left the tape recorder running."

"She took a long time to die," said Montone. "He wanted us to hear it."

"Supports the suicide," said Feany.

"The scratches on her neck are from her trying to loosen the rope. The more she struggled the tighter it got. While he stood there and watched."

"Cocksucker's going to burn in hell, Jimmy."

Montone struggled to keep his mind focused, sifting through the apparent facts, searching for pieces that fit.

"Think she knew him?" asked Montone.

"If she did she never mentions a name. Seems like she had the opportunity."

"Maybe he negotiates that with her, when she thinks he might let her live."

"Maybe she does say it. Maybe he goes back and erases it."

"Or maybe she's just too damn scared. We'll go over it, word by word; maybe she tried to—"

Montone jumped when he heard a metallic bang inside; caught a glimpse of the gurney through the window as the attendants guided it down the steps at the front door. He turned away quickly, the thought of her as cargo in the meat wagon searing him.

"You reach the family?" asked Montone.

"Got a number from her modeling agency. Talked to her sister, lives upstate in Syracuse; she wanted to tell the parents herself. They're in Miami; older people. Father's health isn't real good. The sister said she'll fly down to the city tonight."

"What's her name?" asked Montone, without really knowing why.

"Her name's Erin. Erin Kelly."

"Older or younger?"

"I'd guess older. Sounds strong. Sounds smart."

"Holly told me about her. She's a psychologist. Can you call her back, give her my number? I'd like to talk to her myself."

"Sure, Jimmy." Feany paused and lit another cigarette. "Frankie says there's come on the sheets upstairs."

Montone didn't answer.

"I talked to Mike," said Feany, letting him know that he knew. "How we gonna handle this?"

"Tell the truth."

"You want the brass to know you were intimate with her?"

"I got nothing to be ashamed of, Patsy."

"Didn't say you did."

"This is the same guy who did Dennis. No way it's a copycat, no way it's anybody else. Same perp. Same case."

Feany stubbed out his cigarette on the rail.

"Except you weren't sleeping with Dennis."

"What's that supposed to mean?"

"Hey, it's downtown's call, not mine."

"Meaning what, Pat?"

"You think they're gonna let you run the case now, Jimmy? What if the press gets this? You think you can keep it from them? They'll fucking crucify you, man."

"What's done is done."

Feany seemed to regret his outburst. He waited. A hot pulse of sunlight flared off the badge of one the deputies walking the beach.

"We'll back your play, Jimmy. Whatever you want to do, just say so. This fucker wants to do a number on you, that means he takes on the squad. We straight?"

"Yeah."

Feany rested a hand on Montone's shoulder without looking at him, then went back inside.

Montone placed calls to Lieutenant Coxen and Captain Dan Jakes on the drive back to the city. They were waiting for him at the precinct when he arrived at eight o'clock that night. Montone asked Murphy, who'd driven back with him, to sit in as he laid out his relationship with Holly Mews to their commander.

He showed them the ring, in an evidence bag, that they'd taken from Holly's finger and the photograph of it from Dennis's office. He showed them the threatening notes she'd received and played the recordings from her phone machine, told them about the man he'd chased off from her apartment. He laid out the time frame for her murder, how the killer must have known he would be gone long enough to commit the crime. Showed them a photograph of a sheltered stand of trees about a quarter of a mile from the beach house, the only nearby cover, where the killer might have watched him leave.

They didn't say much or betray any reaction; Jakes told them he would have to take the situation to the Borough Commander. Any determination on Montone's status would come from downtown. Their tone stayed matter-of-fact, no slack given or asked for, none of Murphy's or Feany's comrade-in-arms support. This was department politics, heavyweight division; careers, if not lives, hung in the balance. Jakes asked Montone to comb through his case files, check recent prison releases, look for a perp that might be carrying some kind of vendetta against him, while they awaited the decision.

"In the meantime, am I off the case?" asked Montone.

"You slept with her once, Jimmy," said Jakes gently. "You weren't engaged to the girl."

"You did know both victims, though," said Coxen.

"Am I a suspect?"

The question hung in the air a half second longer than Montone would have liked.

"Absolutely not," said Jakes.

"Keep working it," said Coxen, taking his cue from Jakes. "Don't talk to reporters and for Christ sake keep yourself off television."

"Do we make an announcement that they're linked?" asked Montone, stopping them at the door.

"Wait," said Jakes.

"I only ask because if the son of a bitch releases that tape of her, like he did with Dennis, and there's gotta be a good chance that he will, Captain, the press is gonna make us look like we're way behind the curve."

"He took a couple of days the last time, didn't he?" asked Jakes.

"Yeah."

"Wait till you hear from me. "

Coxen followed Jakes out. Montone stayed at his desk, fatigue weighing on him like an anchor as he stared blindly at the contents of his message box, spilled across the desk.

"You wanna eat something?" asked Murphy.

Montone shook his head. The immediacy of Holly's memory rattled through his senses; the sheen of her skin, the clean smell of her hair. He'd been with her this morning. Only twelve hours ago—

"Jimmy, you gotta eat. I'll get takeout, whatever you want. Maybe some soup'd be good."

Montone didn't answer. He'd long ago learned how to block from his conscious mind the indelible images of death that came with the job.

Her bare legs dangling.

Not tonight.

Eyes stinging, barely able to focus, he blinked at a business card he found buried in a stack of phone messages. He labored to make sense of what he was reading.

"Jimmy?"

"Who's Peter Henshaw?" he asked.

"I give up, who is he?"

"Inspector, Scotland Yard?" Montone held up the card.

"Some guy came by to see you last night but you were gone already. Coulda been him."

"Why didn't you tell me?"

"I didn't know who he was. Ida handled it."

"Ida," said Montone, shaking his head.

A message on the back read, "Please contact me regarding a matter of some urgency," along with a local phone number.

Montone picked up the phone and dialed. A woman answered; a switchboard operator at a large midtown hotel.

"Peter Henshaw, please."

Montone waited through a long, irritated silence as the call went to the room, before a rough male voice that sounded as if it had been stirred from sleep answered.

"Peter Henshaw."

"Mr. Henshaw, this is Detective Montone at the Nineteenth Precinct. I just got your message."

"Yes, Detective. Thank you for calling." A pause; he heard the man trying to quickly wake up. "I know it's late but would it be possible for us to meet?"

"You want to tell me what this is about?"

"A man named Terence Keyes."

Montone rubbed his forehead, a sharp pain organizing itself there, his thoughts mired, connections misfiring. "Can it wait until tomorrow?"

"That's entirely up to you."

Montone named a coffee shop near the man's hotel and agreed to meet him there in twenty minutes.

A thick greasy drizzle slicked the streets. Murphy parked the car under a sputtering neon sign while Montone went inside the restaurant. Aside from a few solitary coffee drinkers the place was empty, cheerless, the same dank mood that had emptied the sidewalks worming its way in through cracked caulking, badly sealed doors.

The old man sat in a red vinyl booth along the rear wall, facing the entrance. He raised a hand when Montone walked in, seemed to recognize him. The man stood up as he approached; tall, slightly stooped, rail-thin. Clothes clean but noticeably worn. Large head, a memorable face: high, broad cheekbones, taut and polished as a cigar store Indian; electric pale blue eyes arched by gnarled eyebrows that matched the close-cropped skullcap of white hair on his head. He had a strong grip and held Montone's gaze without challenge or yield.

"Foul night," said Henshaw.

"Thought you'd be used to this kind of weather."

"I don't mind the rain. There's a smell to it here. Metallic or chemicals. As if you'd done your washing up in it."

Montone sat down across from him, ordered coffee, swimming upstream against waves of exhaustion.

Henshaw laid his police service badge down on the table between them. Montone glanced at it politely as Henshaw opened and closed the sleeve.

"Spend much time in New York?"

"First visit."

"Still on the force over there?"

"Retired. Five years."

Murphy came through the doors, surveyed the two men, heads lowered at the table, and took a stool at the counter.

"Inspector," said Montone. "That's like detective rank."

"The same."

They waited in silence as the waitress set down Montone's coffee. He stirred in two packets of sugar.

"Not here on vacation are you, Mr. Henshaw?"

"No."

Montone waited.

"You know him," said Henshaw. "Keyes."

"Yes."

"Some years ago, in Blackpool, he killed a woman."

"He told me."

"I was the arresting officer," said Henshaw.

"The woman under the pier."

"You've heard his side of it, then."

"What else should I know?"

"Have you read his book?"

"No."

Henshaw looked out at the empty streets. "How long have you been on the job?"

"Twelve years. First five in uniform."

Henshaw turned back to look at him. Montone wondered if he'd ever seen eyes possessing such intensity and focus.

"I had fourteen years before that night. Promoted to inspector two years prior. Not a lot of trouble in that town; enough to keep the job interesting. That summer we had three killings in two months. Women. Prostitutes. Crimes of shocking brutality; vicious mutilation. Of a sexual nature. The same hand had clearly done the job and in each instance left not one shred of evidence. Ever work this kind of case?"

"Yes."

"Never seen anything approaching it, before or since. We don't get many like that over our way; at least we didn't then. It's a different world now, isn't it?"

"Seems so."

"I was on the pier that night by chance. Taking a long walk, trying to clear my head. I heard a scream somewhere below and ran down to the beach. Found this boy Terry Keyes not far from the body, lying in the surf. Said he was drunk, the woman had attacked him. When he pushed her away, she fell back and hit her head on the rock escarpment. Said he didn't even know she was hurt."

"His friend was watching. Supposed to be some kind of prank."

"It was five in the morning. I didn't see anyone within a mile of that place."

A chill ran through Montone.

"Was he drunk?"

"It was on his breath. By the time I got him to the station he seemed sober enough."

"Did he resist?"

"No."

"Did he try to run?"

"I clapped him in handcuffs before he had the chance."

Henshaw waited patiently for Montone to assimilate the information, form his questions.

"The girl was a hooker?"

"An artist's model. Local girl. Very pretty. Never been in any kind of trouble."

"The friend supposedly arranged for them to meet."

"This friend, if there was one," said Henshaw, "never came forward."

"You interrogated Keyes?"

"Yes. His story never varied. Not one word. I heard him tell it a dozen times. Total self-possession."

"And you didn't buy it."

"I believe he followed her out there under the pier and assaulted the girl. Opportunistically. When she resisted he got rough with her and she died."

"He pleaded guilty."

"To a lesser charge than he was guilty of. Because he knew it was his main chance."

Montone stirred some milk into his coffee. "You liked him for those other murders."

"I never believed his story. As I ran toward him under the pier, I saw him throw something into the sea. He denied it. I had the area dragged; nothing was recovered."

Now Henshaw paused, folding his hands around his cup, staring down into the black.

"The three other women had been found in the open air, near public places, like this one. Cut with a razor. I think he'd dashed this girl against the rocks because she fought back. He was just about to go to work."

"You're saying he tossed the razor."

"Yes."

Montone thought about that for a while.

"He was a bright kid," said Montone. "Rough background, lot of hard knocks."

"And a long juvenile record."

"But he's straightened himself out. He was about to go off to college, right? Some kind of scholarship?"

"Yes."

"So why would he throw all that away?"

Henshaw studied Montone dispassionately for a long unblinking moment; he could well imagine any perp squirming under the old man's icy gaze.

"I'd only seen it once before in a man's eyes. Just a glimpse as I sat with him in that interrogation room. When he didn't know I was looking." Henshaw leaned forward across the table, lowered his voice. "The bottom dropped away. With it, whatever cherished idea you might hold about what makes a human soul; gone. No limits. Nothing but dark. Have you ever looked into eyes like that?"

Wendell Sligo lumbering toward him out of the woods. His wide, black, buttony eyes . . .

"Yes."

"That's what I saw in that boy. He wasn't made; he was born that way. I knew in an instant that he'd done those crimes. And when he saw me watching he knew that I knew. He smiled at me. Then the look passed from his face. Not a word spoken."

Montone set a picture of the adult Keyes he knew—sober, agreeable, confident—beside that one in his mind; the two visions seemed impossible to reconcile.

"He killed her," said Henshaw, returning to Montone's question, "because he wanted to. And he thought he could get away with it."

"But you couldn't tie him to the other killings."

"Nothing physical. His alibis stood up."

Montone sipped his coffee.

"He did twelve years."

"Sentence was fifteen. Early release."

"Why such a long stretch?"

"A television reporter from London took an interest in the case. Brought a lot of attention. Public outcry. Report from the psychologist that examined him played a part in it as well."

"What did he say?"

"She. That Keyes was dangerous. Prone to violence. Full of grandiosity. Not the sort of thing he wears on his sleeve, but other people aren't real to him. He can simulate human sympathy, he just can't feel it."

Montone thought it over.

"Still," he said. "That was a long time ago."

"That man's nature, what I saw, Detective, doesn't change. Perhaps the manner in which it's expressed, but not his being."

"They profiled him again, did evaluations?"

"The man is one twist of DNA away from genius. He can shape the conclusion of any test to fit whatever he wants them to think. That's not the point. What he learned in those twelve years inside was the ways and means of how to do crimes. That's what a prison like the Scrubs teaches and you'd best believe he applied himself with diligence. This thing he's made himself into, this 'celebrity.' That's his real fiction."

"Still. Not a lot to go on."

Henshaw looked impatient, almost annoyed. He set down a three-ringed notebook on the table and slid it toward Montone.

"By the time Keyes earned parole the first book had already been published. The one about his wretched childhood; how he'd been victimized by society. His second book was already in the works. Movie stars paid him regular call, trying to buy the rights to his life story. He had the press, the liberals, all those bleeding fancy publishing nobs queuing up outside the prison walls."

Montone opened the notebook: newspaper clippings, articles and photographs from English newspapers. Stories about Terence Peregrine Keyes. (The tabloids had settled on "Terry-Perry" as his headline nickname.) Paeans to the success of the rehabilitative system. The lost soul of an artist reclaimed by institutional clemency.

"I spent my last five years in service attached to Scotland Yard. By the time he got out of the Scrubs I'd taken my retirement. Health problems; I've got diabetes."

"Sorry to hear it."

"Like I said, Keyes used the time inside to transform himself. Polished to a high sheen. Sounded educated now. Talked a good game. It was clear from the start he had them all fooled. Going on television. Toast of the town. I watched him. Let him know I was there. Waited for the man I'd seen to show himself."

For the first time it occurred to Montone that the man might be a crank. He'd seen it before in retired officers, their lives emptied out, drifting bitterly toward obsession to fill the void. The weight of his weariness suddenly doubled.

"This doesn't prove anything," said Montone.

"Turn the page."

A lower-class kitchen; a crime scene photo. A middle-aged woman's body, kneeling, slumped inelegantly, arms draped on the floor, before the open door of an oven. The face turned away. Montone could almost smell the gas.

"Ruth Chadney, fifty-three. Lived in Norwich. Six months after his release."

"What's the connection?"

"She was his mother."

Suicide. Keyes had said he didn't know if his mother was dead or alive . . .

Montone couldn't even form the word; the room started to spin, he felt light-headed. He put a hand on the table and the other to his forehead, trying to steady himself.

"She'd worked twelve years in a jam factory. Quiet little mouse, lived alone, kept to herself. That same London TV reporter tracked her down, identified her as the abusive tart Terry-Perry had written about in his best-selling memoirs."

"Did she leave a note?"

"I wouldn't call it that. More like a confession. How she'd mistreated him as a child. Why she felt responsible for what he'd done."

A hammer pounded the pit of his stomach. Montone looked down and away, trying to conceal his reaction.

"Course he had an alibi for that night, too," said Henshaw. "He came to America not long after that. On a book tour, I gather. Made the rounds. Got the clever set here all in a lather. Nothing like a reformed murderer to spice up a smart dinner party."

"That was last fall."

"Here two months. Then back to London, where I picked him up again. When the papers announced he was coming back to this side of the briny for as long as a year, I packed up my kit and followed him." Henshaw paused, taking note of Montone's reaction. "I take it he introduced himself to you."

"He's doing research. Writing a book."

"That may have been what he told you but he didn't come to write, son. Keyes sat in that cell for twelve years. I know his mind. He was planning something. And you'd best believe he's thought it through down to the last detail, the slightest gesture."

"Why would he come here to do that?"

"England's too small a country for him now, he's too well known. America's wide-open ground. He came to hunt."

Hot tears burned Montone's eyes, threatening to spill.

Holly's legs . . .

Henshaw turned the page of the notebook again. A society photograph of Keyes standing behind Mackenzie Dennis at a party.

"He told me they'd met," said Montone.

"He'll tell you a lot of things."

"There's no proof."

"Ask him where he was that night."

"I know where he was. With me until eight o'clock. Then at a party. With a woman."

Montone looked up. Henshaw saw the depth of the anguish in him for the first time. His cold blue eyes replied with surprising compassion.

"That was his story on the nights those three women died in Black-pool. Different girl each time. Repeating his words like parrots. They were terrorized. I think he'd drugged them."

The vacancy in Tyler's face as the car drove away from the beach house . . .

Anger welled up inside him and Montone found a place to stand. He swallowed the pain, wiped a hand across his raw eyes and looked directly at Henshaw again.

"You all right, son?" asked Henshaw.

"Have you seen the news tonight?"

"No."

"There's something I have to tell you."

"Hallo?"

"Terry, it's Montone."

"How are you?"

"All right. Actually I was calling for Tyler."

"Sound asleep, I'm afraid. The chemist's sent over some medicine that's knocked her right out, poor thing."

"Does she know about Holly?"

"I haven't told her yet. I don't think she'd have the strength to deal with it."

"What does the doctor think is wrong with her?"

"Frankly? Pills and red wine. Seems she's got a bit of a problem in that area. Kept it well hidden. I'd never seen it before, God knows."

Montone looked back from the pay phone to Murphy, who had joined the old man in the booth.

"Anything I can help you with?" asked Keyes.

"No, thanks. I'll call tomorrow."

"Right. I'd offer to keep you company, old boy, but it looks like tonight's my night to play nursemaid."

"I'll be fine. Just going to try and get some sleep."

Keyes heard the kitchen echoing in the background, registered the perceptible reserve that had crept into Montone's voice. He reached over and activated the caller ID device he'd attached to the phone line.

"Best thing for you. Sounds like you're out. Not alone are you?"

"Murphy's with me. Grabbing a quick bite."

"Good. Any message for Tyler, Jimmy?"

"No message."

"Get some rest, okay?"

"We'll talk tomorrow."

Keyes hung up the phone, punched two keys and read the number of the incoming call on the readout. He took from his wallet one of the business cards he'd stolen at the precinct house and dialed another number from memory.

"Police operator."

"This is Detective Lopez, badge number four-seven-six-nine, One-nine squad," said Keyes, falling into Lopez's soft Puerto Rican accent. "I need an ID on a local number, I think it's Manhattan."

He gave her the number from the readout.

"That's an interior pay phone. Location is Nine sixty-five Madison Avenue."

Fifteen blocks away. He was out the door in thirty seconds.

Murphy had moved over to the table with Henshaw while Montone made the call.

"What would he say if he saw you in New York?" asked Murphy, as Montone rejoined them.

"He already knows I'm here," said Henshaw.

"Keyes was there," said Montone. "Says the girl's asleep."

"Have you spoken to him?" asked Murphy.

"No," said Henshaw. "He's seen me, though, I've made well certain of that. He's already changed hotels once. Do you know where he's staying now?"

"I don't," said Montone.

"What if we put you with him? Arrange some kind of meet, have you show up unexpected."

"You could wear a wire," said Montone.

Henshaw shook his head. "You'd get nothing. You can't take him head-on. He'd shake my hand, talk about the weather."

"What would you talk about?"

"He's right," said Montone, laboring to keep his thoughts sharp and detailed. "If what you're saying about him is true the best thing we have in our favor is that he doesn't know we've ever met."

"Agreed," said Henshaw.

"If he's involved, obviously that's his reason for wanting to stay close to me and the investigation. We need to keep him there, in reach, see if what you're telling us checks out."

"If it sticks we'll drop a fucking safe on him," said Murphy.

"Anything I can do to help," said Henshaw.

Montone wrote something down on his business card and handed it to Henshaw. "Call in to the precinct twice a day. Use this name."

"Charlie Squires," said Henshaw, reading the card.

"He's a retired officer from the squad, lives in Florida. If Keyes is in the station I don't want them shouting your name."

"Understood."

"You ought to think about moving hotels yourself. If he's trying to keep a tail on you, let's not make it easy for him."

"I'll move tomorrow."

"Let us know where you land, Peter. I may need you to talk to some people."

Montone gestured to Murphy, who slid out of the booth and headed for the door. Montone and Henshaw got up to leave.

"I'm very sorry for your loss," said Henshaw quietly.

Montone hadn't confided in the old man about the depth of his feelings for Holly, only the facts. But Henshaw had over the years been the bearer of tragic news to too many families, spouses, friends.

"If you're right about this," said Montone, his voice husky with emotion, "you've already done more than I can thank you for."

Montone could only hold the man's gentle gaze for a moment, then hurried out of the restaurant ahead of him, where Murphy was waiting with the car.

"I'll rack up at your place tonight," said Murphy.

"Go home to Donna. I'm okay."

"Not tonight you're not," said Murphy, as they pulled away.

Henshaw walked outside, turned up his collar against the mist and started back to his hotel.

A taxi on Madison slowed as it neared the coffee shop. Inside, Keyes could just make out the gleaming white cap of the old man's hair as he turned the corner.

Calculation, instantaneous: Henshaw and Montone had made contact.

The cab glided to a stop. Keyes watched Henshaw disappear into the dark.

Getting too sure of yourself, old man. This almost amounts to an inconvenience.

He considered taking them both out, tonight. Easy enough to accomplish, but it would nullify everything he'd already set in motion. All that work. He'd have to disappear and start all over again.

No. Out of the question. They'd taken everything from him once, stripped him of pride, possessions, hope. He would never let it happen again.

You have the Plan. You built it to last; trust it to work.

Positive thoughts. Once the old man showed up here, you knew they were bound to meet eventually.

Keep moving forward. What are you worried about?

They're only the police.

Confidence, a quality of ease returning. His mind clicked down a list of options: He would need some of the equipment he'd set aside for just such an occasion. And he'd better get it now before they put a tail on him.

"You want to get out here?" asked the cabbie.

"No," said Keyes. "Drop me at the subway."

Montone and Murphy got back to Montone's apartment just after eleven. Montone found a message on his answering machine from Dan Jakes; they wanted him for a meeting at Chief of Detectives Bill Foley's office, One Police Plaza, nine-thirty tomorrow morning.

The second message was from Erin Kelly, Holly's sister, who said she had arrived in New York earlier that evening. She left her hotel number. Montone went into his bedroom alone, dialed the number and was put through to her room.

"Miss Kelly, this is Detective James Montone."

"Yes. I had a message from one of your colleagues that you wanted to speak to me," she said, her voice crisp and authoritative.

Montone hesitated; he hadn't really thought of what he wanted to say to her.

"I'm in charge of the investigation. I wanted to express my deepest sympathies to you and your family."

"You don't remember me, do you?" she asked. "We've spoken before."

"Sorry, I—"

"On the phone. I interviewed you for a book I was writing four years ago. We talked about Wendell Sligo."

Montone's memory grew slippery. Those months in the aftermath of the Slug's arrest tended to blur; he couldn't place her. Her voice had sounded instantly familiar but he had assumed it was because she sounded somewhat like Holly.

"I wouldn't expect you to remember," she said. "You must have done a hundred interviews about that case."

"You're the psychologist," he said.

"I'm on the faculty at Syracuse. I teach forensic psychology. The book was called *Criminal Intent*. I believe I asked my publishers to send you a copy."

Montone's eyes searched his bookcase on the wall.

There it was. He plucked the hardcover book off the shelf. He'd never opened it before.

Inside he found an inscription: *To James, Many thanks for your cooperation, Erin*. He saw his name listed on an acknowledgments page near the front.

"Yes," he said. "I remember now."

He opened the back flap and saw her photograph. The woman bore a remarkable resemblance to Holly. Her features varied from the perfect symmetry of her sister's face by only millimeters; the difference between exquisite and attractive. Older, early thirties, hair a few shades darker, her face more marked by time.

Something tried to link up inside his exhausted mind but he couldn't piece it together.

"I was at my cabin in the Adirondacks when I got the news. I drove home and caught the last flight down."

"Right."

"I take it if you're involved you believe Holly's death was a homicide."

So much he wanted to tell her. So tired that he didn't trust his instincts.

"I'd like to talk to you in person, Miss Kelly."

"I'm at the Sheraton Towers, midtown. Room seven-nine-five."

"I'm on my way."

Montone called Erin on the house phone and waited in a quiet corner of the lobby. He stood when he saw her come off the elevator and walked toward her. For a moment he couldn't accept what his eyes were telling him, dismissing the sight as an accumulation of stress, sleeplessness, desperation. His heart raced and adrenaline shot through his body at the irrational thought of seeing Holly again, but as they moved closer his vision clarified.

Dressed smartly, stylishly, but more conservatively than Holly. Tall, self-confident. The same sea-blue eyes.

"Detective Montone," she said, extending her hand.

"Miss Kelly. I'm very sorry for your loss."

She looked at him searchingly. He felt transparent under her gaze, as if she knew everything already. He gestured for her to sit with him.

"I did remember speaking with you before," he said. "I found my copy of your book."

"Good. I'm never sure if they send them when they say they're going to."

Montone felt strained, excessively formal, and didn't know how to break through.

"I have to confess I didn't get a chance to read it," he said.

"You didn't need to. You lived it. I can't imagine you'd want to go through all that again."

"No."

But I feel like I am anyway.

"I called our parents this afternoon before I came down. They live in Miami. They moved after I was already in college. Holly went to high school there. I never could get used to the weather down there. Anyway, they're both quite ill. Certainly not well enough to make this trip."

He could hear the pain in her voice but was still astonished at her self-possession. She radiated strength.

"Miss Kelly, I wanted you to know, before you see any newspapers or hear anything on the news, that we're investigating Holly's death as a homicide."

"As opposed to . . ."

"The circumstances might have suggested that she took her own life."

"That's not possible. Not Holly."

"I agree with you."

"Did you know her?"

"Yes."

He felt the weight of her scrutiny again, penetrating and straightforward.

"I spoke to her two nights ago," said Erin. "She said she'd met somebody that seemed very special to her. She sounded optimistic and happy. Everyone always took one look at her and assumed she had everything, but she'd never had much luck with men."

Behind it all, the unspoken question: *Was it you?*

He nodded, but couldn't answer. Not without telling her everything else and he didn't know enough yet to be certain.

"The department will do everything it can to help you," he said, taking out a card and writing on the back. "I'll give you my cell phone and pager number."

"Are they performing an autopsy?"

"That's standard procedure."

He looked up when he finished writing. Her eyes were closed. She was biting her lip, fighting back tears.

An image of Holly lying on that cold steel table.

"I'm so sorry," he said.

A soft involuntary cry escaped from her. One tear rolled down her cheek. He reached out to her; she grabbed his hand and held it tight. Montone couldn't speak, using all his control to keep from breaking down himself. She fought back the grief, willing it away, bringing her breathing back into rhythm. Opening her eyes, she let go of his hand and dried them briskly.

"I'll have to make the arrangements," she said. "I've got the name of a mortuary. We want to bury her back home. Her home. Miami."

"Of course."

"Can we talk again tomorrow? I think I should probably try to get some rest."

She stood up urgently, trying to hold herself together.

"Call me anytime," he said.

She squeezed his hand and walked quickly back to the elevators. He wanted to give her her privacy and headed for the lobby. Glancing back once, he saw her entering the car alone, doubled over, face turned to the wall, as the doors closed behind her.

8

PARTIAL INVENTORY

bank records: checking accounts in the following cities:

Miami, in the name of J. Thomas Sylvester: $25,560.00
Atlanta, in the name of Charles C. Hardy: $18,652.00
Los Angeles, in the name of Robert Terry: $15,579.00
New York, in the name of Howard Kurtzman: $43,621.00

*: found among personal effects in the Brooklyn apartment rented by Terry
Keyes under the name Howard Kurtzman*

The meeting convened the next morning at nine-thirty in the downtown office of Bill Foley, Chief of Detectives, at One Police Plaza. Detective Mike Murphy waited outside while Montone sat with Foley, Lieutenant Coxen, Captain Dan Jakes and Borough Commander Will Flannigan. Foley had decided the Chief of Police's attention was not required; not yet.

Montone detailed his short-lived relationship with Holly Mews. He told them that they could expect to find evidence of their brief intimacy from her postmortem. As far as he knew, no reporters had any information about a connection between them. Although her "suicide" had made the papers that morning, most of the Sunday editions had already been put to bed when the news broke from Suffolk County. None of the stories that had appeared linked her death to Mackenzie Dennis, but the precinct had already been besieged that morning by the tabloids, both print and television, eager to strip-mine any sensational aspects of the tragedy. This was clearly shaping up to be their "hot" lead for the upcoming week, and Montone's involvement with the girl, the brass had concluded, would inevitably break the surface.

They agreed that the evidence clearly indicated the two crimes had been committed by the same perpetrator, but for the moment Montone withheld any mention of what Peter Henshaw had told him about Terry Keyes.

As he'd thought about it through a sleepless night, he had held out a slim hope that Henshaw was nothing more than a zealot with a personal axe to grind. He had placed calls to London early that morning asking for confirmation of his assertions and expected a response by the end of the day. If Henshaw was wrong about Keyes, Montone knew it would take some of the weight of Holly's death off his shoulders. If Henshaw was right, Montone didn't intend to play that card until he knew it was in his hand. Let the brass make the first move.

Bill Foley laid down the department's decision: Montone would have to remove himself voluntarily as head of the task force. If he took this step today, peremptorily, before any information about his affair with Holly became public, they felt they could keep damage to a minimum. This would allow the department to initiate its own investigation and, as they anticipated the facts would allow them to do, absolve Montone of any impropriety. He would be kept on a desk at the One-nine, at full pay, pending its outcome. Assuming the determination was favorable, at this time his return to the task force would not be ruled out.

Montone displayed no surprise: this was, best case, how he had anticipated they would react. He suspected correctly that the text of a press release explaining his removal from the investigation was already sitting in Foley's desk. He expressed his sincere appreciation for their "understanding"; sympathy would have been too disingenuous a word. Then he played his bluff.

"I realize I'm in no position to ask for a favor," said Montone quietly.

"You're among friends, Jimmy," said Foley.

"Chief, if you would be willing to delay making that announcement for twenty-four hours, I can name you a solid lead and I can give you a plan on how to wrap him up."

The brass looked around at each other; only Foley kept his eyes on Montone.

"For both crimes?" asked Foley.

"Yes."

The looking around intensified, but Montone kept his focus on Foley.

"What do you need to make that happen?" asked Dan Jakes.

"Just what I asked for. If you want to prepare a statement for me in the meantime, I'll sign it for release. Noon tomorrow, if I can't deliver. But I think I can."

"When's the autopsy?" asked Foley.

"This afternoon," said Montone.

"We can hold back results," said Jakes. "If need be."

Good; Jakes had backed him. He knew Lieutenant Coxen was over his head at this level and wouldn't put himself on the line one way or the other. Will Flannigan had become more politician than cop. This would be Foley's call.

"Whatever you decide, sir," said Montone. "You have a lot of other issues to consider."

The ticking of the Delft porcelain clock behind Foley's desk filled the silence.

"Would you excuse us for a moment, Jimmy?"

"Of course."

Montone waited outside with Murphy. They smoked cigarettes in silence until Lieutenant Coxen opened the door and waved him back inside.

"Ten o'clock tomorrow morning we release the statement," said Foley.

"Can we meet here at nine?" asked Montone.

"Yes."

"Terry, it's Jimmy."

"I was about to call you. How are you doing?"

"Better today, thanks."

"Sleep all right?"

"Some. How's Tyler feeling?"

"Much improved. Sitting up. Getting her appetite back. For such a skinny little thing she's a surprisingly strong girl."

"Good. Listen, Murphy and I are working today. Can you meet us for coffee? We've got some pretty interesting stuff, I thought you'd be interested to hear about it."

Montone shifted the cellular to his other hand, glanced at the facsimile of Tyler Angstrom's driver's license he'd received from DMV, then up at the number on the front of her Madison Avenue apartment building at the corner of Seventy-third Street.

"I think she's well enough by now that I could get away."

"Can you meet us at the Silver Star, corner of Sixty-fifth and Second, in about fifteen minutes?"

"I'll be there."

"See you then."

Montone crossed the street, moved a few doors down and waited inside a small bookstore that had just opened for business. When he saw Terry Keyes exit the front of Tyler's apartment building and turn south on Madison, Montone hit the flash button and dialed Murphy's number; he answered during the first ring.

"Jimmy?"

"He just left. Looks like he's walking."

"I'm across the street from the restaurant," said Murphy. "When I see him go in I'll follow him."

"Let Pat and Frankie know what you're doing. I'm going up," said Montone.

He cut off the call, waited until Keyes disappeared around the corner, then pocketed the phone, leaving it switched on, and crossed to Tyler's building. He showed his badge to the doorman, said this was a police emergency and asked him to call upstairs to Tyler Angstrom.

Tyler didn't answer.

He asked the doorman to bring his passkey and they took the elevator to Tyler's floor. On the ride up the doorman volunteered that at one o'clock yesterday afternoon he had helped Ms. Angstrom from her car to her apartment; barely conscious, seriously ill. Her friend, Mr. Keyes, had seemed very concerned.

"What's your name?" asked Montone.

"Sal," said the doorman. "I'm the weekend guy. I got a brother's a transit cop, out in Queens."

No one responded to their ringing the bell or knocking on Tyler's apartment door. Sal the doorman opened the lock with his passkey. Montone asked him to hold the elevator and wait in the hall while he went inside.

The apartment was large, prewar, high-ceilinged. Shades were drawn in the living room, shrouding it in shadows. He stepped cautiously through to the closed bedroom door and knocked again, softly. He heard a moan inside.

When he pushed the door open he didn't notice the long, blond human hair that had been placed across the threshold. It moved as he entered.

This room was equally dark; a humid sickbed smell permeated the air. He could make out a form lying in the four-poster bed and heard another faint moan.

"Tyler?"

He moved to the bedside, reached over and turned on an art deco lamp. She rolled over to face him, her face a ghastly, ashen gray. Damp, matted hair plastered to her feverish forehead. She flinched from the light, warding it off with a raised hand, then looked at him searchingly, filled with confusion.

"Tyler, it's Jimmy Montone."

"What is it?"

"Are you all right?"

"I'm really sick."

"Have you spoken with your doctor?"

"Terry did."

"Did he send you some medicine?"

"Yes." Her voice sounded small and childlike.

Montone looked over an array of prescription bottles on the bed-stand; Xanax, Valium, some penicillin, an antibiotic, a strong pain medi-cation. He found one vial dated the day before, labeled "Ativan" and issued from a nearby pharmacy.

"This one?" said Montone, holding up the bottle.

"Yes."

He casually removed a single pill from the vial, wrapped it in a tissue and slipped it in his pocket.

Tyler's hand reached unsteadily for a glass of water on the table; Montone guided it to her. She took a small sip, her lips swollen, pain-fully chapped. Montone noticed that the ringer on the phone by her bed had been turned off. He lifted the handset: no dial tone. He traced the line to the wall jack and plugged it back in, then turned the ringer back on to its lowest setting.

"Did he say what's wrong with you?"

She shook her head; she appeared to be on the verge of tears. As she raised a hand to her face he noticed a circle of livid bruises rim-ming her right elbow.

The phone in Montone's pocket rang, startling her. He turned away and quickly answered: Murphy.

"He hasn't shown."

"Stay put," said Montone quietly. "Call Pat and Frankie, have them make a few passes between here and there. Maybe he stopped to buy a paper. Call me back in five."

Montone ended the call and turned back to Tyler.

"Where's Terry?" she asked.

"I don't know, Tyler. Just lie quietly for a second, all right? I'll be right back."

He patted her hand. Montone moved quickly out of the room, opened the front door and gestured Sal the doorman to him.

"Wait downstairs. If Mr. Keyes comes back into the building, do not say anything to him. If he gets into the elevator and starts up, you call me on the house phone."

"House phone's tied into the regular line."

"Good. You call me, Sal."

Sal got into the open elevator, keyed it on and started down. Montone hurried back to the apartment, locked the door behind him, moved to Tyler in the bedroom, sat beside her and took her hand.

"Tyler, I promise you you're going to be all right. We don't have much time and I need to ask you some questions. It's very important that you not tell Terry that we've spoken. Do you understand?"

"Why?"

"I'll explain later; just give me your word that you'll do as I ask."

She nodded.

The elevator arrived down in the lobby. When the doors opened Sal came face-to-face with Terry Keyes.

"Mr. Keyes."

Keyes smiled pleasantly. "Forgot something, Sal. Beautiful day out," he said as he walked past him into the elevator and pushed the button for Tyler's floor.

Sal tried to return the smile, then as soon as the door closed he hurried to the house phone.

The phone beside her bed rang, startling them both. Montone picked it up but didn't say anything.

"He's coming up," said Sal. "He was already here."

Montone replaced the handset, turned off the ringer.

"Tyler, there was a party, the night before you introduced me to Holly. You were there with Terry."

"The night before?" she asked, confused.

"Where was that party?"

Montone heard the bell ring as the elevator arrived on Tyler's floor. Keyes exited and started for the apartment.

"The Plaza," said Tyler.

"Pretend you're asleep."

Montone turned off the bedside lamp and had started for the bedroom door when he heard the sound of a key in the front door. He moved to the bedroom closet, got himself inside and closed the door just as Keyes entered the apartment. Montone looked out through a narrow slit and saw Keyes open the door to the bedroom.

Keyes looked down at the floor of the threshold, then kneeled, searching for something Montone couldn't see.

"Tyler? Have you been out of bed?"

Her back to him, Tyler didn't move and didn't answer.

"You know the doctor said you're not supposed to be on your feet, sweetheart."

Tyler's open eyes sought out Montone in the darkness through the crack in the hinge. Keyes stepped closer to the bed.

"Tyler, are you sleeping?"

She stirred slightly and murmured.

"I got halfway there and discovered I'd forgotten my wallet," said Keyes, standing directly over her.

Her eyes stared at Montone, wide and fearful.

"If you're going to insist on being up and around you really ought to be wearing your robe."

Keyes moved across the room, glancing behind a tall decorative Japanese print screen before starting toward the closet door. Montone reached for his gun.

"Could you get me some more water?" said Tyler, a shaky hand holding out the glass.

Keyes stopped one pace away from the closet.

"Of course, darling."

He took the glass from her hand, staring down at her for a long moment before he left the room.

Montone waited until he heard water moving through the pipes, then quickly moved out into the bedroom, nodded at Tyler, then settled behind the Japanese screen against the far wall.

Keyes walked back in holding a full glass of water. Tyler turned in bed and accepted it from him as he looked down at her, standing very still.

"Thanks."

Montone saw his head turn as his eye followed the phone cord to the jack in the wall.

He'd forgotten to unplug it.

"Were you using the phone, darling?"

Tyler finished a sip of water and leaned back before she weakly replied, "I tried to call my mother."

Keyes picked up the phone and idly glanced at the position of the ringer. "Weren't you able to reach her?"

"I left a message."

Montone suddenly remembered he'd told Murphy to call him back in five minutes. Pinned between the wall and the screen as he was, if he made any fast movements his arm would jostle something and give him away; he inched his right hand toward the cellular in the inner pocket of his jacket, willing it not to ring.

Keyes set the phone down, waited another long moment, then moved to the closet and opened the door. As his hand reached his jacket, Montone edged an inch to his left and peered around the end of the screen. Keyes was leaning down to examine something on a shelf just inside the closet that Montone couldn't see. Then Keyes stepped out into the room, lifted a white terry cloth robe off a hook on the back of the door, closed the closet and laid the robe across the foot of the bed.

"You make sure you bundle up if you get out of bed again, darling. We don't want you catching your death."

"I will."

"I'll be back very soon."

"Okay."

Keyes made no effort to touch her and walked out of the room, closing the door behind him.

As Montone's hand finally reached the cellular phone in his pocket it chirped; he switched it off midring.

They both froze. No sounds came from the other room. Montone didn't dare to breathe until he heard the apartment door close and the lock engage.

He waited another full minute before whispering to Tyler.

"Reach over to the phone and turn the ringer on. Answer it if it rings."

She did as he asked. They waited in silence.

Ten seconds later the phone rang. Tyler immediately picked up the handset.

"He's gone," said Sal the doorman.

"It's Sal," she said. "He's gone."

Montone unfolded himself from behind the screen, walked over and took the phone from her.

"Sal, walk outside, make sure you can't see him, then come back up to the apartment right away."

"You got it."

Montone hung up the phone. Tyler started to say something but he held a finger to his lips to silence her. He went to the closet, opened the door and turned on a light. Tyler watched him anxiously.

Inside a shoe box, on the shelf Keyes had looked at inside the closet door, Montone found a palm-sized Nagra reel-to-reel tape recorder; the same model used in police surveillance operations. The reels were moving. Montone traced a cord through a hole in the box and down along the base of the wall to a dot microphone concealed behind the headboard of Tyler's bed.

As he watched, the reels stopped.

"What is it?" asked Tyler.

The reels started silently revolving again.

Voice-activated.

Montone used a pencil to turn off the recorder, then hit rewind.

"Jimmy, what's going on?" she asked.

Montone sat beside her again and took her hand. "Has he hurt you in any way?"

Her face contorted, near tears again. She shook her head.

"Are you frightened of him?"

"I don't know what it is," she said finally. "He's been very nice to me."

"But you're scared of him."

She nodded, tears falling.

"Tyler, you did a fantastic job when he was here. You won't ever have to see him again if you don't want to. Is that what you want?"

More tears. "Yes."

"One other question now: Do you remember anything about driving back in from the Island yesterday? Do you remember stopping or the car being parked for any length of time?"

She looked bewildered by the question. "I don't remember."

A sharp knock at the front door; Sal called out, then let himself into the apartment. He appeared, breathless and eager, in the bedroom doorway.

"One second, Sal," said Montone, as he took out his cellular and dialed Murphy's number.

After the first ring: "Jimmy?"

"He came back, Murph. He's on his way there now. Call Patsy, have him pick me up downstairs in two minutes. Go inside, wait for him. I'm there in five."

Montone terminated the call. As he spoke he found a pair of socks and shoes for Tyler and she put them on.

"Sal, here's how it is: A few minutes after Mr. Keyes left the building, you got a call from Ms. Angstrom. She said she was feeling seriously ill and she asked you to call an ambulance. You called nine-one-one, then you came up here and helped her downstairs. You waited with her for the ambulance in the lobby; when it arrived the paramedics came inside and took Ms. Angstrom to the hospital."

"Which hospital?" asked Sal.

"Lenox Hill," said Tyler. "That's where my internist is."

"Do you have the story straight? Because when Mr. Keyes asks you, and he will, that's exactly what you have to tell him."

"I got it."

"He has to believe you, Sal."

"I'll win the fucking Academy Award."

"You feel strong enough to do this, Tyler?"

"Yes."

"You're safe now. I'll have officers waiting for you at the hospital," said Montone, helping her on with her robe.

They both helped Tyler to her feet, then Sal walked her toward the door.

"Here we go, Ms. Angstrom," said Sal. "Piece of cake."

"Leave the front door open, Sal. I'll be down in a minute."

Montone waited until he heard them reach the elevator, and walked back to the bedroom. He turned on a radio on the bedstand near the hidden microphone, then went to the closet and hit the record button on the Nagra. As the reels started to move, erasing all his conversations with Tyler, he carefully replaced the top of the shoe box and left the apartment without making a sound.

Pat Feany and Frank Fonseca pulled up in front of the apartment building just as Montone walked outside. He could hear the siren of the approaching ambulance.

"Drop me off a block from the Silver Star," said Montone as he got into the backseat. "Let's try to beat him there."

"What're we looking at?" asked Feany as he floored the sedan away from the curb.

"Who's got a contract at the Plaza?" asked Montone.

"I do," said Fonseca. "Head of security, food and beverage guy."

"That's our Frankie; the king of contracts," said Feany.

"Check it out," said Montone. "They had a party the night Dennis went out the window. Keyes was there with his girlfriend."

Fonseca took out his cellular, looked up a number in his daybook and started dialing.

"Send Lopez and a patrol to Lenox Hill Hospital," Montone told Feany. "Have Hank set up a twenty-four-watch on Tyler Angstrom; get plainclothes over there to relieve the patrol as fast as possible. If Keyes tries to get in to see her we don't want a lot of uniforms hanging around. And you tell the doctors to tell anybody who asks: No visitors."

They made the drive to Sixty-fifth and Second in under three minutes.

Montone hustled through the doors of the coffee shop and spotted Murphy sitting alone in a corner booth, when he felt a strong hand come down on his shoulder.

"Right behind you, my friend," said Keyes.

"Hey, Terry." Montone hoped he was able to keep the surprise off his face.

"Saw you run in outside. No need to hurry on my account."

"I'm late, I got hung up at the station."

"I just got here myself," said Keyes, keeping a hand on Montone's back as they walked to the booth. "How are you feeling?"

"I'm better, thanks."

"God, what a terrible ordeal."

As they sat down, Keyes shook Murphy's hand and sat across from him, while Montone slid in beside his partner.

"I went ahead and ordered," said Murphy.

"I was thinking about you all last night," said Keyes. "It's bad enough as it is, certainly. But how much worse this all might have been for you. You know, if you'd actually gotten involved with Holly."

"Amen to that," said Murphy, playing along.

"The same thought occurred to me," said Montone. "But you know what made me feel better? Knowing that I'm going to find whoever did this to her."

Montone held his eyes for a fraction of a second longer than comfort allowed but Keyes's expression didn't change; still amiable, self-approving, supportive.

"Of course. That's your job, isn't it?"

"I was meaning to tell you this the other day: you know what the real secret to police work is?"

Keyes shook his head, poised and interested.

"Grinding. That's a sports term. Means constant effort. Never let up. The bad guys may be smarter than you, they may have more resources, they may seem like they're always one step ahead, but if you put your head down and keep pushing and tell yourself all that matters is that whoever did this is not going to beat you . . . they will eventually make the one mistake that lets you take them out."

Keyes nodded sagely, displaying deep interest. "So it's a matter of will. Whose is stronger."

"Don't you think, Murph?"

"Absolutely."

"Interesting," said Keyes.

Keyes took out his notebook and wrote something down. Montone watched him and sipped his coffee.

"I didn't mention this to you earlier, Terry, but since you've been through this with us from the jump, I feel like you should be the first person to get it."

"I appreciate that, Jimmy."

"It hasn't made the papers yet, so our confidentiality agreement still applies, okay?"

"I hope that goes without saying."

"It looks like this crime and Mackenzie Dennis are connected."

Keyes eyes widened. "Are you serious?"

"In fact, we're almost sure of it," said Murphy.

"That's incredible. How can you be certain?"

Montone glanced at Murphy; they had talked through each of these moves beforehand. "We really shouldn't go into too many specifics."

"I understand."

"But I can tell you this; we've also got our first solid lead," said Montone, leaning forward. "Like I said before, so far this guy hadn't made any mistakes. Until yesterday."

"What happened?"

"A witness came forward. Local resident was walking on the beach yesterday morning. Says he saw a car parked behind a stand of bushes in the sand about a quarter-mile from the house, right about the time we think Holly was killed."

"Did he see anyone?" asked Keyes.

"We haven't talked to the guy ourselves yet," said Murphy.

"He called Suffolk County police late last night," said Montone. "After he saw it on the news."

"That sounds encouraging," said Keyes.

"We'll see," said Montone, unable to discern whether the lie was having its desired effect; he decided to up the ante. "He did say it looked like a newer-model car and that someone may have been waiting in the passenger seat."

"No sign of the driver?"

"Maybe Holly saw him," said Montone, looking straight at Keyes.

"Maybe so," said Keyes, shaking his head.

"Anyway, we thought you'd be interested," said Montone.

"Very much so."

A waiter set down a couple of plates on the table filled with sausage, fried eggs, pancakes.

"Here, help yourself," said Murphy, hauling in one of the plates.

"We were going to head downtown for the autopsy after this," said Montone, digging into some pancakes. "If you want to join us, we should know a lot more after we have those results."

"You know how I am with all that," said Keyes.

"You don't have to come in the room with us," said Murphy, with his mouth full.

"Wait outside, like last time."

"I really ought to get back and see how Tyler's feeling."

"Why don't you call her? Here," said Montone, offering his cellular.

"I would, thanks, but I think she's got the phone turned off. Trying to sleep."

"Tell you what, we'll drive by, you can run in, make sure she's okay before you come with us."

Keyes smiled. "You're very persistent, aren't you?"

"Hey, we like to help people," said Murphy.

"You know what?" said Montone. "We needed to get her finger-prints anyway, maybe we'll come in with you."

"That's right," said Keyes. "You needed mine, too, didn't you?"

"Just routine," said Montone.

"You've got your kit with you, don't you, Murph?"

"Oh, yeah. Come on, eat, it's on us," said Murphy, shoving one of the plates toward Keyes.

When they left the coffee shop, Murphy went to retrieve the car while Keyes and Montone waited outside.

"Listen, there's something I need to tell you about, Jimmy."

"What's that?"

"It's rather embarrassing, actually. I'd appreciate it if this could just stay between you and me."

"Sure."

"I've been getting some disturbing phone calls the last few days."

"What kind of calls?"

"I think they're related to a problem I had in London last year."

"What kind of problem?"

"When my second book was published in England I had to make a number of public appearances; bookstores, radio, television, that sort of thing."

"Pretty standard, right?"

"They were until a man started showing up at all these events, trying to disrupt them."

"Some wacko."

"I wish it had been that simple. I didn't even recognize him at the time, but the man turned out to be the police inspector who arrested me for that incident I told you about when I was nineteen."

"The manslaughter charge?"

"The same man. Shocking. He was recently retired now and he'd somehow gotten it into his mind that my publishing career was some sort of elaborate charade to cover up my secret life as a deranged killer."

"What in the world gave him that idea?"

"I couldn't begin to tell you. Of course he hadn't an ounce of evidence to substantiate any of it; I'd been a model prisoner, early release for good behavior, unanimous support from my parole board, not to mention all quarters of society, but he caused such an uproar at so many of these book signings—shouting, making unsupported accusations to these poor people waiting to meet me—that I finally had to obtain a restraining order."

Montone felt his heart sink. "You're kidding."

"I wish I were. The judge ruled the man was not to come within a hundred yards of me, the disturbances stopped and I thought that would be the end of it. Anyway, the point of my telling you all this is I think he's followed me here to New York."

Montone's cellular rang.

"You've seen him?"

"Outside my hotel the other day. And I'm fairly certain he's the one who's been making these phone calls. Long silences, hang-ups, never speaking—"

Montone answered the call. "Montone."

"It's Peter Henshaw."

"Charlie, how great to hear from you. How've you been?"

"Is he with you?" asked Henshaw.

"That's right," said Montone, glancing casually at Keyes, gesturing that the call would just take a minute. "How's Florida? Where are you calling from?"

"I've checked into the Mayflower Hotel—"

"Sure, I know where that is. Listen, can I call you back when we're done here? I really want to talk to you."

"I'll wait."

"Let me get that number."

Keyes alertly opened his small notebook and handed it to him along with a ballpoint pen. Montone wrote down the number Henshaw gave him, then ripped the top two pages out of the notebook before Keyes could see it and handed back the book as he ended the call.

"Sorry," said Montone. "This sounds like a real nuisance, Terry."

"I'm sure he's harmless enough."

"If you want I could look into this for you. What's the man's name?"

"Peter Henshaw. But I really couldn't ask you to go to all the trouble."

"No trouble. You have a copy of that restraining order?"

"I didn't think to bring one with me, but I'm sure I could have my lawyers fax one over."

"Good. Have them send it to the station. Have you seen him again recently?"

"Not in the last few days."

"Where are you staying now?"

"With Tyler over the weekend. I moved out of the hotel when I saw him there."

Murphy pulled up beside them in the sedan.

"The problem, of course," said Keyes, "is that a restraining order from a British court doesn't carry the force of law over here."

"Maybe I should speak to this Henshaw myself," said Montone, as he opened the car door.

"You've got enough on your plate. I'm sure my publishers can recommend an attorney if it comes to that. I just wanted to let you know the man was here, in case he tries to contact you."

"We'll keep an eye out for him."

Following Keyes's directions, they drove to Tyler's building on Madison, double-parked and waited as Keyes went inside. Montone got out of the car and lit a cigarette, making sure that Sal the doorman could see him from the lobby.

Sal stopped Keyes before he could reach the elevator; observing their body language, it seemed to Montone as if Sal might have a chance at that Oscar after all. Moments later, looking genuinely shaken, Keyes hurried back out to the car.

"They've taken her to the hospital," he said.

"Jesus, you were just with her."

"She said she was fine, I don't understand. They had to call an ambulance."

"Come on, we'll take you," Montone said, holding the door for him. "Which hospital?"

"Lenox Hill."

"Practically around the corner."

Murphy stuck the bubble on the dash and turned on the siren as they screeched away from the curb.

Montone was pleased to see two plainclothes detectives already in place. Dressed as interns, they folded seamlessly into the mix flowing through the intensive care unit. While Keyes went into an office to speak with her doctor, trying to get an explanation of why he wasn't being allowed to see Tyler, Montone asked Murphy to get an update from Hank Lopez, then showed his badge to a young resident behind the desk and asked to speak with him privately.

They moved down the hall and around the corner. Montone took out his handkerchief and showed the resident the white pill he'd taken from the prescription vial on Tyler's bedside table.

"Can you identify this?"

"What did the label say?" asked the resident.

"Ativan."

"That's an antianxiety. This is Rohypnol. Two-milligram. Lot of it going around."

"What is it?"

"Sedative. About ten times stronger than Valium."

"Legal?"

"Not here, but in about sixty other countries. Before the FDA cracked down foreign travelers used to be able to bring in three months' worth at a time for personal use."

"As a sleeping pill?"

The resident nodded. "That's what the box says. It's a party drug. Think it started in Florida, Texas, we're starting to see it up here now. Kids call 'em roofies, roach, the forget pill."

"Why?"

"Perfect accessory for date rape. Add a couple shots of alcohol, you get complete memory loss. One hundred percent blackout."

"Thanks for your help."

Montone returned the pill to his pocket and went back to the waiting room just ahead of Keyes, returning from the ICU looking deeply concerned.

"She's still unconscious," he said, slumping into a chair. "They had to pump her stomach. Some kind of overdose. Maybe sleeping pills."

"Had to be accidental."

"I hope so. She was in a terribly fragile state."

"I'd say so."

"You know, it just occurred to me; maybe she turned on the television, saw the news about Holly, and that set her off into some sort of downward spiral."

"You still hadn't told her."

"I didn't think she was strong enough."

"Did they say what kind of drugs?"

"I didn't think to ask."

"Did you see any in her apartment?"

"She had a number of bottles by her bed. I know she took more than a few of them with her this weekend. Maybe she just mixed the wrong ones or got confused and took too many, I don't know."

"The doctors probably ought to know which ones she was using," said Montone.

"He mentioned that. God, I feel so guilty that I didn't see this coming."

"I could have a patrolman swing by the building, the doorman could let him in to collect the bottles."

Montone thought he noticed the briefest moment of calculation cross Keyes's features.

"That's very kind of you, Jimmy."

"Not a problem."

"Hell of a weekend for both of us, I guess," said Keyes, looking up at him with a rueful, battle-weary smile.

"You said a mouthful."

Murphy witnessed the autopsy of Holly Mews alone. Montone stepped into an adjoining antechamber before Dr. Lee even exposed the body on the table. He saw no need to add any nightmare material to the images already crowding his mind.

Through a porthole window in the door connecting to the morgue corridor he periodically glanced out at Terry Keyes, occupying the same stone bench on which he'd waited during the Mackenzie Dennis postmortem. Keyes sat quietly, writing in his notebook, seemingly unaware of Montone's proximity.

Keyes appeared to be lightly rubbing a pencil back and forth across the page, as if he were filling in a sketch.

As he waited, Montone paged through a file with the findings of the tests Dr. Lee had conducted on Mackenzie Dennis. He found a handwritten note from her scrawled next to the result he was looking for.

You were right—positive for amobarbital.

Dennis had a bloodstream level of six hundred milligrams at the time of death; equivalent to six standard-prescription amobarbital capsules.

Judging by the degree of biochemical degradation, Dr. Lee estimated the barbiturate had entered Dennis's body within an hour of when he died. She found no traces of undigested gelatin in his stomach or intestines.

Conclusion: The drug was administered by intramuscular injection.

Montone didn't expect Dr. Lee to find any drugs in Holly's system. She might have been surprised to see Terry Keyes walk back into the beach house but she would have trusted him, long enough to let him get close and overpower her without an injection.

He glanced out the window at Keyes again, then used his cellular to call the Mayflower Hotel. As instructed, Peter Henshaw had checked in under the name Charlie Squires.

"Hallo."

"It's Montone. We can talk."

"He still with you?"

"Nearby. Peter, did Keyes file a restraining order against you in London?"

"Is that what he told you?"

"Is it true?"

"Does he know we've spoken?"

"I don't know. Is it true?"

A pause. "You know what these lawyers can do," said Henshaw.

"Why didn't you tell me that?"

"It doesn't apply here—"

"How did it happen? What were the circumstances?"

A longer pause. "I approached him outside a Piccadilly bookstore. After one of his bloody book signings."

"For what reason?"

"Wanted to give him my regards, let him know I was interested to see him. Before I said a word to him he saw me coming and started screaming bloody murder. When people came running he claimed I'd physically assaulted him—"

"Any witnesses to that?"

"We were alone. The magistrate chose to believe the word of a convicted murderer over that of a police officer. He produced a threatening letter he claimed I'd sent him."

"Did you?"

"Abso-bloody-lutely not."

This time Montone waited.

"When did he tell you this?" asked Henshaw.

"About an hour ago."

"Unprovoked?"

"Yes."

"He knows."

"That's impossible."

"You don't know him. Why else would he bring it up to you now? I promise you he does nothing by chance."

Montone glanced out the porthole window again: Keyes was gone.

"Call you back," said Montone.

As he hung up Montone heard a loud crash behind him. He spun around, half expecting to find Keyes sneaking up on him.

A morgue attendant was wheeling an empty gurney through the hallway.

Montone pushed through the double doors into the marble corridor. No sign of Keyes.

Turning a corner, he stopped when he saw Keyes ten paces away, standing and talking with a woman whose back was to him. As he approached she heard his footsteps and turned.

Erin Kelly.

What did Keyes want with her? A whiplash of anger surged up inside Montone, protective instincts flaring. He struggled to conceal those feelings as he reached them.

"Detective Montone," she said, extending her hand to him.

"Miss Kelly."

"I see you've already met," said Keyes.

"Last night," said Montone.

She looked at him in slight confusion. Montone wondered what Keyes had said to her. Keyes backed slightly away, offering privacy.

"How can I help you, Miss Kelly?" asked Montone.

"The man from the mortuary was supposed to meet me here half an hour ago. I made the arrangements this morning by phone."

"I understand." Montone touched her gently by the arm and guided her back to the stone bench around the corner, away from Keyes.

"They came highly recommended." She mentioned the name of the firm.

Montone gestured and they sat down on the bench. She stared at the floor, exhausted, less confident than last night, slightly lost.

"I had a rough night. Reality of what's happened sinking in," she said, almost abstractly. "I've never lost a close family member before. Thought they might let me see her."

He nodded, acknowledging but not wanting to address that idea at the moment. He had no intention of letting Erin see her sister before the mortician had done his work.

He had no intention of seeing her that way either.

"What was the name of the mortuary again?"

She told him; he wrote it down, along with the name of the undertaker.

"We'll get in touch, see what the delay's about," he said.

"Kelly was my married name," she said, distracted, looking at her hands.

No ring. Montone sensed she'd had her fair share of sadness and disappointment.

"What was Terry talking to you about?" he asked.

Erin shook her head slightly, then seemed to focus on him for the first time.

"I'm sorry?"

"Terry. The man in the hallway. What were you talking about?"

"Holly. How fond he was of her. He said he was one of the last people to see her."

"That's true," said Montone.

Maybe the *last.*

"And he was just saying how happy she'd seemed. That something really positive had happened in her personal life. The same sort of thing she'd told me the other day."

Montone didn't know how to respond. The thought pierced him like an arrow.

"Did I tell you that already? It sounds familiar."

"Yes," he said.

"He asked if he could come to the funeral. Wanted to pay his respects."

"You said the funeral's going to be in Miami."

"That's right."

Calculations rattled through Montone's head: What does Keyes want in Miami? He didn't like the idea.

"What did you tell him?" he asked.

"I said that would be fine. If he was her friend he should be there."

She looked at him more searchingly. Montone hoped he hadn't given anything away.

"I didn't know that much about Holly's world. I think she felt in some way that I didn't approve. That it was . . . I don't know, the whole industry she'd become a part of was somehow irrelevant. All I wanted was for her to be happy and fulfilled by what she did. My opinion meant so much to her. Maybe too much. I don't why I'm telling you all this. I'm supposed to be the expert on understanding your feelings, but I've never felt like this before."

"It's all right."

He wanted desperately to tell her about their relationship and what she'd meant to him.

Not now. Not with Keyes right around the corner.

"It's like being stuck in a bad dream that you can't wake up from. You keep hoping the next moment's going to bring relief, that it's all a mistake, but it doesn't change."

She slumped to the side against Montone; all the effort of holding herself together could bring her to this point but no further. He put his arm around her shoulders and held her tight. She sobbed, deep and guttural, muscles contracting violently, her head resting on his chest, one hand weakly grasping the lapel of his jacket.

Around the corner, Keyes sat in an old-fashioned, accordion-door phone booth. He perked up when he heard the woman sob, thoughtful but unmoved. It never failed to amaze him how one individual's pain, compared to what he had suffered, seemed so weightless and insipid. Trapped inside their own consciousness, unable to hold on to the larger truths in the face of the slightest hardship. He could only regard such self-involvement with cold curiosity.

He examined a piece of paper from his notebook, the one he'd been tracing his pencil across on the bench earlier. The faintest outline of a phone number, the one Montone had written down outside the coffee shop, appeared in white in the middle of the tracing. Montone had torn off the top two pages to prevent this, of course, but the pen Keyes had handed him to use was almost out of ink; he'd had to press down hard on the paper.

Keyes dropped a quarter in the slot, dialed an operator and asked for directory assistance in Florida. When the call went through he told the operator he wanted her to check a number for him in a few different area codes. Although instinct told him it wasn't a Florida number at all—that it was in fact a local number or why else wouldn't Montone have written an area code?—from the sound of things around the corner, he had some time to kill and it never hurt to be overly thorough.

When her first wave of grief had worked itself out, Erin continued to hold onto Montone, motionless, exhausted as the survivor of a shipwreck clinging to a reef. She accepted the handkerchief he offered, wiping at her eyes.

"I was nine years older than Holly," she said finally. "You never saw a sweeter little girl in your life. She was so sincere. So connected to other people. Almost angelic. I'm not just saying that. Everyone felt it about her."

"I believe you."

"Her room was next to mine, once she was old enough to sleep alone. When she was about five she'd wait until she thought I was asleep, then she'd come into my room, kneel down by my bed and say her prayers. I always told her I was too grown up for prayers, so she said them for me. Always whispering; she didn't want me to know. I never told her I knew. I'd lie there, eyes closed, listening to her.

" 'Now I lay me down to sleep, I pray the Lord my soul to keep . . .' "

She looked at him, drained, somber, self-accusing.

"I never prayed for her."

Terry Keyes dropped one last quarter in the slot and dialed the faint number on his notebook page without a prefix or area code.

"Mayflower Hotel, how can I help you?" said the operator.

"What is your address please?" he asked.

"Central Park West at Sixty-first Street."

"Thank you so much."

His finger found the hook. He destroyed the piece of paper. He directed his senses to the conversation taking place around the corner, listened for an appropriate lull and then walked around to join them.

Shortly after Dr. Lee completed the autopsy, the undertaker Erin had been waiting for finally arrived. Montone handled the arrangements with the morgue for the transfer of the body to the man's custody. A hearse collected the sealed travel casket at the building's loading dock.

Montone stared at the black steel box as it slid onto the rollers in the hold.

Holly's not in there.

You'll never see her again.

As they closed the doors of the vehicle, Montone made certain that Erin had gone back inside, out of earshot, then he took the funeral director aside.

"Where are you doing the work?" he asked.

"At our facility here in town."

"When?"

"Tonight. The family's requested an open casket. They would like her to be ready to travel tomorrow."

Travel. As if she were a passenger.

The man's false piety infuriated Montone.

"Where's the funeral?"

"Services will be held in Miami on Tuesday."

"You're doing the job yourself?"

"We have a number of very capable people—"

"Who's your best?"

The man's smile began to falter. "I suppose I have the most experience."

Montone got close to the undertaker, a Mr. Gabriel; soft, middle-aged, habitually servile, a slight hint of decaying food on his breath, inadequately masked by peppermint.

"This was a beautiful girl—"

"So I understand—"

"No, you don't understand. You're going to do everything you can to give her family some decent memory of who she was to them. She didn't like makeup; don't paint her like a hooker. You put some kind of lace or collar on her neck so they don't see the rope burns—"

"Officer, I can assure you I know how to do my job—"

Montone took hold of the man's tie and pulled him even closer. "And I know all the shortcuts you could pull. And if you try to cut any corners or you disappoint these people in any way I will make it my business to find out. And you will hear from me."

The man stared at him, mouth agape, eyes wide.

"I understand," said Mr. Gabriel faintly. "I understand."

Montone let go of the man and he stumbled away. Montone walked back inside where Murphy waited with Erin.

Before he joined them, Terry Keyes appeared from an intersecting corridor and took Montone aside.

"Any results, Jimmy?" Keyes asked, gesturing toward the morgue.

"No surprises. Cause of death was hanging. Everything she found supports the facts we've got."

Keyes shook his head sympathetically, then glanced back at Erin and Murphy. "The sister all right?"

"Well as can be expected."

Keyes looked at Montone. "Jesus, this is awful. How are you, Jimmy, you holding up okay?"

"I'm not as good as I'm going to be."

"You look better than you did earlier in the day. More color in your face. Eyes are clearer."

"Getting back to work helps."

"You're sure you're not trying to take on too much?"

"Nothing I can't handle."

"You know your own limits, I'm sure. Listen, I'm going to run back up to the hospital, see how Tyler's coming along."

"That's a good idea. I almost forgot, did Mike remember to get your fingerprints?"

"We took care of that over an hour ago. Second time you've asked."

"Right. Forgive me, I'm still a little scattered."

"Don't worry about it. Completely understandable," said Keyes, patting him on the shoulder.

"You gonna stay at Tyler's place tonight?"

"I hadn't really thought about it."

"In case I need to get in touch with you."

"You can always leave a message there."

"Thanks, Terry," said Montone, trying to sound convincingly sincere. "We really appreciate all your help."

"Sure, buddy. Least I could do. You take care now."

Keyes paid his respects to Erin and Murphy. Montone watched him walk away until he was out of sight.

Montone and Murphy drove Erin to her hotel, the huge conventioneers' Sheraton in midtown. Montone walked her to the front entrance and stopped before she went inside.

"What are your plans?"

"Tonight?" She sounded surprised. "I wasn't exactly planning on taking in a musical."

"I mean, were you thinking about seeing friends, going out to dinner?"

"I'm thinking about room service, a call to my parents, a hot bath and a couple of margaritas."

"Anybody you know can keep you company?"

"I'd prefer to be alone."

"And tomorrow?"

"Wait for the mortuary to call. Fly down to Miami. I've got an open ticket. Why?"

Montone took a deep breath.

"Miss Kelly . . . Erin, I was involved with Holly. We only met a few days ago. I didn't even know her that well. All I can tell you is I felt very strongly about her."

He couldn't quite decipher her reaction.

"I'm sorry, I feel badly that I didn't tell you earlier but last night didn't seem right and today didn't seem like the appropriate time or place."

"No, it's all right," she said, looking away, taking a deep breath. "So you were the good news."

Montone shrugged. "That would have been my hope."

"I'm sure it's true."

Neither spoke for a moment.

"I'm going to find who did this, Erin. I don't want you or your family to have any doubt about that. I promise you."

She looked at him closely, clear-eyed and centered. "Are you sure you should be taking on that responsibility right now?"

"I can't let it happen any other way."

"I know you're capable of it. More than capable. I ought to know, I wrote about you."

Montone felt more compassion from her than he could bear. He turned away.

"I also know what you went through the last time," she said.

"That was different."

"This is personal," she said.

He waited while she thought it over.

"Do you know who killed her?" she asked.

"I have an idea."

He reminded himself to remember how smart she was.

"Do you know why?"

"Not yet."

She paused.

"My feeling is you're going to pursue this regardless of what anyone tells you to do."

"Yes."

"I'll help you any way I can," she said. "I've consulted with police on cases before, testified at trials—I think you know that."

"Yes. You can start by inviting me to the funeral."

"Should I ask why?"

"Better if you didn't."

She considered for a moment. "I will help you and I won't ask why until after we bury her. There's more than enough to cope with between now and then. But when that's done you have to promise that you'll tell me what you know."

"Agreed."

"You don't need my invitation to the funeral, Jimmy. You should be there anyway." She wrote down a phone number on a business card and handed it to him. "That's my parents' number in Miami. Are you flying tomorrow?"

"I'll call you when I get there. I think it's a good idea you stay in tonight, like you planned. You're not in any danger but I'm going to put an officer outside your door. Just a precaution."

"If you think that's necessary."

"I do."

She nodded and looked at him for a long moment. "I'm glad it was you. I'm glad for her."

Montone didn't know what to say. Erin briefly hugged him, then turned and entered the hotel.

"Is he there, Hank?"

"He's here," said Lopez, crouched in a hospital room adjacent to Tyler's, the phone in his hand, peering out the window in the door. "He's in the hallway talking to the doctor. They're telling him she's still too weak to see anybody."

"He buying it?" asked Montone.

"Seems like he is. I could have one of the plainclothes guys talk to him."

"I don't think he's gonna hang around."

"You want a tail on him?"

"We don't do anything to tip him. I want you to set up across the street from Tyler's place on Madison, I think that's where he's going next. Apartment six-oh-five, south side of the building facing the street. Get there ahead of him, check in when he shows."

"I'm there," said Lopez, hanging up.

Murphy turned onto Park Avenue and headed uptown into the crush of traffic. Streetlights blinked on as dusk approached. A stiff wind freshened the air.

Montone made one more call, to Pat Feany, and arranged to have the rest of the team meet them at the hospital.

At six-fifteen Terry Keyes walked around the corner and entered Tyler's building on Madison. Sal the doorman had gone off shift; the weekend night man nodded to Keyes as he walked to the elevator.

Keyes had felt the eyes on him outside. He switched on all the lights in every room of the apartment except the kitchen. He turned on the television, cranked the volume high and moved to the kitchen window. Looking down from the dark, he spotted the detective's unmarked car, parked just around the corner on Seventy-third.

He checked the tape recorder in the bedroom; the tape had spooled all the way to the end. He played it back in a few places; five hours' worth of radio broadcast. Either Tyler had left the radio on by mistake or someone had discovered the rig. Suspecting the latter, and knowing this would be his last night in her apartment, he disassembled the recording kit and took it into the other room.

He removed a cheap black canvas backpack from its hiding place behind a false panel he'd installed in the front closet and dropped the recording equipment inside. He took out the night-vision scope, walked back to the kitchen window and trained the sight on the windshield of the sedan on Seventy-third.

Hank Lopez, a detective from the 19th, looking up at the lit apartment windows.

Keyes moved to the bedroom, changed into the clothes he'd packed in the bag, added the eyeglasses and the touches of makeup he'd planned. He put on leather gloves, a reversible black leather jacket, and took a moment to adjust the baseball cap in the hallway mirror.

Picking up the backpack, he made certain no one was in the corridor outside, left the apartment without locking the doors, moved swiftly to the fire exit and took the stairs to the alley behind the building.

After Montone questioned Tyler Angstrom again in her hospital room, the task force officers convened over a hasty dinner in the cafeteria. Hank Lopez called in to report that, as Montone had anticipated, Terry Keyes had arrived and gone up to Tyler's apartment, where he still remained. The doorman, who had taken a pass on the sixth floor during his break, reported hearing a television set on inside.

After Feany and Fonseca reported what they'd learned from Frankie's contact at the Plaza, Montone summarized what Tyler's doctor had given him about her medical history.

"He prescibed Ativan for general anxiety about three months ago.

Tyler says she doesn't know how the Rohypnol got into her Ativan prescription bottle."

"Good," said Feany.

"The bad news is that in the last two years she's been in detox three times, and hospitalized twice for what she called accidental overdoses. Once on Rohypnol and cognac."

"She's a fucking medicine cabinet," said Murphy.

"Claims she's been clean for three months," said Montone. "Doesn't understand how this happened."

"Any way to verify?" asked Fonseca.

"It's bullshit. That night at the beach she killed a bottle of cabernet by herself and she'd smoked at least one joint before we got there."

"Cleopatra, the queen of denial," said Murphy.

"So then he was feeding this shit to her," said Feany.

"Maybe the pills. Maybe he was dropping them in her wine. She has no recollection."

"That's why he picked her, Jimmy," said Feany. "He knew she was all junked up."

"Maybe. On the night Dennis was killed she thinks they got to the Plaza about nine and were separated at the party for a while, but her memory's a little hazy."

"No shit," said Murphy.

"What about the hotel room?"

"He checked in at nine forty-five under his name, used his own credit card; it's a Visa from a London bank," said Fonseca, handing around a copy of the receipt. "One night. Room service, champagne and caviar at eleven-thirty. Breakfast for one at seven. No phone calls."

"Any baggage?"

"Bellboy thinks maybe a garment bag."

"His or hers?"

"His."

Montone rubbed his eyes with the palms of his hands, trying to will away the fatigue.

"Did he go up to the room by himself, or was she with him?" he asked.

"Alone when he checked in. Probably during that time they were apart from each other."

"Which we don't know was for how long," said Murphy.

"Nine forty-five to eleven-fifteen," said Feany. "That's his window."

"It fits for Dennis."

"And she's his alibi."

"So probably he dropped something in her drink before he left the party."

"Maybe so. On the drive back from Long Island she was lights-out too," said Montone.

"She doesn't remember stopping?"

Montone shook his head.

"Is it enough?" asked Feany.

No one responded. They already knew the answer.

"Let's hit the squad, type up what we got," said Montone. "Meeting's at nine, Foley's office. I want everybody to keep the next couple days wide open, don't make any plans with the family. If they go for this we're putting in some serious time."

Montone stood up and stretched, desperate to find a second wind. He headed to the coffee station for a refill. Murphy and Feany followed him over.

"What about Henshaw?" asked Murphy.

"I'm still waiting for a callback from London."

"Five hours later there," said Feany, glancing at his watch. "Doubt we'll get anything tonight."

"Henshaw admitted to me the restraining order was for real. I don't know if we can use him, Pat."

"Leave him out of it. You can use what he told you, anyway."

"Without attribution? I don't think so."

"You want to talk to him again?" asked Murphy. "You said last time you got cut off."

"Maybe we should."

"I'll try to get him," said Feany, heading for a pay phone. "You said the Mayflower?"

"Charlie Squires."

Feany picked up the phone and dialed.

"You know Keyes is our guy, Jimmy," said Murphy, lowering his voice.

"Just on instinct. That's all Henshaw has anyway."

"But you *know*."

"Yeah. I know."

Feany turned to them urgently, the phone in his hand. "There's a fire at the Mayflower."

After he crossed through the park on foot, Keyes turned south, keeping to the park side of the stone wall paralleling Central Park West. At the corner of Sixty-second he reversed his jacket, concealed the black backpack behind a low hedge, hopped the wall, unseen, and crossed the street at the intersection.

The Mayflower Hotel occupied the entire block of Central Park West between Sixty-first and Sixty-second, an aging dowager anchoring the southern end of the upscale avenue. As Keyes approached he saw the hotel's entrance swarming with tourist traffic, more than adequately occupying the doormen and bellhops. Keyes lowered his head, moved through the revolving door and into the lobby unnoticed.

He walked to the bank of elevators on the right side of the building, purposeful, confident that no one would question his presence. He pressed the down button, waited until he got an empty car and rode the elevator to the basement.

Later, only a few people would even remember seeing the police officer in the lobby and not one of them could provide a detailed physical description, let alone the number on the badge he'd stolen from the 19th Precinct. That the officer wore a trim mustache and a pair of black-framed eyeglasses was all the most reliable of them could recall.

Keyes searched around the corner from the elevator bay until he found the on-site laundry facility. He heard the sound of people working inside but no one saw him wheel a laundry basket back toward the elevator shafts, out of sight. He removed a small hand-crafted incendiary device from his pocket, activated the timer and buried it in the basket under a loose cover of sheets, then calmly exited via the service stairs, bypassing the lobby, to the second floor.

He waited in the empty hallway for two minutes, checked his watch, then located the floor's fire alarm box, smashed the glass panel and tripped the lever. Bells and sirens began to sound throughout the hotel just as smoke from the smoldering fire in the basement began to swirl convincingly up and out of the elevators.

Keyes hurried down the stairs to the lobby. Alert personnel at the front desk manned the phones, already well into organizing an orderly evacuation.

As news of the fire spread rapidly through the hotel, Keyes took up a position near the front entrance. When guests and visitors began to stream down into the lobby he authoritatively directed them through the revolving doors and out onto the street. He could hear the sirens of approaching fire trucks in the distance and he anticipated other police officers would arrive momentarily. His sharp eyes darted through the crowd flowing around him, searching for that one familiar face.

At exactly that moment, Detective Feany placed his call to the Mayflower switchboard, one of the last incoming calls the operators answered before leaving their posts to join the evacuation.

Feany held the phone, waiting for Montone's response.

"Let's move," he said.

Montone bypassed the elevators and led the four detectives in a race down the nearest stairs to Seventy-seventh Street and into their units. They turned the bubble light on, stuck it on the dash, hit the sirens and headed for the Seventy-ninth Street transverse through the park. Montone radioed ahead for patrol backup to meet them at the Mayflower.

Peter Henshaw appeared in the lobby amid a knot of excited schoolteachers from South Carolina, in town attending a convention. He wore a belted trench coat over a set of sweat clothes and a pair of tennis shoes without socks; the emergency had woken him up. As the group funneled out the front doors, Henshaw passed within three feet of the policeman directing traffic but never looked at his face.

Keyes waited until Henshaw reached the sidewalk, then quickly exited out a side door, pulling the radio from his belt and holding it to his ear as if he'd just received an urgent call. Moments later the first NYPD patrol to arrive on the scene walked through the hotel's main entrance. They did not notice the other officer leaving.

Montone and Murphy, in the lead car, accelerated through the hard left at Eighty-first, clearing traffic out of their way as they fishtailed onto Central Park West. Feany and Fonseca made the turn seconds later, narrowly avoiding a collision.

The first fire engines pulled up in front of the Mayflower, with two additional police units close behind. Firefighters poured off the trucks and into the lobby, quickly tracking the smoke, while patrol officers fanned out to manage the rapidly expanding crowd; traffic heading north on Central Park West had ground to a standstill behind the cluster of vehicles and displaced tourists spilling out of the hotel, snarling the streets all the way back to Columbus Circle.

Keyes took off his NYPD cap and badge and knifed into the crowd, keeping the tall white cap of Henshaw's head in view some twenty paces away. All eyes, including Henshaw's, remained fixed on the hotel facade, watching the wisps of smoke that escaped from the lower floors, searching for flames.

As he slowly maneuvered through the crowd to Henshaw's rear, careful not to jostle anyone, attracting no attention, Keyes's right hand moved slowly to the large pocket he'd fashioned inside the left breast of his jacket.

At Sixty-seventh Street the congestion further ahead brought traffic moving south on the avenue to a sudden halt. Montone revved the siren and leaned on his horn but there was nowhere for the cars ahead of them to move. He could see the spinning lights of the police and fire trucks sending flashes of color up the sides of the buildings six blocks away.

With the street obstructed at Sixty-first, most of the northbound vehicles had passed and the lanes to their left suddenly cleared. Montone yanked the car to the park side of the road and continued south in the northbound lanes, siren wailing, into the teeth of the remaining traffic. Pat Feany made a hard left and followed him. Cars skidded and swerved to move out of their path; a taxi went skidding into a bus.

Hidden in the heart of the crowd, Terry Keyes grasped hold of the syringe concealed in his pocket and closed the last step toward Peter Henshaw. He pretended to stumble and as he fell forward he thrust the needle forward through his jacket, penetrating Henshaw's trench coat and sweatpants and stabbing him in the left hip. Keyes slammed the plunger in the moment it made contact with his flesh, then withdrew it before Henshaw even turned around, by which time Keyes was already burrowing back through the crowd toward Central Park. Not one person near Henshaw noticed the syringe and no one could provide a decent description of the man in the black leather jacket they'd seen.

When the thousand milligrams of adrenaline shot into his bloodstream and his weakened heart began to jackhammer, Henshaw summoned the energy to call out once for help before the force of the stimulant knocked him off his feet. As he gasped for breath, his pulse stuttering, fracturing into a deadly arrhythmia, his knees hit the pavement and the crowd around him began to scatter out of his way, realizing something had gone terribly wrong with this man.

Organizing his final clear intention, Henshaw's hands clawed desperately into the pocket of his raincoat. As consciousness failed and his face hit the ground the last thing his mind registered was a slice of symmetrical grillwork cut into the sidewalk, one open eye staring down into the blackness of the subway tunnel as the rush of a train passing below obliterated the world.

With Feany's car not far behind, Montone hit the brakes and skidded to a halt on the edge of the crowd at Sixty-second; the other detectives were out of the vehicles moments afterwards as they hurried forward after him.

Terry Keyes reached the far edge of the gathering on the eastern sidewalk, turned and casually backed up against the wall fronting the park. To his right he heard sirens and the squeal of brakes. Stepping up onto a bench, he spotted Montone and the other detectives moving away from their cars toward the hotel. Keyes eased over the wall and dropped to the ground inside the park. Staying low, he retraced his steps northward and slipped behind the cover of the hedge where he'd hidden the backpack.

He stripped off the leather jacket and policeman's uniform, revealing the running shorts and sweatshirt he wore underneath. He exchanged his heavy black brogans for a pair of Nike cross-trainers, removed the mustache and glasses and tossed them into the bag with the uniform. Less than a minute after he'd gone over the wall Keyes emerged from behind the hedge, hefted the backpack over his shoulders and began jogging to the north and east across the park.

He glanced at his watch as he ran and estimated that he had, at best, ten minutes to cover the mile across the park and get back inside Tyler's apartment.

By this time Montone and the detectives had worked their way through to the center of attention in the crowd. Bystanders had already summoned two paramedics from one of the ambulances; they had turned Henshaw onto his back and were aggressively administering

Eric Bowman

CPR while they waited for their ambulance to back up to them through the mob.

Montone flashed his badge to the paramedics as he approached and saw Henshaw lying on the ground.

"What've you got?" he asked.

"Cardiac arrest. Full stop."

"Anyone see what happened?"

"I don't know." The medics kept working.

Henshaw looked dead; eyes blank as slate, pupils dilated, his face mottled by stark shades of white and blue.

Montone turned to the crowd; ambivalently watching, fascinated and shamed.

"Anybody see what happened here?" asked Montone.

"He just fell over," a woman offered.

"Did anyone touch him? Anybody hit him or come up to him? Was he talking to anyone?"

No one answered, shrinking back from his intensity, but the crowd's sheepishness did nothing to deter their morbid interest in Henshaw's suffering, and it made Montone furious. He reined in his anger and forced himself to concentrate on the body sprawled on the sidewalk.

Henshaw's right arm, splayed back over his head at an unnatural angle, lolled back and forth as the medics worked on his chest.

The fist of his right hand was clenched tight.

Montone kneeled down beside him and pried the fingers of Henshaw's hand apart.

He held a key.

Montone noticed an anxious look that passed between the paramedics; one of them shook his head ever so slightly but they continued to work.

"Did you know him?" asked the lead medic. "Detective? Did you know him?"

"Yeah, I knew him."

The paramedic's vigorous rocking of Henshaw's body sent the key sliding out of his lifeless palm. As Montone grabbed for it the key clattered out of his reach onto the grille in the sidewalk, slipped through the gap and fell into the darkness.

Montone stood up and turned to the other detectives. "Mike, get Lopez on the phone. Pat, Frankie, take the scene, see if they know yet where the fire started and start taking statements from these people."

Feany stepped toward the crowd, held up his badge and raised his raspy voice, cutting through the chaos like a bullhorn.

"I need anyone who saw or heard anything about this man's injury to come forward."

Moments before Mike Murphy dialed his cell phone number, Detective Hank Lopez stepped out of his sedan at Seventy-third and Madison for the first time since he'd begun the stakeout. He walked ten steps to the corner to stretch his legs and smoke a cigarette. He left his phone on the front seat of the car and, as an ambulance passed by on Madison with its siren blaring, Lopez didn't hear it ring.

Nearing the Sixty-fifth Street underpass as he reached the middle of Central Park, Terry Keyes slowed his pace when he spotted a garbage truck making collections ahead of him on the East Drive.

Keyes edged up slowly behind the truck, slipped off the black canvas backpack and, as the attendant riding on the running board jumped down to empty the next garbage can, flung the bag up into the open maw of the tailgate. Without missing a step, Keyes cut sharply to his right, passed the truck and accelerated onto the bridle path that paralleled the road, heading north.

Murphy turned back to Montone, the phone in his hand. "He's not answering."

"God damn it. Try Tyler's apartment."

"You got the number?"

Montone paged through his notebook and pointed at a number. Murphy dialed.

With the help of two firemen, the ambulance attendants attached an oxygen mask, lifted Peter Henshaw onto a gurney and loaded him into the vehicle. He showed no signs of life.

"Take him to St. Luke's-Roosevelt," said Montone.

"Machine," said Murphy. "I'm getting the machine."

"Come on, Mike," said Montone.

Montone ran for the car, Murphy followed. Montone cranked the engine and stood on both the brake and accelerator, spinning the car around in a tight pivot, then sent it screaming north along Central Park West.

Murphy saw the look on his face and fastened his seat belt.

"Try Hank again," said Montone. "Keep trying him."

Montone ran two red lights, siren wailing, leaning on the horn, then took a controlled slide as he made the turn onto Sixty-fifth to cut east across the park. Murphy had to stop dialing halfway through the number and hang on to the strap above the door. Once they reached the straightaway he finished the call.

Lopez answered on the third ring.

"Where the fuck have you been?" yelled Murphy.

"Right here—"

"Hank, get to the doorman in her building," Montone shouted over both of them. "Have him call upstairs to her apartment on the house phone. Now!"

"Okay—"

"You stay on the line, Hank, keep this line open."

"I'm heading over."

Lopez held on to the phone and hurried across Madison Avenue toward Tyler's building.

Six blocks away, Terry Keyes heard the siren of Montone's car crossing behind him at Sixty-fifth and picked up his pace. He ran along the inner wall of the park, hidden by the trees and foliage that bordered Fifth Avenue, until he reached Seventy-second. He waited for a break in the traffic on Fifth, then crossed the street, ran one block north and turned to his right.

Montone's car shot into the air across the intersection at Sixty-sixth and Fifth, trailing sparks as the muffler scraped the pavement on landing, then negotiated a sliding left turn onto Madison, heading north. Murphy could hear Lopez talking to the doorman over the open phone line.

"He's trying the apartment," said Lopez into the phone. "What's he supposed to say if he answers?"

"Tell him he has a visitor," said Montone.

Montone swerved around slower-moving traffic on Madison like an Indy car driver, banging on the horn to open up holes in the flow, then punching through them.

"No answer," said Lopez.

"No answer," said Murphy.

"Wait for us there, Hank," shouted Montone as Murphy held up the phone. "Call the elevator down to the lobby and hold it. We're a minute away."

Montone cut the siren as they hit Seventieth, using the horn to get them across Seventy-second against the light.

Terry Keyes opened the rear service door of Tyler's building. He saw the spinning lights of an approaching police car on Madison, removed the duct tape he'd earlier placed across the dead bolt and started sprinting up the stairs.

Montone's car jammed to a stop in front of the building. He jumped out, ran through the lobby past Lopez and the doorman and went straight into the elevator. Murphy ran into the lobby after him.

"Stay there," said Montone, pointing a finger at Lopez, then called to Murphy. "Take the back door."

Murphy headed for the back of the building. Montone pressed the button for six. The elevator doors closed. He unholstered his pistol and held it in his coat pocket, taking a series of deep breaths to steady himself.

The elevator opened on the sixth floor. Montone walked quietly to Tyler's apartment. He could hear a television on inside and nothing else. When he heard the creak of a hinge behind him he wheeled around, the gun in his hand.

The door to the fire stairs closed.

Montone put the gun away and rang the apartment's doorbell. No response.

He counted to ten, then rapped loudly on the door. He heard someone whistling inside the apartment.

A lock turned and Terry Keyes opened the door, wearing a dark bathrobe, hair wet, a towel wrapped around his shoulders. Keyes smiled broadly when he saw him.

"Hey, Jimmy, what's up?"

"I tried calling from downstairs," said Montone, trying to cover his surprise.

"Sorry, I was in the shower."

"I called on the way over. Got the machine."

"You leave a message?"

"No."

"Tyler's phone. Rings off the hook. I screen calls when she's not here; I'll only pick up if it's for me." They looked at each other for a moment. "Are you all right?"

"Sure."

"You want to come in?"

"Thanks."

Montone entered. He kept his right hand on the gun in his pocket. He heard a loud ticking sound.

The stopwatch from *60 Minutes* filled the screen of the television in the living room.

"I was just finishing up at the station," said Montone. "Thought I'd swing by, see if you wanted to grab a bite."

"Bad timing; I just finished a pizza," said Keyes, smiling quizzically. "You want something to drink?"

A pizza delivery box sat on the coffee table in front of the set. Two slices uneaten.

"I'm good, thanks." Montone pointed toward Mike Wallace on the screen. "You watching this?"

"Wouldn't miss it." Keyes picked up the remote and turned down the sound on the set.

"My favorite show. What was on tonight?"

"You know, the usual stuff; exposing injustice, holding the feet of the corrupt to the fire. That old crank bitching about his phone bill."

"Andy Rooney," said Montone, glancing at his watch: 7:43. "He doesn't come on till the end of the show."

"Right, well, we don't know what's put a bug up his ass this week yet, do we?"

"It's always something."

Keyes leaned against the threshold of the bedroom door, smiling and relaxed. "You sure you don't want a drink? Tyler stocks a pretty decent bar."

"Could I use the bathroom?"

"Sure," said Keyes. "In here."

He turned and walked ahead of Montone into the bedroom.

Keyes's sweat-soaked running clothes lay on top of the bed. Terry whipped the towel off his shoulders and casually tossed it over them just as Montone entered behind him. Keyes pointed him toward the bathroom. Montone went in and closed the door.

Keyes scooped up the wet clothes, threw them under the bed and replaced the towel. He kicked his Nikes out of sight, walked back into the kitchen, pulled a steak knife from a butcher block on the counter and concealed it in the pocket of his robe.

Montone quietly locked the door, ran the faucet in the bathroom sink, then examined the shower. Water had beaded on the sliding glass door and the interior tiles were wet, but no condensation had formed on the medicine cabinet mirror. Keyes had been in the shower, he concluded, but not long enough to miss that call on the house phone.

Montone flushed the toilet, eased his right hand back to the gun in his pocket and walked back out to the living room. Keyes was sitting on a footstool directly in front of the television, eating a slice of pizza and drinking a beer.

"I'd really like to go out with you, Jimmy, but I think it's going to be an early night for me."

"I should probably do the same."

"Wish you'd called fifteen minutes earlier." He paused to wash down a bite of pizza. "But between you and me I'd just as soon put this fucking weekend from hell behind me."

"I'll leave you to it."

Keyes set down his beer, stood up to see him out and slipped a hand into the right pocket of his bathrobe. Montone kept both hands in the pockets of his raincoat as they reached the door and stood facing each other on either side of the jamb.

"Listen, Terry, I was talking to Holly's sister after you left. She mentioned you were planning to fly down to Miami for the funeral."

"Least I could do, isn't it?"

"I was thinking of maybe going down myself."

"Really?"

If Keyes felt any surprise he concealed it completely.

"She said the services are going to be on Tuesday," said Montone.

"Yes. You sure you can get away?"

"I'm going to try."

Well played, Jimmy. You're making my job easier than you can imagine.

"I'm sure it would mean a great deal to her," said Keyes. "We could fly down together, if you like. I'd welcome the company."

"Let's talk in the morning. Maybe we can grab a flight in the afternoon."

"I'll call you first thing. In the meantime, do try to get some rest, old boy."

"Yeah, you too."

"Goodnight, Jimmy."

Keyes locked the door after him. He took the knife from his pocket, ran his thumb along the edge of the blade as he studied it for a while, trying to chase down a troublesome line of thought.

How much does he know?

Montone rode the elevator down to the lobby, ignored a contrite Lopez and went right to the doorman.

"Did six-oh-five have a pizza delivered tonight?"

"No, sir," said the doorman.

"Are you sure?"

"Hey," said the doorman, swelling with pride, "anybody brings a pizza into this building I'm gonna know about it."

9

When did you start wondering why, Jimmy? Was it that night in the apartment after I topped the old man? That's when I first saw the question in your eyes.

"Why Holly? What did he do her for? Was he trying to get to me somehow? If so, who's next?"

You were turning that around, too, weren't you? I'm curious: Were you thinking of the sister already?

Did it burn into your mind, Jimmy, that question? Why? Murder for its own sake is one thing but you knew I was up to more than just sport.

Do you know how many whys I lived with for twelve years?

No, not for sport. You figured that early on. Had to. Not that kind, was I? Not like poor old Sligo, killing for sex, enacting the same adolescent scenario of rejection and rage over and over again.

Pathetic, predictable. American as apple pie. Mass murder's a staple of your culture, every bit as common as Elvis and white trash. Indiscriminate killing's a key symptom of the peculiar disease you've injected into the bloodstream of the world.

Indiscriminate killing was the last thing on my mind.

Need a clue?

Twelve years in prison and how do they subdue our incorrigibly criminal natures? Bombard us round the clock with American films, television, music. Brainwashing, pure and simple.

Why? Because America discovered the secret to pacifying the human animal; overwhelm the poor beast with fantasy, images of sex, money, sleek material goods. Stun their forebrains, reward them with occasional objects of desire, and they'll line up like cattle for the slaughter.

And what did your cultural imperialism teach us? That affluence is the norm, that possessions solve problems. Women are sexual objects of instant and eager availability. Justice is swift and certain. Athletes are gods, untouchable, worthy of worship. Psychologists, the high priests of your secular religion, hold the secret to understanding all human behavior.

That fame, gained for whatever specious reason, is valued more than genius.

Are you still wondering why, Jimmy? Look around. Look inside yourself.

Do you honestly think you deserve all that you've been given?

: from an untitled manuscript by Terry Keyes, found in the Brooklyn apartment rented under the name Howard Kurtzman

At nine o'clock Monday morning Montone, Murphy and Pat Feany entered Chief Bill Foley's office. Foley, Will Flannigan, Dan Jakes and Lloyd Coxen were waiting for them, along with Dick Eberle, a high-ranking deputy district attorney.

"Our suspect's name is Terry Keyes," said Montone. "Resident alien, from England and a convicted felon with a twelve-year stretch for manslaughter. He's a writer. He's supposed to be here working on a book, came in six weeks ago on a six-month visa. Department PR office steered him to me; they say he asked to meet me specifically, for research purposes. I met him about three hours before Mackenzie Dennis was killed."

He distributed copies of the customs forms they'd received from INS, along with Keyes's police record and parts of his case file which had arrived by fax early that morning from Scotland Yard. Montone waited for the brass to digest the information before proceeding.

After showing them the photograph of Terry with Mackenzie Dennis in the notebook they'd recovered from Henshaw's hotel room, Montone walked them through a thorough account of Keyes's movements on the evening Dennis died, backing it up with the statement he'd taken from Tyler Angstrom.

"They arrive at the Plaza at nine. Sometime around nine-thirty Keyes leaves the party in the ballroom, and checks into a suite at nine forty-five. He goes up to the room without the girl. He's got a garment bag that he carries himself. Once he's alone we think he changes clothes, leaves the hotel unseen, moves through the park to Sixty-ninth, then over to Lexington. Which puts him at the scene at, say, ten-fifteen."

"Anything connect him to it?" asked Dick Eberle.

Montone displayed the single scale of red confetti in a plastic envelope.

"We found this on the roof of the building next door, from where we think he gained access to Dennis's building. Plaza source confirms there was confetti being tossed around at that party. We've talked to the outfit that organized the party, got the name of the manufacturer, we're checking this morning to see if it's the kind they were using."

Eberle didn't seem overly impressed, but Montone knew that was his usual stance. "What else?"

"Dennis went out the window at ten forty-five. The girlfriend says she didn't see Keyes at the party again until about quarter past eleven. Gives him time to make it back into the hotel room, change clothes, get back downstairs and make it seem as if he just lost her in the crush for an hour and a half. Then he takes the girlfriend upstairs. They order room service at eleven-thirty. He leaves before she wakes up the next morning."

"You have witnesses that put him outside the hotel during any of this?"

"Not yet."

Eberle glanced at Foley, not encouragingly.

Montone explained the genesis of his relationship with Terry Keyes. How Keyes had insinuated himself into the squad's confidence, uniquely positioning himself to receive information about any progress they made on the case. He laid out how Keyes had suggested and encouraged his introduction to Holly, then nudged them together by arranging the weekend in the Hamptons.

Eberle asked what they had that physically linked Keyes to Holly's death.

"His prints are all over the house," said Montone.

"So are yours," said Eberle. "What about where it helps us; the banister, the chair, the tape recorder? The notes she got in the mail?"

"Nothing."

"Any ideas about motive?"

"We're working on it."

"You knew Dennis, too—right, Jimmy?" asked Dan Jakes.

"Yes."

"You think you're the connection here?"

"I do. I don't know how yet."

Dick Eberle looked around impatiently during the pause that followed.

"Come on, Jimmy, you know you gotta do better than this," he said.

Montone went on to relay his meeting Inspector Peter Henshaw, briefly outlining Henshaw's history with and suspicions of Terry Keyes. He mentioned the restraining order without assigning it too much weight and showed them a copy of Henshaw's medical discharge from the London force, detailing the fragile heart condition that had resulted from his diabetes.

Then he showed them Henshaw's death certificate from St. Luke's-Roosevelt Hospital.

"You're alleging Keyes is responsible for this, too?" asked Eberle.

"Somebody fell or bumped into him about thirty seconds before he went down."

"But, let me guess, you don't have anything to tie Keyes to this directly."

"Not yet."

"No witnesses? In the middle of a fucking crowd?" asked Foley incredulously.

"People were looking at the fire. Arson investigator says it started in a laundry basket in the basement. We think Keyes set it to smoke Henshaw out of the hotel, then he came in through the crowd and hit him with something that stopped his heart. Doctor at St. Luke's-Roosevelt says there's an injection mark on his right hip."

"He had diabetes. There may be quite a few injection marks," said Eberle.

"Keyes knew that, too. Forensics will tell us if it's fresh. The autopsy's this morning."

"Even if he *was* injected you've still got nothing that puts Keyes next to him."

"I found a key in Henshaw's hand. As he's dying I think he was trying to tell me he knew exactly who'd done this to him."

"Key? As in Keyes?" asked Coxen cynically.

"Was it his hotel room key?" asked Eberle.

"I think so. It fell down a subway grate."

Eberle rubbed his forehead, paged through the documents they'd given him again, shook his head.

"It's not nearly enough," he said, looking at Foley, flicking a finger at the confetti in its envelope. "We can't indict on this, Bill. I can't even recommend an arrest."

Foley and the brass stared at Montone disapprovingly.

"That's what I thought you'd say," said Montone, standing his ground.

Dan Jakes spoke for the group. "So what are you asking for, Jimmy? Search warrants? You want to brace this guy? Tap his phone?"

"No," said Montone. "First thing is, I want you to suspend me, pending a full investigation. Without pay."

"Why?"

"Because I was involved with the girl and failed to inform you in a timely and appropriate manner. Take me off the case. I want you to call a press conference and spread it all over the newspapers."

The brass looked at each other quizzically.

"You know what you're letting yourself in for, Jimmy?" asked Jakes.

"Yes."

The call from Erin came in over Montone's cellular as Murphy drove him back to his apartment from Police Plaza.

"I'm at Kennedy," she said, barely audible over a shaky connection. "The mortuary delivered the casket directly to American Airlines cargo."

"The funeral director, what's his name—"

"Mr. Gabriel."

"Right, he handle everything himself?" asked Montone.

"Yes. He rode out with me this morning. He's been enormously helpful."

"I'm glad to hear that. When's the flight?"

"About an hour."

"It look like I'm going to be flying down there myself later today."

"You'll call me? I'll be at my parents' place tonight."

"I'll definitely call."

A full silence followed.

"I felt good about our talk last night," she said. "I'm glad you confided in me, James. About you and Holly."

"Hmm."

"What?"

"Sounds funny. Nobody ever calls me James anymore."

"You mind if I do?"

"No, not at all," said Montone. "I'm glad we talked, too. Erin, you may see some things on the news, or maybe in the papers about me, the next day or so. I want you to know there's a reason for all of it. And I'll explain as soon as I can."

"I trust you—" she said.

The call cut off.

The first tabloid headlines about Montone's relationship with Holly ("TOP COP 'UNDERCOVERS' WITH DEAD MODEL") were already hitting the newsstands that afternoon when he reached the Delta terminal at Kennedy. Once he saw the story he kept his dark glasses on, hoping no citizens would recognize him from the photographs accompanying the story. At least the clerk at the counter didn't seem to take any undue notice of him. Montone had booked his reservation to Miami under Murphy's name and paid with cash.

Just as his flight began to board he noticed an overweight photographer wearing a brace of cameras around his neck pass through the security area; paparazzi were commonplace at the airport, but the personal statement Dan Jakes had read for Montone at the press conference a few hours earlier suggested he might be going out of town. It occurred to him that this time *he* might be a target.

Montone watched the photographer waddle down the concourse, scrutinizing the travelers waiting at every gate. When the man headed toward the gate for Miami, Montone stood up and moved to a nearby pay phone kiosk, leaning behind the privacy partition while he pretended to place a call. Out of the corner of his eye he sensed the photographer notice him and move in to investigate.

Montone leaned forward, holding the phone. Moments later he saw beneath the opposite side of the kiosk the photographer's shoes—

lime-green, mildly orthopedic—and half expected to hear the snap of the lens as the man confronted him.

Another pair of shoes appeared beside the photographer's. Montone heard a familiar voice.

"We've met before, haven't we? Your name Andy?"

Keyes.

"Andre," said the photographer.

"Right, Andre, I think you took my picture a couple weeks back. Outside the Harley Davidson Cafe? Terry Keyes, the novelist. I was with Elle MacPherson, some other people."

"Yeah, sure, Terry."

"Look, I'm catching a flight to LA in about twenty minutes at the end of the concourse. I don't know if you're interested but this cop they just suspended is on the same flight with me. I'm supposed to meet him at the gate."

"Jimmy Montone?"

"He's a friend. I'm sure he'd be happy to give you a shot if you asked him politely. Gate forty-two B. "

"That's a good lead, thanks."

"No problem. See you there."

The photographer hustled away, cameras clattering. Montone hung up the phone as Keyes came around the kiosk, holding up a copy of the *Post* with Montone's picture on the front page.

"Thanks," said Montone.

"You're a marked man, buddy."

"I was hoping to get out of town before this caught up with me."

"I'm afraid your cover is, as they say, blown. Fucking beasts. I had one in England that used to camp on my doorstep."

"How do these people sleep at night?"

"Hanging from the ceiling like bats. We better get on board before he doubles back."

"They haven't called my row yet."

Keyes produced two first-class tickets from his pocket. "I took the liberty. My treat."

"I can't let you do that."

"Of course you can, it's the least I can do. According to this impeccable journalistic source, they've taken away your paycheck, my friend."

"If it's in the *Post* it must be true."

"Then I hope you won't put up a fight if I take care of the hotel, either. I've already made the reservations."

"I hadn't even thought that far ahead," said Montone, as they walked toward the jetway. "I just wanted to get the hell out of Dodge. I barely had time to pack."

"Fabulous place, right on the water in South Beach. Friend of mine owns the place."

"You've been to Miami before?"

"On my book tour, last fall. You?"

"Never been."

"Nowhere else like it in the Western world."

They took their seats in first class, the first time Montone had ever flown this close to the nose of the plane. Montone sat by the window. A flight attendant offered champagne and orange juice as the plane rolled back from the gate.

"Erin gone down herself yet?" asked Keyes softly, the *Post* spread out on the seat-back table in front of him.

"This morning. She called me from the airport."

Keyes raised an eyebrow. "Did she see the papers?"

"I told her about this yesterday."

"You never told *me* you slept with her, Jimmy."

"Was I under some kind of obligation?" asked Montone, clamping down on the rage that leaped up inside him.

"Of course not. I'm just surprised, that's all."

"Why is that?"

"I thought something as personal as this you might have confided in me."

Montone felt a hot pulse of anger in his chest. "Never had the chance, did I?"

"Of course not. I'm not judging you, Jimmy. Everything happened so quickly. I'm sure I would have done exactly the same."

"What, sleeping with her or not telling anyone about it?"

"Since you asked, both most likely. No offense, old boy. What man wouldn't have responded to a girl as beautiful as Holly? You're only human, like the rest of us."

Not like you.

Montone ached to take him apart, right there in his seat. Shatter his smarmy complacency. Knock his teeth down the back of his throat. He called on every reserve of control he possessed to contain himself.

"Let's talk about something else," he said.

"Sure. I'm sorry if I upset you."

Montone sat back, put his dark glasses on and closed his eyes as the plane began to taxi for takeoff.

Could he do this? Keyes knew exactly what buttons to push. Could he maintain this front without strangling the son of a bitch?

He had to.

No way to tell how much he knows that I know.

Don't show him anything.

Once they were in the air Montone took Keyes's book from his carry-on and began to read. He noticed Keyes glancing over at the jacket and could sense he was dying to ask for his reaction. Montone gave him no opening and kept his nose buried in the book.

He could push a few buttons too.

When the seat belt sign blinked off Keyes got up to use the bathroom. Montone glanced over and noticed that he'd left his travel bag, an expensive saddle leather satchel, open under the seat. Montone could see the top of a matching kit bag resting inside.

He waited until Keyes entered the lavatory by the cockpit entrance, two rows in front of their seats. He set the book down casually reached over and rummaged through Keyes's satchel; two airplane paperbacks, a change of clothes, a laptop computer. He unzipped the kit bag, spotting nothing out of the ordinary.

As he replaced it he noticed a stack of files at the bottom of the bag; the tab on one of them read "MONTONE."

He heard the lavatory door open ahead of him, stayed low and swung over to his own bag as Keyes came back to his seat.

"Looking for something?" he asked.

"Aspirin. Got a headache."

"Here, I've got something."

Keyes reached into his bag and produced two Advil from his kit bag. Montone washed them down with the last of his orange juice, sat back and closed his eyes.

"How's the book coming?" asked Montone.

"With all that's been going on? I've hardly had a moment to work on it."

"Probably a lot more about murder than you actually wanted to know."

"To be honest, Jimmy, right now I think it's still too painful to write about."

"That'll change with time. You're a professional."

"I like to think so."

Montone angled in his seat to face him. "What do you think is in this guy's mind, Terry? What's he after?"

"The killer?"

"You said you considered it part of your job to understand criminal behavior."

"True."

"You've probably run across a few psychopaths in your time. When you were inside."

"I'd say we've both known our share."

"So help me out here: Why's he doing these crimes?"

Keyes nodded, considering the question seriously. "This confession the newscaster made. I think that might be the key."

"How so?"

"We agree those were the killer's words, not the victim's."

"Absolutely."

"So with a great deal less effort, whoever killed him could have left a note or message at the scene claiming responsibility. In his own voice, explaining exactly what he'd done and why. But it was obviously critical to him that his victim appear to be making this 'confession' on his own."

"Why?"

Keyes paused thoughtfully. "If he's passing a judgment, he wanted the accused to acknowledge its legitimacy. A confession validates the charges made against him."

"Even if it's coerced?"

"That doesn't seem to matter. Apparently he's trying to say something that he deeply believes."

"Does he have to kill to do that?"

"Maybe. Maybe he needs to carry out this sentence, this punishment, for the act to feel complete. If he sees himself as judge and jury he might as well make himself executioner in the bargain. And I think his method, the crime itself—his medium, if you will— allows him to reach a larger audience. Its shock value helps spread the word."

"Maybe that's why he's chosen these high-profile people."

"If he kills John Q. Citizen, why should the media pay any attention? Graveyards are full of nobodies."

"So he wants publicity for his message. Whatever that may be."

"Perhaps you ought to consider it at face value. That he means exactly what he says." Keyes turned to him and lowered his voice. "I hadn't asked. Did you find anything similar with Holly?"

"You mean a confession?"

"Whatever you want to call it."

"Yes."

Keyes nodded sagely. "This makes some sense, then. Similar kind of tone?"

"I can't go into specifics."

"I understand. Withholding details again."

"Right."

"But still, you're off the case, aren't you?"

"Doesn't change the rules."

"Fine. Let's presume for the moment that the message he coerced from Holly ran along the same things, some sort of social critique couched as a personal confession—don't feel obligated to confirm or deny that, I'm just speculating."

"Okay."

"If the killer follows the same pattern—and from what I understand about these sorts of crimes, they almost always do—he'll find a way to get her words, his message, to the public."

"Because . . ."

"That's why he's doing it, Jimmy."

"The publicity."

"Not for him. To express his point of view."

"And that is . . ."

"I couldn't begin to tell you without hearing Holly's tape."

Yes. Got you.

Montone worked hard to look confused. "Did I say it was a tape?"

"Didn't you?"

"I don't think I did."

"Anyway, I just assumed. What with the last one."

"You didn't hear it from me."

"No, well, a written confession just wouldn't have the same impact as the victim's own voice, would it? Just an assumption. As I said, these things tend to follow the established pattern."

Keyes looked right into his eyes, smooth, unblinking.

Montone held the look. "You think this guy's crazy?"

"Not really my area."

"What's your gut tell you?"

Keyes paused, as if thinking it through. "No. He's not crazy."

"Is he finished?" asked Montone.

"What do *you* think?"

"If he's sane I think he could stop and walk away at any time."

"Do you think he will?"

"No."

"Why?"

"He likes it too much. I don't think it has anything to do with passing judgments or getting a message to people. I think he likes to create fear in people and I think he likes to kill. That's the pattern I see. Doesn't matter why. He's a sick fuck who's not going to stop until somebody puts a bullet in him."

Keyes paused, as if considering the idea for the first time. "Perhaps you're right."

"It's *my* area of expertise."

"Shame you won't have a chance to catch him."

"Those are the breaks."

"Maybe they'll come to their senses. Reinstate you."

"I'm not holding my breath."

"You really believe that?"

"You don't know the department."

They rode in silence for a while.

"Really no need for you to be back in New York now for a while, is there?" asked Keyes.

"I guess not."

"With all due consideration to the fact that we're on our way to a funeral, maybe we should stay down here when it's over, spend some time, try to put this behind us."

"I'm open."

"Good. Because I don't think we should let anything get in the way of our enjoying ourselves," said Keyes.

Montone looked at him and smiled. "I'm not going to let anything get in the way of that."

Tropical heat drenched their shirts the minute they walked out of the terminal. The heavy air smelled like a greenhouse built in a sauna. A candy apple sunset painted the western sky behind them as their cab angled onto the Miami Expressway. The city looked strange to Montone's eye, a foreign landscape, low, sprawling, decayed by sun and sea, punctuated with palms.

The tail car picked them up as they left the airport.

Night had fallen by the time they reached Collins Avenue in South Beach, a narrow strip of commerce across the causeway from Miami proper. A riot of neon lit up the parade of pastel deco hotels, rescued from ruin, reborn as a hedonistic playground.

The cab dropped them at the Delano, a deluxe trendsetter's flagship in the heart of the district. The help, inside and out, dressed in severe white unisex uniforms. The guests prowling the lobby all looked like millionaires. Keyes, dressed impeccably, casual and cool, seemed right at home. In his crumpled black New York suit, Montone felt like a monkey at the Oscars.

The bellperson, a tall, tan Swedish girl with a buzz cut, showed them to adjacent quarters on the eighth floor. Everything in the room—furniture, wall treatments, curtains, linens, even the television sets—was done in pristine white. The only patch of color was a single green apple resting on a small silver shelf by the door.

After they'd unpacked Keyes invited Montone over to his room, a spacious suite, decorated in the same monchromatic white. A narrow balcony overlooked the hotel's pool and, beyond it, the beach. Colored spotlights splashed garish accents across the sand. A heavy bass beat throbbed from somewhere nearby.

"Feels like a party's about to start," said Montone.

"It's like that every night down here," said Keyes. "The party never ends."

They made plans to meet for dinner in an hour. Keyes headed down for a swim. Montone went back to his room and waited for a call that came five minutes later.

"Where are you?" he asked.

He received directions, took a file out of his suitcase, locked the room and rode the elevator to the lobby. He walked to the entrance to the cabanas and made certain that Keyes was still in the pool before exiting the front of the Delano.

Crossing Collins Avenue, he entered the Imperial, a smaller, more modest deco hotel directly opposite the Delano, walked up the stairs two floors and knocked on the door of room 312.

Mike Murphy, in shirtsleeves, eating a fat sandwich, answered the door.

"Sorry, Jimmy, we couldn't set up until we knew where you was gonna check in," said Murphy.

"I didn't know until we got there. How's your flight?"

"We beat you by an hour. Your fuckin' cabbie nearly lost us coming across that bridge. Good thing Frankie knows the area."

"How we doing?"

"Just getting started. Talking to the locals."

Pat Feany waved, holding a phone near a streetside window, looking over at the Delano.

"Where is Frankie?"

"Downstairs with two guys from Metro-Dade, they're setting up the tag teams."

"I got Hank at the squad," said Feany. "You want him to work anything?"

"Keyes says he's been here before. Have Hank run a check with his publishers in New York," said Montone. "Get an itinerary for his book tour last fall. We want to know every move he made, everywhere he ate, everywhere he stayed and for how long."

Feany relayed the message to Lopez.

"You made plans with him for tonight?" asked Murphy.

"So far only dinner."

"Teams'll be ready by then. Frankie's contracted in pretty good down here."

"You say that like it's a surprise." He handed Murphy the file he'd brought. "Hang on to this. It's Keyes's case file. I don't want it in my room where he might find it."

Montone took out his cellular and dialed the number Erin had given him. She answered on the second ring. He could hear voices in the background.

"We've got a bunch of people here," said Erin. "All the relatives from out of town."

"Should I call back?"

"It's going to be a pretty busy night. Let me give you the address of the church. It's in Coral Gables, not far the house. We're in Coconut Grove."

He wrote down the information.

"I'm glad you're here," she said.

"I'll see you tomorrow."

As he hung up he heard a soft knock at the door. Frank Fonseca entered with two officers from Metro-Dade PD.

"Jimmy Montone, this is Lieutenant Hector Galindez, Detective Lee Bower," said Fonseca, in his boyishly earnest way.

Galindez, a stout, jovial middle-aged Cuban, dark circles under sleepy brown eyes, Jimmy liked immediately. Bower was the junior partner, thin and pockmarked, a background guy.

"First thing is we got to get you some new clothes," said Galindez. "That suit's going to fucking kill you."

"Frankie says you're the man down here, Hector."

"I love this kid," said Galindez, laying a big affectionate hand on Frankie's neck. "We got some good history, did he tell you? Collared up a gang of high-end Cali cowboys in East Harlem two years ago. Frankie was our NYPD liaison. Beautiful bust."

"Caught a couple breaks," said Fonseca.

"He didn't tell me," said Montone.

"As you know, Frankie's too modest. With his help this whole operation opened like the petals of a lotus. We made him our honorary cousin."

"That's why we call him the king of contracts," said Murphy.

Fonseca, looking bashful, almost blushed.

"Appreciate you ramping up on this so quickly, Lieutenant," said Montone.

"Call me Hector. This is the modern world, my friend; inter-departmental policing is the wave of the future. This territorial bullshit is an evolutionary throwback."

"That's an enlightened postion, Hector."

"Do you think so? I've been reading these books by Deepak Chopra. Are you familiar with his work?"

"No."

"He is of the opinion that everything we see around us is made up of nothing but energy and information. So if I understand him correctly, what he's saying is that what we call reality is just a matter of how your consciousness interprets these wavelengths or particles or whatever the fuck they are."

"Keeping you up nights, is it?"

"I'm a fat, middle-aged Cuban policeman, so if I'm going to reach enlightenment I feel like I got to work pretty fast, you know what I'm saying?"

Galindez laughed infectiously.

"Teams are ready to roll, Jimmy," said Frankie.

"I'm giving you six of my best pistoleros. Two shifts, three men apiece," said Galindez. "Pair 'em up with your guys or use them separate, that's your call. We supply cars, radios, fax machine, whatever else you need."

"You think your boy'll make a move while he's here?" asked Bower.

"We'll be ready if he does."

"Feds interested in this guy?" asked Galindez.

"So far everything he's done is strictly local."

"Good. Who needs those limp dicks hanging around?" said Galindez. "You take him out to dinner we'll toss his room. I got this beautiful new bug we can stick in there that's so sensitive it'll pick up what this *hijo de puta* is thinking."

"You get a judge to write that up?"

"We don't need a judge for this, Jimmy, we already got a bellboy," said Galindez, lighting a big cigar. "You want to wear a wire?"

"Not yet. Maybe later."

"How long's he planning to stay?" asked Bower.

"I'm playing it loose with him. He thinks I'm on suspension. We'll see after the funeral tomorrow."

"He killed that beautiful girl?" asked Galindez.

"Yes."

"She was one of ours, you know. Went to high school here. They put her picture in the papers. Just for that I'm going to work this case with you myself. You say the word we'll send a charge through this guy. I'd like to beat his fucking contemptible face in."

"Frankie told me I was gonna like you," said Montone.

"Why would Frankie lie?" asked Galindez, handing over a couple of thick cigars. "Have a Macanudo. Best cigar you'll ever smoke. Take one for your friend across the street. He lights this up we'll smell him for a fucking mile."

After his swim, Keyes had exited out the back of the Delano Hotel pool area onto the oceanfront, as if to take a turn on the beach. He walked two blocks south to a small residential hotel called the Beachcomber and let himself into the second-floor apartment he'd rented the previous fall in the name of J. Thomas Sylvester. The landlord hadn't seen his new tenant since, but since Mr. Sylvester was a businessman who traveled extensively out of the country, he hadn't given the matter a second thought. Six months of rent in advance, no mail received and no questions asked bought a lot of cooperation.

Keyes removed the false ceiling panel he'd installed above the kitchen. He pulled down a black duffel bag that held the equipment for the Miami phase of the Plan he'd purchased during his November book tour visit. He assembled the components of the device he had designed, making certain that every part was in working order before carefully replacing the bag and walking back to the Delano.

None of the other residents saw him enter or leave Mr. Sylvester's apartment; the Beachcomber was one of the last buildings on the oceanfront that still catered to elderly retirees, and Keyes knew that most of them were shut-ins.

Montone was back in his room, and changed into his lighter-weight suit, by the time Keyes knocked on his door. Clean-shaven, hair slicked back, wearing a light citrus cologne, a black and pink flamingo silk shirt and white linen trousers, Keyes looked like a Miami native.

"That suit looks a little more sensible," said Keyes.

"Nobody wears a tie down here," said Montone, as they walked to the elevator.

"We should carve out some time to take you shopping. You want to feel relaxed, you have to look relaxed."

The two men caught a taxi in front of the hotel. Montone spotted one of Galindez's men waiting in a parked car at the end of the drive. As the cab made the turn onto Collins the detective reached for his radio.

The first team, Fonseca partnered with Galindez, tailed the cab to Joe's Stone Crab at the south end of the beach. The second team, the other two plainclothesmen from Metro-Dade, took over and parked across the street while Keyes and Montone were waiting for a table.

Joe's Stone Crab did not accept reservations but after a few words with the girl at the door who seemed to recognize Keyes, they were seated at a prime table near a window. The waitress set down a couple of beers in frosted mugs, and two platters of cracked crab quickly arrived.

"You given any thought to what you're going to do if the department doesn't want you back, Jimmy?"

"I'll worry about that when I have to."

"I hope it doesn't come to that. But it seems to me you have a choice here, too."

"You mean walk away?"

"Let me give you my perspective: This is the thanks you get for the twelve years you put in? Wounded in action. Putting your life on the line every day. And here you were, trying to help somebody in trouble, and this just landed on you? I'll tell you what they can't do; they can't fault your intentions." Keyes slammed a crab shell with the wooden mallet on the table and picked out the meat with his fingers. "You ask me, their whole attitude toward you stinks."

"What else would I do?"

"I've been giving that some thought. You've got some phenomenal material, Jimmy, all the cases you've worked on. I understand you feel a certain loyalty but it all happened to you, the NYPD doesn't own any copyright on your experience. You've already got a high profile, plus there's the way you present yourself. In crass commercial terms, my friend, you are definitely marketable."

"You mean write a book?"

"A book, a movie, maybe even a television series. Why limit your-self? You'll never know unless you give it a shot."

"I wouldn't know where to start."

"You could start by asking me. I'll help you any way I can. Set up some meetings. Introduce you to agents, publishers. Scouts from the movie studios are always sniffing around for good stories."

"Doesn't sound like me."

"Don't you want to leave something behind for people to remember you by, Jimmy?"

"Is that what *you* want?"

"That's what everybody wants. A little slice of immortality. Your gift to the people who come after us. Something you've accomplished that no one else could have done."

"I'm not anybody special. I'm just a cop."

Keyes paused thoughtfully. "Don't misunderstand, I'm not trying to push you somewhere you don't want to go. I'm just putting it out there. You might lose your job and there's money to be made here, if nothing else. And I want you to know that if there's anything I can do for you all you have to do is ask."

"Let me think about it."

"I hope you do. I'll try to come up with some names for you. The offer stands."

Montone studied Keyes across the table. Grinning, eager to help, wearing one of those goofy lobster bibs, up to his elbows in crabmeat and butter. The best friend you could ever ask for.

They took a walk along the beach after dinner and smoked the fine cigars Galindez had given him. Without looking for them, Montone felt the surveillance team watching from the darkness. He wondered if Keyes felt them too.

"What time is the funeral?"

"Church services are at ten," said Montone. "I've got the address back at the room."

"The sister seems awfully bright, doesn't she?"

"She's a professor. Syracuse University."

"Handling it all right?"

"Seems pretty tough. I knew her from before."

"Is that right?"

"She wrote about the Slug a few years back. Interviewed me at the time."

"Isn't that a coincidence?"

Is it? Montone wondered.

If he could find the answer to that question the mystery of Terry Keyes might solve itself.

"You aren't familiar with her work?" asked Montone.

"I didn't know a thing about her."

"She wrote a book called *Criminal Intent*. A study of the criminal mind. Right up your alley."

"Really? What's her point of view?"

"Every crime is a choice. No excuses, no explanations. Every criminal makes the decision to turn that way for themself."

"Positively Darwinian. I'll have to pick up a copy."

Montone watched him as they walked in the semidarkness. Found his expression impossible to read.

"Up for a longer evening, Jimmy?"

"What'd you have in mind?"

"This city doesn't even wake up till after eleven. Whatever you want. Show you a few places."

"Maybe tomorrow. Long day."

"Think I'll stay out awhile. Savor the sea air. Finish this excellent smoke."

They agreed to meet in the hotel lobby the next morning at nine. Keyes continued strolling along the beach. Montone waved down a cab and took the short ride back to the hotel.

When he got to his room Montone called Murphy at the Imperial Hotel across the street.

"First team's still got him," said Murphy, holding the phone in one hand and a walkie-talkie in the other. "He's on foot. Heading up the beach toward the club district."

"Has he made the tail?"

"Frankie says no. They're switching off every few blocks. These local guys are good."

"Where's Pat?"

"He helped one of Hector's guys put the bug in Keyes's room. They're standing by in case we need 'em on the tail."

"Anything from the squad?"

"I just got off with Lopez. He spoke with Dr. Lee about Henshaw's autopsy. You were right; injection mark on the right hip was fresh. Just a second."

Montone heard Murphy say something into his radio, then he came back on the phone.

"He's gone into a club on Ocean Drive, about three blocks from the hotel. Both teams are on it."

"Tell 'em I'm coming down."

"Just a second." Murphy spoke into the radio again. "Club is called Papillon. Frankie's across the street, the Palm Cafe, Five-ten Ocean. Stay on your radio, Jimmy."

"I've got it with me."

Montone strapped on his shoulder holster, grabbed his radio from under the mattress and tuned it to their talk channel. He left the hotel and walked the three blocks to the restaurant.

He found Fonseca and Hector Galindez in the Palm Cafe bar, under the arching canopy of an artificial rain forest. Both men nursed umbrella drinks, head to head, speaking rapid-fire Spanish, sitting by a window with an unobstructed view of Papillon, the nightclub across the street. Both men wore their radios concealed inside their jackets, a coiled wire feeding into discreet earpieces.

"He still inside?" asked Montone.

"Take a look," said Galindez. "My latest toy. Sharper Image. They sell better shit off the rack than the CIA."

Hector handed Montone a small steel tube no thicker than one of his cigars. He held an end fitted with a rubber gasket to his eye and discovered he was looking through a compact, powerful telescope. Pointing it at the opposite building, Montone pulled focus when he found Keyes's distinctive black and pink shirt.

Alone, standing perfectly still with his back to the picture window, Keyes held a glass of white wine in his hand, watching the crowded room. People all around him danced and swayed to a melody that didn't reach across the street; they heard only the muted pounding of a distant backbeat.

"Used to be a gay bar," said Galindez. "Of which I don't approve because I'm Catholic and as a man in Cuban culture we don't go for that, right? Except my wife's brother, he was inclined that way and he dies of that disease which shouldn't happen to a fucking dog and since my spiritual studies I'm definitely more open-minded. But I mean, still, you have to wonder, what were these boys thinking, that taking it up the ass twenty times a night would be good for them?"

"There's a lot of women in there too," said Montone.

"This is South Beach, my friend: the *maricones* start the hottest dance clubs, word gets around and pretty soon they're letting all the riffraff in. Success spoils everything."

"He talk to anybody?" asked Montone.

"Not a soul."

"You want a drink, Jimmy?" asked Fonseca.

"O'Doul's."

Frankie moved off to the crowded bar.

"You send the other team inside?"

"Look to the right," said Galindez. "Under the neon butterfly."

Montone swung the tube over and irised in on the two Metro-Dade plainclothes detectives standing by the bar, bathed in the red glow of the neon.

"Say *buenas noches* to Detective Montone, Raul," said Galindez into the microphone concealed in his sleeve.

One of the officers at the bar glanced out the window toward their position and slightly raised his glass.

"You were in love with this girl," said Galindez.

Montone lowered the viewer and looked at him.

"Frankie tell you that?"

"He didn't have to."

"You don't even know me."

"Tell me and I'll mind my own fucking business. I don't mean to make you uncomfortable. "

Montone considered. "Maybe I was. I never had the chance to find out. What difference does it make?"

Galindez shrugged expressively. "Maybe you feel personally responsible."

"This part of your spiritual studies, Hector? More advice from Six-pack Porkchop?"

"Deepak Chopra. He's Indian. As in a from-India Indian. Very spiritual culture."

"Whatever."

Galindez smiled at him sadly. "He writes that one of the most important spiritual disciplines, if I understand this correctly, not that I'm any expert, is to practice detachment in all things. To observe the world around us and not react."

"Meaning?"

"If you'll forgive the observation. If this *comemierda* in his fancy fucking shirt is as smart as you say he is, and you let yourself get caught up in what he did to her, a moment's going to come when that's all the distraction he'll need to take you out."

"I know that."

"I know you *know* it. My question is, can you *do* it? I'm not asking for an answer. I'm just asking."

Montone could detect no malice or challenge in Galindez's attitude and backed away from his defensive response.

"Fine. You made your point."

Galindez looked over toward Keyes again. "You read this guy's books?"

"Enough of them."

"They give you anything that helps us?"

"He doesn't give anything up. They were performances, designed to get him out of prison. He says he did the crime that put him inside, but you're supposed to come away thinking it's not his fault."

"Let me guess: society?"

"Cops, doctors, lawyers, the media. The victim, naturally, she never should have been there in the first place. And his friend who put him up to it."

"*Coño.* And for this they put him on television. What is this fucking world coming to?"

Galindez shook his head sadly.

"There's a lot of options here, Jimmy. If you want a confession from this *hijo de puta* we could marinate him in a holding tank for a few days with some flavorful pieces of meat. He'll be popping party favors out his ass for a week."

"He did twelve years. Lockup won't put a dent in him."

"Fuck it, then. He's not a citizen. We'll just take him off the street and beat it out of him."

"Not very enlightened, Hector."

"A stone-fucking killer like this? Who gives a shit? We should just make him disappear. This is Miami, man. Stick him in a rental car out by the airport, let the homeboys take care of him. By morning he's a fucking statistic."

Fonseca returned with Montone's drink. Galindez put a hand to his earpiece.

"He's moving," said Galindez.

Montone looked through the viewing tube again and picked up Keyes walking directly across the dance floor toward the two detectives. One of them turned away, the other glanced briefly out the window toward their position, as if looking for advice.

Fonseca pulled his radio and unplugged the earpiece so Montone could hear the transmission.

"Would you care to dance?" said Terry Keyes.

"Me? No thanks," said the detective.

Keyes smiled, turned and walked slowly back to his position by the window.

"What is he, a *puto?*"

"They're burned," said Montone.

"Maybe he just wanted to dance," said Galindez.

"He made them."

"Cabrón," said Galindez, the sense of who they were up against dawning on him. "So he likes to play games."

Keyes lingered another hour in the Papillon bar, ordered one more glass of wine and spoke to no one else. After fifteen minutes had passed, Galindez ordered the detectives to exit separately and called in the third team to stand by outside.

When Keyes finally left the club shortly after midnight, Montone hustled out of the rear of the Palm Cafe, making certain that he made it back to his hotel room before Keyes did. Galindez fed him updates over the radio of Keyes's whereabouts; walking slowly along the beach like a tourist without a care in the world.

Montone waited until he heard Keyes unlock the door to his room before switching off his radio for the night. He put a glass against the common wall between the rooms and listened to Keyes use the bathroom, heard water running in the sink, then the drone of the television set.

Montone flipped on his own television to cover the sound, then checked in with the nerve center at the Imperial by phone at one o'clock, whispering so his voice wouldn't carry.

"Bug's working great," said Feany. "He's watching HBO. We can't get that over here."

"He make any calls?"

"No. Elevators and stairs are covered. Looks like he's buttoned up for the night, but if he makes a move we'll call you."

"Use the radio, he might hear the phone."

"Get some sleep, Jimmy."

Montone crawled into bed at two, turned off the lights and listened as the murmur of the television next door blended with the ocean outside until he drifted into dreamless sleep.

Keyes sat waiting for him in the hotel dining room at nine, wearing an appropriately funereal suit. They ate a quiet breakfast, then took a cab to an old Spanish-style Congregational church in Coral Gables. The day shift team of Metro-Dade detectives followed at a distance; Montone had already given them their destination.

A crowd of over five hundred people gathered for Holly's memorial service. Montone and Keyes found themselves seated among a group of her high school friends. Montone wondered if any of these people recognized him from the sensational news stories that had followed him to Miami. If they did no one made a point of letting him know it.

He spotted Erin in the front pew between her parents, both of them well into their seventies, frail and somber. Her father slumped in a wheelchair parked in the aisle next to Erin, breathing with the help of an oxygen tank.

Erin addressed the assembly first with a loving tribute to Holly, impressively maintaining her composure while still conveying powerful emotions, before a moving eulogy was delivered by the minister. Montone steeled himself not to shed a tear. He couldn't bear the thought of

Keyes watching him give expression to the anguish he felt. Keyes, under no such restrictions, wept freely throughout the service.

A long procession, with police escort, led to the cemetery, where an orderly sea of black limousines formed outside the gates. The graveside ceremony was mercifully brief; the grieving open and widespread. As the last words of the service were spoken a cooling breeze rustled the overhead palms, cutting the oppressive humidity. Concealed speakers played a recording of Louis Armstrong's "What a Wonderful World." Muffled sobs issued from throughout the crowd.

When Holly's father, who had appeared stunned and disbelieving all morning, struggled to rise from his wheelchair and place a single white rose on his daughter's casket before it was interred, even Montone could not hold back. He hadn't allowed himself to fully register her loss until this moment. As the casket descended into the grave he lowered his head, covered his face with his hands, and his body shook with emotion.

Keyes laid a hand on the back and Montone felt so bereft for a moment he almost accepted the comfort, until the thought of who was giving it snapped him instantly back to cold reality.

As the crowd wandered slowly back to their cars, Montone separated from Keyes and made his way to Erin, who was accepting condolences under a green canopy beside the grave. He stood at the end of the line, waiting to be alone with her.

She embraced him gratefully and even managed a smile, her strength all the more impressive as it carried, and didn't deny, the weight of the mourning.

"I don't know why," she said, looking at him with absolute honesty. "I'm as glad to see you here as anyone I've known all my life."

"Thanks."

They drew apart. She took him by the hand and led him a short distance away. She took off her dark glasses and looked at him frankly.

"Those stories about you and Holly in the newspapers. They're there for a reason, aren't they?"

Montone hesistated.

"You're supposed to level with me now, James. Isn't that what we agreed to?"

"Yes. Yes, they're there for a reason. The man who did this, I wanted him to think I'd lost my job."

Her gaze drifted past him and found Terry Keyes some distance away, standing alone among the graves, looking solemn.

She knows. Somehow she knows.

Montone saw it in her eyes.

"I brought his case file with me," he said. "I've written up everything we have. The pieces don't fit yet. I want you to take a look at it."

He glanced over his shoulder at Keyes, who was not looking at them, as a way to confirm her unspoken assertion.

"How quickly can you get it to me?" she asked.

"I'll bring it by tonight."

"I gave you my parents' address, didn't I? In Coconut Grove?"

"Yes."

"People will be stopping by the house all day. Come whenever you can. But don't bring that man with you."

Montone nodded. They understood each other perfectly.

"Come meet our folks, James."

Erin took his hand again and walked him over to where her parents were sitting under the green canopy. She waited for an elderly couple to leave before introducing him.

"Mom, Dad, this is James Montone," she said, raising her voice; at least one of them was hard of hearing. "He's a good friend of Holly's from New York."

The father's grip felt surprisingly strong and he looked Montone straight in the eye. "You're the detective."

"Yes sir."

"You gonna find who did this to our little girl?" he asked, his thin voice husky with emotion.

The mother began to gently weep.

"Yes sir, I am."

They rode back to the hotel without speaking a word. Once, when Montone leaned forward, Keyes laid a hand on his shoulder again, a show of support. His touch felt like an dagger of ice but Montone fought the impulse to shake it off.

"Instead of honoring the natural gifts I was given, I have allowed my beauty to be used . . . by an industry built on deception and the exploitation of women's emotional vulnerability ... I've sold my physical gifts to the highest bidder ... like a common whore."

He intially thought he was hallucinating but it slowly dawned on Montone that he was hearing Holly's voice, issuing faintly from the cab's radio, tuned to an all-news station.

A reporter's overamped voice broke into the recording. "The shocking tape recording arrived this morning by mail at a New York radio station. We'll have more on this story as it becomes available—"

Keyes leaped aggressively forward at the driver. "Turn it off. Turn it the *fuck* off."

The flustered cabbie switched off the radio.

Montone couldn't speak. As they rode on in silence, a volcanic rage twisted up inside him with noplace to go.

"Good God," said Keyes, staring grimly out the window of the cab. "Terrible."

A few blocks before they reached the Delano, Montone barked at the driver.

"Stop the car. Stop, right now!"

"You all right, Jimmy?"

Montone didn't answer until the cab pulled over and he climbed out.

"I need to be alone."

"You don't have to explain—"

Montone slammed the door and started walking.

"Take all the time you need, buddy," said Keyes, as the cab drove on. "I'll be at the hotel. I'm there if you need me."

Montone headed for the beach, eyes fixed, unseeing. He needed desperately to get away; one more consoling gesture from Keyes and he wouldn't have been able to stop himself from crushing the man's throat with his bare hands.

Detachment.

Galindez was right. He needed it more than air right now. He was too close. It mattered too much. For the first time in twelve years on the job, the first time in his life, he came close to giving up, dropping the entire operation without a word to anyone, cabbing straight to the airport, flying out of this miserable hothouse.

Anywhere away from this monster.

Montone walked for blocks, up and across the beach to the lee-ward edge of the bay, without regard for direction, waiting for the fury to let go of his gut.

He tried to talk his way through it.

This is what he wants you to feel.

This is how he wins.

This is why he does it. The anwer is in here.

Keep grinding: do not give in to him.

The grip of his anger finally loosened as he sought refuge in a flood of memories of Holly; the curve of her neck, her long graceful hands. Fragments of her voice, the sweet immediacy of her fading already, losing texture and shape. This after only days; what would he be left with months or years from now?

Not enough time. Not enough time to know how much she might have meant.

What was stolen from him.

What he did to her.

She isn't coming back.

"How could I let this happen?" he whispered to himself. "How could I let him get this close?"

Another wave of grief overwhelmed him and he squatted in an alleyway like a beggar, ashamed to show his face.

A kinder voice came into his mind. He was reminded of Erin's cool thoughtfulness.

This is how it's supposed to feel. If you keep this much pain locked up inside it'll kill you, too.

Remember what happened the last time.

When the feelings passed he found his way back to the security of facts: a stigma of uncertainty still lingered around Holly's death. He'd sensed it from these decent churchgoing people at the funeral, unspoken but still vivid. Suicide remained a cardinal sin and, in the absence of any other knowledge, they suspected her of it.

That demanded answering. He owed her that much.

The tears on her mother's feathery cheek, the delicate weight of her father's hand in his.

The promise he'd made them.

When his vision cleared and his thoughts ran cold and clear again, he found himself a mile from the hotel, his shirt, his black suit soaked in sweat. He pulled off the coat and tie and called the Imperial from the next pay phone he found.

"Is he tailing me?"

"He's sitting by the pool," said Murphy. "Drinking a piña colada. Slapping on sunscreen."

"He make any calls?"

"No. He's reading *Vanity Fair.*"

"I'm heading back to you."

"You okay, Jimmy?"

"You don't want to know."

Montone hung up the phone.

Terry Keyes left the hotel for an hour and half in the afternoon and the Metro-Dade teams tracked him. He walked to a nearby cluster of upscale shops in South Beach, bought a bright yellow Byblos silk shirt, a teal-colored Florida Marlins baseball cap, then sat in an ice cream parlor and ate a bowl of frozen yogurt.

He used a pay telephone to place a call the detectives were not able to overhear, making an appointment to see a prominent Miami defense attorney in his downtown office at nine o'clock the following morning. During a second call he confirmed a long-standing appointment for an interview at the hotel with a German television crew, also for tomorrow morning.

On his way back to the hotel he stopped in an old-fashioned neighborhood barbershop for a shave and a trim. He called Montone's room twice when he returned, then read through a stack of newspapers and watched television in his room.

Working from their suite at the Imperial, the detectives spent the better part of the afternoon on the phone with Hank Lopez back in the New York squad room. Lopez had learned that Holly's suicide tape arrived in a package identical to the one that had held Mackenzie Dennis's video; similar handwriting, no return address, no prints, postmarked the day before. Montone concluded Keyes must have mailed it from midtown just before leaving for the airport.

And as in the previous instance, radio station executives had felt no obligation to notify the police before spreading Holly's torment indiscriminately across the airwaves. Their only show of restraint: cutting off the broadcast before she actually began to strangle.

At three o'clock the information Montone had requested from Lopez about Keyes's American book tour came over the fax line. Keyes had stayed at the Delano for five days last November before moving on to Atlanta. Montone asked Galindez and the Metro-Dade officers to canvas local banks and businesses in a six-block radius around the hotel to see if he'd made any purchases, opened any accounts.

At four they received the results of toxicology tests from Peter Henshaw's autopsy, confirming Montone's suspicions; Dr. Lee had discovered massive amounts of adrenaline in the tissue surrounding the injection mark on Henshaw's hip. That should be enough to perk up the DA's attention.

Montone crossed the street at five o'clock and knocked on Keyes's hotel room door.

"There you are. I was starting to worry about you," said Keyes.

"I'm all right. I must have walked about five miles."

"Probably the best thing for you."

"So I'm down in the lobby just now, trying to buy some toothpaste." Montone held up a small bag. "Twelve bucks for some Swedish crap you can't even read the label. They ever hear of Colgate?"

"The cost of catering to all these terminally hip Eurotrash. They don't feel special unless they pay eighty percent over retail."

"I need a drink."

Keyes opened the mini-bar, poured a Coke for himself, a vodka tonic for Montone. Montone carefully watched him handle the drink.

"Find out anything more on that tape?" asked Keyes.

"Haven't spoken to anyone."

"That's bloody unbelievable, isn't it? Hearing her voice over the radio like that. Christ, it made my blood run cold."

"You were right, Terry. The words he's putting in their mouths is what's important to him. Who the victim actually is seems almost secondary."

"Except for their symbolic value. Representing the area of society he's criticizing. Bit of an anti-American theme emerging there, I think," said Keyes, opening the door to the balcony.

Keep talking, you son of a bitch.

"I meant to ask you; anything further on the witness who saw that car near the beach house?"

"You know what, Terry? I haven't heard a word about it and it's not my case anymore. I think you hit it right on the head; what you said about the department? Why should I knock myself out if this is how they thank me for it?"

"That's certainly how it seems to me."

They moved out to the balcony. Montone looked down at the pool area below and considered how easy it would be to throw Keyes over the edge. Concoct a story. Make it look like an accident.

But then you'd never know why, would you?

Montone set his drink down on the ledge and shoved his hands in his pockets. Keyes lay back on a wicker lounge and folded his arms behind his head.

"Do you feel like doing something tonight?" asked Keyes.

"I'm going to go see Erin," said Montone.

"Really?"

"She called, wanted to get together and have dinner. Maybe we could go out afterwards."

"Only if you're up to it."

"What about you, what are you going to do?"

"I don't know. Dinner. Maybe hit some clubs. Take in a movie. I'm easy. I'd like to take a few days and recover from all this, to be honest."

"I would too but got to be honest with you, I don't like it down here. Too fucking hot for me. I don't feel much like going back to New York just yet either."

"A man without a country."

"What's that supposed to mean?"

"No offense intended. You've just had all your familiar systems of support taken away. The job. Your colleagues. The city. Has to be a little unsettling."

"Sure, whatever."

Keyes locked his hands behind his head and considered the idea.

And that's just what you wanted me to feel, isn't it, Terry?

"I was actually giving that some thought this afternoon," said Keyes. "Identity. What makes a man what he is."

"Is it what he does or who he is?"

"Exactly. Which comes first? Which determines the other?"

"It's his nature," said Montone. "It's what's in his nature."

"But that's the hardest thing to know of all."

"Why is that?"

"It's hard enough for a man to know what's in his own heart. Let alone somebody else's."

"You think so?"

"Absolutely. But when a man comes to understand that about himself, he knows what's in every man. Intimate knowledge of his soul is the key to all other understanding."

Montone hesitated. "Something to think about."

He stood up and waited for Keyes to go ahead of him, suddenly reluctant to expose his back to the man.

The razor edge in his voice. That superior self-regard surfacing like the tip of an iceberg.

The answer was there, inside Keyes, tantalizingly close.

Montone changed clothes in his room and left the Delano. After checking in with Murphy on his radio and making sure that Keyes was still in his room, he doubled back and entered the back door of the Imperial across the street.

Feany let him into the nerve center. Murphy, Fonseca and two of the Metro-Dade guys were playing bridge by the window. Montone picked up the case file he'd left earlier, to take down to Erin.

"So what's up, Jimmy?" said Feany. "He going after somebody?"

"He set something up the last time he was here," said Montone. "It's like Henshaw said, whatever he does he's got it all worked out. And it's going down tonight."

One of the Metro-Dade detectives drove Montone down to Erin's parents' house in the upscale enclave of Coconut Grove. The detective waited in the car while Montone walked across a wide, open expanse of lawn to a rambling Spanish-style ranch house. The door stood open; visitors and well-wishers still filled the front rooms, grazing from an extensive buffet.

Erin spotted Montone across the crowd and led him back to her father's office in an isolated wing of the house. She turned on a brass desk lamp in the cool wooded room, put on a pair of reading glasses and opened the file he'd brought to show her.

Montone sat quietly while she read, looking at the titles in her father's library. He pictured Holly as a teenager curled up on this same couch, talking on the phone. He checked his pager to make sure it was on, glancing over at Erin, engrossed in study. He'd included everything they had; the crime scene analysis, the dossier on Keyes they'd received from London, even Dr. Lee's autopsy findings.

"Did you realize how similar your backgrounds are?" she asked without looking up.

"Whose?"

"Yours and Terry Keyes's. No father figure. Foster homes. History of juvenile delinquency."

"I hadn't really thought about it."

"My guess is that he's thought about it quite a lot," she said, taking off her glasses. "I'm trying to remember: Didn't you have some kind of scholarship to college?"

"Hockey. Small school upstate. You did your homework."

"He had a scholarship as well," she said. "Revoked after his arrest."

She sat still, gazing thoughtfully at the ceiling, then went back to the file.

"Jesus, his test scores were off the map."

"What are you getting at?" he asked.

"He'd turned his world completely around, just like you did. Not many kids make it back that far from where you were. The effort, the self-discipline that requires is enormous."

"Tell me about it."

"He was leaving for Cambridge the day they arrested him. His life was just about to begin; it's right there in his grasp, he can feel it. You remember your first day on campus?"

"Greatest day of my life."

"Only hours from fulfilling his dream and it's all stripped away from him. Dragged back down to where he started. Worse. Prison. Public humiliation. How cruel that must have seemed. Devastating."

"Henshaw thought he'd already committed these other murders."

"I suppose it's possible, but to be honest? I don't think so. Those were sex murders. He doesn't fit the profile. He'd lifted himself too far from absolute zero."

"What about the mother?"

"Maybe. That was years later, wasn't it? He changed inside, no question about that. Or maybe she actually killed herself."

"So what happened that night under the pier?"

"I think it's worth considering that his version of the story is true, James; that his friend, the athlete, had set him up with this girl, the model, and that it just somehow went horribly, tragically wrong. He was drunk, when she rejected him he overreacted, she fell and hit her head on the rocks. The policeman, Henshaw, happened to be nearby and saw what he wanted to see. The friend ran off, refused to testify, and when the bad publicity started, with all the television coverage the case took on a life of its own. He was socially stigmatized. Made a public example of, perhaps excessively or even unfairly. And it broke him."

Montone's beeper sounded. He phoned in on his cellular.

"He's on the move, Jimmy," said Fonseca. "Maybe you want to meet us?"

"Where?"

"Same place as last night; the Palm Cafe."

Montone ended the call.

"I need to go," he said.

"May I keep this?"

"Of course. I'll call you."

She showed him out a side entrance and he trotted back across the lawn to the car.

By eight o'clock the temperature had cooled to eighty-five. Rain was in the forecast. While Montone was on his way down to Erin the detectives watched a Marlins game on television. Hector Galindez arrived at the nerve center at nine with some spectacular takeout Cuban food and a collection of the filthiest jokes they'd ever heard.

They listened to Keyes order and eat a quiet room service dinner, heard him take a shower and dress, then heard the door close as he left the room.

Keyes walked out of the Delano at nine-thirty, turned left on Collins Avenue and headed south. He wore the shirt the detectives had watched him buy that afternoon, bright yellow silk adorned with palm trees filled with red and purple parrots, a pair of khaki pants, white tennis shoes without socks and the Marlins baseball cap. Around his waist was a black leather fanny pack.

The first team picked him up and followed him to a Latin dance club a few blocks south on Collins. He bought one glass of wine, spoke to no one but the bartender and watched the dance floor from a stool at the bar until shortly after ten.

The second team took over when he left. Keyes walked west to Ocean Avenue and as the first drops of rain began to fall he entered the dance club Papillon again.

Hearing that, Galindez and Fonseca left the Imperial and drove back to the Palm Cafe. Fonseca placed the call to Montone while they were still in the car.

The rain was coming down hard when they arrived at the restaurant. Galindez said a few words to the manager; he hustled a group of college kids out of the way and the detectives took the same table near the side window.

Keyes ordered a glass of wine and stood in the same spot he'd been in the previous evening, at the edge of the room with his back to the window. From their post across the street, his bright yellow shirt flared out through the rain like a traffic signal.

Galindez held both teams back in their cars parked outside of the club, covering both exits; no sense in sending them inside only to have Keyes burn them like he had the night before.

An hour passed. Montone joined them shortly after ten-thirty. He sat silently, lost in thought.

Across the way the club filled up rapidly, the heavy rain hustling traffic in off the sidewalks. Keyes didn't move.

"Papillon. That was a movie, wasn't it?" asked Fonseca.

"Steve McQueen," said Galindez. "He plays a prisoner who escapes from Devil's Island or some shit. And Dustin Hoffman plays this near-sighted accountant embezzler fuck with glasses like the bottom of a Coca-Cola bottle."

"Is his name Papillon?" asked Fonseca.

"No. McQueen is Papillon, but that's not his name either. It's his nickname because he has a tattoo of a butterfly on his ass or his elbow or somewhere."

"I think I saw it when I was a kid. He eats bugs or something," said Fonseca.

"Cockroaches. In solitary."

"He never escapes," said Montone. "He keeps getting caught."

"Which is some tragedy we're supposed to feel bad about? He was a fucking low-life *cara de culo*," said Galindez.

Fonseca laughed, but all further attempts at conversation at the Palm quickly stalled. Galindez attributed their difficulty to a new level of intensity in Montone but thought better than to comment on it. Montone never took his eye off the yellow shirt in the window across the street.

The thoughts Erin had started turned in his mind like tumblers in a lock.

The parallels between them.

The death of the girl changed everything. The utterly different directions their lives traveled from that moment forward.

At eleven-thirty the steady rain turned into a downpour, hammering on the roof. A humid film formed on the windows, obscuring the view between the buildings.

Keyes set down his glass and moved away from his place at the window. Montone followed him with the viewing tube through the crowd to a door on the far side of the dance floor.

"Bathroom," said Montone.

The girl on the beach was an artist's model.

Two minutes passed. Montone looked at his watch. Another minute. A line began to form outside the bathroom door.

"The door's locked," said Montone.

"Stand by," said Galindez into his microphone.

"You want to send somebody in?"

"There he is," said Fonseca.

Montone looked for the men's room door through the tube again but couldn't immediately find Keyes.

There, a flash of yellow and red as a gap opened on the crowded dance floor. Through the shifting bodies Montone spotted the birds on Keyes's back and the teal baseball cap as he returned to his position at the picture window.

Keyes ordered a second glass of wine from a circulating cocktail waitress and settled back to watch the dancers.

Keyes had told him: A television reporter from London picked up the story. A series of reports appeared on the national news.

Erin's phrase: socially stigmatized.

Broken. Changed inside.

Montone felt the tumblers falling into place.

The rain let up at eleven forty-five, then intensified again at midnight as another squall line passed through.

Keyes looked at his watch, set down his wineglass and headed straight for the club's front door.

"He's leaving," said Galindez.

Just as Keyes walked outside a cab pulled up at the entrance to let out three young women. They passed him and moved toward the club. Lowering his head to dodge the rain, Keyes dove right into the back of the cab and it quickly drove away.

"Carajo!"

"Let's go," said Montone.

"I'll get the car," said Fonseca, heading for the door.

"Both teams take the cab," said Galindez into his microphone. "We'll catch up with you."

As they waited in front of the restaurant for the car, Galindez put a hand to his earpiece and provided Montone with a steady report on Keyes's location.

"He's heading north on Collins. They've got him."

Fonseca pulled up in Galindez's black Cadillac Seville, then slid over as Hector took the wheel. Montone jumped in back. Galindez used the car radio to let the other teams know their location and left the channel open for updates.

"Cab's turning left," said the first team. "Heading for the Kennedy Causeway."

Galindez flipped on his running lights and accelerated around traffic on Collins, using both sides of the street, popping the siren briefly when he needed to open a lane.

"Turning right onto Ninety-five."

"Where's he going?" asked Montone.

"North," said Galindez.

Galindez negotiated a shortcut to reach the expressway and

jumped across to the speed lane. The speedometer never fell below eighty-five as they slalomed their way between the slower cars.

Holly was a model.

Mackenzie Dennis a television reporter.

"Crossing into Broward County."

I caught all the breaks you never got. I'm a cop. A cop put you away.

A cop ruined your life.

The answer opened to him.

The model.

The reporter.

Henshaw.

Me.

You're getting even with us, aren't you?

Within twenty minutes they caught up with the second pursuit car. The detectives waved them forward. Galindez tapped the gas until they pulled up next to the first car and could see the cab's brake lights six car lengths ahead of them.

"We'll take the lead," said Galindez over the radio.

The first car dropped back. Montone used a light from the glove compartment to examine a map.

"There's another airport up here," he said.

The cab passed the airport exit, then slid over into the right-hand lane. Its right-turn signal stayed on.

"Broward Boulevard," said Montone, reading the next exit on the map.

"He's going to Fort Lauderdale," said Galindez.

The cab took the exit and turned. right onto Broward. Galindez slipped into the flow of traffic two slots behind.

"What's up here?" asked Montone.

"He's driving toward the marina."

The cab turned right and then left onto Las Olas, a narrower street that led them through a quaint shopping district with residential neighborhoods branching off to either side. Suddenly they found themselves in the middle of a maze of man-made peninsulas and canals dredged from the bay. A series of bridges conveyed them to the edge of the Atlantic, where the road came to a halt.

The cab slowed, turned off the main road and drove out to the dead end of a long jetty, beside the shell of an abandoned restaurant. Galindez stopped back on the main road; the other two pursuit cars pulled up behind them.

The cab's brake lights came on, then an interior light. They saw the driver turn around and take money from Keyes.

Keyes got out of the cab, walked to the edge of the pier and stood looking out at the ocean.

The cab turned around and drove slowly back along the jetty. As it passed them, Galindez radioed the second team.

"Take the cab. Pull him over when it's out of sight."

The second car followed the cab.

Montone used the viewing tube to watch Keyes. He stood with his back to them, gazing out to sea.

Who else are you after? Who else ruined you, Terry?

The lawyer? The judge?

"What the fuck? He waiting for a boat?" asked Galindez.

A small cruiser came into view in the channel near the end of the jetty, approaching Keyes's position.

"He won't get far," said Galindez. "There's a coast guard station less than a mile from here."

Keyes didn't move. The boat passed right by him, backwash shifting the loose pilings surrounding the dock.

The psychologist?

Keyes turned around.

"It's not him," said Montone.

He handed the tube to Galindez, jumped out of the car and started running down the jetty, pulling out his gun. Fonseca hurried to back him up.

At an order from Galindez the first team's car sped onto the jetty and followed them.

"Police! Get on the ground!" yelled Montone as he approached. "Get on the ground!"

The man saw the two cops and the car speeding toward him and dropped to his knees, raising his hands in the air.

Montone reached the man, grabbed him by the back of the shirt and shoved him the rest of the way to the ground.

"What are you doing here?"

"I don't know."

"What do you mean you don't know?"

Fonseca reached them and, as Montone covered him, quickly cuffed the man and yanked him back up to his knees. The headlights of the approaching car lit them up, briefly blinding them.

The man, who was approximately Keyes's size and had similar coloring but otherwise looked nothing like him, stared up at the two detectives in shock and terror.

"Where am I?" he asked.

10

Mackenzie Dennis
Holly Mews
Cody Lawson
Livingston Parker
Erin Kelly
James Montone

: found in a notebook in the Brooklyn apartment rented by Terry Keyes
under the name Howard Kurtzman

They see you on TV. They see you bloodied up on game day. They
see you selling some shit on TV and you know what? They buy it.
That's the NFL, baby.

We're not gods, but we're as close as they're gonna get in
this lifetime.

I'm in the league twelve years. Nobody, not once, ever said no
to me.

: underlined passage in a copy of My House: Life in the NFL Combat Zone *by*
Cody Lawson, found in the Manhattan office rented by Terry Keyes
in the name of Howard Kurtzman

Keyes had picked his mark out of the crowd on the dance floor at eleven. Approximately the right size and body type, the man didn't drink and, judging by his unassertive social skills, he possessed a suitably weak temperament. After determining that he was at the club alone, Keyes waited half an hour until the man headed for the bathroom, then swiftly followed him inside.

The man went into a stall. Keyes waited for a third man to leave the rest room, then locked the door after him. When the stall opened, Keyes stepped right into the man's path and extended his hand. The man shook it and Keyes held on.

"Hi, it's nice to see you again," said Keyes, focusing all his will into the man's eyes before he could respond.

"Do you notice that? How much lighter your hand feels? I want you to concentrate on the sensations you're about to experience in the hand I'm holding. Your hand is going to become lighter and lighter until it becomes so light that when I let go it's going to float up into the air all by itself. Ready?"

Keyes let go of the man's hand; his eyes clouded over. His hand began to rise.

"That's good, and as your hand grows lighter and lighter and moves higher and higher you're going to become more and more relaxed. That's right."

The man's hand continued to rise up into the air. His gaze became fixed and his eyelids drooped.

"And by the time your hand reaches up and touches the top of your head you're going to be in a very deep, very relaxed, very pleasant state. Can you feel that?"

"Yes."

"You feel deeply relaxed and deeply at peace and now when I tell you to move your hand back down to your side, you'll do that for me, won't you?"

"Yes." The man slowly lowered his hand back down.

"And up again."

The man obeyed.

"Good. What's your name?"

"Eddie Valen."

"Eddie, that's a very beautiful shirt you're wearing. I'd like you to give it to me and in return I'm going to give you mine, that's fair, isn't it? In fact, I think it would be a good idea to trade all of our clothes, would that be all right with you?"

"Yes."

Keyes took off his baseball cap and placed it on Eddie's head as Eddie undid the buttons of his shirt. They finished the exchange in less than two minutes, down to their shoes. Keyes was now wearing black jeans, a charcoal-gray T-shirt and a black windbreaker. He emptied the contents of his black fanny pack, put Eddie's wallet inside, then fastened it around the man's waist.

"That looks very good. Eddie, as soon as we finish speaking you're going to leave this room. When you leave this room I want you to keep your head down, walk over and stand against the far left wall with your back to the big window. Do you understand?"

"Yes."

"Order another glass of white wine and watch the people on the dance floor. Keep your back to the window at all times. At five minutes after midnight I want you to leave the club and get into the first taxicab you see. Tell your driver to take you to the pier at the end of Las Olas Boulevard in Fort Lauderdale. Pay the driver, get out of the cab and wait at the end of the pier. Do you understand?"

"Yes."

"Once you're on the pier, the first time anyone speaks to you, you will forget everything we've talked about. You will not remember why you are on the pier or how you got there. And when I count to three, now, you will come out of this relaxed state and you will not remember a single word of our conversation. Is that clear?"

"Yes."

"One . . . two . . . three."

Eddie's eyes fluttered open and he looked surprised to find someone standing so close to him.

"Excuse me," said Keyes.

Keyes stood aside to let Eddie pass, then went into the stall and closed it behind him. Eddie walked straight to the door, unlocked the bolt and left the bathroom.

From the items he'd taken from the fanny pack, Keyes put on a pair of tortoiseshell eyeglasses, hooked a gold loop earring through one ear and wrapped a blue gangsta-rag bandanna around his head. From a plastic envelope he carefully removed a black mustache and goatee and applied them to his face.

After waiting three minutes in the stall for the glue to set, he flushed the toilet, walked out and stood in front of the mirror combing his hair until the other two men using the room headed for the door. He left the room immediately behind the two men, keeping them between himself and the window until he reached the bar, then turned sharply to his right toward the rear exit.

Picking up an umbrella from a table near the door, he popped it open and headed out into the heavy rain. He stopped to light a cigarette and see if he'd attracted any attention. Limping slightly to vary his gait, he walked right past the sight line of the police surveillance car parked across the street.

No reaction.

Half a block to the north he turned into an alley and entered the side entrance of the Beachcomber residential hotel. He used his key to open the door to the apartment of J. Thomas Sylvester. Shades drawn, he turned on one small light in the kitchen. Opening the false ceiling panel above the stove, he pulled down the black duffel bag, along with a customized replica of his black leather satchel.

Keyes removed Eddie Valen's clothes and stored them in the duffel bag. He dressed in black nylon sweats, black Nike Air Jordans, thin black gloves and a black watch cap. Hefting both bags over his shoulder, he checked his watch—11:38—left the apartment and took the back stairs down to the building's subterranean garage.

A car cover protected the 1994 black Ford Taurus, parked in Mr. Sylvester's spot, that he had purchased last fall for cash. Keyes placed his bags and the cover in the trunk and got behind the wheel. The engine turned over on the first try.

Keyes drove the Taurus up the ramp to the street and turned south onto Collins, then for the next five minutes followed a circuitous route back and forth across South Beach. Strictly observing the speed limit, he checked his mirrors frequently for pursuit. Satisfying himself he was clear, Keyes drove the MacArthur Causeway west to the mainland and turned left again onto Biscayne Boulevard.

Ten minutes later, just as Eddie Valen was getting into the cab outside the nightclub, Keyes entered the residential neighborhood of Coconut Grove, six blocks from Erin's house.

"Where'd you get the shirt?" asked Montone.

"I don't know."

"Is it yours?"

"I guess so," said Eddie, looking down at it.

"You guess so?"

"I don't know."

Montone examined Eddie Valen's driver's license. Behind them, on the radio in the car, Galindez ran him through the system for wants and warrants.

"What were you wearing when you went out tonight?"

"I honestly don't remember. Not this."

"You do any drugs tonight, Eddie?"

Eddie Valen, his hands cuffed behind his back, kneeling on the rough planks of the dock in the center of a circle of cops, lowered his head and began to cry.

"I don't use drugs. I don't even use Tylenol since that poisoning thing."

"What do you do, Eddie?"

"I work in a pet store in Coral Gables."

"You know a man named Terry Keyes?"

"No, am I supposed to?"

"You tell us."

"How much did he pay you to drive out here?"

"Pay me?"

"Don't lie to us, Eddie."

"I'm not lying, I swear. Please don't hurt me," said Eddie, fighting back tears. "I'm so frightened. I swear to God this never happened to me before. I had two margaritas, straight up, on the rocks. I don't know what happened. I blacked out, didn't I?"

"You didn't drink any wine?"

"I don't even like wine."

"We saw you order a glass of white wine, Eddie."

Galindez got out of his car and shook his head at Montone.

Nothing. Montone moved quickly away from Eddie, took out his cel-lular phone and dialed Erin's number. He listened to it ring repeatedly.

"Oh God. This is like *Three Faces of Eve*. I've got multiple person-ality disorder. That's it, isn't it? What did I do? This is too totally *Sybil*. I don't even know anyone in Fort Lauderdale. Please, tell me, Officer, have I done something terrible?"

One of the Miami officers and Fonseca glanced at each other and almost laughed. Fonseca had to look away.

No answer at Erin's. Montone hit redial and listened to it ring again.

"I had attacks of cluster headaches in my late teens, do you think they could be related?"

"You never know."

Fonseca steered him toward the car.

"I've got an aunt with epilepsy. They say that can be caused by brain tumors. This could be the first symptom. Maybe you'd better take me to the hospital."

Montone ended the call and pocketed the phone.

"Hector, get some units to this address in Coconut Grove right now," said Montone, handing over Erin's card, her parents' address written on the back. "I think he's going after the sister."

"Get in," said Galindez.

The two men jumped into Galindez's car. He backed down the pier to the street at thirty miles an hour, spun the car around and headed back to the interstate as he called Metro-Dade dispatch.

Keyes turned off the highway and entered a nest of residential streets near Peacock Park. Relying on memory, he found the street he was looking for, then drove slowly along until the house came into view. Keyes glided past the entrance and turned left on a side street, then left again into an alley that skirted the rear of the property, and parked the Taurus under the dense cover of a large willow tree. He lifted the duffel bag from the trunk and carried it to a spot along the rear fence next to a small utility building that shielded him from the alley.

The Spanish-style house stood fifty yards from the back fence. Unzipping the duffel, he removed the night-vision scope and focused it

Eric Bowman

on the top floor of the house. Lights burned in a number of windows and he could vaguely hear music.

Keyes shouldered the duffel bag and scaled the fence, dropping down silently inside the grounds. He followed a path of flagstones through lush landscaping. Weaving between a brace of koi pools, the path ended at a colonnade that extended along the length of the rear of the house. Keyes moved slowly along, trying each door handle he passed, and found them all locked.

He reached the shelter of the balcony, scalloping out past the line of the verandah roof, and flattened himself against the building. A flowered trellis ran up along the wall beside one of the exterior columns. Keyes took an exploratory grip and judged the structure solid enough to support his weight. He adjusted the duffel bag back over his shoulder.

Scaling the trellis, Keyes carefully hoisted himself over the rail and silently set foot on the balcony. A row of three double French doors, all of them standing open, led into the bedroom. He kneeled down, edged up to the first doorway, and through swaying white linen curtains he looked into the suite.

Three patrol units slammed up outside Erin's parents' house, shocking the last of the guests who were walking across the lawn to their cars. The officers rushed to the front door, weapons drawn, demanding to speak to Miss Kelly.

Erin emerged from the kitchen, where she'd been helping the maid put away food from the buffet.

The officers fanned out to search and secure the rest of the house and grounds.

The senior cop, a sergeant, called in an all-clear on his radio. The phone rang moments later and they put Erin on with Montone, still in the car with Galindez, racing toward their location.

"I tried to call," he said. "There was no answer."

"One of my cousins was talking to her kids in Ohio," she said. "She probably didn't know how to use call waiting."

"Stay in the house. Stay with the officers. We're about half an hour away."

The room was a citadel of sex; the bed, the largest Keyes had ever seen, stood on an elevated pedestal, illuminated by a bank of flattering, recessed spotlights.

A young woman lay on the bed, alone, her naked white skin a stark contrast to the black satin sheets. Legs spread-eagled, the heels of her ankle-strapped black patent-leather pumps hooked around a wrought-iron headboard. Black leather cuffs, bondage accessories lined with sheepskin, ringed her wrists. Propped up on pillows, she stared, pupils fixed and dilated, at her own image reflected in a mirrored gilded wall behind the bed. Her right hand rested on her pelvis, languidly masturbating.

Looking more closely, he realized the girl's ankles were bound to the headboard with lengths of black tasseled rope. Her left arm, draped behind her head, was similarly tied to the footboard.

A snowy drift of cocaine lay on a small mirror beside her on the bed. A fat silver champagne bucket, holding two open bottles, sat on the bedstand. A selection of garish sex toys littered the bed.

As Keyes watched, the woman wet the index finger of her right hand, touched it to the white powder, applied some of it to her nipples, then touched herself between the legs again.

From an archway to the right of the gilded wall Keyes heard someone gasp, then a raspy moan. As his eyes grew accustomed to the dark he noticed another woman leaning against the wall there, avidly watching the one on the bed. Tall and painfully thin, a dark-skinned girl with almost comically inflated breasts, moving in rhythm with a man who was entering her from behind.

The owner of the house, former NFL all-star linebacker and professional celebrity, Cody Lawson.

The man stood an entire head taller than the girl and outweighed her by a hundred pounds. One of his massive black arms, gnarled with muscle, wrapped around her stomach, holding the girl captive. Keyes could barely make him out in the dim light but saw that he had his eyes shut, head angled back, lost in sensation.

When the driving beat of the music faded out, the song ending, the man disengaged from the girl, turned her around, then shoved her firmly toward the bed. The girl stumbled forward up the steps to the platform, protesting lamely, obviously drugged, drunk or both, then fell to her knees beside the bed giggling. Her head lolled around like a rag doll's.

"Get after it, bitch," said the man, his voice thick and heavy. "You know you want to."

He stepped backward out of sight. Moments later Keyes heard water running in the next room.

The black girl leaned forward, sprawling across the bed to reach the other woman, and began to alternately kiss and bite her across the shoulders, down her arms, then onto her breasts. The white girl barely registered the attention, eyes glassy, still pleasuring herself, her gaze welded to the sybaritic image in the mirror.

Keyes lifted a CO_2 powered pistol from the duffel bag, sighted down the barrel and drew a bead on the black girl's haunches. From somewhere in the room he heard a mechanical whir; the sound system changing discs. As the first cut of the next CD began to play, filling the room with a manic rap beat that rattled the doorframes, he fired.

The tiny needle embedded beneath the girl's skin, disappearing. The girl reacted as if she'd been bitten by an insect, momentarily distracted but too wasted to follow the thought to a conclusion. Moments later she seemed to have forgotten it ever happened.

Her attention drifted to the cocaine on the mirror, extending her tongue into the powder, coating its tip, then she leaned forward and lowered her head between the other girl's legs.

Keyes reloaded the pistol, then reached into the duffel and brought out a full-sized syringe and the noose.

He slipped into the suite through the first balcony doorway, crouched low and crept slowly to his left. The room was so large he didn't come within twenty feet of the bed. Neither of the zombied courtesans noticed the shadow in black passing behind them or his reflection in the mirror.

Taking shelter behind a black leather sofa ten feet to the right of the bed, Keyes rested the pistol on the arm, drew a sight on the white girl's left thigh and fired.

Her senses deadened, the girl didn't even flinch. A thin trickle of blood ran down her leg from the insertion point. The black girl was already beginning to show the effects of the drug; head nodding, limbs losing coordination. Both would be out within minutes; the needles would dissolve in their bodies within twenty-four hours.

Keyes stood and walked to the threshold on the left side of the bed, twin to the one that flanked the right. Both led into the suite's eight-hundred-square-foot bathroom, a hedonistic oasis with every imaginable amenity. Dimmers and recessed lights bathed the room in soft pink light. Music emanated from another pair of speakers set in the walls.

Steps led up to an elevated sunken six-foot-square bathtub cut from a slab of Carrara marble, accessorized with solid-gold fixtures. To its right an open-air Swedish shower sent powerful jets of water from twelve identical gold faucets.

The owner of the house—six foot four, sculpted and powerful—stood planted in the center of the spray, his smoothly shaven head thrown back, arms outspread, inundated from every direction.

Keyes looked down at the bed. Through blood-red eyes the white girl was staring up at him, uncomprehending, trying to make sense of this dark apparition. The black girl had already passed out beside her, facedown on the bed. One of her arms had twisted awkwardly to the side as she fell forward and jostled some of the cocaine off the mirror onto the black satin sheets.

Keyes raised a finger to his lips, then smiled at her.

The girl's head sank back into the pillows. Her eyes rolled up, then closed, surrendering to the drug.

Behind him the shower stopped running.

Keyes leaned back and pressed himself against the inside wall. Without looking, his hands snapped open the collapsible steel pole to its full four feet. He readied the syringe and rehearsed the clamping action of the noose.

He heard the man's bare feet padding wetly across the marble floor toward the other archway.

"Bitches ain't making enough noise," the man muttered. "Fucked up. This s'posed to be play, God damn it."

As he stepped through the archway into the bedroom, Keyes moved silently into and across the bathroom behind the man. The music covered his approach.

The man stood on the edge of the platform, glaring down at the unconscious women. He nudged the black whore with his foot but she didn't move.

"Shit."

He tried to brush the spilled cocaine back onto the mirror, then set the mirror down beside the champagne bucket. He lifted one bottle from the bucket and took a long pull from it, then turned the black girl over and poured some of the champagne on her face.

"Wake up, bitch."

He slapped her twice. No response.

"No fuckin' use."

He wiped his finger across the mirror, then rubbed the cocaine across his phallus, using his hand to make himself hard. Breathing heavily he kneeled down between the unconscious girl's legs, spread them apart and entered her roughly.

Keyes stepped forward silently, raised the noose, waited for the man to exhale, then in one quick motion dropped the coil of steel down around his neck and yanked it taut, locking it into place.

For a moment, the man didn't realize what had happened to him, then his hands shot up to his neck and found the cold metallic ribbon. Panic fired adrenaline throughout his body and he shot backward off the bed, away from the girl. Prodigiously strong, his arms thrashed out in every direction, trying to strike his invisible attacker.

Keyes planted his feet and hung on to the pole with both hands, using it as a lever to drive the man to the ground. He fell to his knees, twisted around and caught a glimpse of Keyes behind him. Veins in his forehead bulged dangerously, the whites of his eyes went red, capillaries bursting. He kicked furiously at Keyes, but the length of the pole kept him out of reach. The man reached up, grabbed the pole with one hand, planted his feet and pulled as hard as he could, whipping Keyes around to the other side of the room.

Slamming into the wall knocked the breath out of Keyes and he lost his grip on the pole. With the noose still clamped around his neck, the man scrambled on his hands and knees up the steps to the edge of the bed. Keyes hurried after him but just as he laid his hands on the pole again, the man reached in and drew a handgun from a concealed holster attached to the side of the bed frame. Starting to weaken, he turned and slowly raised the gun at Keyes, who let go of the pole and dove inside the shelter of the archway.

The man attempted to crawl after him but the constriction of the noose finally brought him down. He lost consciousness, fell forward, bounced face first down the platform steps, and the gun dropped from his hand.

Keyes stepped forward, stabbed the man in the buttocks with the syringe and injected the full measure of the tranquilizer. He waited ten more seconds, then gently loosened the coil from around the man's neck. He put a finger to the carotid pulse. Still strong, chest still rising and falling.

The music should have masked the sound of their struggle but he stepped back out of sight and then waited an extra minute to see if anyone responded.

No one approached. If someone else was in the house and had heard the fight they were apparently accustomed to disturbing noises coming from this room. Keyes walked to the bedroom door and locked it. He collapsed the noose, went out to the balcony and carried in the duffel bag. Checked his watch: 12:14.

Using deep breathing to center himself, Keyes surveyed the scene before him. The raw materials of his canvas thrilled him. His imagination began to soar.

The gun on the floor.

The whores.

The drugs.

The sex toys.

The needle.

If he was to keep to his schedule he could allow only twenty minutes. Enough time to do the work.

Hardly enough time to enjoy himself.

Montone jumped out of the car and ran to the door as Galindez pulled up to the curb. Erin came outside to meet him and he guided her down a path along the side of the house, away from the cops.

"They wouldn't tell me what happened," she said.

"We were following Keyes and he got away from us. I thought he might have been coming here."

"Why?"

"If Keyes felt that his life had been destroyed by these other people, ouside forces, as you suggested; the news reporter who publicized his story, the model who rejected him, the cop, the friend who ran off and refused to testify—"

"What about them?"

"Could this be his motive? He's killed a television reporter. He killed Holly. He killed Henshaw. He's going down a list, getting back at them."

"But they're not the same people."

"Except for Henshaw. And then maybe because he just got in the way."

"So you're saying his victims are surrogates, stand-ins."

"You tell me: Does that track?"

They stopped under an ivy-covered trellis as she considered the idea.

"It's supportable," she said. "It's possible he's doing it without even knowing why."

"How do you mean?"

"These confessions he left, the anti-American tracts. He may actually believe he's conducting some kind of moral crusade. To the point where that's obscuring his real intention."

"Bottom line is, none of what happened to him is his fault."

"He can't accept responsiblity for his life going so wrong; he sees himself as the victim. The court psychologist diagnosed him, I think correctly, with narcissistic personality disorder. That wouldn't prevent him from being highly functioning, charismatic, even enormously successful. But there's a gaping hole in his psyche that he can't fill. Not with fame, not with money, anything."

"Nothing short of murder."

She stopped again. "A rage that would lead him to murder the people he perceived as conspiring against him is not inconsistent with that diagnosis."

"So why is he doing it?"

"Hard to say exactly. He's trying to make himself whole. Obliterate the past. Erase the mistakes. Maybe it's just envy, pure and simple."

"Of what?"

"Of you, James. Of who you are. The fact that you're recognized and respected for what you do."

"What does that have to do with you?"

"You're the other component: the one person Dennis and Holly had in common. Whatever else he may think he's doing, you're at the center of his reason."

"Why me?"

"You're who he could have turned out to be. That's what I was getting at about the similarity in backgrounds. He sees himself as smarter, stronger, more deserving, and yet there you are earning accolades, having books written about you while he's languishing in prison."

"How would he even know who I am?"

"Maybe he read my book," she said. "Isn't that why you thought he was coming after me? The psychologist who examined him and testified that he was competent to stand trial."

Out of the corner of his eye he saw Galindez signaling to him from near the front door. Montone excused himself and walked over to him.

"He's back at the hotel," said Galindez. "Walked in fresh as a fucking daisy."

They discussed their response and Montone moved back to Erin.

"We know where he is," said Montone. "We're going to keep some officers stationed here for the night. Tell your parents there's nothing to worry about. I'll call you first thing in the morning."

"I'll think about what you said."

"So will I."

While Montone and Galindez were still on their way back to Coconut Grove, Terry Keyes stopped his black Ford Taurus under a bridge near a tourist lookout spot where the lights of South Beach sparkled across the water.

He peeled off the beard and mustache and changed back into a duplicate set of the clothes he'd been wearing before meeting Eddie Valen. He stuffed Eddie's clothes and all the equipment he'd used for his work into the duffel, along with a twenty-five-pound barbell, and dropped the bag into Biscayne Bay.

The only item he kept from the job was a roll of thirty-five-millimeter film.

Keyes drove into the design district of downtown Miami and parked the Taurus in an alley directly behind a three-story office building. He slipped a lightweight tan jacket over the yellow silk shirt, zipped it to the neck and pulled on a black Miami Heat cap. He carefully lifted the duplicate saddlebag satchel from the trunk, locked the car and stashed the keys in a small magnetized box inside the front right wheel well.

He put the film can into a stamped and addressed manila envelope that already contained a handwritten letter and dropped it in a mailbox as he walked to the nearest bus stop on Biscayne Boulevard. Three minutes later he boarded the one a.m. express, the last run of the night, to South Beach. The bus crossed the causeway, turned right at Collins Avenue, and he rode it all the way down to within two blocks of the Delano.

Waiting across the street until a group of boisterous German drunks congested the entrance, Keyes moved through the front doors into the crowded lobby.

Murphy, on duty across the street, was the first to see Keyes return and immediately called Galindez's cellular.

Keyes dropped the duplicate leather satchel off with the girl on duty at the bell stand, collecting a receipt.

He walked to the nearby stairwell, took off his jacket and cap and ran up the stairs to the eighth floor. Seeing no one outside his room, he went inside and prepared his next move.

Galindez dropped Montone off across the street from the Delano at one-thirty. Murphy came out of the Imperial to meet him and they stood in the street. Galindez listened through his driver-side window.

"He came in about ten minutes ago," said Murphy.

"Anybody see where he went?"

"We heard him go into his room. I think he's back down in the bar."

"I want to bring him in," said Montone, staring over at the Delano.

"For what, swapping shirts?" asked Galindez.

"Let's try it your way. Let's try to break him."

Galindez and Murphy exchanged a sympathetic look.

"Not for nothing, Jimmy," said Galindez, "but I think your read on this guy's the right one. He's not breakable."

"I don't care. I don't fucking care anymore. I want to put my hands on him."

"Jimmy, we're running a blood panel on Eddie Valen. We'll get his statement, show him some pictures, see if we get an ID."

"If Keyes drugged him we'll take him down for that."

"It's not gonna make any difference. He knows what we're doing before we do, what's the point? Let's turn up the heat. Put somebody in his fucking face."

"I'll bring more men on tomorrow."

"Not tomorrow. Tonight. I'm through playing this his way. It stops now."

"It's your call."

After another rueful look to Murphy Galindez shrugged and drove off.

"For what it's worth," said Murphy, "I think Hector's right."

"You sure he's in the bar? Anybody see him leave the building?"

"He's in there."

Murphy saw the cold fury on Montone's face.

"What do you want to do, Jimmy?"

Montone didn't answer.

"What are you gonna do?"

Montone started walking across the street.

"Where you going, Jimmy?"

"I'm going to talk to him."

Murphy followed him to the door of the hotel before he thought better of Keyes seeing him, then hurried back to the Imperial to get Pat Feany.

Montone climbed the steps and entered the lobby, even at this late hour filled with above-average-looking people in designer chic searching for some indelible way to round out their evening. Montone moved through them like Death at a child's birthday party.

The hotel bar stood at the far end of the open lobby, an asymmetrical rectangle of polished teak separated from the rest of the space by billowy white linen curtains that stretched from floor to ceiling. As they rippled in the breeze, lights inside the bar threw grotesque, distorted shadows of the people inside onto the fabric.

Montone spotted the yellow silk shirt in the crowd at the bar. Keyes sat with his back to the entrance, talking to a dark doe-eyed beauty smoking a thick cigar. She looked up, saw Montone standing behind Keyes, and her eyes grew even wider.

He waited for Keyes to turn around.

"Jimmy."

"Hey, Terry."

"How's your evening?"

"How's yours?"

"Super. Extra specially good. This is Immaculata, isn't that a fantastically beautiful name?"

"Excuse us for a moment," said Montone to the girl.

Her high-beam smile faltered as Montone grabbed Keyes by the arm, yanked him to his feet and led him away from the bar.

"Where are we going?"

Montone didn't respond.

"Jimmy, come on, buddy, I was just starting to get somewhere with that girl."

Montone pushed through the double doors that led out to the pool. He moved Keyes around the corner, down a wheelchair-access ramp, shoved him up against the wall and stood back a step.

"What's the problem here?" asked Keyes, half amused.

Montone stared at him.

"Jimmy, give me a clue here—"

"I know what you did, Terry."

Keyes didn't answer. His brow furrowed, his eyes searching Montone's face.

"I know it was you."

A momentary flash of dark cunning in his eyes. For the briefest moment Montone caught a glimpse in that look of the blackness Peter Henshaw had described; emptied out, icebound, as pitiless and unknowable as the eye of a shark. The eyes darted to Montone's midsection.

Montone ripped his own shirt open.

"I'm not wearing a wire. Nobody listening. Just you and me. That is the way you want it, isn't it?"

Keyes didn't respond.

"I know what you did, I know why you did it. You hear me?"

Keyes stared at him impassively.

"If you touch her, if you ever go anywhere near Holly's sister, I'll kill you."

Leaning back against the wall, Keyes lowered his head, then slowly covered his face with his hands. His body began to shake. Montone thought he was crying.

When Keyes finally raised his head again, Montone realized it was laughter. Out of control, close to hysterics. Keyes fought to control himself, wiped the tears from his eyes as he focused on Montone again, slowly grinned and raised both arms to the side. He never said a word.

Shaking with anger, Montone pulled back a fist to strike him. Keyes didn't flinch. They stared at each other. At the last moment Montone withheld the blow.

"This your real face, you sick fuck? This what you really look like?"

Keyes smiled placidly at him.

Montone lowered his fist, took out his handcuffs, slapped one on Keyes's right wrist and roughly fastened the other to the ramp's handrail. Keyes didn't object or struggle, maintaining his passive silence.

"Sooner or later it's gonna come down to you and me," said Montone. "And when you fuck up, and you will, I'm going to take you out."

Montone turned and walked back into the hotel. He stopped in the bar, quietly showed his badge to the girl with the cigar who'd been talking to Keyes.

"You ever see that man before tonight?" he asked.

"No."

"Did you give him your phone number, home address, any way for him to get in touch with you?"

"No."

"Don't ever talk to him again. Go home right now and lock your doors and pray to God it's the last time he ever lays eyes on you."

He got through to her. Visibly shaken, she picked up her purse and Montone walked her to a cab outside. As she drove off he saw Murphy and Feany approaching from the sidewalk.

"Get Galindez on the phone," he said. "Whatever Keyes did tonight is gonna break by tomorrow. We'll wait him out. If he goes anywhere we stay on top of him. If he tries to run we take him down. Soon as we know what he pulled or who he hurt, he's ours."

"Frankie called; they got nothing out of that kid."

"Does that surprise you?"

"They're running the blood. Frankie's saying they think he might have been hypnotized."

"Get a perimeter up. Cover the exits, the stairs and the elevators. No more fucking around."

Montone walked back through the lobby and out to where he'd left Keyes by the pool.

The empty handcuffs hung from the railing.

Montone heard a taunting whistle and spun around.

Keyes waved to him, sitting at a table beside the pool, holding a cocktail and smoking a cigar.

Montone walked over to him.

"I don't think you're getting enough fun out of life, Jimmy. Work, work, work."

As if the previous conversation had never taken place.

"You're going upstairs, right now."

"Beddy-bye time, is it?"

"Get up."

"You're so strict."

Keyes set down his drink and stood up. Montone grabbed him by the arm and herded him toward the door.

"I'm worried about you, Jimmy, I really am," said Keyes. "The department may have been spot on about this; you're over the line. Right at the breaking point."

Montone didn't answer. He led him into an elevator, boarding with two drunken young couples wearing party hats. Montone's intensity, and his grip on Keyes's arms, drew nervous looks from them.

"I've been a naughty boy," said Keyes, leaning toward them conspiratorially.

The couples smirked, turning away to snicker. Montone stared holes in one of the men and he shut up immediately.

As the elevator stopped to let them off, Keyes rolled his eyes at them and the couples behind them broke into laughter. Montone walked Keyes to his door.

"Open it," said Montone.

Keyes slid his key card through the slot and opened the door. Montone took the key from his hand, pushed him into the suite and followed him inside. He ripped the phone jack out of the wall in the bedroom, then did the same to the phone in the bathroom. He carried both phones with him back to the door.

"Don't try to leave," said Montone.

"Really do try and get some rest, Jimmy," said Keyes, with a friendly smile. "No hard feelings; we'll put this behind us. You'll feel better in the morning."

Montone closed the door. He opened his room next door, propped the door open with a chair so he could see out into the hall and called Murphy across the street.

"You reach Galindez?" he asked.

"He's on it. Hotel's covered, top to bottom."

"Keep somebody on that wire. You hear anything from him during the night, you call me."

"Done."

Montone hung up the phone. He set up his chair by the open doorway, sat down and waited for morning to come.

He woke up violently as his head nodded forward, then snapped back as he came around. A pale lemony light filtered through the blinds in the bedroom. He glanced at his watch; Seven-thirty. Montone glanced out into the empty hallway and at Keyes's door, all quiet, then stretched and stepped into his bathroom.

When he'd showered and changed clothes he walked out to the bedroom and noticed the message light flashing on his phone. Following the instructions on the phone, he punched up the hotel's voice mail "message retrieval center."

"You have one new message," said the metallic computerized voice. "Received at seven twenty-five a.m."

Montone pressed the requested button.

Whispered, muffled voices, a scratchy recording, backed by the soft swell of the ocean.

"Was it that leg?"

"Yeah."

Breathing, a rustle of clothing. Then the unmistakable sound of a kiss.

"Should we go inside?" A man's voice.

His own.

"No."

Holly's voice answering.

That night on the beach. The first time they made love.

Keyes had been listening. He'd made a recording.

Montone slammed the phone down. He rushed out into the hall and pounded a fist on Keyes's door.

"Open the door! Open it, you son of a bitch!"

When Keyes didn't immediately answer, Montone kicked the door in, splintering the jamb.

"Where the fuck are you?"

He threw open the bathroom door, the closets, the door to the balcony. The suite was empty.

Montone ran back into his room and called the Imperial. Pat Feany answered on the first ring.

"Where is he?"

"He's downstairs, in the restaurant—"

"I told you to call me—"

"It's under control, Jimmy, we were just about to—"

Montone threw the phone across the room and rushed out to the hall. He slapped the elevator button and rode the car down to the lobby, radiating fury. The other two people inside stopped speaking and instinctively shrank away from him.

As he came off the elevator, Frankie Fonseca hung up a phone and moved toward him from the front desk.

"Jimmy, wait—"

Montone turned and walked directly away from him. Frankie tried to catch up.

"Jimmy, he's not alone—"

Montone didn't even hear him. He burst through the doors into the restaurant, eyes searching for Keyes, a heat-seeking missile.

There, seated at a table in the middle of the room, talking to someone, a woman whose back was to Montone.

His vision narrowed, the rest of the room disappeared. He had a vague awareness of a bright light in his eyes. Montone covered the ground between them in ten strides.

Keyes, in midsentence, looked up, saw Montone, and his expression freeze-framed.

"Jimmy, no!" Fonseca yelled as he entered the restaurant behind them.

Montone lifted Keyes right out of his seat, picked him up and threw him across a neighboring table. People screamed and scattered from their seats, plates, food, cutlery, flew in all directions.

Reaching him before he could scramble to his feet, Montone grabbed Keyes by the shirt collar, pinned him down and jackhammered a series of right hands into his face; short, brutal punches.

Looking directly in Montone's eyes, Keyes offered no defense or resistance. He said nothing. Blood blossomed all across his features.

Montone lifted him again, hooked a right hand under his ribs that knocked out his wind, dug another into his kidneys, then set him for an uppercut under the chin that sent him sprawling back into a section of the buffet. Keyes landed heavily on the table, then slid to the ground amid piles of Belgian waffles, broken glass, and lay still.

The beating took less than a minute. No one, not even Fonseca, dared to interfere. The few other patrons in the room either fled for the doors or sat watching, mesmerized, shocked by the savagery that had shattered the calm morning.

Montone walked over to Keyes, pointed an emphatic finger in his face and landed one kick into his unprotected side, hearing a satisfying crack of bone, before Fonseca finally pounced on Montone's back and pulled him away.

Two uniformed officers rushed into the room and helped drag him back through the wreckage. His adrenaline spent, Montone offered little resistance.

Hector Galindez and Murphy appeared at the door.

In the sudden silence, Montone noticed a television camera pointing at him.

The bright lights.

He'd found Keyes in the middle of an interview.

Montone held on to Frankie Fonseca's arm.

"He left . . . He left a message," said Montone quietly, trying to catch his breath. "Make sure they save it. The switchboard."

"Okay, Jimmy."

A woman holding a clipboard, the interviewer, said something to the cameraman in German. They moved quickly in on Keyes, framing a closeup.

Galindez walked past Montone.

"Get him out of here," he ordered.

Fonseca and Murphy walked Montone toward the door.

"Ask them if he got up to make a call," said Montone, waving a hand at the TV crew. "He's got a tape recorder somewhere."

"Police department, ladies and gentlemen," said Galindez to the room. "I'd like everyone please to move out of this area and into the lobby."

The female interviewer was kneeling beside Keyes, wrapping ice in a napkin, applying it to one of the cuts on his face. He looked up at her, speaking plaintively to the camera.

"I don't know why," said Keyes. "I honestly don't know why. We were good friends."

Galindez yanked the power cable out of the camera; the cameraman protested in German when his viewfinder went blank.

"We will be witnesses," said the woman to Galindez, trying to sound threatening.

"Outside, lady," said Galindez, in a tone that invited no argument. "An officer will take your statement."

The woman and the camera crew backed away. She gave orders, in German, to remove and protect the tape.

Galindez kneeled down beside Keyes and stared at him with a cold and knowing eye. Keyes returned the look, unblinking.

"You need an ambulance?" he asked.

"No."

"You got to see a doctor, anyway."

"No. I don't want to press charges."

"Good."

"I want to talk to my lawyer," said Keyes.

"You got one locally? Why doesn't that surprise me, you piece of shit?"

Keyes shifted the ice from the wound on his forehead. A trickle of watery blood ran down his cheek, simulating tears. He smiled at Galindez, blood from the cuts in his mouth staining his teeth.

Murphy and Fonseca sat Montone down in an isolated corner of the lobby, trying to shield him from view of the finger pointers and witnesses who'd been in the restaurant. Rumors flew thick and fast around them, growing, accruing details. Uniforms moved in and covered every door.

On the other side of the lobby Metro-Dade detectives collected statements from the TV crew. Pat Feany listened to their conversation, then walked over to Montone to report.

"They're from a German television network. He had the interview set up weeks ago."

"Weeks ago?"

"They got the whole fucking thing on tape, Jimmy," said Feany.

"Ask me if I give a shit. I'm sorry I didn't kill him. Did you check my messages?"

"We're working on it, Jimmy," said Fonseca.

"Check the bathroom, that's where he must have made the call."

The doors to the restaurant opened and Terry Keyes walked unsteadily into the lobby, doubled over slightly, his face a pulpy mask. Galindez and two uniforms followed close behind. Galindez spotted Montone and walked over to where the New York detectives huddled.

"He doesn't want to press charges. He wants to see his lawyer," said Galindez.

"Follow him, let's go," said Montone.

"This how you practice detachment, my friend?" asked Galindez with sadness in his voice.

"He made a tape of us, of Holly and me," said Montone, his hands shaking violently as the adrenaline in his system burned off. "Making love. That's what I heard on the phone."

"Just now?"

Montone nodded. "We have to follow him."

"I'll offer him a fucking ride."

Terry Keyes handed a claim check to the bellman at the desk and reclaimed his duplicate leather satchel. He staggered slightly as he shifted its weight onto one shoulder.

Normal activity in the lobby slowed to a halt as every person in view stopped to watch the injured man walk to the front doors, a scarecrow figure, his clothes splattered with blood. Once he nearly lost his balance, righting himself at the last moment. He shrugged away an offer of assistance, then stopped near the doors, collected his dignity and took out a pair of sunglasses. He unfolded them, put them on and straightened to his full height, wincing with pain. The doorman held the doors for him and Keyes walked out of the hotel.

Montone, Galindez and the other detectives followed him outside. Keyes climbed into a taxi in front. Four patrol cars and two sedans stood ready at the entrance and exit. As the taxi drove off, the detectives climbed into the sedans and a procession of police vehicles followed Keyes onto Collins Avenue.

"Ten sixty-two Biscayne Boulevard," said Keyes to the driver.

Keyes looked at his watch: 8:20. The driver, a middle-aged white woman, glanced uneasily at him in her rearview mirror.

"You all right, mister?"

"Splendid. Thanks for asking."

"Sure you don't want a doctor or something?"

"Ten sixty-two Biscayne Boulevard."

The driver looked at the trail of police cars behind them.

"You in some kind of trouble?"

"Why, whatever in the world would give you that fucking idea?"

She saw the expression on his face and didn't say another word.

Keyes took off his jacket, reached into the satchel, took out a wallet that held identification and credit cards in the name of J. Thomas Sylvester and three thousand dollars in cash. He put that wallet in his pants pocket, then slipped his own wallet in the pocket of his jacket.

The cab started across the Tuttle Causeway to the mainland. The police cars continued to trail them, maintaining their distance.

From an inner pocket of the satchel Keyes took out a standard white envelope, addressed to the *Miami Herald,* and laid it carefully on the seat of the cab. As the taxi took the exit onto Biscayne Boulevard he lifted the flap of the satchel's largest compartment and turned something inside.

Ten minutes.

"Where's he going?" asked Montone.

"Somewhere on Biscayne," said Galindez, as they followed the cab into the flow of downtown traffic.

Three minutes later the cab pulled up in front of 1062 Biscayne Boulevard, a unique three-story wood-frame office building designed as a faux Tudor mansion. Without saying a word to the driver, Keyes paid the fare, got out of the cab and, carrying his satchel over his shoulder, entered the structure.

The police cars pulled up and double-parked outside, lining the street. Galindez directed one of the patrol units to follow and detain the cabdriver for questioning. They turned on their lights and flagged down the taxi a block away. The other officers sat in their cars and waited for an order from Galindez.

"Who's he here to see?" asked Montone.

"Parker and Morell, criminal defense counsel," said Galindez. "First class shitheels."

"They dirty?"

"Parker used to be a public defender. He crossed the line about fifteen years ago. He's sprung so many Colombian clients they ought to open an embassy. We've been looking for a reason to take them down for years."

Montone climbed out of the car and leaned on the roof. Through the first floor's large picture window he could see Keyes sitting in the lobby reading a magazine. They waited.

Two and a half minutes later a secretary ushered Keyes into Mr. Parker's office.

As Keyes entered, Mr. Livingston Parker and three associates who were present for the meeting expressed dismay at his appearance. Keyes set down his jacket by the window, draped his satchel over the back of a chair, removed a fresh shirt from a side pocket and asked Parker if he could use their washroom to freshen up before they began. One of the associates escorted him to Parker's private bathroom, which Keyes knew was in the rear of the building.

An urgent call came for Galindez over his cell phone. He quickly got out of the car and whispered to Montone.

"They just found Cody Lawson with two dead hookers and a bullet in his head," said Galindez.

"Cody Lawson, the linebacker?"

"He has a house in the Grove. There's a suicide note."

The football player.

"Take him," said Montone. "Let's take him."

Galindez gave the order and the uniforms swarmed toward the entrance of 1062 Biscayne Boulevard.

The explosion lifted the building off its foundation. The air went white-hot before they even heard the sound.

Concussion blew out the front windows, spraying a deadly fusillade of glass across the sidewalk, killing two of the officers instantly. The three floors of 1062 Biscayne pancaked to street level. The people inside Mr. Parker's office, closest to where investigators later determined the blast originated, disappeared, vaporized.

The force knocked Montone ten feet backward, over the car. He lost consciousness before his head hit the pavement.

CHAPTER
11

To whom it may concern:

I came to give America a gift.

You are the great Degrader, the nemesis of all civilization, culture and compassion. Posing as champion of individual freedom, you are in truth the Adversary which has been foretold in the darkest visions of man, all the more malignant because you protest an innocence which your ignorance and isolation allow you to indulge.

Reduce the population of this world to a village of a hundred people who reflect all ratios of wealth and nationality and only six of that hundred would be Americans. But those six would control 50% of the planet's resources and 70% of her wealth. You were raised to believe this outrage is your God-given right, without even stopping to consider that your good fortune comes at the expense of every other human life.

The price of your precious freedom is the enslavement of the human race.

I have brought you a gift, America.

My gift is this promise: that not riches, nor beauty, not power or fame, not high principles or noble intentions can keep you from His reach when Death comes calling. The denial of death is the central hypocrisy of your empire, for you have visited indiscriminate murder on every other land on this earth.

Bombs from your factories have fallen like rain.

The bile of your materialism stifles out spirits, your cult of celebrity poisons our souls.

The waste of your industries and your excesses chokes our air, despoils our waters and destroys the natural order.

Your science has killed all our Gods.

As history makes clear, no act of diplomacy can stop you, nor any political movement. All hopes that you might reform yourselves are lost in your hedonism and corruption. The end of the world is graven in your image without your even knowing because in this, your American century, you have never on your shores suffered the hoofbeats of the Horsemen.

I'm here to give you back the death that you've bequeathed to the rest of us. Call it a work of art, a message in a bottle, letters scratched in the sand, I have couched it in the only language you can comprehend, in the only form that will penetrate your fractured attention spans.

Death is my medium and my message.

I have come to teach your children they are going to die. Only then, with that truth seared into their consciousness, will they understand how they must change so that the world might be saved from your arrogance and self-esteem.

I am the product of your dreams.

Death and rebirth.

: letter left by Terry Keyes in a taxi outside 1062 Biscayne Boulevard

Montone spent four days in a Miami hospital, for the first twenty-four hours completely unaware of what had happened. He suffered a second-degree concussion, some memory confusion, which his attending doctors believed was temporary, a sprained neck, a dislocated right shoulder and a fifty percent hearing loss in his right ear. Hector Galindez lay in a bed in the next room, recovering from a shattered pelvis suffered when a filing cabinet shot out one of the windows like a cannonball and pinned him against his own car.

Pat Feany and Mike Murphy, still in the second car at the time of the explosion, were only cut by flying glass. Frank Fonseca, who jumped out of the car when the uniforms made their move toward the door, had a broken arm. The two fatalities were both Metro-Dade patrol officers, the first to reach the doors of 1062. Sixteen other officers were injured; five were still listed in critical condition by the time Montone was discharged.

Although they could find only three intact bodies in the wreckage, investigators concluded that seven people inside the building at the time of the explosion had died, including Livingston Parker, his three associates, two receptionists and Terry Keyes. Keyes's wallet and shreds of the jacket and bloodstained shirt he'd been wearing were found in the rubble.

Days later a section of a partial dental bridge was unearthed at the site. Medical records faxed by the prison infirmary at Wormwood Scrubs near London identified the bridge as one manufactured for Terry Keyes while he was still an inmate.

Bomb squad investigators found evidence that Semtex had been the explosive used in the device, a compact, controlled solid substance used by the military in large-scale demolition work. They believed the bomb, approximately ten pounds, had been housed in the satchel that Terry Keyes carried into the building, portions of which were found fused to the handcrafted detonator.

The twin to the satchel that had housed the bomb was found by police in the closet of Keyes's room at the Delano. Inside was the file labeled "MONTONE" that the detective had glimpsed on the plane to Miami.

The pages inside the file were blank.

On his laptop computer they found nothing to indicate Keyes had even been writing a book.

Within days of the disaster, local witnesses came forward identifying Keyes as a man they had known as J. Thomas Sylvester. An empty apartment rented in that name was discovered in South Beach, two blocks from the Delano Hotel. Keyes's fingerprints were found inside.

From ID fragments sifted from the explosion site, investigators subsequently traced the Semtex to an allotment stolen from a military base the previous September. An informant already in lockup on unrelated charges came forward to allege that a man answering Keyes's description had purchased ten pounds of the substance in November, when Keyes was in Miami on his book tour.

A black Ford Taurus purchased at the same time, and registered to Mr. Sylvester, was never recovered.

Competing for headlines in the blast's immediate aftermath was the death of Cody Lawson, discovered on the morning of the explosion in the bedroom of his Coconut Grove mansion. A perennial all-star linebacker for the Miami Dolphins during his twelve-year career, Lawson had also created a playfully menacing off-the-field image that he parlayed into a multimillion-dollar advertising persona.

A South Florida native, Lawson had helped win an NCAA championship at the University of Miami before turning pro a year early after a scandal in the athletic department; two of his teammates had been accused and convicted of rape. Unsubstantiated rumors put Lawson at the scene—some even implicated him in the crime—but he never came forward to testify. A star on the team while the men who went to jail were part-time players, Lawson was followed into the NFL by accusations of favoritism. His carefully calculated image had been tarnished in recent years by an ugly, public divorce trial that generated persistent rumors about a degenerate lifestyle, and a controversial autobiography in which he finally admitted that he had been a witness to, but not a participant in, that infamous collegiate rape.

Lawson had been discovered at eight-thirty the morning of the explosion by members of his household staff. Two prostitutes from a Miami escort service were found lying on his bed, bound and gagged, both dead from massive overdoses of injected cocaine. A large quantity of the drug rested on a mirror beside the bed. Both women's bodies bore repeated injection marks and a syringe was still embedded in one of the girls' arms. Both had been savagely beaten, before and after death.

Lawson was found lying between the two bodies with a single gunshot wound to the head. A .38 revolver licensed to Lawson was still held in his right hand. His suicide "note," scrawled on the mirrored wall behind his bed in the blood of one of the murdered girls, consisted of two words.

"TOO MUCH . . ."

The morning after the grisly discovery a roll of film detailing the crime scene arrived in the mail at the offices of a national tabloid newspaper, along with a copy of the letter Keyes had left in the taxi and a single sheet of paper on which had been printed the question "ROLE MODEL?" Within days those pictures and the letter appeared in print on newsstands across the country, setting off a legal and moral firestorm.

The devastation at 1062 Biscayne, Cody Lawson's sordid bacchanalia, the discovery and publication of the letter left in the taxicab, catapulted the life and message of Terence Peregrine Keyes into the national spotlight in a way that perhaps only Keyes could have anticipated. When the videotape of Montone assaulting Keyes in the Delano Hotel made it onto CNN, inevitable linkages to the suicide murders in

New York emerged and the scope of the story achieved a scandalized immortality.

Melodramatic cover stories appeared in the newsmagazines ("The Dark Angel of Death"), angry words were exchanged by the televised pundits, on radio talk shows, over telephone lines and backyard fences. Keyes's two books rocketed onto the bestseller lists, even as his publishers decried the trail of blood he'd left behind. Psychologists scrutinized his every written word, including the putative suicide notes. As more than one of these experts pointed out, in an irony they decided would not have disappointed Keyes, a lot of money changed hands.

During these early days, representatives from every spectrum of the press tried desperately to reach James Montone. The hospital came under a media siege and the crowd outside grew larger every day. Huge cash offers were extended for exclusive access to his side of the story. Speculation and second-guessing centered on the detective's role in Keyes's crusade. Controversy swirled around him: How much did he know about this man and when did he know it? How many of the fourteen deaths attributed to Keyes might have been prevented if earlier action had been taken? Their conclusions, in response to Montone's silence, proved less than charitable to the detective.

The members of his squad formed a protective perimeter around Montone while he recovered from his injuries and began to piece together the fragments of his splintered memory. From his sickbed, Hector Galindez authorized an around-the-clock police presence in the hospital to hold the press at bay, and his superiors worked closely with the brass in New York to orchestrate a bilateral response.

They immediately scheduled a joint news conference and for the first time revealed, to a limited degree, the operation they had undertaken to apprehend Terry Keyes. Damning him with faint praise, his department began to gently distance itself from James Montone, leaving large unanswered questions about the manner in which he had exercised his discretionary command of the case. Damage control remained their first priority.

On the night after Montone came around he spent a quiet hour with Galindez and Mike Murphy, asking questions, fleshing out the frightening gaps in his memory, before fatigue and painkillers carried him away. During the night he woke, frequently, and cried for reasons he couldn't remember.

The following day Montone felt strong enough to accept his first phone call. He had to hold the phone to his left ear; the damage to the hearing in his right was permanent.

Erin Kelly called from her home in Syracuse. On the day he was injured she had repeatedly attempted to get in to see him but doctors turned everyone away. She had flown home the following day to fulfill an obligation at the university.

"I'll fly down if you want me there," she said. "I can be there tonight."

"No need," he said. "I'm getting out of here soon."

He didn't tell her his real reason: that, to date, her name had been kept out of the papers and he wanted it to stay that way.

The conversation ran dry. He waited.

"The football player who was killed," she said, lowering her voice. "He fits your theory."

"The friend who wouldn't testify."

"The gifted athlete who lives by a different set of rules. Couldn't be clearer."

"I see it," said Montone, rubbing his forehead.

"The lawyer in the explosion, Livingston Parker, he fits too."

"How so?"

"He used to be a public defender. Moves on to a thriving private practice. Turns his back on his disadvantaged clients. Just like the one who talked Keyes into pleading guilty."

A fractured memory of the explosion flashed through his mind; heat, the deafening concussion.

"Have you told anyone else about this yet?" she asked.

"I'm having a hard enough time with the Jell-O."

"You were right, James. All the pieces fit. You had him figured out."

Montone paused. "Being right doesn't mean a whole lot at the moment."

"I understand how you could feel that way. But I don't think there's any doubt he would have come after me and God knows who else. And you stopped him."

"He stopped himself."

She was silent again. Montone heard her softly weeping.

"I'm sorry he hurt you," she said.

"I'll be all right."

"I'm so sorry for all of it." He heard her making an effort to compose herself. "When are you going home?"

"Day or two. Depends on the doctors. Got a hell of a headache. I'm hearing this ringing sound. Tried to answer the phone about twelve times."

Another lengthy pause.

"Can I come see you when you're back in the city?" she asked.

"Let me get up and around first."

She paused. "If you don't want to see me right now, James, I understand. But I think it might help for us to talk. It might help us both make some sense of this."

Montone tried to sort through a complicated welter of emotions. He wondered if she shared his confusion. He felt bound to her, not only through their mutual loss. Something more substantial, more needful, now registered inside him when he thought of her, and it frightened him but the reason why stayed remote, fogged in.

"I'll call you when I get back," he said. "That's a promise."

Senior officers from Metro-Dade visited the hospital the next day to solicit statements from the New York squad. At Hector Galindez's insistence, Montone was spared any pressurized interrogation, spending only an hour with the Miami officers. Murphy remained in the room to prompt him whenever his still-unreliable memory came up short. The other detectives later filled in his sketched outline of events.

After consulting with his doctors, Montone received medical clearance and made plans to fly back to New York the following day. That evening, after a last round of physical therapy for his injuries, Hector Galindez asked to see him privately. Montone sat beside Galindez's bed, wearing a brace around his neck, his right arm still wrapped tight to his body in a protective sling.

Drifting in and out of a medicated haze, the middle of his body immobilized in plaster, Galindez grasped Montone's good hand and would not let go.

"You don't look so bad," said Montone.

"No? I won't be able to fuck for six months," he said.

"How's your wife taking it?"

"My wife? Are you crazy? We have six children, for Christ's sake. It's my girlfriend I'm worried about."

Montone smiled for the first time since the blast.

"You remember what happened?" asked Galindez.

"Bits and pieces. It's coming together."

"You remember pounding the shit out of that *puto?*"

"Yes."

"Good. Hang on to that."

Galindez regarded him for a long time with his sad, sleepy eyes.

"You'll be forever changed by this, my friend."

"I know."

"I don't just mean externally. You go back to your life, it may take you years to comprehend how or why. Don't be in any hurry. This kind of shit is too complicated."

Montone nodded, trying to listen.

"You still beating yourself up?"

"Some."

"You're thinking how could I let this monster into my life? I should have *known.*"

"Yeah."

"That's bullshit. This one, he isn't human, not in the way that could have helped you see. I looked into his eyes, I know."

"You saw it too."

"A walking corpse with the soul of a dead man. Nobody's home. He could be whatever he wanted to show you. Only a fucking saint could have made him."

"Maybe so."

Hector leaned over and whispered. "Jimmy, there is only one way to make yourself feel better about this."

"What's that?"

"Retribution. Old Testament. Straight up."

"How?"

"Nobody knows this yet. . . . We didn't find the car."

Montone didn't know what he meant.

"His black Taurus. It hasn't turned up."

"What are you . . ."

"I'm just telling you."

They sat in silence for a while.

Growing fatigued, Galindez finally let go of Montone's hand, patting him on the arm.

"You come back down and see me when I'm out of this fucking

chastity belt. We'll go out on my boat. Introduce you to my girlfriend, who by the way knows more good-looking women than you could meet on your own in five years."

"Okay, Hector."

"Life is what you make of it. This is a choice we have. That is the wisdom of the fucking ages."

Montone sat with him until Galindez drifted off to sleep.

A wealthy friend of the department arranged a private plane to fly Montone and the squad back to New York. Galindez arranged a decoy police van to distract the media outside the hospital, so they reached the small, private airfield unmolested.

A car met the officers on the runway at LaGuardia and drove them into Manhattan. Feany, only too eager to spend time away from his wife, and Fonseca took turns staying with Montone for the first few days until he craved solitude and ordered them to leave.

The following week Captain Dan Jakes called Montone into his office and explained the department's decision. They offered him paid medical leave for six weeks, provided he didn't grant any interviews; enough time, they figured, for the heat on the story to die down. Jakes gently suggested that in the meantime a few sessions with a department psychologist might help Montone sort out his feelings. At the end of the six weeks he could decide if he was ready to go back on active duty. If not, he could transfer to a desk.

Or he could file for disability and claim his pension; Jakes let him know that the brass would not put up an argument. The police union representative had already told him about the offer, encouraging him to quickly take advantage of the department's unusual largesse. Montone had nearly lost his life twice in five years and brought down a dangerous killer in both instances; as far as both organizations were concerned, he had gone above and beyond the call.

It was also painfully clear to him the department wanted to put as much distance between itself and the public relations nightmare he'd become as decency would allow.

Montone asked for a few days to think it through. Jakes told him to take the whole six weeks if he liked and shook his left hand as they parted; the right was still suspended in a sling.

He spent most of the next week in his apartment, alone, and slept ten to twelve hours a day. He changed his phone number to hide from the press, and at least one journalist a day tried to stake out the lobby of his building. He ordered meals in from the Italian deli on the corner, going out only for long, solitary walks.

On one of those walks he stopped at the 19th Precinct without calling ahead, but after a round of awkward welcome-backs the uninterrupted routine of the squad room—senseless crimes, endless paperwork, the parade of sad-loser perps—felt foreign and stifling.

Maybe Hector Galindez had been right; the cover had been ripped off his life and he couldn't put it back. The possibility disabled him because he had no idea what to replace it with.

He monitored his phone calls, picking up only for Murphy, Fonseca or Feany. He watched a lot of ball games on television and visited the hospital every day for physical therapy on his shoulder and neck. He grew a beard because he couldn't shave with his left hand and it covered the cuts on his face as they slowly healed. On the day he discarded the sling he walked to Times Square and bought a ticket to an afternoon matinee, one of the big summer movies, but he left in the middle because the Hollywood violence looked so phony.

At least once a day he picked up the phone to call Erin Kelly and only once completed dialing her number. When he got her machine and heard her voice he declined to leave a message.

The next day, heat and humidity signaling the early arrival of summer, as he returned from one of his walks, heading south on Eighth Avenue, Montone stopped for the light at the corner of Thirty-eighth.

He heard someone singing. It sounded like opera, a ragged warble filtering up from the grate over the subway tunnel, distorted and off-key. A vagrant's voice, probably cadging for coins or just plain crazy.

He waited and listened, fighting his still-stubborn memory to place where he'd heard that voice before.

Montone quickly walked the block and a half to his apartment. He rummaged through a shoe box of evidence he took from his closet until he found the microcassette tape, opened his answering machine and slapped it inside.

The recording Holly had given him of the silent phone call she'd received.

He hit play, leaned forward and listened closely.

Street noise. The bus passing by. A distorted voice singing in the background.

The same voice.

The call had been placed from one of the pay phones in front of that building.

Montone stood before his living room window, looking out, trying to piece it together, when something caught his eye.

Reflected sunlight. Glinting off something on the roof of a nearby building. He looked up, saw the glare again, then a hint of movement as the light disappeared. His mind worked to place where it was coming from.

The same building.

He moved away from the window. Retrieved his binoculars from the closet, stood back and trained them on that rooftop, ten stories further up. Scanning, pulling focus.

Something up there. Moving? A piece of a shoulder?

He took his pistol from the holster which had been hanging on the back of his bedroom door—the first time he'd picked it up since coming home; the sling had made it impossible to wear—and stuck it in the back of his belt, grabbed his cell phone and left the apartment.

Montone walked back to the building on Eighth Avenue. He spotted a uniform cop on foot patrol outside. A young kid, freckle-faced, red-head. Montone walked up and showed his badge.

"You know who I am?"

The kid—his nameplate read "O'Keefe"—recognized him instantly and got a look on his face like he'd just met a movie star.

"Yes, sir."

"Come with me."

They entered the building. Montone went straight for an open elevator.

"Find the manager and meet me on the roof," said Montone.

"You want some backup?"

"No time."

The elevator closed. Montone rode it to the top floor. He took out his gun and held it at his side as he stepped out.

The corridor was empty. Blinding bright light reflected off the weathered linoleum flooring. Montone carefully walked past a series of ribbed, smoked-glass office doors until he found the fire stairs.

He walked one flight up, slowly opened the door and edged out onto the roof. A graveled walkway circled the outer edge of the building and he followed it around to the south side, pistol raised.

He found a pair of binoculars sitting on the ledge. His apartment building, and the windows of his apartment, were clearly visible to the south.

Pigeons scattered behind him. He turned, ready to fire.

Patrolman O'Keefe and the building manager stood near the door on the walkway.

Montone described the man he was looking for as they walked back down to the penthouse floor. The manager could think of no occupant who fit that description. Montone asked about tenants who had come into the building recently and gave him approximate dates.

"There's Mr. Kurtzman," said the manager. "But he doesn't look anything like what you've described."

"Show me his office."

They walked to the office door.

Montone gestured for silence, looked through the smoked glass for any motion inside. He noticed that his hands were shaking.

"Have you seen him recently, in the last two weeks?"

"No."

"Open it."

"I can't do that without a warrant."

"Open it or I'll break it down."

The manager produced his master key and unlocked the door.

"Stand back."

Montone pointed his pistol and pushed the door open. He edged inside.

Stale air. A heavy accumulation of dust on the furniture.

He walked over and opened the room's closed closet.

Empty.

He lowered the gun.

"I want to see Mr. Kurtzman's rental application," said Montone. "Get it right now."

The manager walked out. Montone took out his cell phone and dialed the squad room.

"Let me talk to Murphy. It's Montone."

The squad arrived within twenty minutes and sealed off the top floor. Detectives from the Crime Scene Unit arrived soon after and went to work. Makeup and padding that answered to "Mr. Kurtzman's" description were found in a locked drawer of the desk.

The closet yielded a cache of controlled pharmaceuticals, including Rohypnol and serum adrenaline. Murphy cataloged a row of books he found on a shelf.

Mr. Kurtzman's rental application listed an address in the Williamsburg section of Brooklyn.

By the time Montone and Murphy arrived, racing across the bridge with lights and siren, the thirty-man Emergency Services Unit had deployed around the building, cleared out the other residents and stood ready to storm the apartment.

Two minutes before the explosion Terry Keyes had removed his dental bridge, dropped it on the floor and climbed out the window of Livingston Parker's executive washroom. He made certain that no police officers occupied the alley behind the building, walked unobserved across to where he'd parked the black Taurus the night before, got in and drove down the alley.

When the bomb went off he was already three blocks away. He heard, even felt the explosion but resisted the powerful temptation to drive back and view the devastation.

Wearing his fresh shirt and sunglasses, he pulled a baseball cap low over his forehead and removed a first aid kit from the glove compartment. He turned onto Route 41, heading west out of town, and switched on the radio to an all-news station. Word of the bombing spread fast and he stayed tuned, hoping to hear details about the number of fatalities.

Once he was past city limits and into the stretch running straight through the Everglades, he cracked open a bottle of water, washed down half a dozen aspirin and, as he drove, assiduously obeying the speed limit, began tending to his wounds.

By noon he reached Fort Myers. News stories about the shocking death of Cody Lawson had begun to compete for radio airtime with the bombing. Within the hour coverage had started to feature the name Terry Keyes as a possible suspect and consensus placed him among the victims of the blast, which early estimates numbered at nine, including two Miami police officers. Detective James Montone, NYPD, was not mentioned. Neither was a black Ford Taurus. No links between the two events had yet emerged.

His cuts closed and bandaged, Keyes stopped at an isolated self-serve gas station and filled his tank. He bought two ham sandwiches and half a dozen sodas from vending machines and a bag of ice which he emptied into a Styrofoam cooler. No one paid him any particular notice.

He drove off, continuing north on Route 41, avoiding the interstate. He ate both of the sandwiches and applied ice to his swollen lips and eyes. In spite of the pain of the beating, and the throbbing of a rib he suspected was cracked, his spirits soared. He passed a number of highway patrol cars, none of which offered him a second glance.

At three o'clock, reaching the outer neighborhoods of Tampa, he pulled off the side of the road behind the cover of a grove of palms. As a precaution he unscrewed the car's license plates, dropped them in the nearby swamp and replaced them with a pair he'd stolen off a car in the garage of J. Thomas Sylvester's South Beach residential hotel. The car belonged to an elderly shut-in who seldom drove and he knew they would not soon be missed.

He used Interstate 75 to bypass the sprawl of downtown Tampa and decided he'd put enough distance between himself and Miami to stay with the convenience of the superhighway. By this time he figured his photograph would have started to appear on television, but after deciding that the effects of Montone's beating actually rendered him unrecognizable, he stopped one more time near Ocala for gas, some sandwiches and a thermosful of coffee.

Seven hours later, nearing midnight, he pulled into the parking lot of an apartment building in suburban Atlanta. He used a security key card to gain access to the subterranean garage and parked in the spot for the apartment he'd rented last fall in the name of Charles C. Hardy. He blanketed the Taurus with the car cover from the trunk, went upstairs and let himself into apartment 4A.

He had previously stocked the apartment with canned goods and enough freeze-dried foods for a week. He made himself a camper's meal of rice, beef Stroganoff and lemonade and turned on the apartment's small television to watch the news.

Within four days his face had sufficiently healed for him to venture outside, wearing the makeup and clothing that transformed him into Charles Hardy. He spent the next three days riding buses and shopping in suburban malls. He watched CNN avidly for any indications that they thought he might still be alive; there were none. He bought and read with amusement the flood of newspaper and magazine articles that appeared about him.

Most presumed he was crazy; all presumed he was dead.

What their endless theorizing missed, what perhaps of all people only Montone, and before that Peter Henshaw, had understood about him, was that Terry Keyes had become, literally, no-man. When his world collapsed around him under that pier in Blackpool the peculiar sum of who he'd thought himself to be resulted in a void, into which had seeped an elemental malevolence so consuming that it eventually destroyed whatever vestigial personality remained. Terry Keyes ceased to exist.

He was able to stand back and regard his own rage and emptiness with a sense of wonder, but it offered him no comfort, no relief. Not until his last years in Wormwood Scrubs did this passion attach itself to a satisfying course of action. He had already written his first book and was at work on the second, his campaign to free himself well under way.

It began when he happened across a book by a female American psychologist, writing about a serial killer named Wendell Sligo and the cop who had brought him to justice.

Outrage enough that the woman had the temerity to suggest that anyone convicted of a crime—for example, himself, an innocent—was responsible for any persecution they subsequently suffered. As Keyes read deeper into the work his astonishment grew at what its hidden messages revealed to him: somehow, beyond reason, this policeman, whose life bore so many striking similarities to his own it couldn't be mere coincidence, had stolen from him the life Terry Keyes was supposed to be living.

At last, an explanation for the cruel fate he had suffered.

There had been a Mistake. A terrible Crime had indeed been committed. Not by him; *against* him.

He read every book he could find on this Detective James Montone. Acclaimed, admired, celebrated in print and on television; a "good man." All damnable lies. Montone had accomplices, certainly, in committing this outrage against him; no one man could have brought off such a monstrous injustice on his own. They'd all been party to his thievery, right down the list, the ones who'd locked him away. From the the corrupt destructive society that had nurtured and rewarded Montone to the woman who'd written this insidious book. They would all be taken to task for what had been done to him.

As part of that blinding insight, Keyes was shown the way in which those who had denied him the life and happiness that was his by right should now be punished. Not in simple acts of revenge. The grandiosity of the offense committed against him would have to be reflected by the scope and gravity of his response. One that would command recognition from the world of his superior nature.

He would begin by speaking with this other man who had suffered so greatly at the hands of James Montone. Wendell Sligo. They had so much in common.

The Plan was born. From that moment forward he devoted every waking moment to its fulfillment.

The following Monday Charles Hardy packed a suitcase, took a taxi to the Atlanta airport and caught a flight to New York City. He rented a room in a midtown flophouse and revisited his old building on Eighth Avenue. Waiting until he was certain that Montone had seen him watching, he left a pair of binoculars on the edge of the roof, then went down and stood across the street and watched Montone enter the building with a young patrolman.

As Montone and Murphy were arriving at Howard Kurtzman's apartment building in Brooklyn, Charles Hardy walked down a jetway at LaGuardia and boarded a plane for Buffalo. The drive to Attica State Penitentiary would take less than an hour.

From there, Syracuse, New York, was not much more than a hundred miles.

The attack team from ESU took down the door with a battering ram. A dozen men with submachine guns crashed the front room as the other platoon came in through the back.

The apartment was empty and had clearly not been occupied in weeks.

CSU took control of the scene. Detectives lifted a large number of fingerprints that would within hours be matched to those of Terry Keyes.

In the drawer of a desk they found evidence of open bank accounts in four different American cities; including Howard Kurtzman, the accounts were set up in four different names. Police in each of those cities would be quickly alerted to investigate. Murphy initiated a check to see if there had been any recent hits on credit cards issued in any of those names. He also called in a phone dump on the apartment's records; they'd have them by morning.

On a coffee table in the living room stood a framed photograph of Holly and Montone, taken on the night they met at the restaurant opening. Beside it stood one from the same night of Montone and Keyes, their arms around each other's shoulders, smiling.

In an unlabeled notebook on the coffee table they found photographs of Mackenzie Dennis, Holly Mews, Cody Lawson, Livingston Parker, Erin Kelly and James Montone.

Inside the notebook they discovered a partial, neatly typed and printed manuscript. The title page read: "UNFINISHED WORK, by Terence Peregrine Keyes." This was the book he'd been writing; not about investigating homicides, but committing them. Some of it was addressed directly to Montone.

Montone immediately went outside and used his cellular to dial Erin Kelly's number in Syracuse. He told her what they'd found; confirmation that she had indeed been Keyes's next target.

"When we hang up, I want you to call a friend and stay on the phone," he said.

"Why?"

"I'm calling the state troopers up there, I'm gonna have them send somebody over to you. They're gonna stay with you, at least until I can get there. I'm coming up tonight."

"What's going on?"

"There's a possibility Keyes might still be alive."

Silence.

"I understand," she said.

"I'm going straight to the airport. I'll be there in a couple of hours."

"All right."

"Erin, probably this is nothing to worry about, but we're not gonna take any chances. Do you have a gun?"

Another pause.

"Erin?"

"Yes. Yes, I have a gun."

"You know how to use it?"

"Yes. We had an uncle who was a policeman," she said.

"Desk sergeant in Providence."

She hesitated again.

"Please hurry," she said.

Murphy drove Montone to LaGuardia. Montone called ahead and secured a seat on an eight o'clock commuter flight to Syracuse. His neck, free of the brace, tensed up tight, nerves raw.

"You sure you saw somebody on that roof?" asked Murphy.

"Maybe's close enough."

"Those glasses could've been up there for weeks. He's gotta be dead, Jimmy. You saw that explosion."

"I didn't see anybody drive a stake through his heart."

Montone made the plane with minutes to spare. He thought it through during the flight, how Keyes might have done it. Galindez's veiled warning came back to him.

We didn't find the car.

He drifted into a dreamless sleep, exhaustion catching up with him. The stewardess woke him shortly before they landed. Montone rented a car at the Syracuse airport, called Erin for directions and made the drive in the dark.

He found Sycamore Street and checked the numbers until he came to her house, a two-story center-hall wood-frame on a tree-lined, upper-middle-class residential block. A state trooper's car sat out front. He pulled up and parked in front of it and walked to the door.

Erin answered the bell. She nearly broke into tears when she saw him.

"Your face," she said, reaching out to touch him.

"It'll heal."

She put her arms around him. He saw the troopers inside over her shoulder, glancing out at them, circumspect.

"I'm so glad you're here," she whispered.

"So am I."

One of the troopers walked toward them, holding his radio.

"Detective Montone?"

"Yes."

"Trooper Don Lafleur, sir; my partner's name is Bostic."

The other trooper tipped his hat.

"Thanks for your help."

"No problem. Detective, we've got a message for you that came in from your office? You're supposed to call Warden Granville at Attica. The number's right here."

Montone separated from Erin and took the piece of paper from him. Erin showed him to the phone. The switchboard at Attica quickly put his call through to the warden's office.

"This is James Montone."

"Detective, thank you for calling. I'm sorry to have to disturb you with this."

"What's the problem?"

"We did a random sweep of our high-security block early this evening? We found some contraband in the cell of Wendell Sligo that I felt you needed to know about? I'm sorry we didn't come across this earlier."

"What?"

"Correspondence to Sligo from this man Terry Keyes. A letter Sligo had recently written to you."

"A letter to me?"

"Written, perhaps as recently as today, but not yet mailed. And we found a copy of an audiotape concealed inside his chess set. We believe it's a recording related to one of the cases you've been working on."

"Which one?"

"The young woman. The model."

"A recording of what?"

"It appears to be the same one they were playing on the radio a while ago. Only this goes further." Granville paused, extremely uncomfortable. "You can hear her strangling."

12

Dear Jimmy Boy,

A friend tells me you've fallen on hard times. In fact, from the looks of things, it seems like your life is fairly well fucked. Maybe now you'll realize to yourself and admit to the world that when you stopped me from my work it was nothing more than dumb LUCK, and that you are the biggest loser.

Because this state does not have the courage to kill the worst of its killers, namely me, even if they are as bad and deserve it as much as I did, I am the one who will have the last laugh. HA-HA. Because I know now even if I spend the rest of my life in this shithole you are the one who is cheated and fucked over in life and I am free.

Which is how it should be.

The day you stopped me from my work was the day you sealed your own fate, as it turned out. Ain't it funny how things work out?

My friend says to tell you you have to take responsibility for your own crimes. HA-HA.

If you really want to know what that means you're going to have to ask me yourself, unless of course you would rather learn your lesson the hard way. Again.

Which you will anyway.

Good-bye and GOOD LUCK.

HA-HA.

P.S. By the way, how did you like seeing her hanging there with your cum still inside her?

: letter found in Wendell "the Slug" Sligo's cell at Attica State Penitentiary

Warden Granville faxed both letters to Erin's house soon after Montone got off the phone with him. They sat at Erin's dining room table and examined the letters together. Montone decided he would drive to Attica in the morning to interrogate Sligo personally. Erin had a graduate class to teach in the morning; the troopers would remain with her around the clock until Montone returned.

Trooper Lafleur stationed himself just inside the front door, his shotgun resting on his knees. Trooper Bostic sat in the kitchen, covering the back.

Erin mixed a pitcher of fresh lemonade and took it out to the porch. She turned off the porch light and sat with Montone looking out into the warm summer evening, the peaceful street. A dog barked somewhere far off. A kid rode by on a bike, spokes clicking. The arching elms on either side of the street swayed in a gentle breeze.

"I've been thinking about his anti-American thing," she said. "Why he hated us so much."

"He talked about how, in prison, all they watched were these American films. American television."

"We're the land of plenty. We represented everything he'd been denied. Particularly for a poor kid in the north of England. Opportunity. Privilege. Freedom."

"I can feel some sympathy for that boy who had his bright future taken away," said Montone. "Maybe he's innocent. Maybe the girl's death was an accident. But everything he's done since was a choice. Like you said in your book. And for that I want to put him in his grave."

"We're not responsible, James. All I did was write the book. You were just doing your job. He went after Holly to get at both of us. That was his choice, not ours."

Montone looked at the scars from the explosion on his hands, livid in the pale light. His breath caught in his chest.

"I was just starting to live again," he said.

"James, it's not your fault."

"No, Erin, I let him in. I have to take that responsibility. I should have known what he was. I saw what I wanted to see because I got caught up in the idea of him writing the book. I liked the idea and I acted against my instincts. That was my choice, nobody else's."

Eric Bowman

"But no one else—"

"Please. That's how I feel."

She stopped, thought about what he'd said. Set down her lemonade and took his hands.

"What I meant to say is this: How you feel is completely appropriate. We both loved her. And I'm not holding you to blame."

His eyes filled with tears. He could only nod a thank-you. They sat in silence for a long while and she held his hands.

"Living again means you have to feel all of it," he said. "All the pain."

"Not easy to do."

"That's what the shrink used to tell me."

"We shrinks are pretty smart," she said.

She kissed him once, gently, on the cheek before she went up to bed. After securing all the doors and windows with the troopers, Montone lay down in the bedroom next to Erin's. He could hear a fan in her bedroom and imagined that he heard her slow, steady breathing as he drifted off.

Montone left in the rental car at nine the next morning and reached the gates of Attica shortly before eleven. He called Murphy at the squad and told him his plans. The day had started fair but as he drove further west, gray overcast skies promised a storm by evening.

Before he entered, as they'd discussed, he called Erin at the university office number she'd given. She answered; she'd finished her class, the troopers were there with her. She'd been waiting for his call and was about to head back to the house. Montone said he'd call her there again as he was leaving the prison.

Showing his badge at the vehicle entrance, he waited while the guard verified his pass. He'd never seen Attica before; maximum security, last stop in the state's penal system. Looking at the massive cellblock walls in front of him, he wondered how many men he'd sent to this dead end, and couldn't come up with a number. Fifty? A hundred?

The guard opened the gate and waved him through with instructions. He passed between the forbidding Gothic outer walls and parked in a circular drive, where another guard waited to escort him to Warden Granville's office in the administration building.

Eldon Granville didn't keep him waiting. A tall, fleshy, serious-minded man, he shook Montone's hand and immediately walked him to a bare room down the hall that contained the collected evidence from Wendell Sligo's cell, laid out on a table.

Montone looked at the originals of the letters he'd read last night. He picked up the audiotape but declined to listen to it in the recorder they'd provided.

"I'm sorry to be the one who had to show that to you," said Granville. "We also found this in his cell."

He handed over a photo album. A scrapbook of local and national newspaper stories about the disgracing of Detective James Montone. Holly's death. His suspension. The debacle in Miami. A number of stories critical of Montone's role in the investigation, including a rabid *Post* editorial demanding that he be kicked off the force, if not charged with criminal negligence.

"Did Terry Keyes ever come here?" asked Montone.

"Wendell only had one visitor in the last two years. He refused to see anybody else. This man."

Granville showed Montone a photograph; a grainy blowup, poor quality, of a heavyset bald man sitting at a square wooden table across from Wendell Sligo. The overhead angle showed only a portion of the man's profile; he wore a bushy beard along his jawline and oversized, square-framed eyeglasses.

"That's taken off video from a surveillance camera in the visiting room. His name's John Stevenson. A freelance journalist from the Buffalo area. This is a copy of his visitor's application. He was allegedly working on a book about Sligo."

"When was he here?" said Montone.

"Three times," said Granville, showing him photocopies of the visitor's logbook. "Once last November. Again about six weeks ago. And yesterday afternoon. Never caused any trouble or drew any attention to himself. He took a lot of notes, his credentials looked authentic. We assumed he was who he said he was."

"Did he ever give anything to Sligo?"

"Like the tape?"

Montone nodded.

"It's possible."

"Anything pass between them on the video?"

"I'm afraid it's only intermittent frames; one every six seconds.

Cost-cutting measure. I've looked at it closely. This was the best image we could pull of him. Seems clear he was aware of the camera."

"What time was he here yesterday?"

"Four o'clock."

Montone looked at his watch. Erin should be just arriving home.

"I'll see him now," said Montone.

Picking up an armed escort, Warden Granville led him through the yard to the maximum-security block, a dark fortress set apart from the main walls of the prison.

Montone waited on one side of the bulletproof glass in an interview room. A guard opened the inner door.

Wendell Sligo ambled in and lowered his bulk into the seat on the other side of the glass from Montone. His long black hair had thinned since Montone last saw him; greased back, streaks of bone-white scalp peeking through. He wore lush triangular sideburns down to his jaw-line. The same black-framed glasses boxed in his dead-fish eyes. His thin lips formed a long, flat, expressionless line.

"You look like shit," said Sligo.

"What did he want, Wendell? Why'd he come here?"

"Oh, he wanted to know all about you, mister."

"For what reason?"

"He hates you almost as much as I do."

"What'd you get out of it?"

"He brought me that tape of your girlfriend. I liked to jerk off to it. Just like the good old days."

He smirked. Montone wanted to break through the glass and kill him.

"That was your deal. A tape?"

"You took all of mine before, you piece of shit."

"What did you tell him, Wendell?"

"That a girl was the way to get you. That after what I done to that Sheila, a girl you hardened up for was definitely the way to go."

"Fuck you."

Sligo laughed and shook his head. "He said you'd come. Son of a bitch is sharp, I'll give him that."

Montone got up to leave.

"You shouldn't have left her alone, Jimmy boy."

Montone called out to the guard to open the door.

"Don't tell anybody and he'll wait for you to get there, Jimbo. You breathe a word to anybody, he'll finish her real quick."

He realized Sligo was talking about Erin.

"Third time's the charm," said Sligo, smiling slyly.

Montone struggled to hide his response; he turned his back, refusing to give Sligo the satisfaction. The guard opened the door and led him back into the yard.

Montone took out his phone and quickly dialed Erin's number.

Her machine answered.

He thought it through. She might still be on the way home. Maybe they stopped for lunch.

Montone said a fast goodbye to the warden and sped out of the prison gates, accelerating back toward the interstate.

When they arrived back at Erin's house, one of the replacements for Troopers Lafleur and Bostic's shift change stood out front, tool kit open, reaching into the open hood of his car, steam rising from inside.

"Damn fuel pump's acting up," said the trooper.

"I'm expecting a call," said Erin.

"Where's Billy?" asked Lafleur.

"He's inside," said the trooper.

"I'll go in with you, Miss Kelly," said Bostic.

They started up the front steps.

"Can you give me a hand?" asked the trooper. "Grab hold of these pliers, keep the clamp on while I get the wrench in there."

"Sure," said Lafleur.

He reached in and took hold of the pliers.

The trooper pulled a combat knife from the tool kit and stabbed Lafleur in the soft tissue below his left ear. He held Lafleur under the hood until he stopped moving, then quickly dragged the body into the backseat of the car and closed the door.

Erin checked the light on her answering machine. No calls. She heard Trooper Bostic on the stairs, calling for his replacement.

"Billy?"

No answer.

Erin moved into the kitchen for a glass of water and noticed the door to the basement stood open a few inches. She was certain they'd closed it before they left.

"Billy, you up there?"

Erin moved to the door. She hesitated, a strange feeling in the pit of her stomach, then opened it.

A trooper lay at the bottom of the stairs, eyes open and fixed, his neck twisted at an impossible broken-doll angle. Just past him she saw another man on the basement floor. Stripped to his underwear. A pool of blood.

"Miss Kelly?"

She turned to him as Bostic entered the kitchen behind her.

Movement behind him. Bostic froze midstep, midword, then dropped to his knees on the floor. She saw a glimpse of the blade, then the other figure rushing toward her.

A trooper.

Somewhere she heard the phone begin to ring.

Montone got Erin's machine again and didn't leave a message. He stepped on the gas, took the car up to ninety on the thruway. The next sign said eighty miles to Syracuse.

He called the squad room and got Murphy on the line.

"Jimmy, I've been trying to call you. We got a hit on one of those names," said Murphy. "Charles Hardy opened the bank account in Atlanta and he rented an apartment with a cashier's check last November; that's when Keyes was there on his tour."

"They check it out?"

"They found the Ford Taurus in the basement garage about an hour ago."

"When was he there?"

"Neighbors put him in the building as recently as four days ago. The Feds are all over it."

"Mike, he had another name set up. John Stevenson, Buffalo." He read Murphy the address from the prison visitor's form. "There's probably a bank account, too. He visited Sligo at Attica."

"When?"

"The first time was last November and again when he came back to the States, about six weeks ago."

"Why, for Christ's sake?"

"He made some kind of deal with Sligo."

"What kind of deal?"

"Sligo tells him the best way to come after me. For that, he gives Sligo a copy of the tape of Holly dying."

"Jesus, Jimmy."

"Destroying my life was their big mutual interest."

There was a long silence.

"Where are you?" asked Murphy.

"On the road. I'm driving back to see Erin."

You shouldn't have left her alone, Jimmy boy.

Montone didn't mention that Keyes had been to see Wendell yesterday.

Don't tell anybody and he'll wait for you to get there.

"Jimmy, is he up there?"

You breathe a word to anybody, he'll finish her real quick . . . Third time's the charm.

"I don't know."

"Jimmy, you call for backup, call some troopers."

"The troopers are already with her. Call the Bureau, get a jump on Buffalo, Mike. I'm driving the other way."

"You check in with me. You be careful."

Montone hung up and tried Erin's home number one last time.

No answer.

Rain started to fall, obscuring his view of the open countryside. His shoulder ached like a bad tooth.

At quarter to two he took Exit 36 off the thruway and drove to Sycamore Street. He cruised past her house; two trooper cars out front. He was about to pull up behind them when he realized Erin's car wasn't in the driveway.

Montone turned into the alleyway, cut the engine, rolled to the back of the house. Trash cans had been left out for collection up and down the alley, except at Erin's.

He got out, peered through a window in the single-car garage. Empty. He opened a gate into the backyard and approached the rear door.

He drew his pistol and tried the doorknob. Unlocked. He pushed it open, raised the gun and stepped inside the kitchen. No sights or smells of recent cooking. He heard no sound from elsewhere in the house and stepped through the kitchen into the dining room.

The blinking light of her answering machine on a desk near the window caught his eye.

He crossed the living room and climbed the stairs, old risers creaking under every step. He nudged open the door to Erin's bedroom.

The covers had been stripped off her bed. On top of the bare mattress lay a large open map. Montone moved to take a look; a regional map of central New York, including nearby Adirondack Park.

A route leading from Syracuse to an area in the park called the Enchanted Forest had been highlighted by yellow marker. Beside the map he found a xeroxed sheet of instructions detailing the way to "Erin's Hideaway"—by its looks and conversational tone, a handout she gave to weekend visitors.

As he picked up the handout something fell from it onto the map.

A bloodied fingernail, torn out at the root. Painted with a coral polish, the color she'd been wearing. Probably ring finger.

He said you'd come. Son of a bitch is sharp, I'll give him that.

Keyes used Sligo to draw him away to Attica. The troopers were dead. They took her car; he pictured Keyes sticking her in the trunk.

The drive to the cabin looked to be about a three-hour trip.

Montone carefully weighed calling for support. The Bureau would jump in with a big move but Keyes might already have made it to Erin's cabin; no chance to stop him on the road.

Don't tell anybody and he'll wait for you to get there.

Keyes would keep her alive in order to get him there alone. He wouldn't hesitate to kill her under any other circumstances.

He thought of her parents at Holly's funeral. He could not allow those people to lose both of their daughters.

Galindez's last advice to him in the hospital came back to him.

Retribution. Old Testament. Straight up.

He took the map and the handout and went downstairs. He stopped in the kitchen and rummaged through the drawers. From her desk in the dining room he retrieved a roll of Scotch tape. He rolled up his pants leg and taped a steak knife to his right calf.

Fifteen minutes later he was back on the thruway, heading east toward Utica. The rain had settled down into a steady drizzle. He stopped for gas once, reached Utica at quarter to five and turned north onto Route 12. Within a few miles the road began its gradual climb into the western reaches of the Adirondack range.

Shortly before six he crossed the border of the park and for the next forty minutes drove through rolling upland forests. Low-hanging clouds obscured the peaks and ridges of the surrounding mountains, enclosing him in a moving capsule of visibility. He encountered few other cars. The rain let up as he neared the first designated turn off the highway on Erin's map.

Five miles down the narrow two-lane road another turn was indicated, a right onto a dirt road leading into deeper woods. Her house and the lake were drawn on the map, another mile further in.

He pulled the car off the side of the road and parked it out of sight behind a copse of trees. He stepped outside, turned on his cellular phone to test it and was not surprised to find he was now out of operable range. As the overheated car engine clicked and pinged he became aware of the overwhelming silence surrounding him.

The sun momentarily broke through the charcoal cloud cover to the west, moments before it reached the horizon of a distant range, bathing the edge of the forest before him in a golden slash of horizontal light. He had less than an hour of daylight remaining.

He walked down the dirt road, between towering stands of beech and ash. When he caught a first glimpse of the house through the trees he moved off the road and circled to his left. The forest floor was blanketed with a spongy cover of pine needles, moss and decaying plants, muffling his footsteps. He crossed a small creek that fed down to the lake, and crept to the edge of the property line.

The house stood in a wide clearing, on a bluff that sloped gently down behind it to a dock on the water. A graceful A-frame brown log cabin, shutters and trim painted Adirondack green. Thirty feet to the left was a two-story barn, painted to match.

Erin's Volvo sedan sat fifteen feet from the front door.

Montone continued to circle to his left, keeping to the cover of the trees.

He saw flickering light coming from a window on the lake side of the house. Tall cathedral windows faced the water, a broad expanse of glass. No sight of anyone inside.

When the barn was between him and the house he stepped out of the woods and crept up to the side of the second building. He stopped to stabilize his breathing, took the pistol from his pocket and switched off the safety. After moving to the edge closest to the house, he scanned the woods in every direction and then the windows for any movement.

He ran ten cautious steps to reach the house and pressed himself against the wall. Edging to his left, he lowered himself beneath each window he passed until he reached the one in which he saw the light. He eased up and looked inside.

The window offered a view into the house's central room, a generous space, twenty-foot ceilings. A fire burned in a massive stone fireplace. Silhouetted by its burnished glow, Erin sat motionless, her back to the window, in a chair at a long wooden table in the middle of the room. Starkly outlined in shadow, a tube trailed away from and above her to something oblong suspended on a hat rack.

An intravenous drip bag.

Montone quickly retraced his steps back around the side of the house until he found the front door.

No other choice. He pushed it open, hesitated, listened, then stepped inside, holding the pistol. The air inside the cabin felt thick and swelteringly hot.

"Good, so you found the place okay."

Keyes stood beside Erin at the far end of the long wooden table, holding a trooper's pump-action pistol-grip shotgun to the side of her head.

"Come in, come in," said Keyes, a parody of the gracious host. "How was the drive? Was the map helpful? You did come alone, didn't you, Jimmy?"

"Yes."

"Just you and me, isn't that the way you wanted it? Happy now?"

Montone didn't answer.

"And how was Wendell? Did you have a nice visit? Terrible place, a prison, isn't it? Not fit for a human being."

His head was shaved to the bone. John Stevenson's black jawline beard and a set of prominent false front teeth gave him the look of a satanic evangelist. He wore surgical gloves and was stripped to the waist, except for a trooper's flak jacket, sculpted muscles glistening with sweat.

"You ought to know," said Montone.

"You never will. That's the shame of it." His eyes glowed with unnatural energy.

"Maybe they put you away by mistake, I have no way of knowing that. But no matter how twisted up you are because of what you went through, she had nothing to do with it—"

"Wait, wait, wait. Do you honestly think talking like this is going to do you, or her, any good? You're not that bloody thick, are you? You know exactly what you did to me and why. I don't want to hear your excuses. You're as guilty as sin. And it gave me more pleasure than I can describe to watch everything you took from me get stripped away from you."

At the sound of their voices, Erin's eyes opened, saw Montone and registered alarm through a heavily drugged haze. Silver tape covered her mouth. Her arms were similarly taped to the arms of her chair. A bloody bandage covered the third finger of her left hand. The tube from the IV disappeared under a patch of tape inside her left elbow.

"Step to the table, Jimmy, take the clip out and lay your gun down there on the corner."

"You don't have to hurt her."

"I'll end it fast for her, that's the best I'm prepared to offer, but only if you're a good fellow and do exactly as you're told."

Montone moved to his end of the table, eight feet away from them. A sheet of paper, a handheld tape recorder and a roll of silver tape were laid out like a table setting. He removed the clip from the Sig-Sauer and set the gun down.

"Take all the bullets out of the clip, save one."

"What'd you put in her arm?"

"Let's just say she's feeling no pain. And, all things considered, be thankful for that."

Montone thumbed the bullets out of the clip, fourteen bullets, until only one remained.

"Throw the bullets behind you into the room."

Montone casually tossed the bullets away.

He made certain that at least two of them landed in the fireplace.

"Take a seat, Jimmy. Slide the clip back in the gun and chamber the round."

Montone sat at the table, popped the clip back into the Sig-Sauer and loaded the chamber.

"Good. Now put the gun down. Take the tape and wrap it around your left arm a number of times, securing it to the chair. That's right, nice and tight."

As he wound the tape, Montone tensed the muscles of his left forearm, trying to create some give under the tape. He glanced at Erin; her eyes fluttered, heavy, her head nodding forward involuntarily.

"Now, lean forward, turn the tape recorder on and read what's on that piece of paper in front of you. Nice and loud, so our audience at home can hear you."

Montone read what was written on the paper. He started to shake with anger.

"Jimmy, your valentine's already got one hundred milligrams of Demerol in her system. The bag holds five hundred, which is more than enough to send her off to her sweet, fuckable sister. I'm going to turn this drip back on now and I'm going to keep it on until you finish reading."

Keeping the shotgun pressed to Erin's temple, Keyes reached over and opened up the valve on the feed tube.

Montone pressed the record button.

"My worst crime was believing that I was a good man. That I was capable of doing only good. That I was beyond the reach of evil. Because that is not true of any man. And when you become a slave to a false ideal, you embody the worst of what you deny. That is what you become. That is what you are."

Montone wiped the sweat from his forehead with a trembling hand. He watched the bubbles rise in the IV bag as the drug continued to flow down into Erin's arm.

Keyes smiled and gestured encouragingly for him to continue.

"I strangled Holly Mews when she refused my sexual advances. Afterwards I planted evidence to implicate my late friend Terry Keyes for that crime. And I falsely accused him of committing the other killings he's been unfairly convicted of in the court of public opinion. When Holly's sister learned of what I had done, I brought her to this place and killed her, too. I cannot carry the burden of these secrets any longer.

"This is my work alone. My only hope is that Terry Keyes, if he were alive, would find it in his heart to forgive my transgressions against him. May God have mercy on my soul."

Montone leaned forward again and turned off the recorder.

"Now, Jimmy," said Keyes, "take your gun, put it inside your mouth and pull the trigger."

Montone looked at the Sig-Sauer, then at Erin. Unconcious. Her head had lolled back against the chair.

Behind them, two shots rang out as the bullets in the fireplace exploded, echoing sharply around the room.

Keyes flinched, momentarily frozen. His eye darted to the door, the windows.

In one move Montone picked up his pistol, sighted and fired.

The bullet struck Keyes at the joint of his right shoulder, paralyzing the muscles in his arm and knocking him back a step. The shotgun fell from his hand and hit the floor beneath the table.

Montone reached down to his right leg and ripped the knife loose from along his calf.

His right arm hanging dead at his side, Keyes dropped to his knees, crawled furiously forward and picked up the shotgun with his left hand, ready to fire.

Montone sliced through the tape around his left arm, ripped free from the chair and dove across the room just as Keyes raised the shotgun at Erin. Montone threw his entire weight into Keyes, dislodging the gun as it fired into the ceiling. Keyes staggered back against a book-shelf, bringing down a collection of china.

Montone used the knife to cut the cord feeding into Erin's arm and kicked over the hat rack. The bag, half full, bounced across the floor, serum spurting out of the severed tube.

With a howl, Keyes ran at one of the room's cathedral windows and crashed through the glass.

Montone furiously sliced at the tape binding Erin's arms to the chair. He felt for a pulse in her neck and found one, slow but still steady. He picked up the shotgun, knocked the rest of the glass from the window frame and jumped down outside.

He listened; no sounds. He followed a dark trail of blood in the dirt leading to the open doors of the barn. He pumped another cartridge into the shotgun chamber and entered.

Deep twilight inside. The trail of blood disappeared. The barn offered a dozen shadowy places to hide. An oil lamp suspended on a wire from the ceiling creaked as it rocked back and forth in the air.

Montone stepped forward, slowly turning to look in each direction. Sweat ran into his eyes and he raised an arm to wipe it away.

Keyes came out of the darkness behind him with a hatchet in his left hand. The blade creased his back as Montone sidestepped and fired, cutting Keyes down across the knees. He collapsed and fell back hard against the wall of the barn, propped up at an awkward angle, his legs and one arm useless, bleeding; unable to move. With a last furious burst of energy he tossed the hatchet. Montone ducked; it embedded behind him in a beam.

Keyes looked down at his wounds, then up at Montone.

"Just you and me," said Montone.

He pumped another shell into the chamber and pointed the shotgun at Keyes's face, above the flak jacket.

Keyes looked at the gun, then back up at Montone, his finger twitching at the trigger.

"For the love of God, please, Jimmy, don't, don't hurt me anymore, I'm begging you."

Keyes wept frantically. Montone didn't flinch.

"Shut up."

A moment later the simulated fear dropped instantly away from Keyes expression, replaced by his dark, sly smile.

"You won't do it, Jimmy," he said confidently. "You didn't kill Wendell when you had the chance. It's not in your nature."

"You're already dead."

Montone fired, reloaded and fired again.

He dropped the gun in the dirt outside and walked back into the house.

The phone line inside had been cut. He removed the needle from her arm, picked Erin up and carried her out to the car, laying her down gently in the front seat. The keys were in the ignition.

He got behind the wheel, started the car and drove out of the woods back to the road, keeping one hand on her head, stroking her hair, talking gently to her.

Five miles on, when he reached the highway he turned left, remembering a detail from her map.

They passed a sign that read "Enchanted Forest, One Mile." He saw lights in the distance, a settlement ahead.

Erin stirred beside him. She reached out for his hand and he held it tight.

"James . . ."

"Hang on to me," he said. "We don't have far to go."

He heard the tires grinding against the worn country road. Windows open, cool air washing over them.

A thought came to him, unbidden.

Somewhere they're playing a ball game right now. Under the lights. Under this same night sky.

Life can begin again.

Not now. Not anytime soon.

Someday.